PRAISE FOR

A DANCE WITH DEATH

"Absolutely spellbinding! Linsmeier makes a name for herself with this sweepingly romantic, enchantingly gothic fairytale. *A Dance With Death* is both beautiful and haunting—a masterclass of love, loss, and sisterhood."

—**SKYLA ARNDT**, author of *House of Hearts* and *Together We Rot*

"Atmospheric, swoony, and unputdownable, this dark fairytale retelling is about loss and love, revenge and redemption, and the desperate measures one woman will take to save her sister. Corliss and Orrin's chemistry—framed by a haunting setting and beautiful prose—absolutely crackles off the page. An incredible first foray into adult fantasy!"

—**KESHE CHOW**, *Sunday Times* bestselling author of
For No Mortal Creature

"With a trio of charming sisters, a demon in the woods, and a cottage by the sea, Linsmeier crafts a curious world en pointe, balancing classic romance against artful twists you'll want to savor as they go dancing by! Perfect for fans of *Practical Magic*, and anyone who grew up desperate to dance in a pair of red shoes."

—**MAGGIE RAPIER**, *USA Today* bestselling author of *Soulgazer*

"*A Dance With Death* is like a night at the gothic ballet. Eerie atmosphere, resonant themes of revenge and sisterhood, and an exquisitely rendered romance leap from the pages. Readers will be riveted as they watch the story play out on a ghastly stage magically set by Amanda Linsmeier."

—**AUTUMN KRAUSE**, critically acclaimed author
of *Grave Flowers*

"Told in lush prose, *A Dance with Death* is a blood-laced gothic romance tied up with a silken bow. Gruesome, grief-stricken, yet ultimately filled with heart, Linsmeier delivers a crushed-velvet triumph of a tale."

—**TEAGAN OLIVIA KING**, author of *Spit Back the Bones*

"Linsmeier artfully crafts a dark fairytale with gorgeous prose and rich worldbuilding. I was enchanted by the seaside town, the mysterious house, and the eerie magic twisting through every page."

—**ANA DAVIS**, author of *My Keen Knife*

"*A Dance with Death* is a delightfully haunting gothic fairytale, replete with vivid, eerie atmosphere, luscious prose, and a love story that's to die for. I was utterly captivated."

—**KALIE CASSIDY**, author of *In the Veins of the Drowning*

ALSO BY

AMANDA LINSMEIER

Six of Sorrow
Starlings

A DANCE WITH DEATH

AMANDA LINSMEIER

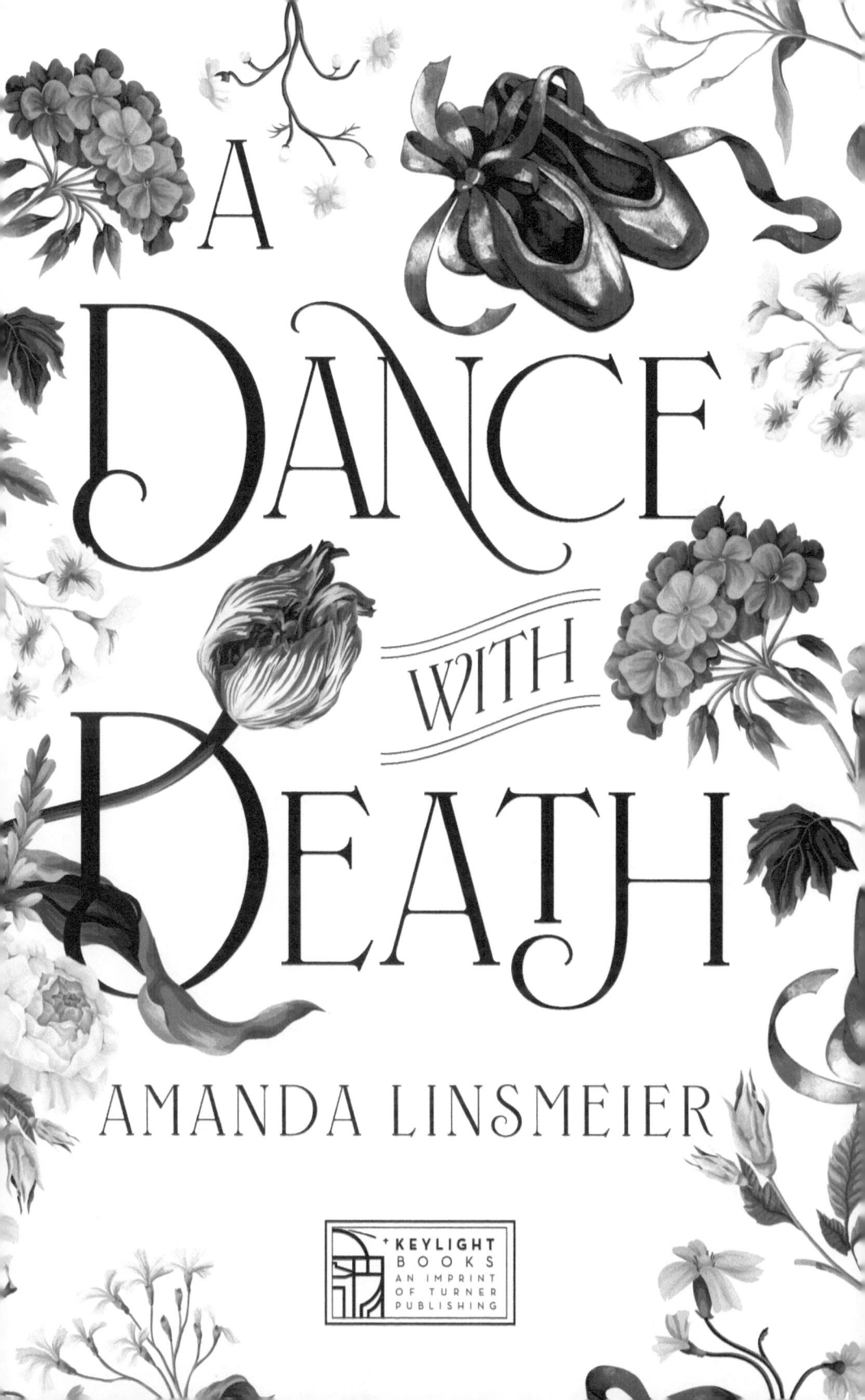

KEYLIGHT
BOOKS
AN IMPRINT
OF TURNER
PUBLISHING

KEYLIGHT BOOKS
AN IMPRINT OF TURNER PUBLISHING COMPANY
Nashville, Tennessee
www.turnerpublishing.com

Page vii: "The Magician's Lover" from *Lace Bone Beast: Poems & Other Fairytales for Wicked Girls* by N. L. Shompole used with permission from author

Cover design by Faceout Studio, Molly von Borstel
Book design by Ashlyn Inman
Map design by Charlotte Slegers

Library of Congress Cataloging-in-Publication Data
Names: Linsmeier, Amanda, author.
Title: A dance with death / Amanda Linsmeier.
Description: First edition. | Nashville: Keylight Books, 2026.
Identifiers: LCCN 2025001802 (print) | LCCN 2025001803 (ebook) | ISBN 9798887980904 (hardcover) | ISBN 9798887980911 (paperback) | ISBN 9798887980928 (epub)
Subjects: LCSH: Ballerinas—Fiction. | Demonology—Fiction. | LCGFT: Romance fiction. | Fantasy fiction. | Erotic fiction. | Novels.
Classification: LCC PS3612.I55476 D36 2026 (print) | LCC PS3612.I55476 (ebook) | DDC 813/.6—dc23/eng/20250313
LC record available at https://lccn.loc.gov/2025001802
LC ebook record available at https://lccn.loc.gov/2025001803

Printed in the United States of America

For the ones with grit, and for the ones losing it.
Keep going. Keep dreaming. And always keep dancing.

Here we are

the sky a mournful blue / my heart / half-struck
unraveling / your eyes pitch black
full / so full
of want

Here we are

pulse like the ninth wave / of a tsunami / caught
between the ribcage & the sternum
caught between / oblivion
& surrender

—"THE MAGICIAN'S LOVER" by N. L. Shompole

CHAPTER ONE

I long for the days before Death touched us, before he crooked one gnarled finger and dragged the ship to the bottom of the sea—and my sister's heart right along with it. With a lump in my throat, I unlock the door to our apothecary shop and enter, twisting back to chance a glance at Aven, but she keeps her eyes downcast as she follows me and our younger sister inside. I used to believe nothing could break her—not the three of us losing our parents and our home, not being moved from place to place with nowhere to live and no one to love us, none of it—but I was wrong.

Aven is breaking more and more every day, every hour, every minute. And I don't know how to mend her. I don't know if she *can* be mended. She moves woodenly beside me, fully aware of how closely I'm watching her. But we both pretend that I'm not.

I've always understood our roles—we've played them well: Aven as the beloved and loving eldest, prone to mothering us; me, the rebel with a stubborn streak and smart mouth; Sélie, the darling baby. Now everything is confused, even these labels we've placed on each other and ourselves. My hands flutter like wounded birds, aiming to stroke down the hair around Aven's pale forehead, but I drop them, uncertain if I should, if she *wants* anyone to touch her at all. Every touch, every look, every encouragement seems to draw more and more grief out of her. Right now, I think she'd prefer to be invisible, to sink into it and be left alone.

Well, that, I refuse.

Determined to keep myself—and thus her—together, I take a solid step forward, pushing myself into action, into this day. The plan is simple, centering our energy around the routine of work—the blessed distraction of needing to be practical. Taking my apron off the hook, I tie it tightly around my waist. Securing my thick, dark waves atop my head, I lock eyes with Sélie, her neat braid hanging in one long length. At two, it trailed past her shoulders; at twenty, it nearly reaches the hem of her ankle-length skirts. In unison, we give Aven reassuring smiles—her first day back at the shop since…everything. She smiles in return, but it's as if her mouth has forgotten how to work, the expression unnatural.

With a shallow breath, I head behind the long walnut counter. Reaching into one of the bottom bins, I scoop up a handful of dried lavender buds and set them onto the clean marble counter-top, sorting through the fragrant ingredient while Sélie flips the sign, keeping myself busy while I try to decide what to do.

For a few moments, I go hazy, letting the aromatic medley inside the shop guide my intentions: flowers, not just the lavender, but roses and primroses, geraniums, and dozens of other varieties. Then there is musk, vanilla, raspberry, mint leaves, oat, orange zest, ground coffee. And strawberries. Their scent haunts the air, impossible to shake—a constant reminder of Darius—his favorite because it was Aven's.

"What today?" she asks as she joins me behind the counter. Her voice is steady though her sapphire blue eyes still hold that terrible pain. "Sachets? Perfume?" she lists, as if everything is normal. As if Sélie and I can't tell her heart has been cleaved in two.

I humor her, answering, "Well, we're running low on rouge." I count the glinting gold compacts on one wooden display shelf. Three left. "My oils can wait."

"I can do the rouge, Corliss," Sélie offers across the white-walled room as she flicks her braid to the side to slip on her apron, tying it deftly around her slim waist. "I know that's your least favorite."

"Thank you, my love." I smile in gratitude, and the two of us converse without words. *What can we give Aven to do? What will lift her spirits the most?* Before I can assign a task, the bell on the door rings and a cloud of lily perfume, mixed by my own hand, enters the shop. Or rather, the woman behind the cloud does.

Loueva Maelin wears her corset so tight, her cleavage spills violently out the front of her green-striped dress. She cools herself with an ornate fan trimmed in lace, though it's more for show than necessity—it's not hot. Summer's been lazy to come to The Pins, drifting in hesitantly, one toe in, one toe out, teasing us all on the daily.

"I need some lip color, dears. In a flash," she says breathily, then mouths, *Milton is waiting*, as though there's someone else in the shop besides us.

As if we'd care that she's the tailor's mistress and his puckered-mouth wife sits at home pretending not to notice their dalliance. No need to whisper here. The Bell sisters know how to be discreet. Loueva, not so much. She furrows her brow, and a soft, little whimper escapes her as she darts a pitying glance at Aven.

Immediately, I elbow my way around the counter, taking the lead so Aven can stay behind and away from Loueva's prying. I lightly tow the woman over to the display, though she knows full well where it is, and say, "There are five shades, or you could wait for something custom? It wouldn't take long."

She swallows and shakes her head, yellow-blonde ringlets bouncing around her silk-clad shoulders. "Oh, no." Shivering involuntarily, her face flashes with unease. "We have too much to do before our trip, and I want to leave town far before the light fades. Already I've wasted half the morning."

"Something wrong?" I can't help inquiring.

"I'd simply rather not pass the Colehart place in the dark."

It takes all of my willpower not to roll my eyes. Not this again. I don't believe in any of The Pins nonsense, and nonsense is all that it is. Things to do with the word *magic*. And—more recently—whispers about that big old house on the edge of town and the poor, judged person who moved in not long ago. How my sisters have fallen so easily into the nonsense is beyond me, all their skepticism seeming to have melted away in the years we've lived here—though, to be fair, I don't know if Sélie ever actually had any to begin with. But Aven should know better.

Now both of them hang on Loueva's every word as she goes on, telling her mostly captive audience, "All I know is I got this *feeling* when we passed the house last time. It was like a rat was scaling the bones of my spine, like something evil was pressed against me. Rumor has it the Devil himself moved in there." Her breasts jiggle like unset custard as she shudders again.

Well, that's a new one. With a half-scoff, half-snicker, I blurt out, "The Devil?"

"Devil, demon, what have you." Loueva eyes Aven very purposefully, and I silently vow I will slap this woman silly if she so much as *mentions* Darius. She goes on, voice low, leaning in, "I hear he's cold as a snake and richer than God. I believe he's dangerous and so should you. I'd steer clear, ladies." Snapping her fan shut for dramatic effect, she looks rather pleased to have shaken up two-thirds of us. My sisters murmur a wary agreement at her warning, but I remain silent. We always stay close to home, our cottage by the sea, and when we do venture anywhere, it's merely into the heart of town, following the narrow forest road that can barely call itself a road, winding its way from our cottage. Only people heading in or out of The Pins on the main road pass by the Colehart Mansion. I haven't been that way in ages. Images of a rundown estate creep through my memory—it's actually just visible from our cottage if you stand at the right viewpoint. And even if we did ever go near it, what could there possibly be to fear? I try to place some sort of horned, hellish creature into that visualization, and even my imagination protests. Mentally, I acknowledge that some very private, possibly eccentric person has moved in, but to these three, a bogeyman has come to The Pins and lies in wait, ready to pounce on anyone who stumbles too near. Now my eyes roll of their own accord.

Turning her attention to the lip stains, Loueva chooses the darkest—a wine-color—and smears it against her thin lips, admiring herself in the hand mirror I procure. "Perfect. You'll charge it to his account, as per usual?"

"Yes, of course," Sélie says, then adds, "Shall I wrap it for you?"

"No, no need, thank you. As I said, Milton is waiting." Loueva tucks the tin into her cleavage and turns to go. At the door, she pauses, turning slowly to face Aven. She simpers, "I'm so sorry, dear. For your loss." Aven chokes out a nonverbal reply, and Loueva's eyes widen, and she corrects, "I mean, *losses*." Then she sashays out, fine skirts swaying.

It's only when the door bangs shut that I unfreeze, my fury igniting. I loosen the hands I've bunched into my apron and lunge forward, set to go after her and give her a piece of my mind. That nosy, no-good—

A touch on my arm, stopping me, just the faintest brush of fingers against my sleeve.

"Don't," a soft pleading, barely audible.

I look up at Aven, swallowing. Calming my temper. A scene will only upset her more. Without pausing to wonder if I should, I ask, "Are you alright?"

Behind the counter, Sélie wrings her hands. She stares over at us, her eyes welling up. *Don't cry, don't cry*, I wordlessly warn her. We have to hold it together, for Aven's sake.

"Oh, yes. I'm fine," Aven answers quickly, too quickly. A lie of course, to placate us, to make us not worry about her—an impossible idea. She tilts her head down, mouth pinched together, as if to hold in a scream. Yet, for as much intensity as wants to escape her lips, it's almost worse catching the lifelessness of her eyes before she turns them away from my view.

It's like she died that day too. The day her husband's ship disappeared.

Like the woman standing in front of us isn't even real anymore. She's just a ghost.

Hours and dozens of customers—and tasks—later, Aven and I have devolved into a half-hearted, age-old argument. I should be thrilled to see some fight in her, however I can only fidget, picking my cuticle to shreds, as she badgers me behind the counter in between customers.

"No, no, absolutely not!" I insist, voice rising to a shrill level.

The man inching around the perimeter of the shop jumps, his hands empty. By the sight of his glossy boots and well-cut suit, I doubt his pocketbook is empty, though he's given no indication he plans to buy anything. Watching him sniff products for the last half an hour has thinned my patience. I curl my lip at him, and he skitters out the door, finally leaving us in peace. Normally, Aven would admonish me for scaring off a customer, but she only sighs.

"You promised—" Aven's strained reply catches me off guard. The two of us lean against the marble top, into the slanted light of afternoon, painting itself in strips across the shop's tiled floor.

I falter. Swallow. How can I deny her? But how can I listen at a time like this? "That was before, and it doesn't matter now."

And it doesn't. Life matters. Death matters. Not this ridiculous dream I should be well shot of at my age, with my lack of skill. I'm not meant for The Red Clover, and it's not meant for me. There are more important things to worry about. I search Aven's face for understanding, but she offers me none—only a pointed stare. If Sélie weren't off delivering an order across town, would she take my side? Or would she give in to Aven? I wish I could give in, but how?

"I don't care about dancing anymore." I lift my chin, shrug. Meet the challenge and push it back to her, as gently as I can. I wave one hand nonchalantly.

When she grabs it, I startle. Her fingers are so cold, and so strong I wonder where the strength is coming from—she's not been eating a thing. Even her wedding ring is loose. It catches the light, and I look quickly up at her face instead.

The dullness in her gaze has been pushed aside—however weakly—by a flicker of something fierce. "You have to try. You deserve it."

"I don't *want* to anymore. I don't want to dance." But it's a lie, and of course, Aven knows it. She knows me better than I know myself at times. She knows how I both love and hate to make deliveries to the Clover, how I enjoy slipping into the dark theatre to catch a peek at the ballerinas practicing on stage. To imagine I am one of them; I revel in my voyeurism. It is safe. It costs me nothing apart from a heart full of yearning.

When I can tell she's unconvinced, I attempt a different tactic. "I'll try another day. Or in a few months when you're...more settled."

Aven lets go of my hand, and I imagine what she's not saying: *I'll never be settled. I'll never be happy. I'll never be okay.*

She shakes her head, not letting me get away with that either. "No, you won't. You'll just keep putting it off like you have been for years. Then one day, when you're very, very old, you'll regret it. Well, I won't let you. You promised you'd audition—you chose a day on New Year's, wasn't it? Just a random date in the future. Well, I may be a shell of a person, but I didn't forget the date—it's *today*. You promised me. You can go now. Sélie and I will close up."

"I don't have my slippers...." But even as I say it, she gives me a *look*.

"We brought them—" Aven gestures to the cloth bag hanging on the pegs where our aprons live when we're not wearing them. I didn't even notice it this morning. They'd snuck it in.

"Of course." I sigh, giving up. Giving in. I can deny her nothing right now. The truth is I would do anything to help her, even if that means playing along with this and getting her mind off of everything, if only for a while.

I reach for a cluster of empty brown glass bottles, to clear them away before I head out, but she shoos me.

"I'll clean up," she says, glancing at the clock on the wall. "Sélie will be back soon. You go, before you're late."

"I wouldn't be late—" I clamp my mouth shut, reading her. I sigh again. Of course, they made arrangements behind my back.

"Julian will be expecting you."

My lip wobbles and I bite it hard, stopping this display. Ridiculous.

Beaten, I peel off my apron and smooth down the skirts of my off-white dress. Did Sélie convince me to skip my fullest crinolette this morning because she knew I'd be dancing? Everything feels wrong, though—my stockings itching the tops of my soft thighs; the nervous dampness under my arms; the feeling that I could vomit any moment now.

I hover at the door, shifting my weight from foot to foot, a warring within me. To dance, to do anything *except* dance. And also—should I be leaving Aven?

She looks up, bottles clanking as she tidies the counter, and still I wait, uncertain, studying her. Her face like faded petals, her hair a deep brown-black, her eyes blue, blue, blue as the sky on a rich, summer night, and aged a century in only a month. Her lips are chapped, split in the corner. She hasn't worn lip stain or rouge in weeks. But she lifts the corners of them now, half-heartedly. Trying.

"Go, on, Corliss," her voice firm. "I'll be fine."

Before I can argue—*you shouldn't be alone*—Sélie returns, empty basket slung over one arm, cheeks rosy, the faintest dusting of golden freckles across her fair skin.

"Oh, good! I caught you," she exclaims, pulling me in for a hug. "Good luck. You'll be wonderful."

Traitor. I murmur some kind of sound, feel their eyes on my

back as I take the bag with my ballet slippers, leave the shop, and head to the Clover without an order. When we do have one, my sisters make certain I'm the one to deliver it every time, a generous yet embarrassing gift I can't bring myself to refuse.

I cross the street, trying to calm my nerves, squeezing the bag of slippers.

"Get away there, you!" a woman hollers, tossing a bucket of dirty water at some miscreant children hassling her. She misses them by a mile, and they run off, giddy with power. Harmless really, but I throw her a sympathetic look anyway. She only glares in return and I drop the unusually friendly smile I had offered and glare back twice as hard, moving past her.

More shouting, more laughing, a fiddle player on a corner. I weave in and out of people as my heart patters with fear—a fear I know is real, despite telling myself it's foolish. I try to put my mind at ease; to think of something else, to ground myself, here, in the physical world.

The Pins is never quiet, never a meek nor mild town. It is always folks bustling down the the streets and through the square, vendors yelling, gulls screeching, boys running. But this time of day, when the afternoon creeps toward night, when the golden light spills warm and colors my skin apricot, when the salty air leaves my lungs refreshed, I love it most.

Yet not even its chaotic beauty soothes me on the way to the dance theatre.

It doesn't matter how unfocused I am, my feet know how to get there.

The Red Clover springs into view, and I stop abruptly, my skirts swinging around my legs. Someone bumps me, making me fumble, barely an apology thrown at me, but I pay them no mind, my focus only on the building, the sign, the advertising posters peppered out front.

The first time I saw ballerinas, I was eleven. My sisters and I had been living and apprenticing with Aunt Mavis for several months. Sélie was set with the task of plucking chamomile flowers in the back room while Aven worked with Mavis on a new recipe. The whole shop had been hot, sticky, so that sweat beaded on our foreheads. Though I was happy to finally be with a guardian we all liked—even in some ways had begun to love—I longed to be outside, exploring The Pins, reading one of my favorite books, doing almost anything but what I'd been told to do—mixing up oil and coarse sugar to soften the skin. I pouted silently as I whipped the large spoon around the mixture, my fingers greasy, my arm aching from stirring.

"Corliss, dear." Aunt Mavis's tone was always curt, even if the words themselves were kind. "Take this package to the dance hall. The Red Clover."

I fought within myself, but finally, my curiosity to see the theatre as well as my desire to get out of the shop defeated my rebellious nature. I cleaned off my oily hands, took the package she handed me, and listened to her strict instructions to return right away with the full payment.

"Yes, Aunt Mavis." I gave her the most innocent smile I could muster.

She scoffed at me like she was neither amused nor fooled, though I caught the edge of her mouth turn up as if in spite of itself. "Get going, and don't dawdle. You know where it is?"

I nodded and she shooed me out of the stuffy shop and into the fresh air. I went gratefully, although I *did* dawdle, meandering through the open market, the scents of hot, spiced nuts and ginger beer making my mouth water. I lingered in front of the sweet shop to eye the delicacies in the window—voluminous cream puffs and dense cakes dripping with shiny chocolate ganache (some said you were guaranteed to remember your first kiss as if it were yesterday with just one bite of those chocolate cakes, but I'd yet to be kissed and didn't believe anyhow). I circled around, going out of my way to ogle the dresses in the dressmaker's store. They hung in the window—a riot of stripes, tulle, gold buttons, fine lace the color of fresh cream skimmed off the top of milk.

When I got to the theatre, I admired the marquee: *The Red Clover Dance Hall*, it said in curling, elegant script. Once inside, while I waited for the owner to return with payment, I watched the stage from the shadows of the theatre, unnoticed, as a dancer with long, sepia limbs finished up her practice routine. She wore pale pink, a blush-colored confection. When she rose up on her toes, she spun like sugar candy, mesmerizing me.

I'd never seen anything so beautiful in my life. For several perfect minutes, time paused. I didn't mind that my sisters and I were orphans. Didn't care that we'd been shipped from home to home. Didn't care that I still wasn't sure where I fit—if I fit anywhere.

At the time, I was too young to audition. Still, I needed to dance, and so I taught myself at first, learning from books, and yes, spying, and years later, eventually, from one beautiful dancer with black curls tumbling to her waist, who became more than just my teacher—Tanna.

Now, as I glide past the poster of Tanna hanging out front, her painted eyes seem to watch me and my nerves jump a notch. Or ten. I can't believe I'm actually doing this—I always hoped I would, eventually. I had worked hard, the desire to someday audition always at the back of my mind, if I only could build up the courage. That courage never arrived, and my dancing has remained private all these years. And even though occasionally I have allowed my family to watch, dancing was mostly for me alone.

I admit the truth that my sisters could see clearly: I wouldn't be here if it weren't for them. With their faces fixed in my mind—knowing how disappointed Aven will be if I turn back now—I force myself forward and reach for the door before I can talk myself out of it. I go inside, and blink several times, adjusting my eyesight to the darkened interior.

"Miss Bell?" Julian appears before me too soon, wearing a crisp suit of cream that complements his topaz-brown complexion, with a lavender tie and shining toffee-colored shoes. He looks at me in slight bewilderment, dark eyes curious. "Right on time. I must say I was surprised to hear you'd like to audition…."

I sound like some kind of monster, the way I clear my throat. My mouth is so dry I think I could spit cotton, but I finally stammer out, "Yes. I would."

Steering me through the lobby, he says, "But you've been taking orders all these years, delivering them to me in person. Why have you waited so long to audition?"

It's a struggle to find the words to satiate his curiosity. It's partly true when I finally answer, "I did not believe I was good enough. And also, I don't like strangers watching me dance." I roll my shoulders back. "But I'd like the chance to try."

When he smiles, I catch peppermint on his breath. "I'd love to see you dance. You have a grace about you—I see it now. A proper audition with music? My pianist is here waiting."

I waver, still so very nervous. Yet, when he leads me through the cool theatre, I follow close behind. Through a door, then a hall, then another door, then some stairs, where we emerge into the wings. Shaking hands, shaking heart, I manage to change out of my boots and shove some lambswool over my toes, then into my secondhand pink slippers. I warm up my body while the pianist plays a lively tune. When he's given me enough time, Julian takes a seat in the front row—dead center. "Ready?" he patiently asks, to which I nod.

As I move to the very middle of the stage, my mind is a blank. I can barely lift a foot to walk, let alone do anything of beauty. Looking out, the limelight blinds me. The empty seats of the red-velvet theatre mock me—if I'm this terrified, this frozen now, how on earth will I ever dance in front of hundreds of people? Their phantom eyes stare back at me. *I'm going to faint* is my first thought. The second: *I cannot breathe.*

"Miss Bell?" Julian prompts from the front. The piano stops, waiting, but the notes still pound through my head, taunting me.

"I'm sorry," I gasp. "I cannot do it. I'm sorry."

I twist and run off the stage, grabbing my belongings. Without bothering to change out of my slippers, I race out of the theatre and down the street then abruptly turn left and dart toward the forest that curls around much of our town, though there's no path to follow home in this area. I run and run north, as though the shame and embarrassment become a thing chasing me, instead of a thing inside of me. All I can think about as I sprint, winding my way through the woods until I come to the dirt-packed forest road that will lead me to the cottage, is how I've disappointed my sisters. Myself. When I can't run any more, I slow, bending over, catching my breath. Brushing my eyes of the hot tears welling up, I tug off my slippers with an anguished cry and toss them through a tangle of trees. After a moment, I move forward again, my head held high, but something bitter roiling within me.

I shall never dance again. It's time to grow up and put foolish dreams aside.

Magic isn't real. Love dies or leaves. And passion is no match for fear.

CHAPTER TWO

I wake up afraid, a knot in my belly that tightens all at once, forcing me upright. It is early, just the faintest of cool light spilling into the room I share with Sélie.

I find her sleeping soundly, her shining hair cascading over the side of her bed like a golden-red waterfall. She's fine. She'll be tired today, perhaps—the three of us found our way into a bottle of whiskey last night—they drank in solidarity with me, as I nursed my regret. My head aches already. But something feels wrong. It's not the acrid aftertaste of my non-audition…but something *else*.

Unsettled, I ease myself up out of my bedcovers and quietly pad across the cottage to Aven's room.

"Aven?" I whisper, pushing her door open. I'm greeted with a pang of emptiness as I spy the boots still standing near the dresser, waiting for a man who will never come home to her, to any of us.

It's unusual to find her bed empty—she rarely leaves it when home, ever since Darius died. But the room is dim and musty, the curtains closed, the marriage quilt undisturbed, like she didn't even sleep.

I don't bother with shoes or a dressing gown—I leave the cottage, biting my lip in worry as I step outside. The air hangs heavy with salt and strangeness, the way it always does in The Pins. Yet it's not the lingering scent of fish and flowers from the market or the garlic paste old women swipe across their sills to keep out bad spirits—the stench *always* seems to drift, even outside of town— but the hint of something else I sense, more a knowing than a smell. The chilly morning breeze whips against my face, making me suck in a breath.

The somber gray waves of the sea soften upon the shore into thick caps of white. I search our land with my eyes until I narrow in on a figure in a nightgown standing waist-deep in the water. My sister's bare arms are wrapped around herself as she inches forward, deeper into the sea. I yell for her, racing down the rocky path, littered with sharp stones that dig into my already-battered feet, until I reach the shore. I keep going.

"Aven!" I kick up the water as I rush to her side, the cuts on my toes stinging from the salt. My heart stutters when she glances over. Will I ever get used to that haunted look in her eyes? Will she ever lose it? I grasp her to me. "What are you doing?"

She stares off into the distance, at the seam where the sky grazes the water. "Corliss?"

"Yes?"

"The ocean hides things." She turns to me again, and I wince at the expression on her gaunt, white face.

Yesterday was, relatively speaking, a good day. She had her downs at the shop, but she'd smiled. She'd laughed, even, when we were a few drinks in last night. Once—then caught herself, immediately sobering. Already I can tell today will be bad. It is already worse than bad.

I swallow hard. "Come on, love." I reach up and push the dark tangles out of her face then tug on her elbow gently, pulling her from the water. "You're cold."

"Why am I here?" Her voice is dull, hollow, though she allows me to draw her body against my side and walk out to dry land. She turns to me, blue eyes imploring, hands wringing. "What am I doing?" For a moment the scent of blood seems to come off of her quivering fingers, as though we didn't wash it all away.

It was on her hands *that* evening. Pouring from her. Into my palms. Afterwards, I moved the rug in her room, to cover the stains that ruined the floorboards—but we all know. We all remember.

I lift my eyes to the sulky sky, as though I'll find answers there. The clouds above us streak like smoke, threatening rain. Despite my fondness for moody weather, I can't help but shiver. It is all so unfair, what she's lost.

"Let's go to the house. Sélie will be worried if she wakes up and finds us gone."

Aven nods at that. We climb up the makeshift path, nightgowns swishing, rivulets of water running down my legs as we make our way to the cottage, beach at our backs.

It seems a lifetime ago that we lit a bonfire on this same beach to welcome 1870, Aven's cheeks flushed, Darius at her side—their babe in her blooming womb. Sélie and I were both tipsy, chipped mugs of champagne in our hands as we toasted the new year, huddled together under a wool blanket near the heat, snow falling on our hair. Not a lifetime, just mere months ago, and yet happiness had been snatched from all our hands since then. The wishes we burned in the fire that night—the dreams we had for our new year—are still buried under the sand. Or maybe they've been washed away. Washed away, like Darius was. The sea took his ship just three weeks ago, all the poor men aboard lost forever. And then the baby—only days after we got the news.

Grief can't just be swept away and driven out. Grief sticks. Grief is walking past our front garden and seeing all the flowers that died overnight, trying not to see the tiny gravestone that stands off the back of the cottage. I've never felt so helpless.

When we reach the top of the hill and step onto our front path, laid with brick by our own hands years before this, I catch a pinpoint on the horizon, way off in the hilly distance. The old Colehart Mansion that Loueva warned us of. I stare for a moment at the isolated place, rather than letting my eyes pass over it as I usually do. Chills wash over me.

As much as I tell myself there's no logical reason to be afraid of a decrepit house or a funny wind, I can't help the unsteady feeling lurking within me. Around me. It's everywhere. I tighten my grip on Aven, the vines on my tattooed arm twining around her, anchoring her, so she doesn't float away. Behind us, down below, the waves fling themselves at the shore, as though aching along with my sister.

The wind whispers against my neck, something secret and horrible. However, the more I try to make sense of the words, the more they slip away from me. Everything feels wrong, and I hurry Aven along until we are almost running the rest of the way to the cottage.

It is still too early, so instead of waking Sélie, we change out of our wet nightgowns, and I tuck myself into the big bed alongside Aven, throwing an arm around her trembling body. I lay still, listening to her breathing settle as she falls asleep again. I feel myself drifting off after her, the salt-air scent of her curling around me.

I dream of the sea, a ship, Darius's face. He is grinning, teasing me and Sélie, his rough hands splayed over Aven's growing belly. He looks happy. I blink and he is gone.

I blink again, and so is Aven.

A clanging wakes me, banging sounds coming from the kitchen.

Pushing myself out of the bundle of covers, I manage a weak yawn, my brain slow to wake. It's late, I can tell by the sun peeking out where the curtains don't quite meet. We should be at the shop by now, I realize guiltily.

"Aven?" I call, climbing out of her bed. I head directly to the kitchen to see how she's doing, presuming she'll be making coffee, or a cup of tea for herself.

Standing by the stove, alone, Sélie looks up, frowning. "She's not out here. I thought you both were asleep in her room. I was going to wake you shortly."

Something in my middle tightens, clenches. Without a word, I turn, run out of the cottage, to see if Aven's standing in the sea again. I curse myself for falling asleep. What have I done? Where did she *go?*

Sélie chases after me, her face drawn, afraid. I shake my head at her, at those big, worried eyes.

"She's not here," I whisper, my gut turning inside out, as I search the ocean, violent now, the white foaming up as each wave crashes, roars, screams. "She's gone."

Door to door, business to business, we go—desperately seeking our beloved sister.

All morning, all day, Sélie and I, some friends of Aven's, Darius's younger cousin—the rest of the Winter family off in Manuette, far too distant to help us. There are old schoolmates that show up to search and ask questions, vendors that know us, customers with sympathetic eyes, lawmen who take pity on us.

"...will get a word out to surrounding cities...see if anyone's noticed a woman of her description...You said nothing's missing? No money?" Constable Elden prodded me when I first went to him this morning, as I paced on the street.

I paused, feeling sick. She didn't even take shoes. She took nothing but the fresh nightgown I'd helped her into when she woke too early, after she went into the sea.

My ears rang, and I shook my head at his question. I wouldn't believe anything but that she would be returned, safe and sound. That she just needed to be found. And so, we search on. The constable and his crew head up the outskirts of The Pins—including the sea surrounding our home, including the houses along the edge of town, including the Colehart Mansion. Meanwhile, I've found myself with Sélie at the heart of town, begging anyone for a sign of Aven, for a whisper of where she might be. If anyone has seen her, if they know where she could have wandered off to.

Hours in and the answers are not forthcoming, but I can't say the same for the rumors that I keep catching in whispers. They cling to me like burrs.

"I heard she walked into the water this morning..."

"Well, losing her husband and baby only days apart...poor thing."

"Poor Corliss and Sélie, now. How much loss can one family handle?"

I hate them for voicing what Sélie and I can't. I should hate the ocean too, for what I fear it has taken, yet there's a part of me that cannot—*that will not*—believe that she would have left us, left the world of the living. I'm not naive—I know some of her *wanted* to. But I can't live without her. I refuse. So, she must return.

I take a step forward, tripping over a loose cobblestone, and Sélie grabs my elbow, her mouth tight, her eyes tired.

"Gettin' dark," someone says behind us. I couldn't pick anyone out of the crowd now—all their faces and voices are blurred together.

Lifting my lantern, I push on. "I don't care. We can't leave her out here all night."

Sélie lets out a little sob, and I shift her hold on me, to squeeze her arm, breathing steadily for the both of us. She's shivering, just a shawl thrown over her shoulders. The unusually cold weather isn't helping tonight. But what about Aven? She was dressed only in a nightgown. I'm too numb to feel the chill, too afraid.

We pass The Red Clover, and I don't even give it a second glance. Was it only yesterday that I thought I'd turn inside out on that grand stage? I feel nothing as I reflect. I just want Aven home. Our search party doubles back to check the alleyway between the nearest buildings, but it's empty of all but shadows.

"—can't see in the dark," someone mutters, just loud enough for me to hear.

I whirl around to snap at them and come face to face with one of the lawmen stepping toward me, his lamp flickering, making his young face look uncertain. Barely more than a child. His carriage is waiting just past us, the door still open. I didn't even hear it pull up.

"What?" I breathe, voice low. They were out searching—

"Constable said to call it a night—bad storm comin' in, and it's gettin' dark."

Frowning, I answer, "I don't c—"

"People need to eat," he cuts me off. Then softer, "They need rest. That goes for you too, Miss Bell." He nods at Sélie. "And Miss Bell."

I raise my brows in dull surprise—I didn't expect him to sound so authoritative, lawman or not.

"You've found nothing?" I ask. "No sign?"

"Not one," the man-boy answers gently. "And it was broad daylight then."

"I…fine." I frown, glancing again at Sélie. She looks like she's about to fall to the ground. Someone else yawns. How much effort will people put into the search if they're this drained? He's right. I hate that he's right. "We meet up early, then. Before first light—I don't care if it's hard to see."

"Yes, Miss," he says, smiling.

I don't return the smile, kindly as he means it, but I do allow him to steer Sélie and me into the waiting carriage, and let it carry us away, watching the group of helpers break apart, scattering into the darkening street. Give up. And all the while my heart is crying out for Aven.

Where are you? Where? What did you do?

And it's so awful that I don't want to hear the answer, but it echoes back anyway over the sound of rumbling thunder.

You know exactly what.

A knock comes as I am dressing for the day.

I drop one of the stockings I was holding, kick it aside, pull my dressing gown across my body. Who would call this early? Unless—

A horse whinnies, and I hurry down the hall to the front door, beating Sélie there as she fumbles with the tea kettle, the exhaustion written on her face ahead of today's search. It's been three weeks since Aven left the cottage—and the not-knowing is all-consuming, overwhelming, torturous. Three weeks of searching and screaming and asking—and still, nothing. We are no closer to finding her than we were on that quiet morning when she first went missing.

There is a saddled horse, just the rump of it visible from the kitchen window.

As I swing open the door, I already know who is waiting on the other side.

Constable Elden enters. I think I must greet him, but my ears ring so shrilly I'm having difficulty hearing a thing, even my own voice.

Time slows. The cottage goes quiet as the lawman steps closer, swallowing anxiously. Even his black-peppered mustache droops.

"Ladies." The constable tips his chin and removes his hat in greeting; sweat drips off his forehead and into the crease of his eye like a tear. Why is he sweating? Is it the humidity that's developed these last weeks—or something else?

Why does he look so nervous?

He and the other lawmen haven't been involved in actively looking for Aven for two whole weeks—*unable to spare the time and resources*. The townsfolk have dwindled off as well. It's just Sélie and me at this point, still holding out hope. Still trying to find out what happened to our sister.

Sélie moves to my side, gripping my hand so hard I wonder how my fingers don't break. He is not here to deliver good news. Something in my soul knows it.

"Aven." I search his face. My lungs can't expand enough to get a good breath.

Constable Elden nods. "A body…" he says, his voice heavy with apology, "washed up on shore in Warring's Cross, matching your sister's description, very late last night. They wired me just after midnight."

Sélie's cry comes out strangled. She buries her face into my neck while I gather her up to me. *No. No. No. No.*

I shake my head. "No. It must be someone else." There've been other bodies, other deaths. Three months ago, a young man washed up near the docks; a year earlier, a woman to the south. It happens. The ocean can be cruel. People drown, and sometimes they're not identified. Such is life in a seaside town.

Constable Elden squirms as though he really, *really* would rather be anywhere else than here. "The body was, see, um, being in the water…it was, well, damaged a bit…but it's a match. I sent them her portrait weeks ago, when she first went—and they confirmed."

Sélie sobs, clutching me so hard my ribs hurt. Everything hurts.

The man's voice is tinny, far away. "They had the body buried within the hour—you are aware of their policies. If you want it returned for a proper funeral, it'll cost. We all know Warring's Cross is full of greedy bastards, if you'll pardon my saying so."

I shake my head. I can't think of funerals. I can't think. Words are exchanged. Voices ring in my head. At some point the constable leaves our home.

Time spreads, evaporates into something hazy, Sélie's tears wetting my dressing gown. Both of us dropping to the cool wood floor. My breath ragged, impossible to catch. As if I'm drowning. Just like Aven. Grief is a wave, grief is salt-thick, grief chokes out my lungs.

I'm going to *die*. I'm actually going to die of a broken heart. I finally open my mouth, let out a cry that doesn't even sound human.

One word repeats itself in my head, over and over again, a whisper: *Aven.*

Chapter Three

On a quiet morning, one week after her body washed up across the sea, we bury Aven's shawl, which has been hanging across the back of her chair all this time. She chose it because it matched her eyes. Ages and ages ago.

I hold Sélie's hand all through the service, tightly, just like a child would cling to a mother. Am I the child or the mother? We are both grown women, but I cannot tell what our roles are now, and I can't seem to let her go. When the service is over, someone—a featureless face—offers us a ride home in their carriage. I say *no, thank you.* I just keep thinking of that blue shawl in the ground, funeral flowers scattered on top. As we step away from the cemetery, warm wind against my skin, I recall little else.

Sélie and I trudge through town, my senses shocked to life, the way everything is just so *normal,* folks crossing into the cobblestone streets to barter with vendors, buy goods, catch up on gossip. The scents are familiar, rich—spiced meat pies, freshly caught whole raw fish with gaping mouths and unseeing eyes, whose scales gleam even in the dull light. We pass a ruddy-cheeked girl on one street corner, perhaps a bit younger than Sélie, offering to sing songs that can make one laugh or weep or fall to their knees in shame, depending on the truths inside their soul.

"Two for one special," she sing-songs as we pass. I face straight ahead, ignoring her.

As we continue moving through town, it's more difficult to ignore how some people watch us, in that sorry way, or worse—as though we're entertainment.

"*Those are her sisters…*" a woman whispers. "*The one that drowned herself.*"

I meet her eyes, hard, and she looks away, ashamed.

She's not even cold in the ground, I want to scream, free hand fisted at my side. With a stupid half-realization, I think, *She won't ever be buried here. We can't even grieve her properly.*

Sélie turns to a passerby offering their condolences, and someone tugs on my sleeve. I stifle an irritated sigh when I see who. Marieta, a fixture of The Pins, known as much for her premonitions as her eccentric ways. She pulls me away with insistence, motioning me down to her level with a crook of her gnarled finger. *Like Death*, I compare without any humor.

Her ragged cloak is wrapped around her, despite the heat, her green stockings split around one bony knee, sagging before meeting her wooden clogs. I've never seen her wear anything else. Normally she's seated at the stoop of the butcher shop, so it's odd to see her here, though I bend down as she bids me.

"I saw your sister last night." Her voice is all raspy from the clove cigars she smokes daily, yet I discern an eagerness in her tone. "The eldest. You were embracing, and she was laughing."

"It's too late," I say, sharper than I mean to. Can she not see the grief pouring from me? I've no patience for her predictions now. "We've just held her funeral. She's dead." I breathe out the last word; I can hardly stomach saying it aloud.

I expect Marieta to be apologetic, but when her eyes meet mine, they are lit with a challenge. "There's dead and there's *dead*. Which is she?"

"Don't. Please," I hiss low, hoping the old woman might lower her own voice. Sélie is mere feet away, and I don't want Marieta to bother her with hurtful needling.

I move out a few steps, and the old woman follows, her dark-brown eyes still pinned on me. "Come now. Haven't you been listening to the rumors of who moved into the Colehart place?"

I grimace, pushing aside the memory of the fear I felt when I looked at the mansion all those weeks ago. "What are you talking about? What does he have to do with anything?"

A screech of laughter, spittle flying. "What do you think?"

"The constable spoke with all the homeowners on the edge of town, including him, when she first went—he wasn't even in town that day. He has nothing to do with her disappearance or her death. Leave the poor old man alone."

"He's not a man," she replies. "He's a demon."

"Oh, Marieta." I sigh, the weight of this day—these last weeks—catching up to me. I'm so depleted I could lie down in the street. I add, "I'm not a child any longer. And I don't believe in monsters."

She coughs out another laugh. "Skeptical girl. Take your time, but miracles don't wait, nor shall your sister. I wasn't sayin' he killed her. I *meant* that he could save her."

"What are you talking about? She's gone…."

"Don't you know? Demons are masters of death. Go to the mansion. You'll see what I mean."

"*Stop*," I say coldly, straightening up. This is pointless. The goddamn Pins and all their goddamn people. I'm sick of it all, the fortune-tellers on street corners, and the myths, and the lies, and Marieta's visions—which have a coincidental habit of coming true. But this one won't. Because it *can't*. My sister is dead. And anyway. Magic isn't real.

Marieta opens her mouth, but I turn away, leaving her standing there alone.

I grab Sélie's elbow just as she finishes her conversation, tugging her along.

"What did Marieta say?" She glances back as we move on from the other mourners.

"Nothing," I say, voice thick. "Only rubbish."

We walk home, silently. Chill against my back. The prediction resounding in my ears.

You were embracing, and she was laughing.

"It's almost empty." Sélie holds a poison-green bottle of dream draught, one we procured from a local midwife who's been making such things on the side for nearly five decades. We sit on our beds. I take in our shared room as if through new eyes. The pickled wood walls, the thin, floral curtains, the golden oak wardrobe, the cut glass vase of wilted grasses we never replaced once Darius died. I could have moved out years ago—I could've rented a little apartment above our shop, but I didn't have any desire to leave my sisters, even after Aven got married and Darius moved in. My lovers took me in their own beds, and I'd return home to a place full of happy memories. But the cottage is too lonely now without Aven and Darius teasing each other or kissing in corners when they thought Sélie and I weren't looking.

The green bottle glints in the light. When I look at her again, I know what she's thinking—the same thing as me: the cottage is strange, unfamiliar. Like a place we are merely visiting and no longer belong to. Not just the cottage, or the apothecary, the whole of The Pins. The world. I blink my eyes, finding the window. The sun, which finally deigned to peek through the clouds, shines through the glass, creating a warm glow all over the room. It's almost ethereal, the way the rays hit Sélie's ivory hand as she stares at the bottle. There's only a scant amount of dark liquid inside. I'm surprised it lasted this long. So many tragedies later. "For tonight then." I finally stand and slip off my itchy black bombazine dress. I toss it in the back of the wardrobe, not bearing to even wash it. I'd rather burn it or throw it away than see it again. I've had enough mourning for a lifetime. "One last dose. I suppose we could buy more, but we can't use it forever. We'll have to sleep on our own at some point."

She nods. A final night of restful sleep before reality sets in. Then tomorrow, back to normal—a new normal. Life goes on. Even after death. We've learned that a few times over. This feels insurmountable, though. How can we live without Aven?

I unfasten my ribbon-trimmed corset, and I ask, "Will you be alright? You can stay home another day if you like."

"No. It'll be good to get back to work," she reassures me as she drifts from the room to give me privacy. Or to go and cry in solitude.

I take a deep breath, exhale slowly, then put on my nightgown, though it's early for sleeping. When I find her near the kitchen, I ask, trying a smile on, "Are you hungry, love? I believe that tin of cookies from Margaux is here somewhere."

Sélie shrugs. I take that as encouragement and search for something for us both to eat, though I have no appetite, and haven't had for weeks. But something will have to sustain us. The thought of savory food is too nauseating, not to mention I'm no cook. Thankfully, kindhearted people in town left dishes at our door to ease us through the mourning. I'm grateful because we had hardly anything left: a few wilted carrots, stale bread, a half dozen speckled brown eggs, a fat purple onion that'd gone soft and smelly, a jar of honey, a hunk of hard cheese, jellies and pickles, potatoes that had grown eyes. I pass over the cream-laden dishes and meat-heavy pies, and move to the sweets instead, which seem more bearable. I rifle around until I come up with a tin. I pop open the lid to stare at the cookies, baked with love—and perhaps a little guilt—from Aven's friend in town. She lasted the longest during the time Aven was missing, but eventually she stopped showing up to search, quietly accepting our sister's fate long before Sélie and I would.

I skip over the chocolate kind, and the ones full of thick, sticky jam, instead picking out two delicate almond cookies shaped like flowers. Then I brew some weak coffee.

When it's ready, I pour the coffee in two chipped mugs, add milk and sugar, and carry everything to Sélie. She waits in her nightgown at the table, hair unbraided in long, loose waves. When she stands, it reaches nearly to her ankles; now, while seated, it cocoons her like a cape. She only drinks half her coffee, nibbles politely on her cookie, but still, it's something. I manage to finish mine though it's like swallowing chalk dust. When she takes out her drawing book, I blow out a relieved breath. She hasn't sketched much since Aven went missing.

"What are you working on?" I ask.

"I don't know. Something light, silly." She doesn't say *something that doesn't matter*, but I understand. If she tried to draw Aven now, she'd break. "Any suggestions?"

"Draw me one of your fairytale scenes."

Sélie gives me a thankful smile and bends her head, crafting a smudgy charcoal outline of a castle, complete with a dragon perched on one turret. She adds a beautiful princess, leaning longingly out the window.

"Which tale is this from?" I try to recall but come up empty. I've always preferred losing myself in romance novels or ballet instructionals rather than that type of story.

She smiles, gazing down at it. "I'm not sure. I made it up. Something with magic."

Tonight, I only nod, instead of scoffing like I normally would when she speaks this way. Ever since we moved here, when Sélie was just eight years old, she's believed in what she calls *possibilities*. She's always said, "There's magic in The Pins" and held fast to that belief, which Aven quietly shared and I've always loudly dismissed. I don't begrudge her fancies. I simply cannot pretend to believe them myself. I don't *want* to believe them.

Only secretly do I ever admit there's something peculiar here that we never saw in any other town we lived—every grandmother in The Pins can mix up a salve to clear away warts or poison ivy; pretty girls flash their eyes in the direction of eligible mates then find themselves married within the week; shadows creep along the walk from our cottage to town, curious and snakelike.

Marieta's face flashes in my mind, her words echoing there, but I will the memory away. Not just from what she told me today after the funeral, but from years ago. *Not real. Not real.*

Instead of hanging on to foolish thoughts, I sit back and watch my sweet sister draw from across the table for several long minutes, sipping my now-cold coffee. When my cup is empty, I light a few candles and clean up around the cottage, and when the moon hangs over the sea, I measure out a spoonful of dream draught, emptying the bottle. There's less than I thought. Only enough for one dose—for one of us, not both.

"Here," I say, holding up the spoon for her to take it from me. "It's late, love."

"In a moment."

"We have to open the shop early," I remind her, playing at being the responsible one.

This was always Aven's role. No matter what guardians we lived with, bouncing from place to place, or even when we settled here with our Aunt Mavis—who wasn't really an aunt at all, but an old friend of our dead mother's dead sister—no matter how old we got, Aven still took care of us. She would have been a wonderful mother. I swallow the thought, and grit my teeth, silencing the howl of agony from the wild beast inside me.

"Fine." Sélie groans a little, taking the spoon and downing the anise-flavored sedative with a gag. Then she sets her drawing aside and stands, stretching her willowy frame. "Are you coming to bed?"

"I think I'll read awhile."

She hovers. Hesitates. "Don't stay up too late. You need to take care of yourself too."

I give her a soft nod, and she leans down to hug me quickly, then heads to the bedroom. I find my book, a love story firmly grounded in reality, one of my favorites, dog-eared pages and a cracked spine. I open it more for the comfort than the distraction, for I know most of the words by heart but they swim before me anyway. I read—or try to—for a good hour, until my eyes are tired, and the book feels too heavy to hold. I blow out the candles. Sit a long time in the dark. When I start to nod off, I finally force myself to stand, go to my room, climb into my bed. My eyes close, and I whisper across the dark room, "Sweet rest."

There's no reply. Sélie's asleep by now, under a mound of Mavis's patchwork quilts. At least in dreams she has peace. Even without any draught, I find my own sleep, a blessed darkness that allows me to forget the ache of grief.

But sometime in the early morning, just as the birds begin to trill outside, I snap my eyes open, something nagging me awake. I sit up, the memory forcing its way to the forefront of my mind, refusing to let me ignore it any longer. Because years ago, Marieta told me of another vision—that she saw our Aunt Mavis in a black dress. Mavis, who only wore autumn colors, shades like the burnished rust of her hair, the olive of her eyes, the warm gold of her lashes.

"She doesn't wear black." I tried to move away, dismissing Marieta easily. At sixteen I had flirtation on my mind, and I wanted to walk past the docks, to see the handsome sailor who kept winking whenever I passed.

The old lady grabbed my apron strings, stopping me. "In my sight, your aunt wore a black dress, a crown of white on her red, red hair. Leaving her body behind for the world of souls."

I scoffed, walked away, but only a fortnight later, Aunt Mavis dropped to her knees in the middle of our cottage. Dead in the time it took for her body to hit the floor.

Aven picked out a fine, black wool dress for the funeral, and Sélie insisted on a wreath of white lilies to lay over Mavis's dark-red hair. I'd barely spoken for the next several days, shaken that Marieta's forewarning had come to pass. It had to be a fluke. Visions couldn't come true.

Now I push my sweat-dampened covers aside, climb out of bed, and fling the door open, careful not to let it slam behind me, though Sélie usually sleeps heavily, and with the dream draught, even more so. I rush out of the cottage, half-wild with adrena-line, half-expecting to see Aven standing right outside, barefooted, nightgown shredded, hair wet. But no. Because she can't. Because she *died*. I reach up and slap myself—hard—across the face. The sharp crack of my hand upon my cheek breaks the silence. My eyes flood with tears, but the pain steadies me.

Marieta's recent words wash over me. That certainty. I shift my gaze in the direction of that mansion and the supposed demon who resides there now. I stand outside longer than I'd care to admit, staring at it, softening my hard lines, willing myself to con-sider the *possibilities*, as Sélie calls them. The unexplainable. The things that I never let myself believe before this. For Aven's sake, I'd believe in magic. For her sake, I'd go to hell and back.

But maybe, just *maybe*, hell has come to me.

CHAPTER FOUR

"The Red Clover's order is nearly ready." Sélie's face is worn, but she gives me a half-hearted smile as we work behind the counter. The hours have ticked away slowly, minutes dripping like honey, slow, painfully so, as we mixed pots of color, crushed violet petals, creating then lining up rows of gold-flecked liner, currant lip stain, sea salt lemon scrub, and all kinds of beauty in a jar. "Would you like me to deliver it?"

Her hesitation is palpable—she knows that my audition was an embarrassment. That I haven't danced since—I wouldn't have wanted to after that, even without the pain of Aven. But I snatch the opportunity.

"No, I'll take it. I have some other errands to run," I tell Sélie, the lie coming out easily. It's for her own good. There's no use getting her hopes up. "You can close without me?"

"Of course."

I'm glad she doesn't ask questions because I don't want to admit the real reason I'm going out. She's more likely to offer to go with me than talk me out of it. But I can't put her at risk. It's dangerous, if what Marieta said is true. Wouldn't a demon sooner kill me than help me?

Nonsense, I tell myself. It's nonsense. A fool's errand. Demons don't exist—do they? But I suppose I'm a fool because I must at least try.

As Sélie starts another order, I leave the shop with the

paper-wrapped package in hand, the black ribbon around it perfectly tied, just as Mavis taught us. When I find a young boy on
the street, I motion him closer and ask him to deliver the order for
me. "Take this to The Red Clover dance hall, please, to Julian."
I toss him a couple of extra coins, which he takes eagerly. "Get
yourself a treat too."

"Thanks, ma'am!" He scampers away, the box under one arm.

I call out, "And be careful with that."

He throws me a cheeky grin over one shoulder, and I trust
he'll do what I asked, even if it's not the usual way we conduct our
business, preferring to hand deliver all our orders ourselves. This
will save time.

Besides, I don't want to go into the theatre, to face Julian after
everything. I have somewhere more important to be. Now that
Marieta has put the idea into my head, I won't be able to settle
until I see who is really living in the mansion. And if—*if if if if if*—
he *is* a demon, can he help me? Can he bring Aven back to life?

As I hurry through the streets, I pass the sweet shop, the general store, the mail office, the bakery. Seagulls swoop overhead,
hoping to catch bits of dropped food from the lingering market
vendors. A horse neighs. Farther away, behind me at the docks, a
ship's horn blares.

The square is still littered with people, but I weave in and out
of them gracefully. When I walk by the butcher shop, I keep my
eyes straight ahead, not only to avoid the bloody cuts of meat
hung in the window, but to avoid talking to Marieta. She'll just
go off spouting things about resurrection and demons. I worry if
she tries to talk to me, I'll change my mind, my rebellious nature
pushing aside the seed of intrigue planted inside me now.

Because I've decided. I'm going to seek out a demon, to beg
him to bring my sister back to life. Even if it costs my own.

The Colehart Mansion is as far from our cottage as you can get without leaving town and entering a bit of nothing before reaching the next village—a small place as bland as The Pins is odd. This area is quite isolated, in the most foreboding sense of the word.

As the sky begins to streak with the golden orange rays of sunset, I arrive at the main road leading to the property. I can't help thinking over what I *do* know about demons, the tales I've heard from Sélie, the stories I was always so certain were fictional. That they're monstrous in form, winged and scaled and tailed, with black eyes and forked tongues. That they can kill you just by looking at you, that they have no soul, are unable to love—not that they'd even want to.

I tighten my mouth and will my feet to move. There's no point putting it off now that I've made up my mind.

Be careful, be careful, my footsteps repeat as the road widens slightly and the house looms ahead. I could just swerve left and cut into the woods, find the curving, narrow road which can barely call itself a road, which starts in the heart of town and leads all the way to our cottage, forged by years of Mavis coming and going in her old wagon. I could meet Sélie there at home. Except, home feels far away at the moment, with the large house so close, too close now for me to turn around and pretend it's not because I'm scared out of my wits, even if there's no one to see me lose my nerve.

I refuse to let fear make me back down, so I continue, only slowing to take stock of the property. The patchy lawn is thirsty, though it's been trimmed recently so there's a shabby neatness about it. With one more breath for courage, I stride up to the wrought iron gate, covered with swirling black vines and iron roses. I push, expecting it to be locked, but it gives immediately, swinging open with a moaning creak. I eye the grand estate ahead of me. It was once grand, at least. Still beautiful, stately, though it's lost a lot of its fineness as it was vacant for so long. There are even a few boarded up windows.

The cream exterior has turned dirty yellow in spots, and it's missing the railing in one area of the porch. Skin prickling, I tread the long brick path which leads straight from the gate to the house, noting that some of the bricks are broken along the edges. Stepping up the crooked steps, I avoid the parts that are sunken in the middle, lest I fall through. I hesitate at the door, swallowing down my apprehension. It's light enough outside, and there's a gentle wind on my face, but nothing feels light or welcoming about this place. Everything is too quiet—you can't even hear the thrashing of the waves from here. A long inhalation and I lift the heavy lion-shaped knocker on the solid door. The sound of the gold ring thuds against the wood, echoing in my ears.

After a moment, the door opens a fraction.

A man's hard-lined face peeks out, a shock of white hair falling over his brow in a wild way. He smells of smoke and furniture polish, his weathered skin like tanned leather. His cold blue eyes flick down to me. "Yes?"

My voice falters. He isn't a demon, but I wouldn't exactly call him benign. Doubtfully I ask, "Are you the man of the house?"

"I'm the butler." His voice a rough timbre from his chest. "I work for him."

"May I see him?"

The man opens the door and stands to his full height—tall and proud. He wears a butler suit, complete with white gloves, but the outfit is strange on him, like he'd be more at home wielding a knife or a pistol than a silver tray.

"He is not seeing anyone," he tells me, voice firm, even a little annoyed.

"Please." I clasp my hands together. I know this man is entirely human, but my instinct is to run back to the road. Instead, I root myself to the porch. "May I see him, please? My name is Corliss Bell, and I've come with an urgent matter."

The butler seems to assess me with a healthy dose of skepticism, and I shift under his critique, glancing down at myself.

My curving figure, waist cinched in a wide corset belt, my leather boots just peeking out below my rose-pink skirts. My updo and the short, puffed sleeves and rounded neckline of my dress leave my tattoos visible, tendrils of leaves inked across my collarbone, vines on my arms, flowers, swirls. There's just a faint whiff of rose perfume and ocean mist clinging to my skin, but surely, he can smell the desperation on me, a hint of sweat and nerves. Then again, most people don't have noses as good as mine. I look perfectly decent, maybe not a *fine* lady, but a lady nonetheless, even if untraditional. I nervously twist the ring on my finger, a gift from Aven. I wore it for luck.

"What do you want?" he asks bluntly.

"I need to see him—"

"I already said no—" He starts to shut the door, and I shove my foot in the crack. He widens the gap in surprise, indulging me. He sighs. "Well then, go on."

"I need *his* help," I say, then add on, "*If what they say is true...*" I let my voice trail off, in what I hope is an intriguing way.

"What who is saying?"

I stall, not sure how to say it. I can't very well ask if his employer is a demon, can I? I look past his shoulder into the foyer, trying to catch a glimpse of the lord of the house in the background, peering around the staircase maybe, or lurking around a doorframe, a shadow slinking across the floor. There's no one else nearby.

Finally, I whisper, "Is he...does he have magic?"

The butler barks a crackled laugh which ricochets in the air. "Don't spread rumors. Some folk are best left alone, dangerous. He's one of 'em."

I snap out, "I don't care if he's dangerous, so long as he can help me! Does he have magic or no?"

"Magic? That's a pretty word for what he does." He laughs again. Like I'm a fool.

I fold my arms against my chest. "Please. A life depends on it."

"Then you should know he's in the business of taking lives, not saving them."

"You mean—"

"Not magic, girl." He leans in, eyes dead set on mine. "*Murder.*"

My mouth falls open. Murder-for-hire then? So, he's not *not* dangerous.

"Now leave and don't come back." Then the unpleasant man nudges my foot off the threshold and slams the door in my face.

Taking a step back in surprise, fury follows. I let out a huff, turn, and make my way down the steps, then to the dark, loamy woods skirting the mansion. Back against a tree, I wait for several long minutes, watching the quiet house through a web of leaves. It feels like forever. My skin buzzes with impatience. Whatever is inside might very well be dangerous, but I no longer care. Maybe it's magic, maybe it's something worse. I feel it and the desperate raging inside me. I want to get into that house. I want it badly, Marieta's premonition resounding through me. Aven's worth the risk.

Leave and don't come back? I don't think so.

Standing in the shadows of the Colehart property, I study the house from a new angle. There's a row of windows, all closed. I pick one at random.

Biting my lip, I pause. As rash as my decisions have sometimes been, I've never broken into private property. Especially not a place rumored to belong to a demon, or someone, as his own butler put it, "in the business of taking lives." But Aven's face comes to my mind, her blue eyes pleading. Even if the odds are slim, I have to try. If it means bringing her back to life, how could I not try to find this demon, beg him to help, barter anything within my means? What would I give up, to bring her back? I don't have much money, but I'd hand it all over. The shop—Sélie would understand, she'd agree. Some jewelry. My body. The problem is I don't know enough about what he'd want to trade me—if he'd consider a barter at all.

A demon wouldn't do something out of the goodness of his heart—he wouldn't *have* one.

I take a breath and race across the land, praying nobody is looking out the windows on the side. Once pressed up against the house, I wait to be caught. When nobody comes, I exhale. With a resolute sigh, I haul a broken pot with a bedraggled clump of roots falling out of it over beneath a window, careful not to make any noise and to stay ducked low. I push the window open with a good amount of effort, the aged wooden frame sticking. Then I heave myself up, lifting my knee until I catch the splintered ledge, tearing my pink dress in the process. I shove the window up even higher, thankful it doesn't squeak.

I climb through, parting the musty, damp curtains—cobalt blue velvet, embroidered with tiny flowers and golden cherubs.

Humph. I eye it wryly. *Cherubs?*

I've entered into a study. In one corner, a forgotten desk, spread with papers and a fine layer of dust. I cross the tasseled rug and peek out the door, holding my breath. There's no sign of the owner of the house—demon or otherwise—or even any servants. Slowly, I leave the room, my entire body on high alert, listening and watching, memorizing the way I came in so I can sneak out safely. If I'm caught by the butler, I'll surely get tossed out by force. And that's the *best-case* scenario. But what is the worst?

Worst-case—the man really is a demon, and he'll obliterate me before I even get a chance to beg for his help with Aven.

Is it any better to think he could just be a really immoral human who murders people for a living and will kill me for trespassing?

None of that sounds like an ideal outcome. I'm no use to Aven if I end up dead too. And whatever would Sélie do? My nerves grow by the second. I listen harder.

Like the landscape outside, the house is eerily silent. No clanking of silverware being polished, no drawers rattling, no talking, no footsteps, no doors opening or shutting. Nothing. An estate this size should be bustling with servants, with noise, with *life*, but everything is just a bit unusual, broken, tattered, faded. Yet I can tell it was stunning once. The furniture is heavy, gilded, the paintings and tapestries abundant, the air of expense everywhere. Old money. Very old money. Our whole cottage could fit in just the foyer. When I reach the grand staircase, with its ornately carved spindles, I raise my brows at it, a little impressed in spite of myself. I've never been in a house as fine as this.

I tiptoe up the steps, running my fingers along the thick, curving wooden banister. Unlike everything else so far, it's surprisingly not dusty. At the top of the stairs, I find the first door to my right open and glance inside. A bedroom, dark and empty, furniture covered with thick white sheets, curtains drawn closed. I leave the room and return to the hall.

The second door on my right is cracked. I push it open, steeling myself to be caught. What if I were to find the demon staring at me from the other side? Would he blast me right here? But it is empty of people—or beings—though the furniture is uncovered halfway, as if someone were in the midst of airing it out. I duck out quickly and continue down the hallway. Goosebumps dot my arms as I come to the third door, which is shut tight. I pause for bravery—or merely in dread—then open it to find an enormous bedroom.

Sighing in relief at its emptiness, I step inside. I'm not sure what I expected to find, but this isn't it. It's the cleanest room I've seen so far, not a speck of dust, not one hint of cobweb. Faded deep-blue brocade papers the walls, and the floor is a shining, worn wood with an intricately patterned rug laid down upon it. There's a massive bed, giant desk, and a cushy-looking chair in navy fabric. A wardrobe stands directly to my right, but it's the windows I'm drawn to. Thick, gold velvet curtains flung open, glass as well, offering a perfect far-off view of the sea. The sight of the dark waves is, even from here, soothing. The sick feeling in my gut returns, though, when I spy our cottage way off in the distance, a humble speck. Just as I can see his home, so he can see ours. If this is *his* room, that is. I cast my eyes around, uncertainly. Would a demon sleep on a bed? Do they even sleep?

If they exist at all, that is. Marieta was so convinced—Loueva too. Being here—it's unsettling. But is anything supernatural afoot?

A frown tugs at my lips as I look around again. It's so *normal*. The bed a rumpled mass of covers yet to be made, and a stack of books teetering on the side table, next to a cup. I peer over the rim, wondering if I'll find flecks of blood inside, however only the ghost of coffee scent greets me when I inhale.

I turn, ready to move to the next room, when voices float in from the hallway.

Quick as a flash, I dart inside the wardrobe, closing the door most of the way, just as two maids enter the room. I hold my breath until I worry I'll pass out. Slowly, I exhale, praying they won't hear the rapid beating of my heart, that they won't open the wardrobe to put clothes away. I don't want anyone to catch me until I come face to face with who I came to see. I don't need any interference here. I watch the women through the sliver of space between the doors. In sharp contrast to the rest of the house, they are clean and neat, wearing starched snow-white aprons and pressed dresses. Where the butler looked out of place and ill-fitting in his position, these two appear comfortable and capable as they change the bedsheets and dust the surfaces, even though the furniture in this room already gleams.

"…been in a mood lately," the younger, skinny one mutters, more a girl than a woman, her hair the orange of carrots.

The one with graying hair, and a thick, pink neck, shrugs back. "I suppose you'd be as well if you thought you were retiring, and it turns out you weren't."

The first maid stops dusting. She leans against a bedpost and wraps her hands around it. "Well, even if he's not, our orders are the same, no? We're to have the house set within the month, as if we can do it all that fast! It took a fortnight alone to do what we done so far!"

The older woman rolls her broad shoulders back. "We need only worry about our own work, Jinny," she says, wearily, as if it's not the first time. "We're making progress, and if he wanted more maids you know very well he could afford to hire them."

"Yes, I know." The red-haired girl sighs. "I'm just tired. He wants his home perfect, I'm thinking. Especially after that speech he gave this morning."

"Perfect. Not a spot anywhere, and especially not in his own chamber. So, let's get to it then, eh? I've got a million things to do before he gets back. Being the housekeeper can be exhausting at times, just between the two of us. Not that I'd say a word against him, dear. After a decade in his employment, I've grown rather fond of him, myself."

"Of course, Mrs. Minthy, he's a fine man, to be sure."

I wait in the hot wardrobe, miserably, while they finish their business, my desperate hope fading as the realization sinks in. There is no way he's a demon. If he were, they would be afraid. In fact, I can't think of how an evil being such as that would ever employ any normal person—they'd run screaming at the very sight of him, I expect. And if he were a killer, like the butler had implied, I think the maids' reaction would be quite different as well.

Embarrassment itches at me. What is wrong with me—how could I have let myself get to this point? Whatever happened to my common sense?

Despite what the butler indicated, it's likely he was in jest—or trying to inhibit me from wanting to see the reclusive man of the house. *In the business of taking lives?* I could almost laugh out loud now if tears weren't threatening to fall. I sought out a myth to bring my sister back—but there's no demon, no danger here. And no hope either. Just a man who likes books and coffee and a clean home. Just a man.

The maids' voices carry as they leave the room and go down the stairs. I was foolish to let myself believe Marieta and everything else pointing me here, to get swept up in fantasy. Aven is gone, and I must accept that. I step out of the stuffy wardrobe, closing it quietly behind me. I walk toward the door—furtively—but the tiny clang of something makes me stop. Looking down at my hand, I gasp at the realization that the too-large ring from Aven has slipped off my finger and rolled somewhere.

"Damnation," I mutter, scanning the room. I could no sooner leave behind the ring than one of my limbs.

I crouch down, looking in every nook and cranny, hairline dampening with sweat as each minute ticks by without finding it. I get on my hands and knees to search under the bed. The pearl glints in the shadows, and I let out a thankful sigh. I grab for it, and my fingers brush against something just beyond, something hard. I slip the ring on and pause. Logic tells me I should get up and get out before I'm caught trespassing. Yet something pulls at me from under the bed—what was that I just touched? Curiosity beats logic, and I reach back under and draw it out—a wooden box. Kneeling on the floor, heart thumping, I open it to find a pair of shoes inside. No, not shoes. Ballet slippers.

I gaze down in awe at the satin slippers, luminous, the deep red of blood.

They look wounded. Lonely. Like they're waiting for me to pick them up. I contemplate for long minutes at how strange they are, just inches from my fingers. They almost feel…alive.

I must put the box away, quickly, and precisely as I found it. Otherwise, the maids—or whomever stays in this room—might guess someone was in here snooping around. Not that I really care now. I don't much fear that a mortal will track me down for intruding, if I'm as cautious leaving as I was coming in. The demon doesn't exist. Yet these shoes do, these beautiful, beautiful shoes…

Leave, I tell myself. I didn't get what I came for. There's no point staying one second longer, risking being found in some rich stranger's home. The last thing I need is to have more rumors about me. Sélie would be mortified if I got caught, and I can hardly guess at the gossip that would follow me for the rest of my life if I were. The Pins doesn't forget things.

Nevertheless, lust floods through me. It won't hurt just to hold them. I graze my fingers against the satin and pull the slippers out. They're splendid, pristine ribbons, toes not even marred; they've never been danced in. They're the finest ballet shoes I've ever seen, much prettier than my worn out, ill-fitting pink ones, which I'd scrounged up secondhand, and which now lie rotting in the woods wherever I last threw them. I don't know how I do, but I already know these will fit me perfectly.

An image of myself dancing in them flashes through my mind. So what if it's nothing more than a selfish indulgence, a little something for myself after so much agony. A trinket to appease my wounds. I want them. I want them more than I've wanted any item in my life.

And if breaking into this mansion to speak to a nonexistent demon was the most outrageous thing I've ever done, I now do the second.

I steal the shoes.

CHAPTER FIVE

I run as fast as I can once I leave the house from the same open window I came in through. A rush of energy sharpens my vision, and my legs ache from the exertion as I escape to the safety of the deep woods, pink skirts fisted in one hand, hopping over fallen branches and sidestepping roots twisting out of the ground, the shoes gripped to my heaving chest.

They beat against my fingers like a heart.

When it is clear nobody is coming after me, I finally slow. Bent over, I drop my head and steady my breathing, wipe my forehead. I stare down at the slippers, a deeper red than burgundy in the shadows of the darkening woods. Something pumps inside me, in my blood. Relief. Fear. Longing. A hungry beast arising from its slumber.

I need to dance.

Without another thought, I slip off my hot leather boots and toss them to the ground. I simply must try the slippers on. Because the hope in my chest has withered away and been replaced with a fierce desperation. Perhaps if I dance, I can forget about this second ripple of grief coming over me. The demon does not exist. It was foolish to wish it so. The path to return Aven to life is no path at all.

She's gone, for real. For good.

I swallow the bitter cry burning its way up my throat and put the slippers on; they fit as if made for me. Tying the ribbons around my ankles only takes a moment. And then, I have the shoes, or maybe the shoes have me. Nothing hurts at all. Even while I dance, I'm feverish with the passion for more. To move, to keep going, to reach some destination I know nothing of. I cut through the woods at the edge of town and dance out to the road, twisting, leaping, gliding with ease, despite my heavy skirts, my heavy heart. I don't care who sees me. The birds, the trees, the leaves, the flowers, the wind, the watercolor-streaked sky—all are my audience; and I put on the best show of my life. Every movement is deliberate, perfect. It is all of my passion and all of my pain pooled together into two pulsing symbols on my feet. I am untouchable. The tears streaming down my face—even they are a kind of grace.

With the slippers, I can reach like never before, can jump higher. It is as easy as breathing, as I dance my way through town, passing staring shopkeepers closing up their stores, gaping market vendors, snickering sailors, and children gobbling spools of pastel sugar that change color in the light. I leap with arms stretched all the way through my fingertips, the dying sun hitting my skin as I move, salt air and sweat clinging to me, the way sadness has hung on me for so long. Though, I don't feel sad now.

With these shoes, I can forget. I can hardly remember what it is I don't want to remember in the first place.

Then, everything comes crashing down. Standing outside The Red Clover dance hall, with his arms folded against his chest and his mouth hanging open, is Julian, Gatekeeper to my dreams. Watching me dance. *Actually* dance this time.

And now I stop with a jolt in the middle of the road, and as some sense returns, mortification follows. I've opened myself up before strangers, making a spectacle of myself in front of half The Pins!

A crowd has gathered to gawk at me. I step forward, meaning to slip off the red shoes in the shadow of some alley, then go home. I'll forget all this ever happened, forget that I went in search of a demon to bring my sister back from the dead, that I danced in the streets, that I stole something—*me*, stole something! But something in me longs to keep dancing. Something in me is still restless for more.

Someone claps, breaking my thoughts apart, and then another, and another. Someone whistles in the background, and I startle when I feel a touch on my arm. I look up into Julian's face.

"May I ask what in God's name that was?"

I finally let loose some of the tension in my shoulders, and a laugh bubbles out of my dry throat as I answer him, "I'm not even certain. I simply had to dance."

He shakes his head, leading me away from the people and toward the Clover's doors. I go willingly, grateful for the chance to escape attention. "It appears your stage fright has eased…if that is the case, won't you try again for me now?"

Within minutes, I find myself back on the stage, all of us in the same positions as before: Julian, front row; the pianist, a woman named Dina, behind me and off to the side; and me, center stage and, this time, more thrilled than scared.

It's a less fevered tempo than what I danced to in my head through the woods and down the road. I count down and begin, sweeping across the floor in petit jumps and piqué turns as the music lightens and quickens, celebrating with the movement, allowing the joy of dancing again—for myself—to rush over me. Because I'm here, because after all these years and a prior failure, I'm finally dancing at The Red Clover. And for some odd reason, I don't care who sees me; I'd let anyone watch. Besides, after all that I've lost, I have nothing more to lose.

The slippers take over. It's as though they *want* me to dance, or perhaps it's just that everything weighing me down falls away like rain, or, like fog, evaporates off me, and I let my body do what it wants. Nothing is planned—not the fouettés I whip out with ease, not the pirouettes I follow with a grand jeté so flawless I even let out a breath of surprise. My skin feels tight and alive. I was born for this.

When the weakness in my legs finally forces me to stop, Julian stares at me thoughtfully from his front-row seat. He doesn't say anything. The pianist rises from her seat with a smile and walks off into the shadows. I stand in the center of the stage, dripping with sweat, fidgeting. Now the worry sets in. Maybe he changed his mind, seeing me dance to music. Maybe I was off beat after all. Maybe I just don't belong here, with my tattoos and complicated past and family drama. Maybe I don't belong anywhere anymore—now that Aven is gone.

Eventually, he stands. "Can you dance tomorrow evening for the show? And come early to get your costumes and set sorted?"

I waver, heart thundering. Hesitation, gratitude, shock all intermingle within me. I close my eyes for one breath. But then I open them and say, "Yes."

"Well, welcome to The Red Clover, Miss Bell."

My hand is shaking when I place it against my heart, a single whisper escaping me, "Really?"

"We've rarely had anyone just come in off the street and audition—and make it," he muses. "Our dancers usually come to us recommended from the schools in Warring's Cross or Manuette. Sometimes further."

"Why do they come here?" I wonder aloud before I can stop myself.

But he only chuckles and shakes his head, slick black hair staying in place. "Yes, The Pins is odd, I know. My grandfather started the Clover many years ago, and I don't think anyone anticipated it doing as well as it has, but something about this place draws people in. I know I never had the heart to go anywhere else."

I nod. "I understand. And thank you…for this opportunity."

"I'm excited to have you, and the audience will be too, when they hear about how you danced on the road, for those who weren't lucky enough to see."

I look away, embarrassed, but then I peep down at the slippers on my feet, at the red ribbons tied up so prettily around my ankles. And I smile.

I stroll through the darkening woods in a daze, ballet shoes flung over my shoulders by the ribbon. My stockinged feet are dusty, my boots abandoned in the woods somewhere between the Colehart Mansion and town. I frown about that now; I'll have to fetch them at some point. As I run the afternoon's events through my head, it seems hard to believe it's still the same day. I know it's *wrong*, but I somehow don't regret breaking into the mansion or taking the slippers. I spend the entire walk home ruminating on this. Why am I not sorry? Perhaps I'm still in shock, frozen in grief over accepting Aven's death. Perhaps I'm broken in some way. Lots of ways.

When I open the cottage door, Sélie is banging about in the kitchen.

"I'm home," I call. "Sorry I'm so late."

"In here! I'm making supper." She walks over, apron dusted with flour, tendrils of hair loose about her face. She stops short when she sees me. "What happened?"

I touch my face self-consciously, I'm sure my cheeks are red, my eyes wild with delight. "Sélie…" I stumble over her name in my excitement; now that I see her, I can't wait to share the news. "You'll never believe it. I got invited to dance at the Clover. Julian hired *me*! He wants me to start tomorrow evening."

Her big blue eyes go even bigger. "You auditioned again?"

As I drop to a seat, the bone-tired feeling catches up with me, my legs sore. "Not exactly. It's a long story, and strange. I was dancing and Julian saw me."

"Dancing where?" Confusion creases her face.

"Um…" I won't lie. She'll hear eventually, anyhow. I admit, "On the street."

I've danced in the tiny back room of the shop, in our cottage, on our beach, for myself, for my family. But never on the street. Never for strangers. Her mouth falls open in disbelief. "On the street, as in, *in town?*"

"I know that sounds odd," I try to explain, though I don't quite understand myself. "It's just, something came over me and I had to dance. I didn't care who was watching me, or how bizarre it was. And then he hired me."

She takes this all in stride, allowing it time to sink in. Her smile is more than a little smug when she finally says, "See?"

"What?"

With a low laugh, she jabs one floury finger in my direction. "I knew you were meant for it. I'm proud of you."

Would you be proud if you knew I was a thief? The thought flashes through me. I blink it away and say quickly, "I'll still be with you in the shop during the day. Shows are in the evenings. I hate to leave you alone so much at night though."

"It's fine. I need to do things on my own too." She scrunches up her face. "For goodness' sake, Corliss. I'm grown now."

"I know." I nod, for she's clearly not a little girl anymore, despite how youthful she looks. But all the same, she's younger than I was at her age, more naïve, innocent. I change the subject. "With the money I bring in, that will help us. We could even send you to art school."

Sélie's mouth tightens. "We've been through this, Corliss. I would never leave you, or The Pins."

I squeeze her hand hard. "I wouldn't want to leave you either. But you should think about it. You're very talented, love. You could do so many great things with your art."

"I can be an artist without school. And I don't want to leave the shop." She waves me away, a hint of irritation at the topic she's clearly sick of revisiting. I don't push it. She's sweet as pie most of the time, but pushed hard enough, her temper has a bite. She goes on, adding, "Besides, can we just focus on you right now? We should celebrate, somehow. I should make a nicer dinner."

I wrinkle my nose at the burnt smell in the air. "What *are* you making—or burning?"

With a shriek, Sélie runs to the kitchen, then she yells, "I ruined the bread. Damn it."

Laughing, I rise, then I walk toward the bedroom. "That's okay. I'm not very hungry."

In the quiet room, I take off my dress and peel down my grimy stockings. I contemplate a bath, which I desperately need, but I'll have to manage it in the morning instead. I maneuver myself out of my corset and chemise, dab at my skin with a wet, soapy rag at the basin, then slide on my nightgown, tugging my old silk dressing gown atop that.

Sélie's voice is far away, in the other room, but the words feel too close. "Oh, where'd you get the red slippers?"

Here is where I lie, though I hate to do it. I gaze admiringly at the shoes. Find myself calling back, "Julian gave them to me."

I set them aside until tomorrow—when I'll return to The Red Clover—and I join Sélie in the next room. After dinner—passable, but nowhere near as good as Aven's cooking, a fact which we both politely ignore—I watch Sélie draw, her work coming to life. Pride glows from within me, and still, deep down, the enduring worry I've always held for her. She's taller than me now, but I can't help remembering her as a small, sickly-looking child.

"What a fearful, skittery thing!" one crotchety old guardian had exclaimed as little Sélie stood in between me and Aven, Sélie's face white, eyes wide, hands shaking in ours. She was always like that with other people, until the year we came to The Pins to live with Mavis. When we moved into Mavis's tiny cottage, Sélie began to flourish, running up and down the rocky path to the ocean, swimming, gathering wildflowers in the woods. She grew freckled under the sun, and strong, learning to speak her opinions—and she had surprisingly many—out loud. And her art flourished here too. Our father, John, had been an artist, like her. I wish I could remember him, would give anything to recall our mother, Mercedes. I wish…for so much.

Forcing away the sorrow, I will myself to celebrate my blessings. *This* moment. *This* sister. *This* good.

Since Sélie cooked, I offer to clear the table and clean up the kitchen. She draws on as I tidy the cottage, my mind busy elsewhere. I'm glad she doesn't seem to notice my restlessness, so enraptured with her work as she is. I can hardly think of anything but dancing—but the shoes. I would like to turn back the day, to go back to the moment before I stepped onstage. I'd like to do it all over again. Tomorrow, I will.

When we go to bed, my sister's soft snores fill the room in no time, while I lie awake, thinking, dreaming until the breeze cools, until the crickets' sounds float in through the window. What will I dance tomorrow? The next night? The next? What will I do in the shoes?

They don't belong to you, a voice in my head says. I disregard it. They're my shoes now. I was meant to find them, to have them. To distract myself, I open my favorite novel once again, to read while the ocean waves crash gently through our open windows, but I can't lose myself as I usually do. I can't fall asleep, no matter how tired I grow. Tossing restlessly, turning, sweating in my twisted sheets.

It's not until I get up, bring the shoes down to the length of sand and begin to dance that the restlessness stops, that I find peace. But it's more than peace—it's a consumption. An unraveling. A euphoria that borders on pain. I might dance myself to death, if given the chance, but, what a sweet death it would be….

The water stretches before me as I leap along the shore, moonlight reflecting off the soft ripples of waves, shining like diamonds. I dance until my mind and heart are full, my body tired, my eyes heavy, and then I return to my bed. Yet even in my dreams, I dance, feverish, lost. Found.

With a cry, I sit upright, awake as fear alights my senses. *Dreaming*. I was dreaming. I swallow the scared feeling down and go in search of a drink of water. Yet as I tiptoe through the cottage, the shadows creeping on the floor send me rushing back to the bedroom to take cover under my blanket, an eerie sense, as if I'm not alone, as if someone is watching me, something whispery and dark which feels like it's creeping up to nuzzle my neck. A sickening fear clinging to me.

I'm not afraid of the dark, I tell myself sternly. *It was only a dream.*

"What's wrong?" Sélie mutters sleepily.

"Nothing. A nightmare." I lie down, try to think of what it was, of what has me shaken. All I recall is a lion, mane painted red. Paws dripping blood. And a voice—deep, cold.

I'm coming for you.

I'm coming for you.

CHAPTER SIX

I t's an exceptionally quiet morning at the shop, and more than
once I've caught Sélie frowning. She's doing it right now. At the
moment, her head is bent over an old arithmetic book, back
from when all three of us attended school, which had been rare
and random as we moved from place to place. When we came
to The Pins, Mavis said we'd learn more from her than in the
stifling old schoolhouse, and that was that. Our formal—albeit
sporadic—education was over, although that didn't mean any of
us gave up on learning in our own ways.

As Sélie studies the difficult figures—for fun!—I take note of
how worn her dress is. This gives me a good excuse to get out of
the shop, for I'm far too restless to do anything productive. All
day I've just been fiddling around with new recipes, but nothing
feels right—I'm too excited and nervous about my performance
tonight. Patting her shoulder, I say, "Let's close the shop for a bit.
You're in desperate need of a new dress."

Sélie frowns at me, then turns back to her pages. "I'm not sure
we can afford it."

"You need one, Sélie." I stare meaningfully at her hem, several
inches too short. I tug on her sleeve and say, "Besides, Bricksbee would do well to consider taking our order on tab, for all the
makeup we've sold Loueva."

"Alright then." She shuts her book hesitantly.

I set the new tins of lip stain I just made on the display shelf, lining each one up perfectly straight, and then we hang up our aprons and hook arms.

I flip the sign and lock the door behind us, then, side by side, we head to the tailor. *Bricksbee's Fine Tailoring and Dress Shop*, reads the wooden sign.

We push open the door and enter the store, which smells of lavender and clean linen. The ready-made dresses hang on one side, on dress forms, or in the windows to lure customers from the street: a chocolate silk with ruffles and a cheeky polka-dotted underskirt, a spring-green muslin with a gathered skirt and citrus-hued piping along the hem—it even has tiny lemon-shaped buttons. I gaze hungrily at a dove-gray brocade with tassel trim and a matching parasol, though my practical mind says I have nowhere to wear such a fine dress, and anyhow, I like a little rain on me. Nonetheless, I give it a backwards glance. The color would match my eyes perfectly. Maybe with my first payment from the Clover, I'll treat myself. But this trip isn't about me. It's about Sélie. Next to me, she runs her fingers around the frilly-ruffled bodice of a cornflower-blue dress.

I say to her, "Lovely. Do you want that one? I'm sure it could be altered to fit."

She lets her hands drop. "I was thinking something white for summer. Simpler."

We wander over to the fabric side of the shop, and she quickly narrows in on a bolt of white cotton with skinny black lines.

"Oh, that's pretty," I encourage. "I bet you could do a simple lace trim too."

Milton Bricksbee walks over, his finely tailored coat unbuttoned over his round belly. He asks blandly, "May I help you ladies find anything?"

I say, "Yes, my sister needs a new dress for summer. She likes this fabric."

He takes the bolt, his eyes so dull I wonder if he ever gets truly excited. I suppose Loueva Maelin would know. Then I try not to laugh as he continues, "It will take three days, as I'm short a seamstress right now. Also, payment is due promptly at pickup. I usually require half-down."

I see precisely the moment he realizes all the times we've let him settle his bill for his mistress after the fact. Recognition flashes across his russet-brown face. He adds, a touch warmer, "But for you, ladies, that won't be necessary."

With an appreciative nod, I say, "Thank you, Mr. Bricksbee. I think we'd like to get two dresses. Perhaps that blue ready-made with the ruffles as well?"

Sélie protests, tugging gently on my elbow, face rosy with discomfort. "I don't need anything so done up, and one new dress is more than enough."

"Don't argue. You deserve it." I turn to Bricksbee. "Could the blue be altered to fit her?"

"Of course. However, I do have a fabric in a very similar shade, which we could start fresh from. It would be a better fit, and I could alter the style if it's not to your liking, Miss Bell. Fewer frills, if you so wish." He addresses the last part to Sélie.

"I suppose." She looks at me. "Corliss, if you're sure?"

I answer, voice firm, willing to bully her if need be. "I'm quite sure."

Bricksbee motions to her. He leads her to the center pedestal and has her step up.

"I'll just have to take your measurements now, Miss. It won't take long. Would you be wanting a protective charm sewn into the hem?"

I hold back from saying such trinkets are a waste of money and politely decline.

While he measures Sélie, I wander the shop, passing by the windows. A movement on the other side of the glass catches my eye. A crow perched on the shop sign. It stares at me. I wait for it to fly away as I move closer, but it is still as a statue, glittering eyes pinned on me, hard, almost…almost *mean*.

I step back, bump into a dress form, nearly knocking it over in my clumsiness.

"Alright over there?" Sélie calls, arms stuck straight at her sides.

"Fine." I clear my throat, return my gaze to the window. The bird holds its pose for a moment longer before finally flying away, and even though a window separates us, I swear I can almost feel the way the air moves in the wake of its wings.

Soon enough, Sélie is finished, and as we move through town, I scan the skies, pensive. When Sélie asks if I'd like to pop into the bookstore, a delight I'd usually revel in, I make an excuse.

The whole way back to our shop, it clings to me, a tingle on my skin, a sour taste in my mouth, the sense—the *knowing*. The eeriness pressed around me, the sense of someone off in the shadows. It hangs on so long I can't ignore it. Someone is watching me.

"Corliss Bell." Julian eyes me like a puzzle he needs to put together as we walk together to the costume room, hours ahead of my first performance. Pausing outside the door, running his slender fingers along his smoothly shaved jaw, he repeats, *"Bell."*

He studies me so intently I look away, already anxious enough.

What if they don't want me to wear the stolen shoes? What if they prefer something more traditional? The thought has me biting the inside of my cheek. I'll just tell them I need the red slippers, that they're good luck, that they fit me perfectly. Because I can't dance without them here. I know I can't. They make me better.

"Yes?" I fiddle with the shoes in my hand, twining the ribbons around my fingers. It will only be minutes until I can put them back on, I hope. All day at the shop, it took every ounce of my willpower not to head over to the Clover early, to dance again. Sélie finally shooed me out, with a good luck kiss, proud tears in her eyes as she promised she'd see me later at the show.

"Bells!" Julian snaps his fingers, jarring my gaze back to him. Today he's in a pale gray suit with a vermilion bowtie. "We'll give you bells. You'll be a feast for the eyes and for the ears."

He must see my cringe when he says "feast" because he chuckles. "Not that way. Not for me, and definitely not for our customers. We're not that kind of establishment."

"I didn't think you were." I smile nervously. Not because I doubt his word. But because I'm here. I'm *here*, and it's almost time to get ready.

"We just like to add a little something extra for the show. When you're done getting your costumes, Becka will send you to get your music set—you can practice for a bit while Dina plays. Nobody will be there yet, so you'll have the stage to yourself."

"Is it just piano?" I'm too flustered to recall the information I might know already. Of course, I've only seen snippets of practices—never full shows.

Julian almost looks affronted. "There are several musicians nightly, for big shows a full orchestra. The show starts at six. You should be ready quite before that, of course. The set is listed backstage. We'll have you go between Pearl and Lysander. We do full ballets twice a year, with more structured themes, choreography, all that, though typically it's more of an individual set of acts that work beautifully together. For tonight, you'll do your best." He rattles off the information. My head feels like it's spinning. Looking past my shoulder, he adds, "Here comes Becka now."

Then he reaches out to take my hand, his gold cufflinks glinting. His smile is earnest. "Also, I apologize for not saying it sooner, I was saddened to hear of your sister, as well as the loss of her husband. I'm afraid I made it to neither funeral."

Aven's funeral is still a blur, though I know there were plenty of somber faces, hushed voices. When Darius and his crew were mourned—twenty-eight empty graves—most of The Pins attended. Weeping mothers, bereft fathers, sweethearts in every corner. Sélie and I held on to Aven, her belly stretched full as she swayed on her feet, face white as a ghost. I hardly noticed anyone else there. To Julian now, I say, "I understand. But thank you."

Before he can add anything else, the costume mistress, a small woman at under five feet tall, nudges me gently aside while she opens the door. She waves me in with an impatient but lovely smile, her tortoiseshell eyes bright beneath a pair of wire spectacles. "Alright, I'm here. New girl, come on in."

Before she shuts the door behind us, Julian calls out, "Her stage name is Bell. Give her bells."

Becka purses her lips at his instruction, then leads me through the packed room, a chaotic array of color, every surface flung with tutus and hangers, spools of ribbon scattered on tables, rows of accessories, shelves full of sparkling costume jewelry. Her voice is brisk. "Come, Bell."

"Corliss Bell is actually my name, or just Corliss is fine."

Turning back, she gives me a dry grin, spread wide. "You're Bell on stage, may as well be backstage too. I can't keep up with real names and stage names, both."

"Alright." I let out a laugh then pause, holding up the slippers. "May I wear the red?"

"Of course." Becka shrugs and stops in front of a large trunk. She begins to rummage through it, and behind her back, I release a deep sigh of relief.

She goes on, "The costumes don't belong to you—they're on loan. I make a new one for each dancer every few months, so if you have ideas tell me. Don't take them home, or for God's sake, try to fix anything you break or rip. Just bring it right back and I'll take care of it." She comes up with a belt, tiny silver bells dangling from it. "This is all I have with bells for the time being. Now, let's get costumes."

Taking the belt, I follow, anticipation blooming in me, despite my nerves for what's ahead. When she leads me to the racks, I can't help but gasp aloud. "Oh, how beautiful they are!"

I move closer to get a better look. Some tutus are stiff and unyielding, others soft and gossamer-like. They come in every color of the rainbow and some colors I've never seen on clothing before, even in Bricksbee's fine dress shop. There are dark and rich shades: mulberry, inky blue, a green almost black. Then the pale colors: bone white, blush pink, ice aqua. Some have beads that catch the light, metallic threads, lace, embroidery, even feathers. On one costume, buttons as white and tiny as a child's tooth all up and down the back. There's velvet, and tulle, and fabrics I'm not even sure the names of. Some of them even seem to subtly change color as I stare at them. I blink away the unsettling sense. Just a trick of the eye. In any case, they're stunning.

I can't believe I'll get to dance in these.

Yet even with the red slippers, the pull of wanting to put them on right here, right now, there's a bit of reality sinking in. In mere hours, I'll be onstage in front of an audience—one used to high standards—and before that, I'll see the other ballerinas. One particular face nudges its way into my memory. Tanna, who taught me so much of what I know. Her black curls. Red lips. The touch of her cool hand as she pushed me deeper into my stretches, as we learned each other's bodies in the shadows of her rented room above the cobbler shop. She'll be here tonight, won't she? Will she be surprised to see me, or will Julian already have told them all about me? Will she have heard the whispers of how I danced in the streets?

I hide my apprehension and look at Becka expectantly.

She reaches up, fastening the bell belt around me. "Small waist, quite round hips, certainly en vogue. But busty. Let's make sure you don't fall out the top, huh?"

I grin. "I'd appreciate that."

She looks over my pale, cool skin, my clear gray eyes, my dark-brown hair. "Hmmm. What shall we put you in?"

When I leave the room I have two costumes in my arms. I will rotate them, with a promise from Becka to make a custom costume for me. I didn't tell her, but I know I'll request a blue costume—Aven's favorite shade. I'll choreograph a routine in honor of my sister, in memory of her. The grief shoves its way into my body, and I roll my shoulders back, squeezing the heap in my arms for strength.

Becka sends me to go find Dina to get my music set. Once there, I carefully place the costumes across a small table off in the wings. I tie the long ribbons of the slippers up my ankles, and when I'm warmed up, walk out on stage, where Dina looks up at me from the piano.

"What would you like?" she asks. "It's just me for now; the other musicians will arrive within the hour."

"Can you play what you did yesterday?" I ask. "I'll improve upon that."

In answer, her long fingers start up on the keys.

I take a quick breath and begin. Each beat of the music is matched in every perfect arabesque, every bourrée, every turn, the curl of my fingers. But I need to finish the routine, so for the last part of the music, I simply play with some steps and sear them into my memory for the show later. I don't even notice when Dina gets up and leaves until I find myself alone, humming the melody under my breath, losing myself in the movement, in the feeling of flinging myself wide open, in the quiet of the theatre. The musicians haven't arrived yet.

I feel like I have the whole world to myself.

Except—a shadow catches my eye, off in the red velvet seats of the audience. It's so far away, and with the gaslights shining in my face, I can only make out a black outline. The theatre is quiet as I continue my work, though the person in the audience makes me nervous, somehow. Julian is busy in his office, but maybe it's a benefactor of the theatre, a nosy patron who shouldn't be here yet, or even a guest of Julian's, hoping to catch him before the show. Self-conscious, I stop humming, and mark out the steps, trying to avoid glancing in the shadows at the silent figure.

I pause, debating between an ending pose en pointe or one sweeping downward, body bowed like a swan, when the stranger in the shadows speaks.

"You dance beautifully." His voice is very deep, measured. Where have I heard it before? My skin tingles with apprehension.

I jerk up my head and squint to make out his figure, his face, his identity.

"Thank you? Mr....?" I step forward, holding a hand above my brow so that the glare of the lamps is out of my eyes. I look to where I saw his outline before. But he is gone.

When I enter the dressing room after practicing, I'm acutely aware of the other dancers getting ready, eyeing me with curiosity. I drift to an empty chair, hands clammy with nerves, and lay my costumes across the back.

Is Tanna here? I wonder, refusing to turn around and check.

Someone speaks behind me, the faintest hint of an accent I can't place, "There's a wardrobe for your things."

"Oh." I turn, nodding my thanks to the tall girl who broke the silence. She looks about my age, maybe a bit younger—closer to Sélie's age, maybe nineteen or twenty. She's striking with vivid hazel eyes and glowing fawn-brown skin, legs so long they go on forever. I add, "Thanks."

She reaches out her graceful hand, grinning as we shake. "Of course. I'm Pearl, by the way." Pearls decorate the bodice of her shimmering turquoise costume, and she wears her black hair twisted up in a thick braid coiled around the top of her head, held in place with a large jeweled pin shaped like a shell.

"And I'm Corliss Bell. Just Bell for the shows."

"I've seen you before, haven't I?" She cocks her head. "You bring our cosmetics. You work at the apothecary, no?"

"I do. I run it with my younger sister." It hurts not to say sisters, plural.

It was Aven's dream to run the shop after Mavis died six years ago. She convinced me and Sélie not to sell it to the mustachioed gentlemen who'd wanted to turn it into a bank and "let The Pins finally turn into a modern town." Sélie and I had wavered. The sum they'd offered had been more money than we'd had in our lives. We'd considered traveling, sending Sélie to art school (despite her resistance), me having proper dancing lessons (despite mine). However, Aven insisted. "We can do it on our own, just like Mavis did, only better." So we did. We kept the shop, and the name—*Boutique d'Apothicaire*—though people began to call it "The Three Bells Apothecary" even after Aven married Darius and took the surname Winter. We were still the Bell sisters. We still are, will always be.

"I love that place. Or rather, I love your products! I use them for our shows. I've been meaning to come into your shop for ages," Pearl gushes, adding, "I've always liked cosmetics and find it fascinating, how you create such beauty."

My cheeks warm at her flattery. "Thank you. Come any time you like, we'll give you a tour."

She opens her mouth to go on, but someone clears their throat impatiently.

"Corliss?"

I stiffen. I know that voice. *Here goes.* I look past Pearl to the woman seated in front of a mirror, drawing wings from her dark eyes.

"Tanna." I smile tightly. "Or, what is it again?"

She gives me a tiny twist of her mouth. "It's Flame here. Surprised you forgot."

As if I *could* forget, especially with her posters papered on the outside of the building. It's the first time we've been face to face since she married. But it doesn't bother me as much as I thought; with Aven gone, this pain is like a crack in the heart compared to having my heart shattered whole.

She adds, "I'm more surprised to see *you* here, though."

Her hand, the one drawing the charcoal along her lids, holds a large diamond ring that glints in the light. She must keep it on while she performs.

So what if she's married now? Good for her.

"Yes, I decided it was time. Anyway, you look well," I answer casually, admiring her sunset-colored tutu, the drops of rubies hanging from her earlobes, her bronze-kissed face. She's beautiful. As always. Half-teasing, I ask, "Still eating fire?"

And hopelessly romantic girls for breakfast? Before you spit them back out? But I'm not angry, and I try to be gracious. She's partly made me into the dancer I am today. *Her, and the red shoes,* I ponder uneasily.

"Mmm," she says, continuing her makeup. "What will you be doing?"

Picturing the bell belt, I deflate. It's no fire-eating. "I'll dance. Just dance."

Before she can question me further, I turn back to Pearl, who's watching us both with curiosity. I ask, "What about you?"

"Ah. I sing while I dance. Lysander uses aerial silks."

"Star has nothing but her dancing," Tanna interrupts. "She's so good she doesn't need anything extra. I'm guessing that's why you only have bells. You always did have a natural ability…" She twists up her hair with two golden clips shaped like dragonflies. Their eyes wink at me—rubies. She gives me an inscrutable look. Not unkind. But…something. I'm probably imagining the flash of regret. Could she be sorry she can't celebrate this milestone with me?

I waver, unsure what to say to that. *Thank you for helping to train me? But damn you for hurting me?*

"Anyway, we should let you get ready," Pearl says kindly.

I throw her a smile of thanks. Going to the wardrobe, I hang up the two costumes Becka gave me. One is the white of a swan with rhinestones dotting the bodice, the other a dark gray, with a long, pitch-black underskirt, silver threads embroidered around the bustline. I'll look like a princess in these, like an enchantress. I'll look like a real ballerina.

While the other dancers finish readying themselves, I grab a few palettes that came from the apothecary from a table in one corner. It's always the same set for the Clover dancers: face powder from a warm reed brown to seashell white; rouge with both cool and warm undertones; vivid lip colors; sparkling eye stains in indigo and gold; chalky color sticks. As I walk back to the dressing table, I admire the products; it's somewhat surreal, having these two aspects of my life colliding in this moment.

I set the cosmetics among my personal belongings: my rose-salt perfume oil; hairpins; ribbon; and earrings of miniature silver vines. My hands shake as I clip them on. I started dancing late, I've trained mostly on my own and only have a fraction of the experience the others have. What if it's not enough?

I sit, overwhelmed, and a bit lost.

Staring into the mirror before me, I gauge my feelings. I'm nervous, yes, almost sick to my stomach with it. But underlying that is such excitement. I'm here. *I'm at The Red Clover!* And soon, I'll be dancing. Is it wrong to be happy when I'm still missing Aven so much? Is it wrong that I've forgotten to be sad for a moment? I push away the guilt. Aven would tell me to stop. To enjoy myself. To move on. Of course I'd argue with her, the way I always lovingly did, but I can't deny the truth: this moment is a good one. I only wish she were here to share it with me.

"Need some help?" A voice interrupts my thoughts, and I look up at the softest face I've ever seen. Round curve of the chin, golden apples for cheeks, the nearly white-blonde hair, the sparkling eyes that crinkle at the corners, the even brighter sparkle of the hefty, star-shaped earrings. If I'm not wrong, those are real diamonds.

"Star?" I recognize her from her poster.

"Ah, the very one." Star gracefully slides her full body into a chair and scoots it closer to mine, then picks up a brush without me asking. "Close your eyes." She smells like vanilla, apple, and some sweet flower that I can't quite place. Nobody has done my face up since Aven. I didn't realize I'd missed it until I swallow the lump in my throat. This woman feels motherly, in the same way my sister did.

"Nervous?" Star asks.

I open my eyes to gaze at her. Her voice is mature, though her face is unlined. She can't be more than thirty years of age, but I'd suppose she's the most senior of them all. I'd guess Pearl is the youngest here, then maybe me next—twenty-two this past spring. "A little."

"It'll be nice to get some new blood around here. The patrons will like it too. All done."

I smile as I turn back to the mirror. She did well, the rich look stands out, perfect for the stage. "Thank you."

Star squeezes my arm. "I'm off to warm up." Then she gives me one last friendly wave before she leaves the room, blowing kisses at the others. "Bye, girls."

"I'm worried I'll forget my choreography—I only just made something up. Is that a problem?" I ponder aloud as the room quiets. I don't even care if I sound vulnerable in front of Tanna. I know Julian said it was fine, but haven't they all been practicing their sets for a week or more? Months even?

Pearl says, "It's your first night. You can do something on the spot if you forget, can you not?"

The way I danced before, unbidden, the way it just came to me, makes me nod in agreement.

"We work on routines and come up with show sets each month,

sometimes as a group, but usually alone. Try not to be nervous," she encourages. "Also, be certain to curtsey at the end. Julian gets angry if we forget." Her hazel eyes twinkle with mischief—as though she sort of likes the idea.

"Oh, and don't smoke or anything outside the theatre. We're supposed to be on our 'best behavior' while we represent the Clover." Tanna makes a face.

How much will she be scrutinizing my technique? Recognizing my movements as things she taught me not that long ago? I picture the strangers that will be staring at me from the crowd. What if I fumble? What if I freeze? My stomach does a backflip.

It's not until I tie on the red shoes and warm up again, waiting for my turn to dance in the show, that my nerves truly fade away. I watch from the wings along with Lysander, a handsome, muscled dancer with curly hair and one blue eye, one green. He tosses a grin at me like we're fast friends, and I can't help but return it. My anticipation takes precedence over everything now.

Pearl finishes up her routine, and it is so exquisite I have to stop myself from joining her, the beauty of what she's creating with her movements and her song inviting me in. She's the picture of pure joy as she twirls, her extension flawless.

"She's good," I breathe.

"She is," Lysander says, nodding then charmingly tossing his hair. "You're up next."

I fasten the bell belt around my waist, and against the gently swaying tulle skirt, it rings pleasantly. I adjust my costume and check myself over in the mirror hanging in the wings for last-minute touch-ups. My eyes dressed in silver and black, my cheeks rouged, a crimson stain on my lips, pronounced when my mouth stretches into a smile. And there's nothing pasted about it.

Pearl swishes offstage, breathless, face dewy with sweat. "Good luck, Bell."

"Thank you." I beam at both her and Lysander and take one last deep breath.

Then I am onstage, performing for the first time as Bell of The Red Clover, in my scarlet slippers and white costume.

The whole performance is like a dream. When I am finished, the audience gives me a standing ovation. Flushed from exertion and a humble—almost disbelieving—gratitude, I dip into a deep curtsey, and, when I glance up, I find Sélie in the front row, tears running down her face. She is the last to sit. It takes everything in me not to cry as well. Out of love, of thanks, of wishing so badly Aven hadn't missed this moment.

When I see Sélie after the show, she stares with awe. "You were so beautiful, Corliss."

Hugging her to me, I squeeze hard. "I'm glad you came."

She tugs on the belt around my waist and says, "These could have been louder, though."

I release her and laugh, pulling her toward the rest of the performers, everyone making their way back to the dressing rooms. "Don't tell Julian. I don't want to wear any more of these. I feel a bit pathetic. Most everyone else has something so flashy…"

When we catch up to the other dancers, I introduce her. "Everyone, this is my sister, Sélie. She came to watch the show."

"It was wonderful!" Sélie says, smiling widely at them all. "All of you, just wonderful."

"I like you already." Lysander smirks, shaking her hand.

Pearl reaches her hand out as well. "It's nice to meet you."

"Your voice…" my sister praises. "It was so amazing."

With a delighted smile, Pearl says, "Thank you."

Then Sélie is sure to compliment each one of them in turn, so that nobody feels left out. So that they all know how much she enjoyed the show.

I feel such a rush, the euphoria from dancing still running through me, and I'm afraid of the questions that might lurk when it wears off. I reluctantly pull away to change out of my costume before meeting my sister in the hall, and once ready to go, the two of us head out of the theatre.

"Can I come again to watch you?" Sélie presses.

"I'll get you a ticket anytime you want, love," I promise as we leave the building, the marquee still shining. "But I think you should wait until I get my next routine set. I want to surprise you."

"Wonderful. Now, a treat maybe? We haven't gotten one in so long. The sweet shop is still open…"

"Alright." I nod, no coaxing necessary. Not that I'm hungry—but that she is.

We move through the streets, Sélie chattering away. We pass market vendors selling fresh flowers, trinkets, jewelry, scarves of cobalt, cream, a burgundy stitched with gold threads that coil like snakes, and fruit pastries. But there's something in the air pressing against me…leaving me cold and anxious. Why? I had one of the best nights of my life.

If only Aven were here to share this moment with us.

A sudden shame fills me, slamming me back to reality.

I stole the slippers. Even tucked away in my bag now, they call to me, enticing me. But they're not really mine, and neither is the glory they're bringing me. I already know my poster will hang out front soon enough. Already know that wasn't my last standing ovation.

I don't deserve it, any of it.

That feeling from when I left Bricksbee's returns, dotting chills up and down my skin. Like someone is watching me.

Sélie waits on the stoop of the sweet shop, waving me in. Flustered, I take the steps quickly and follow her inside. The air is yeasty and sweet, like fried donuts. In the display case, miniature cookies and pastel petit fours are lined up neatly in rows, just like we do with the compacts at our store. Then there's the famous dense chocolate cakes rumored to make you relive your first kiss, taking center stage in the display case, dripping with shining ganache. I've never had one, in all these years. I've resisted out of sheer, practical protest.

"I'd like a sugar twist, please," Sélie says, smiling at the girl behind the counter.

"And for you?" the girl asks me.

I answer without meaning to, "I'll take a chocolate cake. With the ganache."

Sélie looks at me in surprise, while the shopgirl gives me a knowing smile and places each of our treats in a paper bag. I pay for our purchase, and as soon as we leave the sweet shop, Sélie bites into her twist, closing her eyes in pleasure, scrunching up her pert little nose, some of the sugar dusting her lip. "Mmm. That's so good. Aren't you going to eat yours?"

Why did I pick a kiss cake now? Perhaps to prove to myself that it's still ridiculous. All of it. That there's no such thing as the fantastical. No such thing as magic.

As demons.

I take the cake out of the bag, feeling the delicate weight of it, noting the fluted edges, the shining ganache, the rich and bitter scent of dark chocolate. Though my stomach turns, I bite into it as we walk.

And there it is: Wil the sailor, pulling me forward by the hand, coy smile on his face, dipping down to kiss me. As if it were yesterday, the memory comes to me: the pressure of his laughing lips, the swirl of his tongue on mine, the flutter in my middle, the longing, the rush of it. Once again, for just a moment, I am sixteen.

"Well?" Sélie pokes me. "Anything?"

The chocolate sits like mud in my mouth. I swallow. The memory fades.

"Nothing," I say, dropping the dessert back in the bag. As we walk, I glimpse Marieta on the butcher stoop, chatting with two women who lean over her. I skip past as quickly as I can without arousing suspicion. She might see right through me. Might notice how rattled I am.

My sister's face falls. "Oh well. It's not like I have a kiss to remember."

"Give it time," I say absentmindedly, keeping a sharp focus on the people wandering the streets. Will I catch someone staring at me?

"I'll be an old maid before I know it."

"You're only twenty," I say. "And we don't prescribe to that ridiculous notion."

As we near the spot off the square where we usually turn off the town road to head home, I notice a man. He looks out of place to me, although he's simply standing on the corner, not walking, or talking, or doing anything at all. And yet, fear trickles down my spine, freezes in my veins, punches me in the gut. He doesn't seem to notice me. Yet I can't help but wonder, *Is he the one who's been watching me?*

I hold my breath, waiting for something to happen.

It's fine, it's fine, I tell myself. I keep my eyes glued to him all the same.

The man turns suddenly on his heel and walks away, and that's when I glimpse the blood, where he stood only moments ago, pooling out onto the street. A group of children kick a leather ball down the road, chasing it in giggles, and it rolls right across the puddle of blood.

"Stop!" I call out as a shrill warning before they run through the red. "Wait!"

"What?" Sélie turns to follow my gaze. "What is wrong?"

I choke back a scream as the children chase the ball, making bloody shoeprints through the street, up the sidewalk. I bite back further warning, because it's pointless. I can tell by the lack of response that nobody sees anything wrong. The man is gone, as if he were never there. The children laugh, while blood spatters on them, dotting their pinafores and trousers with bright red. An omen, maybe. Or a warning. It must be my imagination—all of it—including the echo of the music I danced to tonight, ringing through my brain. Like the orchestra is inside my skull, pounding away on their instruments. The red shoes seem to pulsate from inside my bag, begging me to put them on.

I am lightheaded as I force myself to move.

"Corliss?"

"Nothing. Nothing is wrong," I say to my sister, over the haunting music. *Nothing. Everything.*

Twisting her lips, Sélie watches me in concern. She definitely knows something is wrong with me, though she doesn't know *what*.

Because she doesn't see anything. Nobody sees it but me. Nobody hears that music but me. I can hardly catch my breath.

Now, standing just ahead, coming into view as people weave around us, is a shadowy figure, face cloaked in darkness.

The figure flickers in and out of focus in the middle of the street, as people move around us, as if everything is in fast motion. Only the two of us are in clear relief, everything else is a muddy haze. I can't see his hellish features, but I feel his malevolent stare. I know who this is. I know what it is. Something roars in my mind, and I turn from the square in a violent about-face, dragging Sélie along.

"What happened? Why are we walking so fast? And why are you crying?"

I shake my head fast, willing myself to believe it was only my imagination. Not real. "I'm sorry. It's stupid. I simply felt scared."

"Of what?"

My fate, I want to say. Instead, I whisper, "I don't know."

"Corliss, tell me!" She pulls her arm out from my grip and faces me, expression stern. Beneath it is worry, clear-cut worry.

"Nothing. I...I'm sick. I must have a fever. I need to go lie down. I feel ill."

She leads me away, and I don't have to pretend. The sickness wells up inside me, the memory of all that blood, that...figure. Right outside our shop, I bend over and lose my chocolate cake.

CHAPTER SEVEN

When nothing happens to me overnight, apart from some nightmares slick with blood, I tell myself to relax. Nobody is watching me—it's merely my guilt at play here, the uncomfortable truth I've been avoiding facing. I took those slippers, and I'm worried I'll get caught is all. Satisfied with my realizations, determined not to allow it one more thought, I leave Sélie at home, trying her hand at pastries this morning since the shop is closed. Alone, I walk into town, ultra-aware of my surroundings. But nothing happens on the way to the theatre, and once I'm settled in the dark wings, pulling the ruby-red slippers on, I put the incident from yesterday out of my mind.

Incidents. Wasn't someone watching me after the dress shop? Someone in the audience while I practiced? And then…the bleeding man. The dark, haunting form right after.

Pushing it aside, I stand by myself while Lysander practices alone on the stage. It was all, all nothing. I'll return the slippers. One day…

Today, a Sunday, is the final practice before we break for summer holiday for the week—the one time a year The Red Clover is closed that long, partly due to the annual Pins carnival which occurs later in the week. And it's a shame, really, because I've only performed one show, and now I'll be forced to pause. I admire Lysander as he finishes practicing his routine. His arms shake as he holds himself up, muscles taut and strong. He is graceful yet powerful as he swings off the silks. I whistle from the wings, awed by his strength and beauty.

He gives me a mock bow when he comes offstage, muscles taut, skin glistening with sweat. "Why, thank you."

"You were wonderful. I love the routine."

"What about that last leap, though? Was it too much?"

"Not at all." I smile. "I loved it. So, are you heading anywhere for the holiday?"

"I am, thank God." He gives me a boyish grin. "I do need to get going, wish I could stay and watch you."

"You can see my routine when you get back. It's barely anything now—I only have a few rough counts, but I'll practice every day while we're closed."

"Rough? I doubt that very much. You are perfection, Corliss." He refuses to call me Bell, which I rather like about him. I anticipate us becoming great friends.

Cheeks warm, I shake my head. "Hardly."

He gives me one last smile before he departs. I wonder if I imagine the look of longing he throws toward Julian's office on his way out. I've felt the expression of unrequited love on my own face before.

"Corliss!" Pearl gives me a wave as she jogs over, her thick hair pulled up into a twist, her face unmade-up yet as lovely as when painted with cosmetics. "How are you? How is your sister—she really seemed to love the show?"

"She really did," I answer. "And we're both good." And in this moment, it is true. Conversing warmly, the two of us stretch together as more dancers trickle in and out throughout the hours, practicing and packing up their things for break. When I leave the Clover—the last one to go besides Julian, still locked in his office—I sling my bag over my shoulder and ease into the fresh air.

It's a perfect summer night, with the deepening blue sky, the heat, the light floral aroma mixed with ocean. The Pins is at its peak, warm, nearly balmy, or as balmy as we can get here. Even now, there's a moodiness to the air. The sticky feeling of future rain.

The breeze suddenly seems to whisper my name.

Corlissss—

I start, nearly stumbling over a curb.

Wary, I cast my eyes around the street, half-expecting something to jump out at me. Everything appears normal, however. There are a couple of shopkeepers locking up, a few sailors coming off the docks, lovers strolling along, a lanky young man promising messages from heaven or hell, from "the dead relative of your choosing," and he'll take payment in kisses or coins. I pass him with a look of contempt, but nothing accounts for this ominous feeling. I hurry along my way.

It's fine, I tell myself, though I'm still certain I'm being watched. Behind me, I sense it. That shadowy feeling, only worse, a hundred times worse, a thousand. The further I move forward, the more intense it becomes. Even more awful than yesterday, with that bleeding man. With that other man...the haze of him as the world stopped and it was just us two.

Except he wasn't a *man*, that second one....

Scanning the square, I zero in on a squat old woman standing at the corner. She wears black, her white hair haloed around her papery face. She snaps her pale eyes my way so deliberately I take a step back. I've never seen her before, but she seems to know me. My stomach drops as I wait for her to do something. She looks... wrong. There's an unnaturalness about her—not quite human, not quite animal. *Wrong.*

I force myself to stare back, tensed for an attack.

The woman doesn't move at all, bust resting on her ample stomach. We look at each other for minutes while I hardly breathe, my stomach clenched so tight I worry it'll twist itself inside out. All at once, she opens her mouth wide, wider than humanly possible.

In horror I stare as her lips form a silent scream and a murder of crows flies out of her maw, tearing their way across the square right at me.

I throw my arms up and duck when they swoop over my head, letting out a strangled cry.

Someone snickers as they pass me, huddled here, shaking like a tree in a storm.

"What's the matter with her?" they say.

The crows fly past, and finally I rise, my legs weak as a newborn foal. Nobody else moves, they just stare at me with curiosity, and some level of suspicion.

Nobody else saw them, I realize. I am frozen in one spot, gaping at the birds cawing in the background, at the woman, whose mouth they flew from. How could nobody see that?

In slow motion, the woman turns her eyes to me again. She flashes me a sinister smile.

I don't wait to see if anything else comes out of her mouth. Staggering backwards, I bump into someone in my haste.

"Watch it," a voice hisses at me.

"Sorry," I say thickly. Normally I'd hiss back. Normally I'd push back even harder. But not tonight. Instead, I turn and rush toward home with my bag banging against my hip, the townspeople parting for me. I run like the Devil is on my heels.

Just before I leave the woods, with the cottage in view, I stop to catch my breath. I finally toss a glance behind me, to make sure nobody is going to jump out. The only movement is a squirrel, chittering away up on a branch. Still, trepidation prickles my skin.

Did I imagine it all? Am I going mad? *No.* My senses have never failed me before. Not my ears, nor my mouth, nor my nose, and certainly not my eyes. I saw what I saw. I saw the birds flying out of that woman's mouth, there's no way I imagined the evil way she stared at me.

Something is after me. Maybe that something even knows where I live....

Panic grips me at once, as one name flashes in my mind: *Sélie.*

I tear through the final stretch of wood and across the short grassy area before I get to the cottage, throwing the front door open.

"Damn it!" Sélie yelps from an overstuffed chair near the window. She puts her hand to her chest, delicate fingers splayed over her heart. "You scared me to death, Corliss, banging in here like that! What's wrong?"

"Sorry," I breathe weakly, noting the state of the cottage and my sister—all as it should be. "I just, um, nothing. Sorry. I didn't mean to throw it open so hard."

"Are you sure you're okay? Did you get sick again?"

"No, I'm fine. I'm hungry." The last word is a lie. Another lie. I haven't been hungry in weeks. But I can't tell her the truth—she'll think me mad. Maybe I am.

Her face lights up, and thankfully, she doesn't ask questions about the way my hands grip my bag, how my shoulders are drawn up tensely, how false my smile must look.

"I made dinner. There's a plate for you."

"Wonderful," I say as I pass. "Sorry for scaring you. Go back to your drawing."

And she does, disappearing into her art, and I take a seat to remove my boots. When she tilts the page to show me, my heart skips at the image. It's me, all in grayscale, in the middle of the stage, leaping in the red slippers—the only thing in the picture she's used color on. My nerves soften. "Oh, Sélie. That's so damn good."

She turns it back to herself, and eyes it critically. "It was better in person. Your costume was beautiful. The white with the red shoes was really striking."

I watch as she starts another sketch, this time capturing Pearl from memory, on her toes, frozen in a moment where her song swelled with tenderness and her face was open, lit up.

"She's really something, isn't she?" I muse.

"Definitely," Sélie answers with her head down, her hands moving swiftly as she captures whatever made this impression on her. "I can still hear her voice. It was so angelic."

While she continues to work, I pretend to eat the food she left out for me: roasted chicken, lumpy potatoes, and a pear tart with a soggy crust. It is kind that she made the effort, but my stomach turns too much to take more than a couple bites. Sélie is fine. I'm fine. But something is coming. I can feel it in my gut.

And I know who it is, and I know why.

It's the Colehart demon. Because he *does* exist. Because he wants his shoes back. What have I done? This isn't worth it. All the dreams I had, the goals, they turn to dust. I'm not going to keep dancing in stolen property. Knowing this, I'll probably not be able to continue at the Clover, not without the confidence and boost in skill the ballet slippers give me. But it doesn't matter—I've made a huge mistake.

As soon as Sélie falls asleep, I slip out of the cottage, into the night, sky dotted with stars as far as the eye can see, ocean licking the shore. Everything at peace here in our corner of The Pins. Everything except me, of course. I walk down the rocky sides, careful not to slip in my bare feet as I carry the stolen shoes in my arms. I don't look at them, though. I don't want to see what I've done. I have to let them go, yet I hate, *hate* how much it hurts.

If only if only if only, my poor heart pangs. *If only I could keep you.* I clutch them tightly to my chest, one last time. But they're not mine. They belong to someone else.

Standing by the edge of the water, I say out loud, just in case he can hear me, "I'm sorry."

Trusting that they will make their way back to him somehow, I fling the ballet slippers into the ocean.

When I wake up in the morning, the red shoes are back. Cradled in my arms, like a baby.

CHAPTER EIGHT

I told Sélie I'm too sick to work today, my lies piling up. She insisted on staying home with me; *I* insisted I'd be fine, that it was just the stomachache from the night I threw up back again, and as I said it, my hand shook so hard I spilled the water she brought me, right down the front of my nightgown. She assumed it was from illness. I knew it was from a bone-deep trepidation.

"I don't think I should leave you." She frowned, lingering at the door as I peeled the sopping garment off.

"Go. I'll be alright," I croaked, throwing on a clean chemise and climbing back into bed.

"I suppose I could pick up some ingredients to make you soup later."

"That would be nice, thank you." I didn't think I could eat a thing, but I smiled anyway.

Then she went to the shop, and I was left alone with my fear, with my thoughts, and mostly, with the ache of regret over my foolish actions. I run it all through my head once more, twice more, a dozen times more. I've been sitting here the whole day, just ruminating over it all.

I stole from a demon. All because of those damned shoes.

Alone in the cottage, I lean over and grab the slippers from where I tossed them on the floor hours ago, and I stare, hating the sight of them, how red they are, how beautiful, oddly enough not even a hint of wear on them, despite all the dancing I've done.

Even flinging them into the ocean hasn't ruined the satin. Inside, a deep, insatiable hunger grows. I'd like to put them on and dance away from this fear. Instead, I deliberately shove them in a cotton sack—I'll figure out what to do with them later. For now, I leave the cottage, walk down to the beach for a change of scenery. But mostly, to get away from the slippers and the hold they have over me. I pretend it isn't painful to walk away from them.

Sitting on the sand, I trace my fingers through it, letting myself breathe. For now, I have peace and safety. But probably not for long. I gaze at the water, the way it inches closer to my bare, bruised toes, the way the waves keep coming whether I'm ready or not. I need to think. I *have* to fix this. Sélie will be home from the shop in an hour or two. If only I could fix this by then.

Some way or another I have to get the slippers back to the Colehart Mansion before the owner comes for me again. Perhaps I could pay someone to deliver them at the doorstep. From what I hear, they have a shop boy bringing food from the grocer. Except it's too irresponsible pulling anyone else into this mess. I've already put myself—and worse, Sélie—in danger.

I'll have to do this alone. I could go very late at night, and toss the slippers on the porch? The thought of even being out in the dark near his home has me quaking. I still haven't gone to fetch my nicest boots, the ones I left near there, as though, subconsciously, I knew that it was dangerous. I knew deep down that I'd made a mistake. I lean my face toward the hot sun. If Aven and Sélie were here, we'd lie in the sunshine, tracing our names in the sand. We'd dive into the water, splashing each other, diving deep, pretending, even if *I* didn't admit it aloud, that we were mermaids.

I push myself to my feet, and, clad only in my chemise, wade into the warm, salty water, dropping onto my back, closing my eyes, and letting the gentle motion of the waves soothe me. I drift, living in this moment. I am safe, the ocean reminds me. The feel of my own beating heart is steady and calm. The world is big and wide, and I am oh, so small. In this moment, my problems feel small too.

Instinct warns me—*danger!*—the sea shifting around me, and I open my eyes the same moment I gasp at the sense of someone near. Too late.

Strong hands grab me about the waist from behind, jerking me through the water, and I suck in a cry of terror. As I struggle, shocked, I go under, swallowing a mouthful of saltwater, swinging my arms wildly.

I'm dragged to the surface again, choking and sputtering. I scream as I'm yanked up, and a rough hand covers my mouth. I bite down instinctively, tasting the tang of blood.

Too desperate to be disgusted, I rasp out another cry, "Help! Help me!"

A low voice grumbles in a frightening sort of laugh, a sound I vaguely recognize. I can't see his face; his arms are wrapped around me from behind as he hauls me away, out of the beautiful sea and to who knows where. "Scream all you like."

Immediately I place the stranger's voice—the one from the theatre. Oh, God. I've run out of time. It's *him*, isn't it?

Scream all you like, as though no one will save me anyway. Even if someone were near enough to hear me—he's a demon. He could end us all. But I do scream, ragged and breathless. Flailing violently, I'm dragged off the beach, gagged, and my face is covered with a thick dark cloth. My entire body seizes up in fear. *I'm going to die. He's going to kill me. Sélie will find my murdered carcass when she gets home.* He carries me up away from the sea, away from the safety of my home. Before I know it, I'm tossed onto something soft and upholstered. A carriage seat, I'm guessing. Then my hands and feet are tied—*like an animal*, I think, enraged. If I focus on this deep anger my heart won't stop from sheer terror. I'm helpless, wet, in nothing but my shift, tied up. My chest is tight, almost painfully so.

"Where are you taking me?" My voice comes out strangled through the cloth around my mouth, so much so I wonder if he's able to make out what I say. "What's going to happen to me?"

"Don't worry," he mocks me, clearly able to decipher my sti-fled words. "Better than you deserve."

A door slams. Then movement.

Muffled sound or no, pointless act or no, I scream as loud as I can.

My cries for help drown out any other noise that might be audi-ble, yet I can't help that voice in my nightmare, echoing through my mind.

I'm coming for you.

And he did.

When the carriage halts abruptly, I am nearly thrown off the seat. As I wait for the door to open, I ready myself to fight for my life. Though what can I do? An awkward kick? The ties around my hands are too tight, my wrists already raw. I start to feel dizzy and remind myself to breathe so I don't pass out. I clench my jaw, my throat dry.

The door opens, and I'm lifted up and out of the carriage with-out a word. It's quiet, just the stifled sound of breath as he carries me, slung over his shoulder like a sack of flour. I hear more doors open and shut. After a few minutes, with a grunt, I'm deposited onto a chair. My bare feet are untied, and then my hands too. I prepare to strike, though he's surely ten times stronger than I am, but before I even have the chance, the hood is lifted from my head and the gag removed from my mouth.

Immediately, I jump from the seat and blink as the light hits my eyes.

"What do you want?" My hoarse voice comes out small in the large room; it's empty save a piano in the back and the chair I was placed upon. Unlit candles line the paneled wall on gold sconces, and three elaborate chandeliers hang overhead. There are tapestries on the walls. It looks like a ballroom, or as close to one as I'd imagine. I spin, reeling with disbelief. I've always wanted to go to a ball, spend time in a majestic room lit with the glow of soft flames and the sparkle of romance. I've never thought about dying in a ballroom. I try again, searching for anyone else—someone must have untied me—"Why am I here?"

Behind me comes a harsh laugh. Shrinking around, I shift my eyes to the tall male figure at the head of the room who I either just missed or who only now appeared, along with another, grander chair. He stands with his back to me. Long seconds go by without him turning. It's him—the demon. I know it's him, even though he's not how I pictured. He has a thick mess of black hair that brushes his shoulders. Even facing away from me, his power radiates my way.

When the figure turns around, my heart jolts.

I give a low gasp of shock. With a stifled breath, I take a step back, tripping over the chair behind me. His eyes are black as ink, with no whites at all. I stare back at him for what seems like eternity. It's ghastly, but hard to tear my gaze away all the same. I vaguely register other details, the dark slashes of his eyebrows, the slightly tapered, elegant shape of his eyes…but it is the unsettling lack of whites, the hatred within them that captivates—horrifies—me.

I finally notice the rest of him, the great height, the control, and my shock wavers into confusion. Because apart from the uncanny eyes, apart from the general fright of him, he looks oddly, unexpectedly human. No tail that I can see. No scales or wings or horns, though a forked tongue isn't beyond the scope of possibility. Still, he is *so* human-looking. He stalks around an upholstered chair at the front of the room as if it were a throne. Instead of robes like a king, he wears black trousers, a buttoned white shirt, crisp and snowy, the sleeves pushed up slightly on his arms, but no vest, no coat, no tie. His clothing is dry, so he must have quickly changed between stealing me from the water and now. His movements are easy, casual, but there's nothing casual about the way his lip curls at me, the way he glowers. Not only does power exude from him, but fury too.

The beat of my heart increases the longer he stares at me, so rapidly I wonder if it might just give up and stop. Can a person die of fright?

With a shaky breath, I take another clumsy step, trying to get further away from the demon, moving to stand behind the chair, as if some wooden rungs will keep him from wringing my neck. I wish I were wearing a dress, sturdy boots, a full suit of armor… anything to protect me, anything to separate me from him other than my stupid, wet chemise. It's plastered to my curves, nearly see-through. It shows my soft body, the flowers on my skin. A few escaped tendrils of hair stick to one cheek and I couldn't feel more vulnerable if I tried. I steady my hands anyway, clench my shaking fists tight, ready to swing if need be, to claw out those demon eyes if I must. But what will my frail hands do against the evil he's surely capable of?

He runs a hand along the back of his chair, and I notice the ink around the one wrist—bracelets of black that work themselves up into thicker, solid bands near his forearm. The other arm is almost fully inked, from wrist to elbow, with only a few skinnier bands on the end, near his wrist. The tattoos are clean-lined, good work, but something about them feels ominous just the same. Under the furrowed brows, those onyx eyes stare holes in me. They should feel empty, but they don't: they seem to glow from within, backlit with some impossible energy. But there is nothing good there, nothing kind. Like hatred. Like the crow from the dress shop, I realize.

Before he opens his mouth to speak, I know every word the butler told me about him is true. Menacing anger rolls off the demon in waves. His laugh still rings in my ears. It was strung with warning.

I move back yet again, carefully maneuvering around the edge of a faded rug so I don't trip. If I fall, I'll look weak. This sort of predator feeds on the weak, don't they? It's a miracle I'm standing, still breathing. I know this.

"Are you afraid of me?" He smiles at me coldly.

I wince, hearing that deep voice again. It's not that I didn't believe it was him—I knew it even as he dragged me through the sea, even as he mocked me for screaming—but it's still so alarming to hear it face to face. The timbre of it, the contempt threaded within it, sends chills up my spine, and those eyes. I worry he'll swallow me whole; I can't look any longer.

"Answer me."

I flinch at the command. If I lie, he'll likely know it. *Obviously*, I'm afraid of him. Though if I admit it, he'll probably enjoy my death even more.

Instead of answering I lift my chin, forcing bravado as I again meet his white-less eyes. "What do you want with me?"

"Can you think of no reason?" He tosses a sack at my feet. One I recognize. "Open it."

The sharp line of his jaw is like a blade, the strokes of him cut with precision, from his head to his toes, his shoulders tapering to the narrow V of his waist, a lean yet powerful body. He walks like a man, moves like a man, looks like a man—a dangerous one— except for those eyes. I know he's not a man.

Soulless. Murderer. In the business of taking lives. Master of death.

I ignore the cotton bundle, refusing to move. My eyes skirt past the faded murals on the wall to the door, measuring the distance. What if I ran? I wouldn't get far. He'll kill me before I could possibly escape. Wisely, I follow his order and reach for the sack with trembling hands, and then I open it.

Unsurprised, I pull the slippers out, ruby ribbons falling from my hands. Even now, they wrench at me. Even now, I would put them on and dance. Even now, I'm hungry for what they give me, for what they take from me. "My shoes," I say, without thinking.

"*Not* yours," he counters. "Shoes you so thoughtlessly *stole*."

"I could hardly help wanting them!" I cry. "What did you do?

Enchant them?" Now, seeing him, I know *he's* real. I'm sure his magic is too.

Shaking his head, his untamed hair falls against his collar as he glances at the pair of slippers. "They were not yours to want, let alone take. They are *mine*."

"I wouldn't think they'd fit you." The saucy reply comes out before I can stop it.

He snaps his bottomless eyes to mine, and I shrink back in alarm.

"They are *mine*," he repeats. "You have no idea the harm you might have done, had I not found you and those shoes, the harm you've already caused. For your punishment—"

"Punishment!" I croak in panic. "I only danced in them! Just a couple of times is all!"

"Punishment," he once more repeats himself, going on as if I haven't spoken. "You will dance for me every night as penance. You will be my companion of sorts, willing or not. If you try to escape, I will kill you as easily as a spider."

The demon takes a step toward me, then another, then another, until his breath is against my cheek, the smell of him—wild and herbal like the night, rich like red wine, and coppery, *like blood*. Standing next to him is standing in the dark, in the forest, under a wave thick with salt. I'm drowning. I can't breathe.

"Why don't you just kill me now?" I manage to choke out. I regret it instantly—though it's not a taunt. It's curiosity.

His laugh in my ear is cruel. "You're lucky I'm bored. Otherwise, you'd already be dust."

Fear turns to resistance, despite my predicament. I say to the demon, with my chin raised, "You can hurt me all you want. You'll never break me."

He sneers. "I don't care enough to break you. You're just the entertainment."

I hold my tongue from arguing, Aven in the back of my mind. Perhaps this is a blessing in disguise. After all, I'm in the mansion.

I'm in front of a master of death. If I can dance for him, play his helpless prisoner, maybe he'll do what I need. If I play at being good long enough, maybe he'll eventually trust me. I can turn this to my advantage. I clamp my smart mouth shut as he speaks again.

"Tomorrow night you will dance for me. You will dance, or you will die. Your choice."

He laces his fingers into my hair and slowly draws me in, his powerful hand gently threaded into the wet strands. I whimper, from fear more so than pain. It doesn't hurt. But each word is enunciated as he warns, "Do. Not. Ever. Steal. From. Me. Again."

Then he releases his hand, turns his back to me, and walks out of the room. I breathe hard, stunned by everything that's happened. The butler comes and yanks me forward, pulling me out of the shock.

And then, we are walking.

Chapter Nine

"You're hurting me." I scowl at the older man as he drags me up the staircase, fingers biting into my arm.

He ignores me. He walks faster than my legs can keep up with as he hauls me to wherever we're going. It's not as if I have a say in the matter. We go down the corridor, past the rooms I sneaked into my first time here and further into the belly of the house. I stumble and nearly fall but for his grip keeping me semi-upright.

He loosens his hold but gives me a condescending frown, as though I'm pathetic. Then under his smoky breath he says, "Your own fault."

"I'm sure you know very well I couldn't help it," I say indignantly. "Those damn slippers are bewitched." And somehow, I fell under their spell.

The man only smirks and walks faster.

We continue through the second floor until we come to another, narrower staircase, and then on up to the third floor. Everything is darker up here, the air thicker, hotter. The butler's white hair glows in the dim light, an eerie contrast against the shadowed hall.

"Why is he doing this?" I ask, not expecting him to answer.

"You should know enough not to steal from someone like him, no matter how pretty the treasure is." Stopping outside a door, the man cracks his knuckles as if that's supposed to intimidate me. It does. I certainly won't let on to it, however.

Crossly, I snap, "You made me think he wasn't that bad! I asked you if he had magic."

"I told you he was dangerous. I told you to leave." With a shrug, he opens the door to a bedroom. Nudges me inside. "Don't try to escape. Don't even think about it."

"I wouldn't dare," I answer with more than a touch of sarcasm, just as he shuts the door in my face—for the second time! "You brute!"

His laugh is rough. "Sleep tight," he whispers from the other side, so I can just barely hear.

Goosebumps erupt over my damp skin, and I back away as the lock clicks. This is really happening. I turn to look at the room. It's not exactly a prison, and if the foyer was big enough to hold our cottage, this room is grander yet. Unlike many of the dusty and forlorn rooms I spied before, this one's been scrubbed spotless. It smells of freshly laundered linens, wax, lemon oil. I shouldn't think so, but it's beautiful.

Across the room, standing regally, is a gigantic four-poster bed crafted with a dark-brown wood, roses and gryphons carved into the headboard. The bedding is cream and rust, with deep-red curtains pooling down from the canopy on all sides. Another time I might find it romantic. Next to it, a dressing table with mirror attached, inlaid with mother-of-pearl and painted with flowers, a velvet stool placed in front. On the other side of the bed, a washbasin and pitcher stand at attention. Near an ornate fireplace, there's a pair of chairs flanking a small table on which a domed tray holding what smells like a delicious meal is set. I ignore the food and continue my careful surveillance of my surroundings.

Most of the wooden floor is hidden by a large carpet in shades of cream and rose and sage but the boards that are visible are pleasantly worn beneath my naked feet as I walk the perimeter. The curtains are thick, partially shut, but I open them wide, along with the windows themselves, to look out, to let the afternoon daylight and air in. Nothing and no one is visible on the grounds.

I lean over the sill of one of the three tall windows. If this fails, and I need to get out quickly, could I jump? I gaze down, the high distance twisting my stomach. This is the third floor, and there's no balcony. I'd break both my legs, if nothing else. Then the demon would kill me. I can't exactly dance for him if I'm badly injured, and I can't save Aven if I'm dead.

Still, I look longingly out, take a deep breath, hoping to catch the scent of the ocean. All I can glimpse from my vantage point is a long stretch of patchy grass leading to what looks like a dilapidated greenhouse. There's a large fountain in the middle of a forgotten garden, and then trees, many trees, for miles. I wish I'd been placed in a room on the other side of the house, so I could have spied the sea, or better yet, my home. I push off the sill and circle back, trying to puzzle out what bothers me so, despite the obvious fact that I can't get out of the room. Even though I'm not here for comfort, I'm pleased to see some semblance of coziness included in my captivity. Obviously, it could be much worse. Nonetheless, there's an emptiness that makes the space cold. No clock, no artwork, no flowers, no décor of any kind. Even worse, I note with a spoiled amount of discontent as I gaze at the empty bookcases along one wall, no books. I suppose *he* wouldn't care to keep me entertained. Still, what am I supposed to do with my time in between dancing for him? I curse under my breath. I'll have to act nice, play his little game.

Just to check, I return to the door and try the knob. Still locked, as expected. There's a low chuckle on the other side, and I stomp back, hating the idea that the butler is out there listening to me, keeping watch over me. All to report back to *him*. I'd prepared myself for the idea of staying, for playing along with the punishment, yet I didn't realize how uncomfortable I would find being locked away.

My throat is too raw to cry, though I'd like to—for the trauma Sélie will endure when she returns home tonight to find me missing.

With a sudden idea, I rush over to the dressing table, which looks wildly expensive—a light wood with legs that swirl to a lion's paw at the bottom—then rummage inside its drawers. I find a quill and an almost empty bottle of ink, as well as a yellowed sheet of paper, ripped in one corner. There's no envelope, but it'll do. The words matter far more than the packaging.

I pause. What to write without saying too much? If I tell Sélie where I am, or who has me, she'll come looking for me. There's no way I can jeopardize her safety that way. I don't want her within a hundred feet of here. However, I can't leave her without answers. The grief would sink her if I disappeared too. Damn this situation! Determined that saving one sister won't mean destroying the other, I dip the quill in the ink. It's only a slim chance they'll even *allow* me to send a letter. I sigh, running a message through my head before I scratch it out on the paper:

Dear Sélie,

I have to stay away for a while. Please don't worry. I hate that I had to go so abruptly, but I have to take care of something important. I wish I could tell you more, but it's better for both of us if I leave it at that.

Please don't mention this letter to anyone. If anyone asks, tell them I went to see Darius's family to handle some things regarding the will. Also tell Julian I'm sorry, so sorry. That I loved dancing at the Clover, and I hope he'll have me back.

I want you to draw a picture every day that I'm away. I'll expect to see them when I get back. I'll be thinking of you each day. Hire someone if you need help at the shop—remember Pearl, the dancer? Please ask her to help you. I think she'd really love the shop.

I love you. I miss you already. Don't look for me.

Here, I choke up. Take a breath. Try not to picture Sélie reading this—though a more likely reality is that I won't even be able to get this letter to her, that she'll just be left wondering. That she'll be abandoned by not just one but two sisters. That she'll presume me dead.

I hesitate over one more piece of advice. It will perplex her coming from me, but given that my cynicism has been changed when it comes to the mystical, I have to include it.

Get some garlic paste to spread on the sills. And have Bricksbee add those protective charms into your hems after all.

Your adoring sister,

Corliss

I fold the yellowed paper into thirds and rush to the door, knocking in a succession of sharp raps. "Hello? Are you still there? Butler?"

I stop myself from calling him something offensive. I'll need his help, if he's willing to give it. There's quiet for a moment, then the door clicks and swings open. The butler stands on the other side and says curtly, "What is it?"

"I need to send a letter to my sister."

He starts to shake his head. I didn't expect any different. But I'm not going to give up.

"I need to," I demand, pulling myself up to my full height, which isn't saying much, though he's not quite as tall as the demon. "She's probably frightened out of her mind, and she'll get the lawmen. They'll come here, eventually, to look for me. People are talking about this place, that bad things are done by your *employer*. There are even rumors he's a demon."

The rude man laughs. "I don't think he's too concerned."

"Please." I grab his gloved hands, startling him. I embrace desperation, allowing myself the vulnerability of looking weak, emotional. My voice cracks, "*Please*. I didn't say where I am. I didn't say who has me. It's just to give her peace of mind. So she doesn't look for me."

"I'd think you'd want to be found." His eyes widen a fraction, knowingly. "Unless you're still after his help. It's why you came here in the first place. You want something."

I don't say he's right. Then again, I don't deny it. "Here. You can read it if you want." I thrust the letter into the butler's hand, adding, "It's completely innocent."

He reads it reluctantly then raises his eyes to mine. About to say something, he hesitates, and, seeing him wavering, I jump at the chance.

"To Sélie Bell at the *Boutique d'Apothicaire*," I say quickly. "If she's not there, to our cottage, which you obviously know the location of, having been a party to my *abduction*. Please."

He gives me a curt nod. "Fine. I'll see what I can do."

"Fine." I echo his cool tone and traipse back into my room. I did my best. I'm relieved he's even considering taking it. I hardly dared hope. Now it's just a matter of him gaining permission from his employer…who will probably say no. I cling to hope—and that it lasts.

The butler closes the door. Locks it. Moving on, I continue my inspection around the room, memorizing the other details: a chamber pot tucked away discreetly and a heavy bench at the foot of the bed, upholstered in a rose-and-thorn pattern.

I open the wardrobe, unsurprised to find it empty. I have nothing except the wrinkled chemise I'm wearing, still damp. And my ballet slippers, or, I correct irritatingly, *his* ballet slippers, which are with him, probably. They weren't brought upstairs with me. I don't dwell on my disappointment over that realization. I assume he'll allow me to dance in them at least, for I have nothing else.

Finished with my path around the room, I go to the table and lift the top of the domed tray—which someone must have brought just before I was hauled up—the smell wafts out in a cloud of fragrant steam. There's chicken fried to a perfect golden crispness; potatoes dripping with butter and parsley; and some sort of fruit tart with a dollop of cream. The meal is still hot. My stomach growls, and I reach out before snatching my hand back. Suppose it is poisoned?

Yet, surely the demon could have just killed me in the ocean. Or in the carriage. Or ripped me to ribbons in the room downstairs. I wish I could forget some of the more gruesome descriptions of demon-induced deaths in the fantastical stories Sélie loves so much. I shake my head to clear the images, the sick feeling dissipating the longer I look at this delectable-appearing meal, the longer I inhale its scent.

He probably wouldn't poison me, reason reassures.

As I devour the meal in mere minutes, I realize not only is it the best food I've ever tasted—even better than Aven's cooking—but I have my appetite back after weeks. I finish every bite as nightfall arrives, and the room grows thick with shadows.

With my belly full and the sky going blue-black, already spread with stars, no candles lit, my eyelids grow heavier by the minute. I snap them open, senses jolting with revulsion, realizing I almost nodded off in my chair. I'm tired, but I can't sleep here. The demon's face flashes in my mind. I shudder, and it's half from fear, half from fatigue. I'd *like* to rest, but what if he comes up here?

I push up from my seat. In the dark, I wander the room, searching for something I can use for protection, grateful for the meager cast of light coming in from the moon. I spy the knife from the dinner tray and grab it, gripping the engraved handle with reassurance. After reluctant consideration, I set it down. I don't want to sleep with it—suppose I accidentally cut myself? It's not like a knife would do much against a demon anyhow. He could peel the skin from my bones as I stand, probably with just his mind alone. Still. Anything is better than nothing.

I finally spot a large candleholder pushed to the back of one bookshelf, much more substantial than the delicate brass holders set around the room. It feels solid in my hands, probably iron, although it's difficult to tell given the lack of light. I hide the taper toward the back of the highest shelf. Holding my new weapon gives me a tiny sense of security. If only I had light, to see more, to think through a plan to survive this place, to stay awake so I'm not so vulnerable. *He* can probably see in the dark, like an animal. I shiver, just envisioning those inhuman eyes.

If only I had a matchbox.

Despite searching through all the drawers again, there's nothing helpful to be found. I have no way to light the candles on the side table, nor the gas lamp atop the mantel, and despite my resistance, my eyes grow heavier yet. I stare longingly at the grand bed, the curtains pooling around it. If the demon is going to kill me, my being awake or not surely won't deter him. Besides, it's unlikely he'll harm me, at least as long as I'm his entertainment. I'm probably safe, I tell myself. I partly believe it.

I climb into the bed and pull the covers over myself. Then I slide the heavy candleholder under the pillow next to me, so I can easily grab it if I must. Finally, I can't stay awake any longer.

I let my eyes shut.

Nightmares assault my mind all night, bits of scattered violence, screams in the dark, my entire being stretched taut with fear. A wolf chases me. I run as fast as I can until I outrun it and then, hours and hours later, when I think I'm finally safe, I fall to the ground, retching. Instead of vomit, only blood, black and congealed, pours from me. When I look up, the wolf is waiting. It leans over, ripping into me. The pain tears into my very soul, and I find my feet dangling out of his mouth, bloody stumps of my ankles wrapped with red ribbons.

I dream of Aven as well, just her sad blue eyes, staring at me, white face shining through the darkness. I wake with tears pouring down my cheeks, sweating everywhere.

The soft blue of barely-morning light streams in through the uncovered windows. I made it through the night. I'm alive. I'm still here. This, at least, was not a nightmare.

I hate to do it. But, finally, I let myself do what I couldn't yesterday—cry. Because there's a strong chance the demon won't be able to help me return Aven—or, much more likely, that he'll have the capability but refuse. Because Sélie is alone, and my foolishness did that. And because I'm here, trapped like a rat. Because even though I tell myself not to be, I'm scared out of my damn mind.

Stop crying, stop crying, I tell myself, though of course, I don't listen.

The muted sound of something like hammering stirs me, and moments later, a sharp knock on the door jolts me awake. I must have fallen asleep weeping. I scrunch up my face and crack open one sensitive eye against the brightness of the room, the fully risen sun shining through the open windows. My head pounds from nightmares and crying. I don't even manage a "yes" or "who is it?" before the door unlocks and opens.

On the other side, not the brutish butler or the dreadful demon, but a skinny maid. I don't know her, but something about her hair is familiar, the exact shade of carrots. I wrack my brain as she wheels in a cart. Ah. She resembles the maid I saw that day I snuck in, Jinny. Close enough I presume they must be sisters.

I climb out of bed as she approaches, fully aware of my stale mouth, tangled waves, and wrinkled chemise. She doesn't seem to notice my disheveled appearance. I stand waiting for her to say something. To acknowledge that there's a hostage under her nose.

"Hello," I finally rasp, my voice half-lost, as though I had been screaming. Then I remember, I *was* screaming plenty, in the carriage.

"Good morning. I'm just here to bring your breakfast, Miss." She sets the trays on the table, lifts up the domed lids, and pulls out one of the chairs next to the table for me, avoiding my eyes. "Come on and eat, now, while it's hot."

"No. Thank you." I fold my arms over my chest. I'll eat later. Maybe. My stomach growls in betrayal, loud enough for the maid to hear.

She says kindly, "You may as well eat your meal, and enjoy it slow for all that. He"—she doesn't need to say who *he* is—"is off on business, so you won't be seeing him until this evening."

"I won't?" A warm wave of relief rushes over me.

"No. So dig in, Miss." She gestures to the food.

"You can call me by my name."

The cap perched on top of her bright hair doesn't move as she shakes her head firmly. "Oh, no. That just wouldn't do."

"Why not? I'm no lady, and I'm a prisoner. I can't leave the room." I laugh bitterly, and she blinks, face blank, as though I hadn't said a word. Something like understanding settles over me. I stare hard as she tidies the room, and, I notice gladly, sets a matchbox beside a candle. Still, she makes no indication she heard me.

"Unlock my door," I demand, more out of curiosity than a real attempt to leave—I know I need to stay put for Aven's sake. "I'm trapped here."

She gives me a glassy smile and motions to the table. "Your food, Miss?"

Interesting. Either she can't hear me when I speak of certain things—most certainly the demon's doing—or she's very, very good at pretending.

Reluctantly I sit, letting my eyes take in the sight of my hearty breakfast: thick porridge with currants and cream; toasted sourdough bread with butter; tiny pots of honey and jam; sliced orange cheese; fresh fruit; coffee and tea; lumps of dark sugar cubes; sugar as white as snow; and more cream, in a miniature silver pitcher. My mouth waters despite myself. How can I be so hungry again after that big meal last night, and in these circumstances? Resentfully, I spread jam on the toast and take a bite. It's delicious.

"The food is good," I say, with a touch of sullenness. "Thank you."

She bobs and walks over to the bed, tugging the bedsheets off into a pile. "It's my pleasure, Miss, to bring it to you. The man of the house does like good food. I'm sure he's happy to share the same bounty with his guests."

"Does he lock all his guests in their rooms?" I raise a brow as I pour myself a cup of coffee. Again, she doesn't seem to hear me. At least this soothes me somewhat. She seems an innocent in all this. Maybe I have someone here I can trust.

"What's your name? And how well do you know the man of the house?" I try.

"It's Hana. And not well, I've only just been hired. Although already I know he's a fine man, handsome and rich." She flushes a little at this assessment and backs the cart toward the door, as if embarrassed for speaking so plainly. Or lying so plainly.

One word she said echoes. Handsome? With those horrifying eyes? If I ignored the eyes…I might call him beautiful. But how could you ignore them?

"Wait," I call. "The handsome man of the house, what color are his eyes? I forget."

She turns. "Green, Miss, like the sea during a storm."

"Right." I nod. "Of course."

Then Hana shuts the door behind her. I hear the cart retreat down the hall, followed by the door being locked from the other side. I frown. The butler must be lurking out there. I stand from my chair, walk around, pacing the room, thinking hard.

Green. But how? I wrack my brain for an explanation.

He must be using magic to manipulate his appearance. Maybe to keep people from seeing things that are there, or, to make people see things that *aren't*.

This would account for not only the demon appearing normal in front of most others but also for the bird woman and bleeding man I saw in town. Nobody else could see them, because they weren't real. Perhaps even the crow perched on Bricksbee's sign was fake.

Or maybe, I ponder with a fearful pinch in the middle, they *were* real but simply hidden to everyone else, invisible to everyone but me. Either way, this demon's magic is powerful. Powerful enough to keep his staff—butler excluded—from knowing I'm being held captive. Powerful enough to make them trust him, see him in a different light.

And if he can do that, what else can he do? What else *will* he do?

I can't fret about that now. I have time to figure out how to get on his good side and persuade him to help me, and I should do that rather than worry. However, I'm too exhausted to think clearly, despite getting at least some sleep, plus I'm famished. I ignore the tea but finish almost everything else Hana brought for me. It's as delicious as the meal last night.

If I keep this up, I'll soon be as round as a dumpling. Maybe that is the demon's plan. Maybe he's just lying in wait, to devour me whole.

CHAPTER TEN

After breakfast, I wash my face in the basin and rake my hands through my messy hair, frowning at the circles under my eyes. When someone knocks on the door, I call apprehensively, "Yes?"

A maid enters. I presume it's Hana again when I catch the red hair, but when she faces me, I recognize the other maid, from the day I snuck in and stole the shoes. They have to be sisters. Clothes are laid across her thin arms, a pair of new boots on top.

"Good morning, Miss. My name is Jinny," she says, unaware I already knew that. "You can get out of that dirty chemise now. I have some new dresses for you."

I wait. Am I supposed to say thank you? I was kidnapped in my underwear. I'd love a bath, but I don't ask for that luxury. Would he even allow it? I move from the washbasin and mirror, watching her. "You are Hana's sister, aren't you?"

"Cousin, actually." She hangs up three dresses in the wardrobe, plus a white nightgown and a pale blue dressing gown with matching slippers. On the shelf inside, she sets down undergarments and the boots. Then she shuts the door of the wardrobe and turns to me, bright smile stretched across her freckled face. "Anything else?"

"Yes," I say. "I was told he was gone for the day. What time will I see him?"

"I'm not sure, Miss. He's off on business matters, I presume."

It's not that I'm looking forward to it. But the sooner I see him, the sooner I can convince him to help me save my sister. "Will he return before supper or after?"

"I don't know, Miss," she answers apologetically. "I am still learning his habits."

"Well, can I have some books while I wait? There's nothing to do here." I can't help the whine in my voice.

"I'll see what I can do, Miss." She bobs into a quick curtsey.

"Do you know you work for a demon?" I test her too.

Nothing. Not even a hint of understanding.

Then she leaves me alone.

Lunch, supper, come and go. I use the time to practice in my bare feet. If I'm going to dance my way into the demon's good side, I'll need to be at my best. Although I fear even with the red shoes, my best will not be good enough.

Just as the sky outside lights with the setting sun, the door opens and the butler enters, uninvited.

"You could knock, at least," I mutter, throwing him a scathing look.

He ignores that, saying, "He's ready to see you."

"Now?" I can't help the crack in my voice as it rises. I remind myself: *this is what you wanted.*

"Now. Let's go."

"Can I at least put one of the dresses on?" I gesture to my crumpled chemise. I haven't changed out of it yet, in protest, but now I'm rethinking that plan. I don't want to see *him* like this again, so rumpled. I will go perform with my head held high, and a clean outfit, if nothing else. A woman on my own terms, or at least close enough. Even if my filthy state didn't already make me regret not asking for a bath earlier, I'd give anything now to have done so. To show up looking pristine. As if to prove how unbothered I am by all of this.

The butler shrugs, turns, folds his arms.

"Get out." I bare my teeth. "I'll just be a moment."

He leaves with an exaggerated sigh and closes the door most of the way. I kick it the rest of the way shut. There's a chuckle on the other side.

I open the wardrobe and *really* look at the dresses. Although exquisitely made, they're just dresses, nothing like my Red Clover costumes. Still, there's a beauty to them in their simplicity I can't help but admire. I move my eyes from one dress to the next, black, cream, green.

It doesn't matter what I wear. If the demon wanted me to be dolled up, he would have provided costumes for me. I grab the black dress, as it is the least embellished. Black with tight sleeves and lace at the cuffs. Black like my mood. Black like his eyes. I clear my head of the disturbing image and shrug off my dirty chemise. I pull on a pair of drawers from the wardrobe and manage to get myself inside the corset provided, sliding the clean undergarments over my dirty skin. Then I put on a small bustle pad, forgoing the fussiness of a crinolette, and finally the dress. It fits perfectly and has been shortened, just like the others—I presume to function more like a dancing costume. At least they're thoughtful, whoever had a hand in this. Was it *him*?

As for the rest of me, there's not much I can do with my wild hair and pallid complexion, but I swish lukewarm water in my mouth to rinse out the sour taste. I paste a smile on my face and try to look obedient. Instead, peering in the mirror above the dressing table, I only appear crazed and desperate. How I wish I had some rouge, at least. I would feel more confident going into this plan if I didn't look so unkempt.

I drop the smile, walk to the door, and yank it open with a satisfying violence. I say to the butler, "Fine. I'm ready. Did you take the letter to my sister?"

"Yes."

"Really?" I can't help sounding doubtful. He had no reason to do me a favor and every reason not to. "Why would he let you?"

As he motions for me to walk, he lets out an annoyed huff. "Perhaps to shut you up." At my look, he sighs again. "I had it delivered. She got it."

"Did she seem alright? Is she worried?"

"I didn't ask."

"Of course not."

"No thank you?"

I offer him a begrudging smile. "Thank you. I really do thank you."

At least she knows I'm okay. If he's telling the truth—though, why would he lie?

As I move forward, I remember what is about to happen. I'm going to dance for a demon. Worse yet, I have to act like I don't mind because I can't make him angry. More than one life depends on it. *Act like a lady. Act like a lady.*

I make my descent from the third floor, down the second-floor hall, then sweep down the grand staircase, which is in the process of repair since I last walked it. If I thought it was impressive with broken rails and a splintered banister, it's magnificent now—and only a small percentage has been transformed! That must have been the hammering I heard while I was locked upstairs. I can only imagine how wonderful it will look in another week or two. We step through the sparkling foyer, which, although still empty, houses a chandelier that I didn't really notice last time—new since the day I broke into the mansion. Dozens of candles shimmer in the reflection of the shining marble floor as we continue on our way.

At last, the butler stops in front of a wide set of paneled doors. He gestures me in.

"How fitting," I say under my breath. It's the empty ballroom where I first met the beast. Of course, I should have known this would be where I would dance for him.

With hesitation, I walk in, readying myself to meet the demon again, face to face. Ready to start working my plan, though what *precisely* it is, I have yet to figure out. However, the enormous room is empty, apart from the piano in the back and a single upholstered chair up at the front—the same one he stalked around yesterday, though there's no sign of the one I'd hidden behind. In front of his chair, the rug, and on it, the slippers. I try *not* to rush to them, to see them, to run a finger along the gleaming satin, hold them against my chest like a lover, though I can't help but walk faster, unable to hold back my eagerness to put them on again. I still crave what they give me, even though I've begun to recognize what they take from me. Not just that they've become addictive—consuming—but because when I am wearing them, I don't want to take them off.

Off on the long side of the room, the tall, sparkling-clean windows lined up in a row are now framed by new thick blue curtains that puddle elegantly to the polished floor. They certainly have been busy in the last day and a half. Through the windows, the sunset is visible—impossibly bright, orange and periwinkle spread across the sky like oil colors, something Sélie would love to capture if she were here. The thought of her is a pang in my heart. But she got my letter. I'm grateful for that.

I grab the shoes but don't sit in the large chair to put them on. The idea of taking a seat in his spot is distasteful. Instead, I move to the floor and tie the red ribbons neatly up my ankles, reveling in the familiarity of the task. I can do this. I can dance for the demon.

"How long do I have?" I call to the butler. "I need to prepare."

"Be quick about it."

I roll my eyes but don't waste any more time, making sure my muscles are warm enough to prevent injury. Still, it's just barely enough before the doors open, and the demon comes striding in.

CHAPTER ELEVEN

y pulse quickens to a frightful pace as my captor crosses the threshold and shuts the doors behind him. I tuck my clammy hands behind my back so I can squeeze them together. So he won't notice how they tremble.

The demon steps to the chair at the front of the room. He reclines in it lazily, like a big cat. I try not to think about my nightmares with lions or wolves, all the blood. I'm sure he could end me with a wave of his hand. I hate the way he looks at me, ink-dark eyes inscrutable, drumming his fingers on the arm of his chair. He appears so bored, as if he's a breath away from stifling a yawn. I narrow my eyes at him, despite my vow to myself to behave.

The keys of a piano start, and I turn in surprise. There, seated at the instrument way in the back, is the butler, gloves set aside on his seat, his large hands almost dainty on the keys as he plays a lovely classical piece. He's even better than Dina.

"You play?" I gape at him.

"Mr. Brown is a talented musician," the demon drawls, bringing my attention back to him. He continues with a condescending sneer. "And you are supposed to be some sort of dancing virtuoso, no?"

I put on a smile and duck my head demurely. *Fuck you and the hell horse you rode in on.*

"I'm tired of waiting. Begin." The last word pierces the air.

He doesn't appear uninterested now, his expression hardened in intensity.

This is an act, I remind myself, *a performance. Dance as if it were any audience in front of you.* The rhythm of the music fills me, and I rise up en relevé, pasting a pleasant yet coquettish smile on my face.

I dance for the demon, pretending he doesn't scare me at all. When I pirouette, he fades away, if only for a moment. I try not to look at him, instead focusing on the movement, and within moments, I don't have to try. I lose myself in the steps, in the bright notes of the piano, in the way the music echoes around the empty room. The slippers take away my fear, all my inhibitions.

When I'm done, I sweep down into a generous curtsey. There is no applause, there are no whistles. Sheer silence greets me. Even Mr. Brown doesn't make a peep.

As I glance up from my prone position at the demon on his throne, my breath catches in my throat at the cold way he stares at me. I rise, the anticipation killing me.

"All that trouble to bring you here. For that?" Each of his words are slow and scathing. "The slippers are wasted on you."

Face hot, I snap out, "Why don't *you* dance in them then, if you think I'm so terrible?"

He rises from his seat so swiftly I swallow a fearful breath. I bite my tongue as he looms ominously before me. Leaning inches from my face, his eyes blaze, the black somehow going even darker, hotter. Distaste—hatred—curls his upper lip. Silence stretches between us, just the rise and fall of my chest with my heart hammering within. What is he going to do?

He raises a hand, and I flinch, scared he's going to crush my windpipe. Instead, he lifts my chin. Gently, which is almost more frightening than if he'd hit me. All I want to do is jerk away from his touch, but I don't dare move a muscle. His fingers are a cool vise. "Do better tomorrow."

"What?" Fear takes second priority; I can't help but be offended.

"I expect perfection. You are wild, and clumsy, and you lack discipline," he insults me, voice rough. "You're going to learn that here, day by day. You're going to dance for me until you're sore, until you're begging me to stop." He softens his tone, a whisper against my crawling skin, "I'm going to make you cry for it."

"I—" But no more words come from my lips—he's rendered me speechless. And now he's walking away, the ghost of his fingers still on my face.

Not only is he a monster, but he's impossible to please. What's the point of my dancing for him if he's not going to like it? I curse at the doors as the demon slams them behind him. I knew he'd be hateful, but never did I think he'd be so *insulting*.

"Come on," Mr. Brown's coarse voice breaks my thoughts. "Back to your room."

Together, we leave the ballroom, go through the first floor, up the grand, sweeping staircase, down the second-floor corridor, then up the narrow third-floor staircase, and finally to my room. My blood pumping hard every step of the way. My ego bruised.

The slippers are wasted on you. I clench my teeth. What an absolute bastard.

Before Mr. Brown lets me in the room, he says, "Whatever you're after, he's not going to help you get it. You stole from him, and he'll never forgive you for that."

"He's a monster."

"Well, that monster will never help you. Take my advice, give up on whatever it is you want from him. Forget it."

My sister's blue eyes flash through my mind. Give up?
Never.

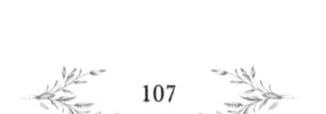

I dance for the demon the next three nights with no more insults, although he maintains a cold contempt that has my blood boiling and my confusion growing simultaneously. Each performance is as though he cannot bear the sight of me—which makes me wonder endlessly why he's even keeping me. I hold back on asking about Aven *yet*. He would never agree, the way he feels now. I play the part, I do what he asks, and still, he hates me. I can only hope that will change in time.

After this evening's performance, which I think is my best so far, he sends me away with nothing more than an absentminded nod. I am escorted back to my room by Mr. Brown, and shoved, rather unceremoniously, though not necessarily roughly, inside. The door locks behind me and my scowl. He's as unbothered as his employer, though in a different way entirely.

I walk forward, noticing there is warm milk with honey waiting for me, lavender-flecked shortbread cookies stacked on a tiny plate beside the giant mug, the fireplace crackling pleasantly, a clock has been set on the mantel. I purse my lips and get undressed, hating how cozy it feels. How comfortable I've grown here in my room in this short amount of time—no, not my room. They even sent a bath up on the second night, which I could have cried for, it felt so good to get clean, though I was shocked he allowed me such a nicety. Every day, I seem to be surprised by something. Every day there are changes to the mansion, which I secretly delight in. The dust lifted, the crannies cleared, the silver shined. I hate it. I hate that I *don't* hate it.

Now, I pull on a fresh nightgown and climb into bed, letting the milk go cold, the shortbread ignored, just out of spite. I think I'm too agitated to do much but toss and turn in the sheets, but I'm wrong, for exhaustion hits me the second I pull up the covers. Sleep catches me quickly, and even while I dream, I know I am dreaming. Even while the dream changes. I can't move…and yet, I *am* moving. My physical body still lies in the bed. But in my mind, I am slinking through the shadows of an unfamiliar place.

I am in a dark house, I realize with a start. I am moving though I cannot walk. I cannot lift a finger, cannot control myself at all. No, something is steering me forward, my dream body as immobile as the real one. Still, I somehow move. Curiously, I watch through stolen eyes as a door is pushed open, slowly. Quietly.

This is a robbery, I almost say out loud, though my lips cannot move. I can't speak.

I stare at the elaborate candelabras and fine paintings, a box with jewels spilling out of it on a table near the bed, a diamond pendant, ruby bracelet. Distracted with the dream sequence, I count a pile of pearls as I—we? Me and my dream self?—pass. I get to fifteen, but there must be a hundred more. I can't see the pearl necklace anymore—we are moving.

Oh, I see. Hear the snoring. A couple, asleep in the bed, silk awnings, thick covers piled high, even in the stuffy heat of the room. No one has opened the windows. Someone has spread garlic paste on the sills, I can smell it somehow, even in this false reality.

A low rumble from my chest, only it's not mine. A chuckle because of the garlic. It didn't matter, did it? He still got in easily.

I stare in horror as a hand raises, lifting from the body that carries me with it. Not my hand.

A knife in it. Blade shining like the diamond pendant only feet away.

And around the wrist, bracelets of tattoos, dark and foreboding.

No, no, I whisper, but no words come out. This is not my body, not my voice to use. My protest goes unheard, soundless.

The knife arcs downward, toward the sleeping couple. Two broad strokes against their throats.

Blood spatters my face, warm and wet. Even into my mouth. I taste it.

This time, I scream, and it works.

I'm still screaming when I sit upright, in full control of my body. I'm in my bed, covers all a tangle.

It was only a nightmare.

I brush at my tired eyes, my heart still thundering, and there's a knock. I call out a faint, hoarse *yes?* A moment later, Jinny wheels in the breakfast cart.

I stare at her hopefully. "Any books?" The other day they brought matches, perhaps today, finally, entertainment.

She smiles. "I've put your request in, Miss."

That horrible beast. I know the request will be denied.

Lifting her head, she smooths her immaculate apron. "Mrs. Minthy ordered another bath for you, Miss, before your performance this evening. We'll be bringing the tub up later, and I'll be back to do your hair after." She blushes. "I think I have a way with styling."

"Thank you. I'd like that." I try to sound casual when I tack on, "Would I be able to get some pins too? For my hair?"

"I'm sure that would be fine."

With a sigh of thanks, I move to the wooden table and Jinny serves my breakfast—oatmeal with peaches and cream, thick-cut toast with butter, coffee and fixings. There is no tea, which I wonder at.

"—noticed you never drink the tea," she's saying, seeming to notice my curious pause. "I'm a coffee-lover myself."

The little thoughtfulness that they've stopped bringing something because I don't enjoy it surprises me. And the fact it was noticed at all. I eat while she tidies up the room. The food is, as always, heavenly. When I'm through with my breakfast, I move from the table to nestle into one of the soft chairs facing the window and sip my coffee. It's become routine to do this, if a bit of a reluctant one. The lawn is still patchy, browning in spots, and the greenhouse looks a storm away from tipping over, but there is the possibility of beauty. It's a vast property, and I suppose it was once lovely.

I am unable to bear shutting the curtains, even as my sensitive eyes squint and water against the sun, and besides, the fresh air coming through the open windows is too lovely. I let the breeze warm me and try to pick out sounds outside, to remind myself there is life beyond this room, beyond this mansion. But, as usual, I hear nothing besides the wind rustling the leaves, and even that is faint, as though Mother Nature is afraid to disturb the demon's atmosphere. The quiet is deeply unnerving, and I could never grow used to it. I miss the sound of the ocean calling, the birds, animals, life. I miss my home. The maid leaves me alone, and I feel it completely.

I wish so hard to be back with Sélie, waking to the sound of her sketching in her drawing pad, grabbing croissants from the bakery on the way to the shop. I miss grinding powders and smearing stains, miss the scents of the oils and flowers, miss the customers, even miss the haughty gossip of the folks in town. I miss the gulls flying around and the lap of the sea on my toes. I miss our home, my books. And, desperately, I miss The Red Clover. However, beyond that, there's only one beat pulsing in my mind—well, two. *Av-en.* She's the greatest desperation of all. For her, I endure. I will learn how to tame the beast. Can I not make do with fate for now? I need his help.

How will I do it? How will I ask? The questions hang about me. But in order to persuade him to answer my questions, I must play the role. Companion. Dancer. Captive. Whatever he likes. I hate even thinking of submitting to him, but ultimately, I have no choice. I'm not going to give up.

So, I wait patiently to dance for him for the sixth time. I take pleasure in my coffee. I let myself be thankful for a good breakfast and a comfortable prison. And tonight, I'll get to dance. Even if my only audience is a less-than-friendly butler and a demon straight from hell.

As soon as I finish my coffee, I put on the red shoes, which he's let me keep with me. *At last!* they seem to cry as I tie the ribbons up my ankles. Just as I have done the last couple of days, I dance in my room in my nightgown. I tell myself it's not practice for tonight, but as I fly through every step on beat, make every graceful turn, I remember his contempt and think, *ha. I'll show you.* I hate that I want to impress him.

Morning dies, afternoon comes and goes, and once supper is done, a copper tub is brought up to my room. After several trips by a parade of staff carrying buckets and kettles—most of whom I don't recognize—the tub is filled with hot, steaming water. When they are through, there is only me left, and one other person.

It's the older woman, the one I saw cleaning *his* room the day I broke in, and she motions to me. Mrs. Minthy. I look her over, a little shyly. Thus far, it's only been Jinny and Hana delivering my food or changing my linens.

"Come now." Mrs. Minthy pushes her sleeves up even further on her soft, thick forearms as she gestures to the tub. "In you go."

"You don't have to bathe me. I managed fine last time. But thank you."

She tsks and says, "No need to be modest, ducky. I would have been here to help you then if I hadn't been busy. In you go."

I laugh, despite myself. I just can't be cool with her, try as I might. She looks like a grandmother, a nice one. "I'm not modest. I'm just not used to being waited on like this. I'm a working woman, just like you."

"Not here. Here you're a guest, and I take care of my guests."

I don't bother arguing that point. If I tell her I'm not a guest—that her employer is a demon keeping me captive—it will just go unheard. Besides, by the time I drop out of my dress, and she unfastens me out of my undergarments, my offense has softened. Perhaps I'm no guest, but I know full well, sinking into the soothing water scented with rose oil, this isn't exactly a cage. I delight in the pleasurable feel of the hot water against my skin.

Mrs. Minthy squeezes a sponge around my shoulders and cleans behind my ears. Lathering up her hands, she begins washing my hair, digging her nails gently in circles on my scalp, swirling the suds through my mass of waves. It feels incredible. I'm glad I didn't send her away.

"How long have you worked for him?" I finally break the comfortable silence, unable to contain my curiosity.

"Oh, a good decade, I'd say," she answers thoughtfully. "This is the fourth residence I've held for him."

"So, you follow him where he goes?"

"Oh no, not everywhere. I stay out of his business affairs, and he's gone quite a lot."

"What kind of business is he in?" I ask, just to see what she says. *Professional demon?* "Something unsavory?"

"You're funny, Miss Corliss." Well, *that* she apparently heard. She goes on, explaining, "He has investments, property. A family fortune, too, though it's not my place to know more than that, however I'm sure he'd explain more if you ask. I've yet to meet a wealthy person who doesn't like to talk about their success."

"Ha," I mumble. Then louder, to her, "Do you enjoy working for him?"

"Yes. Mostly I keep an empty house if I'm being honest, until lately, that is. With him hoping to retire, he wanted to settle somewhere quiet."

"So you came here with him. To The Pins."

"Well, I have no family, and I admit I like being needed."

I place my words carefully. As long as I don't mention my being captive, or him being a demon, it appears they go through. "So he has a vulnerable side then? He needs someone? Even with being so mean?"

"Mean?" Her laugh is slightly incredulous. "And don't we all need someone? Of course he has a vulnerable side. He may be a hard man at times, but I've never known him to hurt a fly."

I sink deeper in the water, miserable. "I think the only one who really knows him is Mr. Brown."

"Oh, *that* man scares me half to death." Mrs. Minthy's voice holds a shiver. "But he's in Mister Orrin's confidence, so I assume he's useful somehow."

I still. "Orrin? That's his name? A first name?"

"Why sure, didn't you know?"

"I didn't think he had a name," I muse, half to myself.

She pours a pitcher of clean, warm water over my soapy hair and laughs again, as if I had made a joke. "Not have a name? I've never heard of a person not having a name. But you folks in The Pins are a bit odd, then, aren't you? No offense meant, of course. It's not that I know many of ya, given we keep to ourselves here. But I've been hearing things."

"Yes," I say after a moment, almost proud of the things in The Pins I've always disregarded, even held in contempt. And suddenly I'm not so sure I can disbelieve—or disapprove—any longer. "We are odd. So…Orrin then? What's his surname?"

"Colehart. Just like the house, didn't you know? I expect you'll learn more as you stay here. I've heard you're a lovely dancer, and so kind, to perform for him in his home, since he doesn't care to go see public performances. Crowds and such. He is such a *private* man…."

"Oh." They know I'm here to dance for him—I didn't even think to wonder what story he'd told them before now. I open my mouth to ask more, but I'm not sure what else I want to know. We drift into a comfortable silence while she tidies the room and I soak until I'm wrinkled and the water turns cold. Mrs. Minthy helps me out and wraps me in a fluffy towel.

"That was nice." I smile with gratitude. "Thank you."

"My pleasure."

She leaves just as Jinny comes in to do my hair. I take my seat at the dressing table while she pulls a comb through my wet tresses. She's less gentle than Mrs. Minthy, ripping through the dark mass, but her fingers are sure as she twists it up into an elegant chignon, with a few well-placed braids threaded throughout. She secures the style in place with a pile of plain pins. I eye them and smile to myself. Finally. Something I can use to my advantage.

"It might fall out when I'm dancing," I say, turning to admire my hair in the mirror, touching with tentative fingers. Even with my untraditional tattoos, with the rebellious twist of my lips, with the fire in my eyes, I look elegant. I look like a real lady, and it will be easier dancing with an updo.

"I'll add more pins then." She shoves them in and tips her head to assess her work. "There, Miss. That should hold you."

"Thank you. I never wore my hair so fancy at home."

She blushes so that her cheeks are almost as bright as her hair. "Well, now, let's get you dressed. Mister Colehart said he is ready to see you."

I roll back my shoulders. Showtime.

CHAPTER TWELVE

Mr. Brown comes into my room abruptly, but I'm ready for him, freshly bathed and clad in the cream dress. This one is short-sleeved, with a powder-blue sash around the waist, and the skirt is fuller than the black or the green, and even shorter—though even if it weren't, the red shoes seem a magical safeguard against any clumsy entanglements with skirts or such things. I look like a cream puff in this frock. I look young. I look sweet. I look like a compliant captive. Maybe it's a good sign. Should I ask about Aven tonight?

Mr. Brown doesn't seem to notice my effort and waves me out to the hall impatiently.

I waltz past him with a breezy nod, and continue down the stairs, already in my slippers, all the way to the first floor, making my way to the ballroom, as though I'm confident. At least I know what to expect after my prior performances. It has all become familiar.

Dance, be glared at, go back upstairs.

Mr. Brown sits at the piano and strums out some light notes while I warm up, my focus narrowed to an almost deadly point. I will dance my best tonight, to show that arrogant demon a thing or two. My nerves are so tight I worry I'll just shatter with the first step. Rolling my neck, I try to stop overthinking. But if I impress him, that is one step forward.

Again, as the sun begins setting through the windows behind

the chair, he enters the room. The demon. Orrin Colehart. The name doesn't sit right in my mind. He shouldn't have a name. For God's sake, he doesn't even have a *soul*. To me he will always be just a demon, a soulless, heartless monster.

Mr. Brown stops playing as the demon crosses in front of me. I stand in the middle of the room, one of the three massive chandeliers directly above me, feeling exposed. He sits in his chair, but he does not indicate I should dance like usual.

So I speak, curiosity getting the better of me. "May I ask you something, *Sir*?"

If he were a fool, he might not notice the hatred-laden resistance in my final word. But he's no fool. Raising a brow, the demon says, in an equally sarcastic tone, "Yes, *Miss* Bell?"

I'd like to rip my name from his mouth. The sound of it shouldn't belong to him. Instead I ask, as politely as I can, "Why can't your servants see your real eyes? Why don't they know what you are? They keep insisting you're harmless, and they can't hear me when I say certain things about you."

"You can see my true form. They cannot," he drawls, indulging me for some reason.

"But…" I stammer here, "It's a glamour, isn't it? A disguise? What about the rest of you? Your fangs and tail and all that?"

He gives me such an unreadable look I take a step back. I think I hear Mr. Brown choke down a laugh behind me.

Then the demon says, "This *is* how I am, and I have no reason to try to hide anything from you. It's tedious and a waste of time. I don't have to pretend to try to get something from you. You're going to do it whether you like it or not. You don't have a choice."

I stand taller, anger pooling in my gut, overtaking the fear, and perhaps my good sense. "I do have a choice. I could say no."

"Then you wouldn't live long."

"I don't think you'd kill me," I retort, a touch of sassiness bursting through despite the warning in his eyes. "I think you just like to scare—"

The demon moves toward me in an instant, faster than humanly possible, suddenly pressing himself against my back. The lights go out that same moment, the candles, the sun setting through the windows, everything. The room—the world—is all black shadows, and I hold back a startled cry as he sets his large hands on my shoulders.

He pushes down slightly, his hair brushing against my bare neck, the hot breath of him too close. That smell of him, rich and dark. Like the underbrush of the forest at night. Like wine that bleeds across a white tablecloth. I can't see anything, senses shrouded in shadows. My body yearns to run away, to hide from the nearness of him. I can't move. I'm a prisoner under his hands, helpless and small.

"Don't think for one minute," he whispers, his voice skittering in the depths of my fear, fingers splayed across my shoulders, "that I wouldn't kill you if I wanted. You have no idea how much I despise you for stealing those shoes, for what you nearly did."

My belly flips as his lips brush against my ear. His voice is so soft, almost kind in tone, but the words he speaks are twisted with hate. "Don't provoke me. I would slit your throat right now if you weren't tied to those slippers. As it is, your death would be complicated. *Complicated*—not impossible—and more tempting than you can imagine. Remember that before you speak so insolently to me."

"I'm sorry," I whisper back. "I'm sorry I took the slippers."

Light returns to the world, the sunset slips back into the sky, candles flick back to life, illuminating the room. He is now facing me, a look of boredom replacing the hatred. "I'm still going to punish you for it. I don't take kindly to thieves."

"I told you I couldn't help it! Obviously you know what they can do. You know the power they—"

"By the way," he interrupts, his voice low, "keep yourself out of my thoughts, and anything else."

"Excuse me?"

"You were there. You were in the house with me. Somehow, you were."

As his words sink in, my eyes widen with shock. "You killed that couple last night. I thought it was only a nightmare! How—"

"Just stay away," he says brusquely. "Don't give me any more reason to hate you."

"Ohh," I breathe, catching how avoidant he is. "You're ashamed of what you did…."

A laugh. The thought of him being sorry made him laugh. He's not sorry. Not at all.

Then he is striding away to the front of the room, and I'm left shaking in fright and ire, warring emotions that won't fade. How did I get into his mind—in his body—in the dream, like we were one for a few, terrible minutes. And how did he know I was there? And why, oh why, did he hurt those people?

"You really—"

He turns and stops whatever else I was going to say with a withering look. "I'm tired of this conversation, and of you. Dance and be on your way, thief."

Once seated, that horrible whiteless gaze sears into me. I'd like to tear that expression off his face, hurt him like I've never wanted to hurt anyone in my life. But I'm a tabby facing a dragon. I hold myself back, squeezing my hands into my cream skirts. I remind myself that I have a plan, feeble as it may be. Get on his good side—*somehow*. Rescue my sister—*somehow*. Aven matters more than anything, definitely more than my wounded pride, even my own mortality.

Sulkily, I glance back at Mr. Brown and motion for him to start. "Play the one from the warm-up, please." I'm sure I've never sounded less gracious.

Mr. Brown nods and his fingers move on the keys. And I dance.

This time, I know I'm better than the first time I performed for my captor. Better than the second time, the third, the fourth, or even the fifth. I know every step is perfect. I know I'm on beat—a lively, quick tune that fuels my steps. I smile pleasantly as I flick my wrists, travel across the empty ballroom, turn and twist and leap. Each step, thinking three words, directed at the demon leaning back in the chair.

I hate you. I hate you. I hate you.

When I'm through, I curtsey gracefully and stand before him.

He gets up from his seat, locks his eyes on me. He gives me a terse, almost resentful nod, brow furrowed. Then he turns and walks out.

I let my hands fall on my knees as I bend over, catching a breath of sheer relief tinged with triumph. I did it. I danced without provoking his wrath. I didn't get a chance to bring up resurrection before he stalked off…but it's a start.

Then Mr. Brown leads me upstairs. I don't even complain as he pulls me along.

"I don't know why you're smiling," he says with interest as we round the corner to my room. "He didn't say you danced well."

"But he didn't say I *didn't*," I say, victorious.

"You're a prideful thing, aren't you?"

"It's not pride. When you love something, when you work hard at it, you want it to come through. If anything, I'm in awe of the slippers, not me. Still." I lift up one curl that has come loose from my chignon, despite Jinny's extra effort, and shove it back into place. "I know I was good too."

"It'll take more than one good dance to please him." Mr. Brown's voice is ominous.

"Undoubtedly." I wave a hand, stepping through my door. "He's dreadful. But I'm not afraid of him." I lift my chin. Make myself believe it.

Mr. Brown grins. "You should be."

Then he shuts the door and locks it. However, that doesn't mean I have to stay trapped in this room at all times. Lucky for me, I've known how to pick a lock since I was seven years old. Mr. Brown usually stays nearby, but despite manners to the contrary, he's human—and even he must take breaks to eat and drink and rest. Given the late hour, and the fact he hovered in the hallway outside my room for most of the day, I'm counting on it. Channeling patience I don't typically have, I wait for hours, until I'm certain the house is asleep. At last, I can have a breath of freedom!

Near the midnight hour, I pluck one of the pins from my mass of hair and kneel in front of the lock. Carefully, quietly, I work at it until it clicks. Satisfied, and maybe a bit smug, I stand.

Our father's cousin—the third guardian we were sent to—may have been a drunk and a gambler, but he knew about useful things—like picking locks. He may not have done anything else for me, but in this moment, I think of him gratefully.

I'm not leaving the mansion yet, but at least I feel less trapped, having the chance to get out of my room. Quietly, I take a step out into the hall, tiptoeing, listening for anyone coming up the second set of stairs. I tell myself that being here is my choice now that I do have the means to get out. And perhaps, if needed, I can make an escape.

It brings me some measure of comfort. Mostly, I'm just nosy enough to want to poke around a bit, and perhaps, the rebel within me wants to defy the demon. It feels delicious, openly disregarding his orders. I creep down the dark staircase, hover at the bottom step to the second floor. When a low voice rumbles in frustration, I shrink back into the shadows of the narrow staircase, hoping nobody has noticed me. I watch, peeking around the corner. The figure comes into view.

It's the demon, with Mr. Brown trailing him up the grand staircase and toward the bedrooms.

His brows are knit in frustration, and he pauses in front of a door—to his bedroom, I presume—the one I snuck into. The one where I found the shoes. He mumbles something, turning to face the butler, waving one hand in front of his shirt. His white shirt, covered with red splotches.

Blood. I blanche. Even after talking to him about it earlier, I'd hoped to convince myself it was merely a nightmare, not based in reality at all. He's not actually going out there and murdering people. Is he? *He is.*

"…because she insisted?" Mr. Brown sighs.

"It couldn't be helped," I think the demon answers. I inch closer to hear better, but then my foot catches a creaky spot on the floor.

They both turn their heads toward the staircase door, and I catch just a flash of narrowed eyes before I whip around and run—on feet as light as I can manage—up the stairs and down the hall, slipping back into my room.

I shut the door behind me quietly, relocking it from the inside with the pin—in spite of my trembling hands. Then I perch on the bed, heart racing, waiting to be caught. But nobody comes up. They must not have heard me. The longer I sit, the more confident I am that I'm safe, that he didn't see me. Even better, I got out, and I can get out again if this plan doesn't work. Remembering how the demon looked, I push up and stand. Wonder over the bloody shirt. Yet another victim?

And did he mean it couldn't be helped, as in he didn't *want* to kill someone else? Then why do it?

Because she insisted, Mr. Brown said. But who in the world is *she?*

It's unsettling to learn he may have committed yet another murder, and more than confusing to try and puzzle out the rest, but what can I do? My body—the slippers—urge me to move through the emotions, and so I dance around the room. I dance until I'm dripping sweat. I dance so hard I wonder if I'm wearing holes in the rug. Still, it is hardly enough.

Out of the corner of one eye, I think I catch a flap of black wings at my window. When I look again, it's gone.

"Your dancing is off tonight." The demon's voice lashes like a whip the following evening.

I flinch without meaning to, indignation and anger rising in me as he interrupts my performance, something he's never done. I fall out of step abruptly, shocked at his interference.

"It is not." I meet his dark look with a challenge, bravado easier to force when I'm offended.

He pushes up his sleeves with a harsh laugh. I stare again at his tattoos, trying to make sense of them: his right wrist has bracelets of inked lines, which seem to get closer and closer, thicker and thicker, until they touch, until from forearm to elbow, it creates a solidly black effect, while his left arm is almost entirely solid, only a few bracelets of ink around that wrist at all. I glance back up as he speaks, noticing the way the sunset's glow behind him throws his face into shadow and the well-formed features catch the candlelight. He *is* handsome. I hate to admit it. He's been so terrible, not just when we're face to face, but trying to dig his way into my mind too, bullying me into submission through my dreams, no matter that he tried to imply I burst into his dream—as if I had such a power! Clearly, he's behind it all. The double-murder I watched him commit without hesitation, the gryphon in my nightmare last night, sinking its talons into my throat, feathers floating through the air as it ripped me apart, the dream during my afternoon nap today—I was too bored to do anything besides sleep the hours away—where I danced until I died. Those were all him. And now this?

I say, "You don't have to be so insufferably rude."

"Rude? Your work is uninspired. You can hardly expect me to grovel at your feet like everyone else, Miss Bell." His smile is taunting.

"Well, *you* can hardly expect me to be inspired!" My temper flares. "I've got nothing to do. You won't let me have any books, for one thing! Good food and a pretty room doesn't change the fact that I'm captive and bored out of my damn mind!"

"You're not meant to be entertained here, you're *meant* to be the entertainment." He rises from his chair and gets close to me, too close. "And besides that, you're meant to stay in your room. When I give orders for the door to be locked, it is to remain that way."

I gulp. I'd hoped I'd gotten away with it, even assumed I had when Jinny came up to do my hair tonight. More pins.

His voice is cold, eyes like shining steel as they cut to my face and then to my hair, the black reflecting the glow of the candle-light...and even *me* to an extent. I look away. He commands, "Give them to me. Your hair will stay down from now on."

I lift a hand to touch the beautiful style put in only a half hour ago. It's her best yet, with even a pink rose tucked into the upswept curls—I didn't tell her it was my favorite flower. "No. I won't do it again, I swear."

"Your promise means nothing. Give them to me. Now."

I resentfully yank pins from my hair until it tumbles around my shoulders. The rose falls to my feet, and I kick it aside.

"I'm certain you don't want me to check," he warns.

Picturing his big hands running through my hair, I shiver. Reluctantly, I take the last hidden hairpin out from the nape of my neck and hand it over with the rest. But I don't back down, even as he shoots a murderous glare at me. I return the expression.

"I didn't do any harm, leaving my room. You might let me out more. I need fresh air. I haven't stepped foot outside in over a week!"

The demon walks along the row of windows, broad back to me—as if to say that I'm so unimportant he doesn't even care, yet I catch the tightness in his shoulders. I'm definitely provoking him. I steady myself, slow my anger to a simmer instead of a boil. *He's a killer, Corliss. Don't be a damn fool.*

"Dance," he utters, without turning.

I roll my eyes, but begin, pretending like he's not even there. Two can play at this game. I finish quickly, and this time, he doesn't interrupt me. I'm not sure if he even was watching. I don't bother to confirm.

As I bend low to curtsey, the air seems to sizzle.

I snap up my head, and there, out of nowhere, is a woman. *No,* I correct myself. Not with those eyes, soulless as his. Immediately, I know. She's one of his kind. And far in the shadows, standing in a corner, a demon man, built like a brick. Never in my life did I think I'd see a real-life demon, let alone three of them.

Orrin has turned to see the strangers, offering a stiff bow to her, ignoring the man in the corner—a servant, or guard perhaps. She waltzes over to Orrin, arms outstretched, catlike smile on her face. She kisses his cheek in greeting, then turns, her long white dress trailing behind her as she heads my way. Above the sinfully low neckline, a long pendant rests heavy, a red jewel as large as a plum.

"So you're the little dancer he's taken in, mmm?" Her voice snakes in my ear, and I startle. She got so close, so quickly.

I gape at her, open-mouthed. Her hair is not blonde, but nearly white, devoid of color—long and shining down her slender body. Her features are cold and hard, like she's been cut from a block of marble. She's definitely not the most beautiful woman— most beautiful *being*—that I've ever seen, yet she's intoxicating. I could study her for years and not figure out that face. The rosebud mouth a bit crooked, the cheekbones blades, too sharp. But arresting, all combined.

"I've been so curious about you," the demon woman purrs, eyeing me from head to toe, smirking at the sight of the red shoes. "You must be a wonderful dancer, for him to keep you all to himself." Here she snickers. "I'll have to return to catch the performance next time."

"She's decent enough entertainment," he says dryly, lounging in his chair now, languid, at ease. Yet there's an edge to his eyes when they look at the back of her. For once, his resentment is focused on someone other than me. I catch this in a millisecond, enough to understand one thing: he hates her.

A lightning bolt of realization. This is the *she* Mr. Brown meant. I still can't speak, she's so mesmerizing, the way the light hits her silvery skin, the red lips that beg to be not just kissed, but *bitten*, the smell of her—charcoal, tart cherries, and jasmine—and something dangerous underlying it all, like a delicious poison that kills. When she moves closer, I spy white bones hanging from her ears, so tiny they might have been the finger bones of a child, and a sickening feeling descends upon me.

She brushes her hand against my cheek, crushing the fallen rose with the sole of her shoe. "So pretty. Perhaps I'll take you as a plaything."

My heart almost stops, and, tearing my gaze away from the emptiness of the woman's eyes, the spell she's laid over me unwinds. Fear dulls everything but her. She's like nothing I've ever seen. Compared to her, *he* is almost benign.

I look back at him, his lips barely a frown, and catch how his face pulls back up into a pleasant mask so quickly I wonder if I'd imagined the way he stared at her. Maybe I just wish he'd find someone to hate more than me. But if she's forcing him—or encouraging him—to do something he doesn't want to do, maybe he really does hate her.

"If you like, my queen." He shrugs to the woman. "Though I'm finding the amusement rather diverting."

"As you wish." She ducks her head, yet the coy bow of her smile belies the action; she is in power here, not him. She could pluck me from this very spot right now, and he would have no say. I know this implicitly.

"Now," she addresses him, "I came for a reason."

The demon makes to stand from his chair, but she waves him down.

"Sit," she tells him, then trails her fingers down my cheekbone so that goosebumps dot my body. "I'm not staying long."

She won't take me. She won't take me. And I can't deny a twinge in me, on me—*through* me—that is sorry. What kind of power does she—and the red slippers—possess that makes reason so completely fall away?

"What can I do for you?" he asks her, completely ignoring me. I glance back at Mr. Brown, seated at the piano. Quiet, rigid. He doesn't look at the woman, at any of us. The air tastes of fear, secrets I'm not privy to. I've never seen Mr. Brown appear timid before.

The woman turns her attention from me again to the demon, saying in a pouty voice, "I need a new valet, and I'd like you to find one for me. I simply don't have time."

"What about Gregor?"

"He became so tedious in the end, I couldn't stand it."

"What happened to him?"

She gives a bored sigh, picking at her sharpened fingernails. "He was tossed out."

He raises an eyebrow. "In pieces?"

Her soft laugh is like tinkling bells, like a shower of stars from the sky, like the sound a delicate lily would make if it were human. I find myself leaning a little closer even as my befuddled brain makes sense of the words. *In pieces.* My stomach drops, and I force myself not to visibly shake. In my nightmare state, I witnessed him slit two people's throats, but even that's not as bad as what she's saying. What'd she do—hack the poor man into pieces or rip him apart? Or, she had someone else do it. Someone else who works for her, like the demon does. He referred to her as a queen. He bowed to her. She has power I can hardly comprehend.

She made him kill someone yesterday. And maybe too, that couple asleep in their bed. It couldn't be helped, meaning he cannot tell her no. Meaning he didn't want to do it. And the way he brushed me off as nothing more than entertainment, in that casual way.

Why do I have the strange, unsettling sense that he's protecting me from her?

Spinning away, she strolls around. "Orrin, you know me too well, darling. Anyway, please don't dally. I need someone soon. A young man, pretty. Perhaps you can take his tongue. Gregor talked *so* much."

I chew my lip; without my constant application of moisturizing stain from the apothecary, my chapped skin breaks easily. I swallow down the metallic taste of blood.

The woman snaps her attention to me, nostrils flaring. She can smell the blood, I realize too late. Just that single drop. She saunters back over, leans in, far too close. "Scared, little one?"

Ice runs through my veins, and my breath catches as she waits for my answer. Managing one slow nod is the best I can do.

She laughs, tilting even closer. "I like you, you know." And she is only a breath away when she darts out her tongue and licks the blood off my bottom lip.

Here my knees almost give out, but I steel myself. I am not really me, I'm simply putting on a show. I lower my chin and eyes, not daring to challenge her in any way.

She snaps her fingers, and the silent man in the corner follows her into nothingness.

Her laugh seems to echo throughout the room long after she's gone. Long after I'm able to move again, to breathe freely again. Now he stands close, staring at me. I tilt my face up, meet his eyes, unafraid now. Maybe he just seems less frightening after her. In those moments, it was clear she had all the power.

I finally whisper, "You work for her. Don't you?"

He looks down at me. A lock of hair falling across his forehead softens him, but his face is hard, his jaw clenched. "Yes."

"She's terrifying."

Only silence is his reply. He's done talking about her.

I clear my throat, take a chance, even though it seems like the worst time to do so. I've spent long days thinking about how to ask him, honing the words over and over again. "I know I have been a bit...contrary at times." While I speak, he moves away from me, returning once more to stare out the windows into the now-dark night. I go on, "You see, it's not just the books, or lack of diversion. I'm missing my sister terribly, both of them. My oldest sister, Aven, she died and I heard that you—"

"I'm not interested in your life story." He doesn't turn to look at me, but his frigid voice cuts off my plea. "Go back upstairs."

I grow more desperate. "But I only wanted to ask—"

"I don't care!" He whips around, shouting, his fury unleashed. "Not about you. Not about your dead sister!"

Angry tears spring to my eyes. "You unfathomable bastard."

He looks so furious he could spit fire. He despises me. "You're *done*. Go to your room."

I let the butler lead me away while I cry silently. All this effort, for nothing. Has my big mouth ruined everything? No. I shake my head. He was never going to help me. Any hope I previously held wilts in me like a dying flower, crushed under a demon queen's shoe. It's pointless. I am afraid of him still; however, I now know that I have found something much worse to fear. And she wants to take me as her plaything?

He'll probably *let* her take me, despite seeming to indicate to her I was rather unimportant. He hates me enough. But why? I still don't understand. I'm through trying.

"I told you, it's no use," Mr. Brown echoes my silent realization, almost apologetically, as we stand in front of my room. "You best just dance for him for as long as he wants. Then maybe he'll let you go."

"You don't sound sure." I look away from him. His rough face. His white hair. How long has he been a puppet for his employer?

He doesn't answer, only motions me into the room and locks the door behind me. Not that it matters. Still, I'm happy to be alone for the moment.

Inside, I wipe the tears with one shaky hand, hating the wet feel on my face. Hating the butler. Hating the sight of the locked bedroom door. Hating the wonderful food and the gentle way

Mrs. Minthy washed my hair. I hate it all, hate the maids, hate the fine furnishings, hate the red shoes. And I hate, hate, *hate* that demon.

I don't care about you. I don't care about your dead sister.

This is futile. He's not going to help me save Aven. His mistress is another threat to contend with now, instinct warns. I have to get out of here, but that lock on the door has never felt more impassable. And with my hairpins confiscated, I've lost any scrap of control I had over this situation.

Then again, maybe I never had any to begin with.

CHAPTER THIRTEEN

ow to do it. How to do it. I pace back and forth in my room on my twentieth evening in the mansion. The Pins carnival has come and gone, I have bled my monthly, I have danced so many times in the enchanted slippers and still, they show no wear. But in this moment, I'm too restless to dance. Even pacing doesn't help, nor does ignoring my supper. I plop back down because I can hardly think on an empty stomach. It's been twelve days since the demon woman came. I've almost forgotten how afraid I was of her. Almost.

I weigh my options as I eat, just as I do so often now that I am certain he won't agree to help me. If my initial goal was to get him on my good side, in the last nine days, my focus has turned into playing the obedient captive—only to throw him off my real intentions. I *am* going to escape…I just haven't figured out how to get past the servants, Mr. Brown's almost-constant presence, and my sad lack of hairpins. I could tie my bedsheets together and climb out the window, a choice I've already considered. But, walking over and eyeing the distance to the ground for about the dozenth time, barely visible in the darkening sky, I ascertain, bedsheets knotted tightly or no, it's likely I would simply fall. My strength is mostly in my legs, not my arms. And it's a long way down.

I slump back to the table and run through other ideas, sullenly chewing my chicken-stuffed pastry. It's delicious. I don't believe I'm able to outrun Mr. Brown. Perhaps I could hit him over the head? But other than the big candelabra in the room, there's nothing else to attack him with that could really do damage, and, as much as I dislike the man, I don't want to kill him. I gather he wouldn't go down with a light thump. I'd have to hit him hard, and he'd bleed. I purse my lips with distaste. I don't even like killing spiders. But if it came down to it, wouldn't I make any of them bleed if it meant saving my own life?

I could bribe one of the maids. Jinny or Hana. As for Mrs. Minthy, as kind as she's been to me, I doubt she'd be disloyal to *him*. However, the red-haired cousins are new, young. The problem is, if they can't hear me when I tell them I'm being held captive, how could they help me escape? I fear nothing I say will help my case.

I turn my attention to the plate of sweets and fruit and bite into an apple aggressively. Instead of bribing Jinny or Hana, I could just overpower one of them. Not hurt them, but grab them and tie them up with something. My eyes drift around the room, to the wardrobe. I could use the sash from the cream dress. This newest idea has merit. So long as I'm not caught escaping...it could work.

I go to the wardrobe, pull the dress out, and lay it on the bed. Then, lacking scissors, I use my teeth to rip the belt loops. I tug on the blue sash, testing it. It's skinny but strong. I could knot it, and it would hold, not for long, probably, but long enough. Unless they scream. My resolve wavers as I consider this. I'd have to gag them. The thought is unpleasant—they've been kind to me. But I can't wait around for the demon to find mercy and just let me go. I'd be waiting forever. He would snap my bones between his teeth before he did me a favor. And if not him, that terrifying creature he bowed to.

Escaping may not be easy, or safe, even once I'm out of the mansion. The demon may come after me, I know this. I'm not *that* naive. I can only hope that I've been such a bother, that he hates me so much, he may just never want to set eyes on me again. The thought settles me considerably. Now that I've decided on a reasonable way of escaping, I can hardly wait to go. I grasp the sash gratefully.

Mr. Brown bangs open the door, making me jump.

"Could you stop that?" I frown, annoyed at his entering without knocking. Yet again. I've only just relieved my bladder! What if I were naked? Indignantly, I snap, "What if I were changing?"

Mr. Brown smirks at my nightgown and dressing gown. I was going to change into my dress for dancing after my meal. "I don't care one way or another what you wear. He wants to see you. He's waiting in the ballroom."

"But it's not time to dance. And I'm not ready."

"I don't think it's for dancing." His voice holds a warning. "He wants to talk to you."

I remember how I snuck out of my room. Remember how I yelled at the demon. What if he knows I'm planning to escape the mansion? What if he can read minds? The thought never occurred to me before, but now, thinking of all the horrible things I mentally called him.... During my performances, ever since the night he screamed at me, he's been frigidly silent, but what if he was only lying in wait. Readying to pounce.

As I step reluctantly toward the door, I ask Mr. Brown, "Has he killed a lot of people? Really and truly?"

"How many is a lot?"

"I don't know," I answer. "More than ten?" I say, just as he says, "A hundred?"

"A hundred!" I cry.

He laughs at my horrified face. "I'm guessing."

A hundred? He has to be kidding. "But you must have an idea...."

"Well, one band for every person."

"Band?"

"On his arms."

It takes me a moment to comprehend. "You mean his tattoos. Each band represents someone he's killed?"

Mr. Brown doesn't answer, though his leathery face holds an amused smile.

I sputter, "But his arms are almost solid ink! Black from elbow to wrist!"

Jerking his head toward the door, he ignores my outcry. "Let's not keep him waiting."

My heart is racing, blue belt still bunched in my now clammy hand. I won't be tying up a maid now. I could very well be on my way to my death. I certainly made the demon angry enough the night the woman came. And though he's not shown his temper since, neither has he indicated any appreciation for my performances. Or my very presence. Has he finally had enough of me? Blood spattered on his white shirt flashes again in my mind.

Following Mr. Brown through the third floor, with each step I search around with wild eyes. What can I use? How can I get away? The hall is empty. Nothing but sconces on the walls. I can't very well rip them off without him noticing. What can I hit him with that will make enough of an impact?

Then the first staircase is upon us. Mr. Brown is ahead of me, taking the first step down, and there's nobody else in sight. Now is my chance. I can't wait. Whenever I go down for dancing, there are never other servants in sight, as though they're all off doing other tasks during that hour—even though it's earlier than normal, I pray that's the case now. This might be my shot to run without someone catching me. The demon will be waiting in the ballroom. I drop the blue belt and reach my hands out toward the unsuspecting butler.

I push him. Hard.

He doesn't make a sound. Just tumbles forward silently. Down, down, down, like a rag doll. He somersaults as I run, gripping the banister lest I fall too, hopping over where he lands. I turn back once to look at him. Slumped on his belly, he doesn't lift his head. A sickening feeling swoops in my gut, but there's no time for regret. I race through the second floor, past the bedrooms, down the grand staircase. In my bare feet, red slippers left behind and tugging at me from two floors above. It's the most irrational thought: *I should go back for them.*

I run on.

This is it. I'm so close. I'm so quiet. Nobody even knows I'm heading toward the door. I'm almost there, cutting through the foyer, which is finally outfitted with a large pedestal table, glass vase of flowers in the middle, their powerful scent sucking the air from the room, making me woozy. I hold my breath and lunge toward the door. Just as my fingertips graze the doorknob, a voice in my ear. *His.*

"Going somewhere?"

I jump about fifty feet, then whip around, meeting the demon's face. I look up at his great height, the feeling of him like a wall opposite me. Choking down a cry, I step back like a trapped animal, until my shoulder blades press against the door. He moves closer yet, standing directly in front of me. My chest heaves so hard I expect he can hear the beat of my heart, but silence hangs around us for what seems like centuries. I look away from his horrible eyes but find myself drawn back. To the dark, the warning of his shining gaze. The rest of his face is impassive, but there's a cold rage radiating from him that has me cowering. I wait.

Going somewhere? he had asked. To my death, probably.

Then, I change my mind. Answer his question aloud.

"Yes," I say, in a haughty way, straightening up tall, though the top of my head hardly grazes his collarbone. I lift my chin to meet his stare, though it pains me. "You obviously don't care for my dancing, so there's no reason to stay. Now, if you don't mind, I'll be leaving." I hope he doesn't catch the tremble in my words, the haughtiness melting to a feeble proclamation.

That obsidian gaze is piercing. "I think you've misunderstood the terms of your captivity, Miss Bell. You cannot just come and go as you please, hence our prior discussion about the hairpins. You are being punished for stealing."

"But you know that wasn't my fault!" I try not to get hysterical. The door is at my back, freedom within reach.

His laugh is harsh, hateful. "Isn't it? That's ridiculous. Nobody forced you to steal from me. You almost—"

"Almost what?" I cry, still not understanding. I know why I hate *him*, but I still don't understand why he's so filled with rage toward *me*. All I did was take the damn shoes. "You can have your stupid slippers. I left them upstairs." Even that has me glancing upward, toward the staircase, thinking of them. I can't help the longing in my voice.

"I don't just want the shoes now," he says evenly. "I want the thief who stole them. You've gotten out twice now. If you try to escape from me again, I'm afraid you won't care for the consequences. I'm sick of you. It won't take much to tip the scales out of your favor."

"Please," I implore him, ashamed of the need spewing from my mouth. "Please just let me go home to my sister. I swear, I won't tell anyone about you or what you are. I just want to leave. Why won't you let me go?"

The demon stares down at me. Then he answers my question with his own. "Do you understand what it's like to be tied to something you hate?"

"No, not at all," I blurt out, the sarcasm thick and impulsive.

"You are either incredibly foolish or purposely provoking me." I swear, for a moment, a growl hovers in his throat. But I don't care.

"Am I supposed to feel sorry for you? For what?" I snarl, all worries of retribution gone. I'm tired of holding back. Let me be a band across his wrist. Nothing I say will prevent or prolong it if he makes up his mind to hurt me. "Actually, you know what? I *do* feel sorry for you! You don't even have a soul! A heart. You're just...empty."

The rage lit behind his eyes has me snapping my mouth shut. I've gone too far this time.

I push back into the door even harder and draw my hands up, defensively. He doesn't touch me, but he does get closer, placing his hands on either side of me, against the wood. He refuses to let me space myself from him, leaving a mere inch or two between our bodies.

He leans in, face so near to mine I see myself reflected in his stare, his cool breath on my upper lip. I gulp, staring at him, his eyes, his mouth. He looks back at me so long I think I forget to breathe. The demon is so close the heat from his body warms my skin. He breathes in, a long draw, almost...

Almost like he's...inhaling me.

My heart catches, something deep in my belly warming despite myself.

Then he moves slightly to my side, so that his hair touches my cheekbone. "You want to push me?" His whisper is a low rumble in my ear, sending chills up my spine. "I will push you harder, so much harder."

Mr. Brown comes lumbering downstairs with a cut on his forehead and blood trickling over one eye. The demon doesn't look back at him but tenses, adding, "Speaking of push, don't even think about harming anyone in this household again, Miss Bell. You're lucky you did not kill him. You're lucky I don't kill you because of it."

I guiltily turn my eyes from the sight of Mr. Brown's injured face.

The demon gives me one last, unbreakable glance, still agonizingly close to me. His voice is jagged, and he closes his eyes, like he can't stand the sight of me. "Mr. Brown, get her out of here. Forget what I said before."

He steps away from me, out of the foyer, and down the hall. He does not turn back to say anything else, does not punish me for harming his butler, nor for trying to escape, nor for baiting him. Confusion fuddles my brain, and I scratch my nails against the wood at my back, hoping to feel the freedom beyond it. Then

Mr. Brown pulls me away. He drags me upstairs and refuses to say a word to me on the way to my room. Yet, I think I catch a small flash of something across his face—admiration, maybe. Underneath the blood dripping from the cut.

"Wait." I catch his eye and cringe with shame. "I'm sorry, Mr. Brown. I didn't want to hurt you."

"Did you think being pushed down the stairs would feel good?"

"I had to at least try," I say, half in a whisper. "Wouldn't you?"

He nods, surprisingly, then starts to shut the door to my room.

"Why didn't he harm me? Why didn't he *kill* me?" I ask, mostly to myself.

Mr. Brown pauses. "Maybe he's tired of killing," he answers in a thoughtful way.

The door closes. I go to my favorite chair and sit, bury my face into my shaking hands. Too tired to kill me? If he's tired of killing, I'll try to escape again. Next time, I could be successful. If the demon is too tired to kill, perhaps he'll be too tired to chase me down.

I wait, but he doesn't call me to dance for him after supper like usual. Too irate, I suppose. And I still don't know why he even wanted to see me in the first place. I move around, nervousness flowing through me. What will he do to me next time we meet? I dance on my own, pushing my edginess into grace, because I have to do *something* with this energy. When night falls, I climb into bed.

Shutting my eyes, I can't help but think about the unsettling way he stared at me, at the way he breathed me in.

Chapter Fourteen

That night I dream again, from inside his point of view. Like last time, I am aware of what is happening, aware that it's not real for me. Aware, this time immediately, that I am merely a passenger inside his body, carried along for the ride. He doesn't seem to notice my presence yet, which explains why he's doing…what he's doing. Body tightened with emotion. I can *feel* it, his sadness, his guilt. I gaze down through his perspective.

He holds a golden locket in one hand, opened to show a lock of butter-blonde hair on one side, and on the other, a fresh-faced milkmaid sort of young woman. Though the miniature portrait is rendered in black and white, I imagine her hair the same color as the curl opposite, her eyes a kind blue.

Deep inside him, the ache of grief fades to make way for the fury. He snaps the locket shut with a sharp sigh. And I think…I dream…that he sighs again, but this time, it is threaded with something like anguish. And it is rounded with the shape of my name.

Damn it, Corliss…

I awake suddenly and sit upright, back in my own body, my own being, my name echoing in the atmosphere. Unsettled is too small a word for what I just saw and felt. Who was the woman in the locket? And why was I a part of…whatever that was?

Soon after breakfast, I learn he's left for business. "Business" being vague enough to be concerning, but I can't help wondering if he is just avoiding me. If he knows I saw him.

If he knows I felt his heartbreak.

Three nights after I tried to escape—during which time I hadn't seen him at all—I'm informed that I will once again be dancing. I know he was only gone briefly for his "business" due to some offhand comments his staff made, but he had not called me down to dance despite being home in the evenings. He *was* avoiding me! That's fine with me. I'm not exactly eager to see him and return to our strained routine.

Mrs. Minthy is quieter than usual as she helps me into the copper tub—which has taken up a permanent spot in my room—before my dance-to-be, though her touch is gentle as she washes my hair.

Finally, I end the silence. "Is everything alright? You seem bothered."

"It's been a day, that's all," her murmur is tired as she rinses me.

"How so?"

"Oh, just normal issues with the staff, plus our cook is all in a tizzy because our order was late and half-missing. I guess there was some trouble in town."

"What kind of trouble?" I ask.

"The grocer was attacked last night, the delivery boy said, and his store was robbed."

"Mr. Links was attacked? How awful!" I frown. "Is he alright?"

"He'll be fine, the boy said. Though he was beaten pretty bad by some rowdy sailors, apparently."

I sit up in the bath, sloshing water about as her words settle on me. "Are the other stores okay? Do you know about the beauty apothecary? My sister works there!"

She nudges me down, tips back my head, but doesn't reply to that, as if she didn't hear. "Don't worry, Miss Corliss. Anyone who comes here to steal will find Mr. Brown with a revolver waiting for them."

Or worse, I mentally tack on.

When she's done helping me, she calls for Jinny, then leaves the two of us.

"Are you tired, Miss?" Jinny says as she twists up my hair into an elegant bun and double-wraps a blue ribbon, like a headband. I wear the cream dress again—sash reattached.

"A little." Tired of this place. Tired of this game. Tired of feeling like prey. And what about Sélie, alone in the cottage? Is she safe? Is she eating well? Is she sleeping enough?

Then I'm being escorted downstairs—the first time since I shoved Mr. Brown. This time he has me go ahead of him. He gives me a broad grin. "Ladies first."

Please don't push me, I implore him silently.

I hold the banister extra tightly just in case. He doesn't lay a hand on me.

Once in the ballroom, I warm up as usual, though my nerves are in tatters, after that last confrontation with the demon. Worry over that demon woman—not to mention worry over Sélie, in town, all alone—plagues me. I move lightly in the red shoes, marking out steps to a routine carefully. It hardly matters. He'll find fault with me no matter how perfectly I dance. And he already warned me about spying on him from my dreams. What will he say about it now, if he knows I know about the mystery woman in the locket? He would detest that I saw his vulnerability.

What if I try to show him through my dancing how I feel? How sorry I am for all of it? How I wish he could forgive me and help me?

Without warning, he appears, standing in the doorway. His gait is smooth as he goes to his chair and takes his seat, draping himself casually across it. Tonight he is clad all in black, a shirt with buttons that shine like his eyes, trousers, and boots so glossy the lights gleam in the leather.

He rakes his fingers through his long hair and says simply, "Dance."

I stare at the tattoo peeking out from under one cuff. One band for every life. So many deaths, they've blurred into one another.

Breathe, Corliss, I remind myself. I have to focus. At least the demon hasn't come to teach me a lesson, I don't believe. Unless he's waiting for me to finish the dance first. One last performance before I die? Or he hands me off to that creature to torture. I let out an involuntary shudder, yet I begin.

I've performed many routines for him—light and lively, short and fierce. Tonight, I choose a slower dance, focusing on my technique even more so than usual. The red shoes carry me, lift me, lead me, pull me. I stretch from my toes all the way through my fingertips, body long and straight, leg pulled up to the ceiling in a striking développé. I let myself fall, let myself collapse and unfold. It's a swan's routine, a butterfly, a doe. It is something gentle and beautiful, something easily harmed.

In a way, it's a plea. *I can't hurt you back. Please don't harm me. Please don't hate me anymore.*

All through it, his face is impassive.

When I complete the dance, the air around me is taut.

"Go." He jerks his head, dismissing me. Something like weariness dragging his mouth down. There is no humor in his gaze, no softness, no kindness. His face holds a fatigue I've never seen before. Whatever business he was off doing has taken something out of him.

Aven, Aven, Aven, her name echoes in my heart. Reminds me. Gives me courage. One last try. I search for any humanity. The other night, I *felt* it in him as he stared at the portrait of the sweet-faced woman. Where is it now?

"If I asked you for a favor," I manage in a brave whisper, out of nowhere, the words coming out of their own accord. "What would it take for you to grant it?"

"I'm not in the business of granting favors, thief." His voice is icy, cruel.

"But—please, can't I explain—"

He growls, "I won't say it again. Go to your room. *Now*."

I feel something inside me break, one final time. One last hope destroyed. I open my mouth to plead but snap it shut. It's hopeless. Just as I feared.

I don't care how risky it is. I'm going to escape, for real, and I won't try running out the front door. I plan to be successful, because I'm certain death will be my punishment if he catches me this time. I'll get Sélie out of The Pins, get us both somewhere safe until the demon is bored trying to track me back down. I'll do whatever it takes because I can't stay at the mansion any longer. And I'm fucking tired of playing by his rules.

After my door is relocked, I yank the sheets off my bed. I rip two of the sheets in half, creating more length. Then, using the sailor's knot Darius taught me years ago, I begin tying them together.

I don't rush. I won't be able to make my move for hours, but, thankfully, the time passes quickly. Everyone must be asleep by now.

I leave the enchanted slippers on the bed. Give them one last caress. Afterwards, I take off the dress I'm wearing and hang it up in the wardrobe. I will take nothing with me I did not come here with. All the less reason for him to pursue me.

With sure and steady hands, I knot one end of the sheet-rope to one of the bedposts, then I carry the other end to the window. I stand there for a long moment, debating whether or not to tie one end to my waist and shimmy my way down the side of the building, but decide I'm not confident in that method. Truth be told, I'm not confident in any aspect of this, but it's all I have now. I slip the sheets down the side of the house, hoping nobody is looking out a back window, and that the demon is asleep—does he even sleep?—in his bedchamber. Mr. Brown and the other staff are probably sleeping in the servants' wing on the other end of the third floor. I hope that is the case, anyhow. It's certainly late enough. The sky is dark, night has come.

After the end of the sheet is left dangling over the ledge of the window, I wait, in case someone comes and pounds on my door. But nobody does.

It's time.

I draw a long breath and inch out the window backwards, my hands grasping the rope of sheets hard, praying the knot around the bedpost holds. I ease my way over the edge, scraping my stomach, my arms, my legs. I curse as I climb down, banging my body against the side of the house as I grip the sheets so tightly my arms scream. It is awkward, muscle-breaking work. I channel Lysander, his graceful strength on his silks, and that seems to help. I go slowly, wrapping my legs around the sheet, desperate to gain safety, finding the knots along the way. It is not easy, not that I thought it would be. Passing the second story windows I hold my breath. As I descend, I notice a window covering on the other side. Dark. I let a tight exhalation slip past my lips and continue on with shaking legs, my entire body aching from the climb. About three feet from the ground, my weakened arms give out. I tumble down and land with a hard thud in the grass, on my thankfully generous backside.

But I did it, and I didn't break my neck.

In the cover of darkness, I stand and then I run like I've never run before. To the woods. Towards home.

I can tell when I'm off the Colehart property because the sounds come at me like an orchestra, the ones missing from my world these last few weeks: the rustle of creatures; the songs of frogs; the strong gust of a September night's breeze; animals burrowing under bushes and up in the leaves; and, farther off in the distance, the roar of the sea. I bend down, catch my breath, my heart thrumming excitedly. I did it. I'm free.

Lifting a branch out of the way, I step forward, relief coursing through my bones, and I walk in the dark, guided by the light of the moon, stepping on moss, cool dirt, soft grass. Clad just in my chemise, I relish the snap of twigs beneath my toes and the scratch of pricker bushes on my bare legs as I move forward eagerly. I relish the feeling of being alive and getting distance from the mansion. I'll be at the cottage soon, with Sélie. And oh, then maybe back to the Clover, if they'll let me. Back to my life, however patched-up it may be at times. It's mine, and I want it back. And now I shall have it!

I ignore the voice in my head—a reasonable one, which says he'll never let me go. He'll come after me again. And this time he'll make me pay for running.

But fear will not make me turn around. Even if Sélie and I have to run, even if we have to hide for a while. I can get away safely, can even call the authorities. Report the double murder that I witnessed—make *him* pay.

I'm so intent on my path back to the cottage that, when I smell a lingering campfire and the odor of cheap ale, I have only a moment of warning before parting my way through a bush and finding two men standing on the other side. By the time I blink, one is just inches away, beefy, bigger than me by a good foot up and two feet across, a sly smile across his whiskered face as he looks me up and down. The other sports a purple bruise under one eye and reeks of the sea, onions, and stale beer. They both wear light shirts and dark-blue pants, fish guts and salt-spray on their boots. Sailors. But they're not local. I've never seen them before in my life.

I clear my throat. With my chin tipped up, I say in as regal a voice as I can muster, "Excuse me. I didn't know anyone was here."

They glance at each other. Smile. Then back at me. "It's fine," the smaller one says. His voice carries a slur. "We were just enjoying some libation."

Stomach dropping, I nod quickly, as though I'm not afraid at all. "I'll leave you to it, then."

These are the men who attacked Mr. Links, intuition screams as I step away, remembering Mrs. Minthy's comments earlier while I was in the bath. I just know it, simply and without doubt. I don't glance back at them, my steps are unhurried, deliberate, the way one walks in front of an aggressive dog, so as not to draw attention.

But then a hand at the back of my neck, so sudden.

I cry out as one of them throws me to the ground.

"No! Get off of me!" I swing at the large man's fleshy face but barely graze him. Fighting back harder, I kick violently with my bare feet, rake his skin with my fingernails. I don't care if I draw blood. I want to draw blood.

"Hellcat," the man grunts, as my foot connects with his groin—though not nearly as hard as I'd have liked. He cracks his palm against my face. My ears ring as my head snaps back and hits the ground. When I blink, I see stars.

"Don't play at being a lady, not with those tattoos, wandering the woods alone at night." The smaller one sniggers, taking a swig of his ale, a glint in his eyes as he watches me fight off his friend. Stroking a revolver at his belt. Laughing as I struggle up. He smirks. "You look like a pirate."

"Go to hell, vermin," I manage as the big one shoves me down again. I bite my tongue. The iron taste of blood fills my mouth.

"You'll pay for that one." He grins, flashing his yellowed, rotting teeth at me.

"No!" I scream, as my hands are pinned to the ground. I fight with all of my might, but still, I can't free myself. I yell, gasping for help, searching the skies above, pleading with the stars for a miracle, but there is nobody to save me. Nobody to help me. The man's mean eyes narrow as he leers over me. I squeeze my own shut, forget how to breathe. Then a sudden whoosh of air and the man atop me is gone, warm breeze and emptiness replacing the suffocating weight of his body crushing my own. A guttural cry. A shattering sound. Like glass breaking. Only I know it's not glass.

I open my eyes to see the demon. His eyes meet mine in one burning stare before he moves again, going after the second man now, who's pissed himself, face white with fright. The man points his gun at the demon, the ring of the shot hardly audible compared to my screams as the demon reaches him, moving faster than humanly possible. Because, of course, he's not human.

I roll over, squeeze my eyes shut, clap my hands over my ears so I won't see the carnage, won't hear the sounds, the screams. Try not to breathe so I won't smell the blood.

It's fast. But it seems like forever.

Now there's only silence. Even with blood roaring in my ears I can tell.

I crack open my lids, darkness filling my senses, my face against the cold ground.

The demon stands next to me, his black, shining boots near my head. Spattered with crimson.

No. No. No. I might say it out loud. Maybe it's all in my mind.

He lifts me into his arms.

And everything goes black.

Chapter Fifteen

I come to just as we're entering the dimly lit ballroom, a few candles glowing. The demon sets me down in the middle of the room, walks away while I sway, blinking. Realizing what just happened. What might have happened. I shut my eyes to lock out the memory of the men's screams. A tiny, secret part of me is glad. Because if it hadn't been them, it would have been me. They surely would have beaten me, perhaps to death. And maybe worse.

"You tried to escape again." The demon's tone is easily discerned, his rage, his resentment. He paces in frustration. "You put me in a position I did not want to be in."

"I…I had to." My voice breaks. "I can't stay here forever…."

"What is so terrible here? Have you starved? Been harmed?" The fury in his eyes makes me take a step back. "You've lived like a queen, have you not?"

"A queen!" I repeat, outraged. "You've shown me no kindness. You won't help me save my sister."

"You never asked."

"You've hardly given me a chance, but I tried to earlier! And I know you don't do favors—you said so yourself. You'll only say no! You've forbidden me to leave."

"And I'll keep forbidding it!" he yells, tossing the red slippers at my feet. "Dance."

"Now?" I jerk my head behind me to find Mr. Brown, waiting at the piano.

"Yes, now," he commands. I turn back and notice the pained expression on his face. The memory of the gunshot resounding through the air returns.

"But you're injured. Bleeding," I say, as it dawns on me. I stare at the blood-splotch spreading across his shirt, just over his ribs, below his heart. There's also a large gash sliced across his temple. I didn't know demons could bleed. The last time I saw blood on his shirt I'd assumed it was not his; it likely wasn't, now that I know he's been off killing people. But I didn't know his sort could bleed. "You *were* shot, weren't you?"

"What care have you for my wounds? Get your ass going and dance. Now," he snaps, surprising me with his language.

The music starts. My knees shake, my face throbs, the back of my head is sore, and I stand in a bloodied scrap of my chemise— mostly his blood, I realize. The chemise is ripped all across the top, falling off one shoulder, thankfully leaving my breasts covered. There's dirt in my hair and under my nails, scratches on my arms and feet. And the memory. Fear covering me like a blanket, the way that man's body did. The way they hurt me.

"Dance." One word. It is not a request. The fire in the demon's eyes makes that clear.

I tie up the shoes, which he jerks his head at, telling me without words to hurry, and I follow his order. I dance, spitefully, each step a mark of regret and disdain. I don't bother smiling at all. I don't bother pretending. I'm too tired to argue. I just want this to be over. All of it.

At the end of the song, I curtsey and turn, expecting Mr. Brown to follow, to bring me upstairs. There, I can fall into my bed and cry. I can count down the hours until tomorrow, when Mrs. Minthy will have a bath drawn for me. I want to wash this whole night off.

"I did not dismiss you, Corliss." The demon's now-restrained voice stops my hand at the door.

I spin around. "Hell's bells. I don't care what—"

"Dance. *Again*. Until I tell you to stop." Some blood runs down his temple, matting his dark hair, and he lets it, not bothering to wipe it away. This is my punishment for running, for escaping. This is the price I pay for him saving my life. I will dance, and I will do it beautifully.

The piano starts once more, and I march to the middle of the room. I push out all the emotions, all the pain in my body, and I let the red shoes carry me. Gliding along in jetés and stepping into passés, I become the music. Spiraling in pirouettes until I am out of breath, whipping my right leg into delicate yet powerful fouettés turns, I dance until sweat runs in rivulets down my filthy arms, until my ankles quiver, until my breath comes out in gasps. The room swims before my eyes and I push on. Everything aches, and I push on. Out of pure spitefulness, I dance harder than I ever have before. He wants a performance? I will make it for myself.

The whole time the demon just sits, watching me with a hard face, anger pulsing out of his inhuman eyes.

He abhors me, more than ever before. At least we're even.

As I stand en pointe in an arabesque that should be unflinchingly graceful, my muscles give up, and my bottom leg buckles. I collapse to the hard floor before I can draw a breath or even try to catch myself. The red shoes have betrayed me, my body has betrayed me.

"Get up."

I try, I do, but my legs give out once more. "I can't." Tears run from my eyes. *Fuck you.* I wasn't going to let myself cry, not in front of him.

"Are you crying?" There's such an emptiness in his voice that it makes the tears fall harder.

"No." I brush my face with one hot, angry hand. Will this night never end?

"Get up and dance. Remember what I said about pushing me?"

I stand, not because he told me to, but to prove to myself I can. I wobble like a newborn foal, and try to rise again on my toes, but both my legs collapse this time, and I land hard, falling on the side of my ankle. The agony of something cracking makes my head spin.

I sob quietly as I lie in a heap on the unforgiving floor. With my bones sore and my spirits thoroughly broken, I close my eyes tight and bow my aching head. His steps are slow, and beyond the pounding in my temples, I make out each one as he comes closer to me.

He will kill me now, as I lie here weak and wilted. He saved me only to kill me.

Somehow, I hardly care. It hurts so badly, my ankle. My heart. Everything. And I'm so exhausted, all this mourning, all the death and hopes dashed to nothingness. My sister is dead, and that's that. All of this was for nothing.

I wait for the strike, for the blow, for the hands around my throat, for him to end me. Instead, he lifts me off the floor. This is the second time I've been in his arms tonight.

Stunned into silence, it takes me a long moment to open my mouth, whisper a weak plea, "Don't kill me."

He stares down at the sound of my words, and I'm reflected in his gaze; it swallows me up. All his anger seems to melt away. He shakes his head. "I don't plan to."

Everything goes bleary. The blood congealing around the cut on the demon's face flickers in and out of focus. But the feel of his arms around me stays steady, the heat of him against me, his lean, strong body like fire against mine. Then once again, like some damned damsel in distress, I begin to faint.

Before the world goes black, it's the strangest thing—I almost think I catch him whisper:

I'm sorry...

I don't remember much about the fire that killed my mother and father. Scattered bits and pieces, memories thick with smoke, ash falling from the sky, the charred bones of our home. In my recollection, I'm standing in the middle of the house, a child of only four, destruction all around me.

But whenever I recalled it out loud, Aven always reminded me that wasn't true, despite her own nightmares about the incident. "We weren't even there."

If we had been, we'd have been killed too, along with our parents. It was only by a miracle that the three of us girls had been sent away to stay with another family while our parents recovered from scarlet fever. If we'd been home, we'd have burned.

Maybe that's why the three of us were so drawn to the ocean when we came to live with Mavis. Why we craved the soothing wet air, the salt on our skin, the way the tides ebbed and flowed against the shore, erasing what had been there moments before, as though the sea could work that way with us—our memories.

I love the water, the way it surrounds me, the way it soothes.

I'm *in* the water.

Coming to this abrupt realization, I snap open my eyes, edge out the fuzzy parts of the lingering dreams, nightmares. I'm in the copper tub in my room, in front of the fireplace. It's filled to the brim with steaming water, thick with soap bubbles and fragrant oil—rose and something herby—something that reminds me of him, the demon. Rosemary.

And it's at this moment I comprehend that he is holding on to me, keeping me from slumping too far into the water, one black-banded arm wrapped around my waist. Blessedly, my chemise is still on. All of this is clear to me in a matter of seconds, yet the shock of it has me slow to react.

I wrap my arms around my chest, pull up my knees, let out a sharp breath.

"I'm not going to harm you." He very deliberately doesn't look at me—not at my face, not at my body. He tries to dab my cheekbone with a wet rag.

I shove at him, fear be damned. "What are you *doing*?"

"You're filthy. I'm washing you. And you wouldn't wake—I thought this might rouse you."

"That's your fault," I say severely, not biting my tongue. Though my trouble waking is probably from hitting my head, he certainly didn't help the matter by making me dance myself to exhaustion!

Finally, he turns his head, those empty, bottomless eyes meeting mine so intently that I blink, but the flames of my rage have died down. I don't recognize the look on his face. I stare, awaiting his answer.

"You argue with everything, usually. I was surprised you listened to me this time," he answers mildly, his fingers gentle as he untangles my matted hair. He looks at my face, only. Keeps his eyes there.

I swat away his touch, then ask with a bitter edge, "How could I refuse? You would have killed me."

He removes his wet arm, sets it on the edge of the tub, face tired. "So, because you think I'd kill you, you'd dance yourself to death?"

I raise my voice. "You gave me little choice! Besides, I've seen you kill someone—two someones! Four, come to think of it! And there were plenty more I didn't see."

If I could stand, I would, even if I'd lose the cover of bubbles. However, I can't move with this tender ankle. Broken ankle, maybe. I pull up my knees tighter, leaning away from him as far as I can, forcing the tears away. I can't tell if they're angry tears or traumatized tears. I flash back to what happened in the woods. The men. Their deaths. I'm not sorry they're dead. Does that make me a monster too? I wish I could have killed them myself.

"I'm not going to harm you," he repeats, scowling. "I was trying to help."

I scoff—on his knees next to the tub, he is almost level with me. "You kidnapped me. You've taunted me with nightmares and visions, been unbearably rude, and downright cruel. You won't help me save my sister. You don't care about anything." Now, tears fall from my eyes again. I've never felt more naked, sitting here before him, weeping.

He doesn't answer my accusations. I stare blankly while he reaches into the tub and pulls out my right foot. His fingers burn into my skin. "Broken?"

My poor foot, skin cracked open in more than one spot, toes bruised and blistered from all my years of dancing, and now this new injury, my ankle swollen and purple. No wonder it hurts so badly.

"I don't know." Why I don't demand he release me, I can't understand. Am I still afraid of him now? He did save my life, even if he was unbearably punishing about it afterwards. But why would he save my life if he was only going to hurt me?

Maybe I'm not afraid of him any longer. Maybe I haven't been for a while. But I still despise him. I want him to leave. I want his hand off my ankle right—

He closes his eyes, pinches his brow and my skin gets hot, pulsing. I cry out and by the time the sound leaves my lips, the pain has ceased. I stare at my ankle in shock as the swelling goes down. The bruising is gone, and it no longer hurts. Not even a little.

"You fixed it," I say. Somehow this makes me angry. Of all the magic he's used against me, *this* is what makes my blood run hot.

He lets go on his own, and my foot sinks back in the water. "I'll help you out now."

"I can get myself out of the tub, and I could have put myself in as well!"

"But you wouldn't. If it were up to you, you'd have gone to bed with bleeding feet and an empty stomach. Besides…you might pass out again." He grabs a towel and holds it up before pulling me out, averting his eyes.

I snatch the towel from him. "I can take care of myself too!"

Whether that's true or not, I don't know. Look at what a mess I've made. Look at how I ended up here. Tonight I would have come to a much worse ending than a hot bath in a mansion had he not been there to save me. I would be dead if it weren't for him. I know it, an ugly, terrible knowing. But that doesn't mean I forgive him for his cruelty.

Miserable, confused, I wrap the plush towel around myself, recalling how Mr. Brown said once that maybe *he* was tired of killing. But, for me (was it for me?) he destroyed two people tonight. Is that, perhaps, why he was so angry? For some reason, he felt compelled to save me, to make those men pay for what they did and what they might have done. Why, though?

"Are you hungry?" He stands across from me. "I can have someone bring food."

I shake my head, hair dripping around my shoulders, and blurt out, "Why didn't you have Mrs. Minthy bathe me?"

He hesitates. "She is asleep. Besides, this seems like my mess to clean up."

"I'm not a mess," I say with a bite to my words. "And I don't belong to you, no matter what you've claimed me as."

His eyes are never-ending, something in them making me shiver. "I'm well aware of that." When I'm silent, he adds, "I'll leave you, then. Rest."

"Thank you," I finally say, just as he is walking out. "For tending to me." Tending me after breaking me. Helping me after harming me. I hate him, still, obviously. Always. I add anyway, compelled to express my gratitude, "Thank you for coming to get me. I know they would have killed me. Maybe worse."

He only stares at me, the look in his dark eyes inscrutable. Maybe there's something I've never seen there before. I think for a beat it might be sympathy mingled with regret. But that's impossible. Demons don't feel, at least not for others. He felt something staring at that locket, though, didn't he? About me?

As soon as he's gone, I peel off the sopping chemise and throw it into the tub. I pull on my nightgown and, tired, spent, climb into bed and burrow under the covers, my ripped-up sheets somehow already replaced with new ones, crisp and cool. I try to sleep, I try not to let the images of tonight creep over my mind, and somewhere, in a small part of my brain, ignore the confusion dusted there that he saved me at all. That he was even *tender* afterwards. Mostly, I let myself feel hope. If the demon has changed in some way, if some seed of pity has been planted inside him in regard to me, perhaps he'll now help me bring Aven back to life. When I mentioned him saving my sister before, he didn't say no. He said that I'd never asked. Well, now I will.

I cling to renewed optimism.

I dream of my sisters.

Chapter Sixteen

"Why are we going to the ballroom?" I ask as Mr. Brown leads me down the stairs after lunch the following day. "It's too early to dance."

I'm not exactly keen to see the demon, either. Then again, he saved my life. That fact echoes in my brain over and over again. But I hate him, I remind myself. I hate even more being in his debt.

"He wants to see you," is all Mr. Brown says before pushing me through the doors and clicking them shut behind me.

He turns to face me, face carefully blank. I swallow nervously, waiting.

When he doesn't insist I dance—now that I can, my ankle all healed up—I walk closer to him, leaving aside any pretense or politeness. "Why did you save me last night? Was it the same reason a cat plays with a mouse before eating it?"

He gives me an unreadable look but doesn't answer. I wait, impatient, for his reply. "Well?" I push.

The demon's voice is a deep thrumming from his chest. "I think if I wanted to kill you, I've had several chances by now, no? I don't need to toy with you."

I narrow my eyes at him. This is true. "I suppose. Though you've toyed with me plenty, I'd say." I look at the front of his shirt—another black one today. I must be imagining it. I can almost smell gunpowder residue on him. "You *were* shot."

"I'm fine. My sort recovers remarkably fast."

"I would think being shot in the stomach might be fatal, even for *your sort*."

"Not the way being hit in the heart is. We only die from certain types of injuries."

"So you can die." I pause, wondering why he's telling me this. Not to mention everything else. "Why are you being so normal?"

"Why do you have so many questions?"

I shoot back, "I usually do. I just don't ask them, or at least, you hardly listen." Then I take a chance. "I have another question I would like to ask, as long as you are willing to listen."

He shakes his head. Dark locks catching the light. "I've said enough."

"Please. You owe me. I know you feel guilty for treating me like that after I was so frightened last night," my voice breaks off, not an act at all.

It's apparent that he's hesitating when he looks away. His jaw tightens. "I have to leave."

"But you're the one who had me brought down here!" I argue.

"Well, I have business. I'll be back tonight to see you dance, if you can. If you can't...I don't mind if you skip it."

"Wonderful." I roll my eyes but bite back a snotty *how kind of you*.

"You may speak to me afterwards, if you like." He pauses for a long moment, then adds, "If you'd join me for dinner?"

A scathing rejection hangs on my lips, yet something holds me back. This is a chance for me to ask him for real, now that I some-how—miraculously—have gotten on his good side, to save Aven. He's sorry for what he did—and I'll use every bit of advantage that gives me. Besides, he didn't order me. For once, he asked. I can almost catch the way he holds his breath for a fraction of a fraction of a moment. Then I recall, too, what he said the first day, *You will be my companion, of sorts.*

He's lonely, I think.

"Fine." I don't smile up at him. I also don't frown. He looks at me, and I can't look anywhere else. I watch him walk away. I can't keep my eyes off the dark of his shirt, his hair, the lean height of him. Can't stop hearing the sound of his footsteps down the hall. The smell of him haunting the air—leather, wine, flame, smoke, dark—is hypnotic. Not in the way the demon woman was hypnotic, against my will, but something else. Like I've never seen him before. I knew he was beautiful, much as I'd like to deny it.... But now it's as if I'm noticing and admiring a hundred new details. Why?

Everything feels off. Even my reactions to him.

When Mrs. Minthy comes up to my room later and does my bath, the strange feelings continue. Everything is intensified. The way the water surrounds my skin—it's as if I've never been in water before.

As Jinny runs her fingers through my hair afterward, I feel each scratch of her fingernails, each jab of the pearl clips she uses. The scent of the oil and soap on my skin. Everything is *more*.

"Are you alright, Miss?" Jinny gawks at me.

"I'm fine. Just hungry." I blame the switch in routine. Usually I eat, then get ready, then go dance. Tonight, things are different—I'm saving my appetite for dinner with the demon. I *am* hungry, maybe. But that's not what this is.

At half-past eight, Mr. Brown raps on my door and opens it. I stand, ready, in my sage green dress and red slippers. Somehow, I felt him coming. I knew it, even before my ears did.

I step past him. "Thank you for knocking."

He nods in answer. "I like to think we're developing a rapport—as much as we can, given you tried to kill me."

He's cracked a rough smile. With indignance, I mutter, "I didn't want to *kill* you."

A chuckle, and we say nothing else until we reach the ballroom. When Mr. Brown's fingers hit the keys for my warm-up, I stop and turn toward him, astounded.

"What?" He looks back at me, his sharp face suspicious.

I stare at him, at the piano, then shut my eyes as the melody reaches my ears. It's so overwhelming, the beauty of it.

He ceases playing suddenly. "*What?*"

"It's lovely, this piece. Did you tune the piano since yesterday?"

"No."

"It sounds different, the music. Play some more." When he doesn't start right away, I add, in exasperation, "Please."

The song comes again, and it is perfect, each note. I stop stretching, and stand, absorbing it, the rise and fall of the music, the way it hits my ears. I can hardly wait to dance to it.

When the demon comes in, he sits and motions for me to start. I thought I'd be consumed with the ethereal music, but I find as I dance, I'm too distracted to notice, too busy looking at him, noting how his chest rises, how he blows out a breath through pursed lips, how his face is creased with frustration. He's distracted too. Though his dark-as-night eyes are on me, on my dancing. What is he thinking? He isn't truly here.

I see this, I feel it. Like the music, I catch each note of him. There's something troubling him. And it's not this performance, it's not my existence. It's…something else.

When I'm done dancing, I pause to ask him, breathlessly, "Will we still speak? Shall I still join you for dinner?"

"Yes." Then he waves a hand to dismiss me. "Give me a few minutes. Mr. Brown will bring you."

I leave the glow of the ballroom and head to the dining room with Mr. Brown. As we approach the set of doors to a room I haven't entered before, I smooth the skirt of my green dress. All I can think about is the way the fabric feels—impossibly soft underneath the sensitive pads of my fingers, the texture of each individual thread. I can't stop touching.

He smirks. "What's the matter with you?"

Glaring, I turn to him. "What do you mean?"

"You're acting funny. I thought you were going to faint when I was playing."

"*I'm* not acting funny." I feel my cheeks heat. "Everything else is."

"The dining room." Mr. Brown's voice reaches my ears in a medley of syllables and tones. I tense, the sensation unsettling. He motions impatiently. "Aren't you going to go in?"

"Of course."

I step inside. It's much smaller than the ballroom but still expansive. The chandelier drips candlelight across the space, reflecting on the surface of a long, dark table, wood polished to a mirror-finish. I stare in delight at the walls—paneled and covered with elaborately painted flowers and vines and trees, like some sort of fairytale land.

"It's enchanting." I blink, adjusting to the gleam and glow of it all. I realize I have a stupid smile spread across my face, and I drop it at once. Turning back to Mr. Brown, I ask, "What's he doing anyway?"

"He'll be along." He shrugs then steps back into the shadows, remaining present but invisible. Though, for some reason, it feels less like he's babysitting me now and more like a normal thing a butler might do. I walk around the table, running my hand along the backs of the fine seats. I choose one randomly and sit down, trying not to appear too eager, too anxious, too…anything.

When the demon enters, he nods at Mr. Brown in the corner. To my surprise, the butler exits the room directly, leaving us alone. I swallow, suddenly wracked with nerves.

Raising one dark brow, he, *Orrin*, casts his eyes on me. Then smiles. Not the cruel lift of his lips like usual, but something almost pleasant, albeit brief. There's a humanness about the expression that draws silence into my mouth in the place of words. He takes a seat opposite me, as I'd expect, which suits me fine. I'd rather have him dining three countries over, but at least he isn't sitting next to me. The more space between us, the better. I push aside the memory of his arm wrapped around my body in the bath. The feeling of comfort I had when he held me.

He saved my life, and he didn't have to. And he didn't have to kill those men so brutally, as though he was punishing them for harming me. Again I wonder, *why?*

"I know that you hate me," he says.

"And I know the same is true for you." Although when I attempt to guess why, I'm still not sure. It's about more than me having stolen the slippers. He has too much rage at me for that simple crime—or he did have.

I narrow my eyes at the empty wine glass in front of me with longing, wishing for something to settle my nerves, this strangeness all around me. Something about the empty glass makes me pause. The way the light hits it. Fractals coming off the shining rim. I blink, and it goes away. The breath I suck in is sharp, tight.

His voice. "What is it?"

I swallow first, then shake my head. "Nothing."

"I can tell something is wrong."

I glance at him, suspicious. "How do you know? Because you're the one doing it?"

When Mrs. Minthy comes in, carrying a bottle of wine, I snap my mouth shut but don't stop wondering if he's behind my stronger senses. From across the room, I can tell the wine is red. Full-bodied. Tart with a smooth finish. I can smell the grapes, can nearly feel the wind from the day they were harvested. My hand hovers, twitchy, while she pours my wine.

"Thank you, Mrs. Minthy," I say softly. I take a long sip. It is everything I guessed it to be, the richness pooling in my mouth. I drink more, and the taste stays with me afterward. It tastes like how *he* smells. The housekeeper bobs and leaves the room.

"Well?" I ask. "What are you doing exactly?"

He studies me with something like curiosity. Sips his own wine. "I'm not doing anything."

I stare at him for a beat, gauging his honesty.

"My senses seem confused, expanded somehow. Do you know why?" Though the onyx shade of his eyes doesn't change at all, something does. Something I can't describe.

"No."

"You're lying." I speak the words before realizing they're true. I look more carefully at him. "You *are* lying, I can tell. But I don't know how I can." It's an unsettling realization. My body tightens in apprehension. It's not like when I was inside of him during that time in the strangers' home or the time with the locket—this is me on the outside looking in, but it's like he's left the window to himself open.

He leans back in his chair, relaxed, drinking his wine without answering my accusation. I drum my fingertips on my wine glass. The sound of my nails hitting the glass bounces around the room, like music. Soft, light, joyful. I sigh in frustration. What *is* this? I don't like it.

Mrs. Minthy returns with our meal, along with Hana and two other servants I don't recognize. My mouth waters at the smells. There's cheese and fruit, meat, fish and potatoes, creamed carrots, rolls, and more, a bounty of food spread all across the table. I close my eyes a minute, taking the scent in, letting it settle against me. The aroma of the spices is so clear. The hint of nutmeg in the carrots, the yeast of the rolls, the black pepper on the meat, cracked fresh. I load up my plate eagerly and take my first few bites sighing in pleasure. The food is delicious, even more so than usual. Heavenly.

When the room has cleared, I look at him seriously. Instead of continuing our conversation from a minute ago, I ask another question, one I can't help but ask again, however much I wish I didn't want to know. "Last night." I hesitate. "Why did you bathe me?"

He holds silent for a few moments. "Because. You asked me to stay."

My fork stills. "I did not!"

He nods, carefully cutting his meat. Looking up at me. "You did."

Though in my gut I know he's telling the truth, I grit my teeth. "*When?*"

"When I tried to put you down. You clung to me and asked me to stay."

"I…I was delirious," I protest.

"You were perfectly lucid." The warm light of the candles reflects on his gold-touched skin, and the words reverberate out of his mouth. "You even called me by name."

"I did not!" I argue, astonishment coursing through me. I've refused to even *think* it. I still can't think of him by name. I falter at it every time. *Orrin.* I add, "And even if I did, you didn't have to bathe me." My cheeks burn at the memory. I was only one step above naked!

It's crystal clear, even now. How I felt in his arms. I remember: the solid feeling of his chest; the way he gripped me. How I felt protected, in a frightened way, like he would kill every danger in the world, but keep me safe. Even recalling it has me fisting my hands in my lap. Because aren't I a traitor to myself if I let these secret thoughts bubble up? I don't want to be comfortable in his arms. I hate him, I remind myself. We hate each other.

He goes on, "You were covered in blood and dirt. I didn't undress you, as you well know. It was just that I felt—feel—in some way responsible for what happened. For what almost happened. And sorry." A heavy sigh. "I felt sorry."

"But why do you care all of a sudden?" I whisper. I search his face for an answer.

He stares at me, an unsettled, angry pitch to his slow words. "I don't know. I'm not sorry about what I did to those two men." Looking away, he murmurs, "It's that I'm sorry I put you in that situation…and for how I treated you directly after. I should have been sympathetic to you—you were frightened, and you had just had something terrible occur. I was upset, and I took it out on you because it was easier than admitting what bothered me so. I apologize. Going forward, I will not be so thoughtless."

"What bothered you so?"

His hesitancy is tangible. "Never mind."

We do not speak again for long minutes. I eat my food, and it's hard to focus on anything else, it tastes so wonderful. I open my eyes after one pleasurable bite of dessert—chocolate torte with whipped cream, served with strong coffee—to find him staring at me again.

"Stop watching me," I say self-consciously, and, after dabbing my mouth with my napkin, return to the matter at hand. "Tell me what is happening to me. My senses are odd. I'm noticing every detail of everything."

"I don't like being told what to do." His brows pinch together.

"Neither do I! And yet you order me about all the time."

An exasperated laugh escapes his lips. "You are hardly an obedient captive, Corliss. I've never met another person so hard-headed."

I grimace.

"What now?"

"I don't like it when you say my name."

He sets down his coffee and sighs again, but faintly, with effort, as if tired. "Would you rather I call you Miss Bell?"

"Absolutely not. It's patronizing when *you* say it."

"Then what? Thief?"

I can tell how hot my eyes blaze. "*No.*"

"You have courage, to always talk back to me so, to look at me with such fire."

"I'm not sure it's courage. I just need answers," I say, running out of patience. "Besides, since you seem willing to engage me, finally, why shouldn't I talk to you? You said yourself you had plenty of chances to kill me. I'm more scared by what's happening right now. Although scared might not be the right word…." I trail off, waiting.

"I suspect," he begins after a moment, "what you're experiencing has something to do with my healing you. I've never done it before, so I didn't expect this. But I think it's magic."

I nearly drop my fork with the thought. "You gave me magic?"

"Not purposefully, and more like an amplification than anything else," he explains, then tilts his head, studying me. "You had good senses before?"

"Yes, a strong sense of smell and taste, especially. It always helped me in the shop."

"Then it intensified the senses you already had, it appears." He leans into his chair, as if it's settled. That's that. No reason to be perturbed by it.

Frustration courses through me. "But this is more. I knew when you lied to me. Also, it's like, I can almost tell what you're thinking or feeling. I get these twinges. And it's not like the dreams I had—" I cut him off even as he opens his mouth to object. "I was simply along with you, somehow."

"I see." He stares at me. "I suspected you were there again, that last time."

"I knew that you knew!" I exclaim, rather pleased with myself, and tack on, "That's why you avoided me for two nights." To which he doesn't confirm nor deny.

When I move to ask him about it, about the woman's portrait, he shakes his head sharply, cutting me off, avoiding my curious gaze. "It's unusual, what you have. A gift. I've known others to have it, though it's rare to affect all the senses at once, including the sixth. It appears you have the ability now to read people in a way you couldn't otherwise."

The idea rattles me. If I let myself accept it—and how can I not, knowing what I do now—I can compare it to other things I've seen. Marieta's premonitions. The fortune-tellers on the streets singing songs and spinning truths. But this is different. And I can't say I like it. I only want to be extraordinary on stage—not in this sort of way.

I grip my coffee cup for comfort, though it's too dainty by half—they didn't bring the proper mugs I've grown fond of using in the comfort of my room. I set it down, place my crumpled napkin on the table. Our meal is finished, but our conversation is not. There's still so much I want to know, to ask of him. I find it hard to say the words right off, in case he says no. He probably will say no. It's the biggest favor I could ask. Instead, I aim for casual curiosity. "I want to know if the myths are true, about your kind. Demons." The last word is a whisper.

He fiddles with his own delicate cup, not holding my eyes. "We don't use that term. We just are what we are. Most of your silly tales are simply myths told to frighten children."

"But you have black eyes, no whites at all. You have powers."

He cocks a brow, looking up. "I already told you, this is how I am. My kind are humans, or in any case, we were—we are not some made-up creature."

"And you can alter your appearance, or make people see things—or not see things—that are and aren't there. Like the bird woman, the bleeding man, the way you made the ballroom dark that one time."

"Yes." His mouth twitches, as if he finds the memories amusing. I scowl back.

"You somehow took me along with you when I was sleeping—"

"I didn't do that. I may have had a hand in some of your nightmares, but I never brought you into my consciousness. You are simply able to connect to me somehow."

"Oh," I say, foolishly unable to think of a response. He offers no explanation but seems to puzzle over it himself, studying me like he might figure it out if he thinks hard enough. After a deep breath, I continue, "I now know you can heal. I know you can harm." The men in the woods, their brutal murders. I cringe. "But are you a master of death? That's what some call your kind."

Pushing aside his own mug, he tosses his napkin down onto his plate. Rises and walks around the dining room, hands behind his back. The ink around one wrist is visible. I count up to five of the single bands before he turns. "That depends on what you mean exactly. I don't have omnipotent power."

"Can you bring people back from the dead?"

There. I've said that part out loud.

He stops behind his chair, looks at me soberly. "You are talking about your sister. The one you've mentioned." It's not a question.

"Yes," I whisper. "I know you have no reason to help me. I know you're still angry with me. I've said horrible things—although you damned well deserved them, so don't try to deny that. Yet, for some reason, you seem willing to talk to me, to listen now. I thought, maybe you might be willing to help me, like you helped when I was attacked, and after. I'm lost without my sister. Please can you bring her back? Restore her to life?"

I hold my breath, awaiting his reply.

He shakes his head, hair falling over his brow. "No."

"Why not?" I cry, feeling the possibility slip between my fingers.

"Because," he answers carefully, "she's not dead."

CHAPTER SEVENTEEN

I stand from my chair so quickly it falls, banging against the floor. "What? No—she can't be alive—"

"She is."

The blood rushes through me, and I wonder if my heart could actually explode from the shock, from the relief. Remembering his words, I grip the edge of the table for support. I might pass out. I lean forward, breathe slow and steady, try to hold myself in before I puddle on the floor in a heap, just like the day I learned of Aven's death. But she's not dead at all. "My God. I hoped we might find a way to bring her back, but I didn't ever believe she might still be alive."

"Well, she is." His expression seems purposefully blank, carefully emotionless.

"But there was a body," I cry, blinking the tears from my eyes. The flowers against her blue shawl, the grave, the pain. "Whose was it?"

"Not hers."

I let that realization trickle into me, slowly. Still in disbelief. Someone else is missing a sister or a daughter, a love. It's a strange, unsettling thought, trading one person for another, trading my grief for someone else's. "How do you know she's alive? Where is she?"

"I've seen her," he admits, and here, some of his stoic façade cracks. He adds, "In the court. You'd mentioned her name—and

I recognized it. She's with Elisavet. The demon queen—you know who I mean."

"What?" I choke out, his answer causing me to collapse into a chair. I can't move except to stare up at him, shocked into silence. *The demon queen has Aven?*

He only stares back, mouth twisted in thought. Candlelight flickering in his dark gaze.

"Talk to me!"

Running one finger along his jaw, he answers, "I'm trying to decide if I should help you. I'm trying to decide why I should."

"But you can't give me that information and not tell me more! That'd be sheer cruelty, even for a…" I trail off. I was going to say, *A thing like you.*

His deep eyes settle on me, narrowed. "I am a beast, it is true. However, you'd do well to remember I'm the only one who can help you. Though, I'm not sure it's worth my trouble. It is dangerous for me to even be talking to you of this."

"You are frightened of Elisavet?" I ask, then pause, a thought occurring to me. "Does she know *I'm* Aven's sister?"

"No," he answers, clipped. "And no, I'm not frightened of her. Not in the way you presume. I'm not afraid of her. Only in losing to her."

"You hate her," I say. "I can tell when you look at her, when you say her name. Not the way you hate me. You really, *really* hate her."

"I don't hate you like that, no. You just make me angry every time I see you. Every time I think of you." His voice is dirty, jaw clenched.

"Well, you don't exactly thrill me either." I cast a hostile glance at him. Just when I thought we were making strides, now we must fight?

Frustrated, I look down at my hands. Stare at the swirls engraved into my skin—the fingertips—turn them over and admire the half-moons on my nails. How have I never noticed how beautiful my hands are? But how human they are! What can I do to help Aven?

"I have so many questions I can hardly think where to start. But my sister is alive." I say what is most important out loud, savoring the truth, the progress. He's talking to me. Perhaps he'll do more if I ask again. "Can you help me get her back, regardless of our issues with each other? I'm desperate. I cannot manage to do it alone."

"It would not be a simple task." He clears his throat, moving about the room. "Elisavet is charming, cunning, as I know you can see. She's a lavish hostess, a generous lover." He goes on, ignoring my raised brow at that detail. "She is also unflinchingly cruel, even for my kind. It will be difficult to get your sister out of Elisavet's court. She's smart, bloodthirsty, and, shall we say, creative? You haven't seen the kinds of deaths and tortures she likes to enact, sometimes just for fun."

"And sometimes you do those for her," I say ruefully. "When you go off on business, you do her dirty work."

"Sometimes, yes. I have killed for her," he agrees with cold resentment. Is he thinking of that sleeping couple now? "I have killed for myself. For others as well."

"Why did you kill those men in the woods?" I finally blurt out the question I've been withholding.

"I didn't like them."

A harsh laugh rips from me. "*You didn't like them?* So you tore them to pieces?"

He mulls that over, eyes reflecting the candlelight. "They were trespassing."

"You're lying." I know it again, a pinch in my gut. The way his dark eyes flash too quickly to catch with mine, then darken just a fraction more than usual, the way his lips purse a scant millimeter. "They weren't on your property. I could tell, there were sounds, nature, animals. There's none of that here, on your land."

He shrugs, as if to say, *Close enough.*

I grow more insistent. "Why did you really kill them?"

"Because." He frowns, sitting again. "Perhaps I don't hate you as much as you think."

"Is *that* what bothered you so?" I press, recalling his vague earlier statement.

"Yes!" his reply is sharp, emphatic. "I never wanted to kill again, but when they hurt you, I wanted to kill them. And if they were suddenly resurrected before me right now, I'd obliterate them twice over."

His admission has me reeling, and apparently him as well. He clamps his mouth shut, as though he's said too much, but I pounce on the opening. "So will you help me save my sister?"

With a sigh, he runs his hand over the smooth, elegant planes of his face. Then, leaning in his seat, he folds his arms and ponders my question before answering. "I will help you save your sister, if possible. But the terms of our arrangement will not change, and you'll stop fighting me every step of the way. Agreed?"

"Fine," I say, meeting his challenge. It's a better deal than I could have hoped for, and maybe, in time, our arrangement can be negotiated. All that matters now is Aven. I go on, still heated, still hating him, and so, I can't help the tinge of sarcasm in my words, "You help me save her, and I'll be your faithful dancing companion. That's what you want?"

He glances away then nods. Looks back at me. At my mouth. I lick my lips. His eyes are hard. Deep. "Yes."

After a rather abrupt end to dinner, while the moon hangs in the sky, I pace in my room, wearing down the floor with my fidgety feet. I can hardly believe he agreed to help me. Oh, God, if only I could let Sélie know about Aven! I'm sick with nervous energy, but I have no outlet. Even dancing doesn't tempt me right now.

I just keep thinking of everything he told me. Everything I didn't even think to ask.

My stomach rolls with questions, and I can't answer any of them, not until he explains more. I force myself into a chair with the mug of warm, honeyed milk Hana brought me. I can't sit here panicking about Aven, making myself sick over it. It won't do either of us any good. I can only pray she's safe, that we find a way to help her before...before what? I didn't even think to ask him *why* Aven's there, what she could be doing with Elisavet in the first place. I was so overwhelmed with the knowledge that she's alive. For now, such a deep and true gratitude fills me. Aven is alive, and he's going to help me get her back.

Sounds drift through my open window. From the grounds below comes a grunt, a smack. A waft of sweat drifts to my room, along with a hint of adrenaline. I recognize the underlying scents of him. Orrin Colehart.

I rise, setting my drink down, and walk to the window, looking to the open stretch of acres below. It's easy to see Mr. Brown's white hair in the full moonlight. He stands there, sleeves rolled up, gloves off, ducking as Orrin—shirtless—punches toward him. Mr. Brown dodges most of the hits, graceful for an older man, until one catches him in the stomach.

Mr. Brown grunts again but recovers quickly. "Come on, sir. You can do better."

He laughs a little, and I stare at the smooth skin of his back, the ink crossing his torso, all kinds of symbols and images, the graceful yet completely demanding way he fights. Spars? I'm not sure exactly what they're doing, but I can't keep my eyes away from him, from his movements, the elegance as he twists and ducks, surprising and sharp. It's almost like a dance. I stand, fascinated at this switch of perspective.

He turns toward the window and glances up, seeming to know I'm watching him. I jerk back to hide myself, though not before I catch the sight of his chest, the ripple of muscles across him, his stomach, the pattern of dark hair trailing down it, how his pants hang indecently low on his narrow hips. I suck in a breath at the beautiful power of his body and pray he didn't see me watching. I shift into the safety of my room, realizing it was more like ogling.

There's another low rumble of a rough laugh from outside. I cross my arms and glower in the direction of the sound, and after a moment, the two resume fighting, or training, whatever it may be. After a moment, my heart rate slows to a normal pace.

For the first time since arriving here, I shut my windows *and* the drapes.

Still, I can hear them fighting long into the evening, can still see the glint of sweat on his skin in the moon's glow. I grimace and close my eyes. But his words, from so many nights ago, come back to me, only this time in a much different context, and in a way, even more concerning.

I'm going to make you cry for it.

I squirm in my bed, my body betraying me with the twinge of desire. Finally, I try to sleep.

I pray for a dreamless night.

Yawning, eyes heavy, I sit up in bed, attempting to orient myself in the comfort of my fine room. I tighten up, remembering. Aven. But hope lightens my heart as I remember it all. Orrin has agreed to help me. A warm flood of faith fills me, and I let out a breath I feel I've been unknowingly holding for weeks. I shift my bleary gaze around, sensing something has changed. My breakfast has been brought, the tray on the table, probably hours ago. I can tell it's late. The sun is high, the curtains have been opened to let the light in, thanks to one of the maids, and it must be midmorning already. I must've slept so heavily I didn't hear the maids coming and going.

But staring at the other wall, I forget all about the food.

I blink in disbelief at what I'm seeing. I wait for it to fade— maybe it's just a vision. Maybe he's teasing me. Maybe. Maybe.

But it doesn't go away.

Slowly, I climb out of my bed and walk across the room in a daze. Because my sad, empty bookshelves have been filled. Not with one or two books. Not with a dozen.

I run my fingers along the spines in disbelief.

I don't bother counting. There are probably hundreds.

CHAPTER EIGHTEEN

I lose myself in books for hours, in novels and poetry and books about languages—even fairytale stories, to feel closer to Sélie. I revel in the way the paper feels beneath my fingers, in the way the words catch the light and float into me.

It is sometime after lunch when I'm summoned. I grab my slippers, uncertain as to why we're going down so early. I say as much on the way to the ballroom.

"*She's* here," Mr. Brown whispers as we walk together. "She wants to see you before she goes."

I almost drop the ballet shoes. Ignoring his apparent fear, I latch onto my own. I yank him to a stop on the second-floor landing, and my voice trembles, asking even as I know the answer, "Who?"

"Elisavet." He says her name quietly. Says nothing more. I clench and unclench my jaw nervously. He leads me into the ballroom, where she is standing next to *him*. Demon. Orrin.

Orrin's eyes fall to mine. "Here she is."

For a moment I forget to breathe. What does she want with me? To take me, like she took my sister? I employ all my willpower not to open my mouth, ask about Aven. To do so could put us both in peril, I understand that perfectly. No. As Orrin said, she doesn't know who I am anyway. He stares past her, giving me an almost indistinguishable head shake. Warning me. The queen moves toward me, her slinking silver-threaded gown pooling across the floor, silk smooth like glass, a strange reflective quality about it.

"As pretty as I recall. But I cannot stay to watch you dance this time. I've just been called. Until next time…"

I wonder at her meaning, but the touch of her hand on my head jerks my attention to the present. She strokes my hair, her bracelets clanking against my ear. I breathe through it, forcing myself not to jerk away. She turns to him. "I'll see myself out."

"My queen." He nods, bending slightly at the waist.

This time, she and her silent, brawny companion leave through the doors of the ballroom. They thud behind them. The sound of it continues in my ears so long I can't move. *Next time.*

What did she mean?

I must say it aloud because he replies, "She has taken a liking to you."

"Um." Such a pointless syllable, but I can't find the words.

"You don't have to dance for me now," he says softly, lifting his gaze away from me, offering me an out. "I didn't call you down for that anyway. You can go back to your room, if you wish."

"No." I shake my head. "It will help. And that was the deal, wasn't it?" I ask but keep my tone light. Put the slippers on. "Be good for you?"

He cocks a brow, mouth tugging at the corner as if he's holding back a smile. Then he relaxes into his chair, waving a hand for Mr. Brown to play so I can warm up. I move to the center of the glossy floor to dance before my new ally. I don't even mind. It is true, what I said. But I also admit, in a way, I want to prove myself to him, still. Even now.

The red shoes are wasted on you, he said once. I hate that he said that. Even remembering fills me with anger. I will it away, focusing on my movements instead.

I raise up on my toes, and I dance, something spirited and joyful, something that feels like freedom. I dance with Aven in my mind. When I'm done, he stands as usual, walks over to me. I ready myself for his disapproval, even though we are on the same side for now.

"Did you enjoy watching me last night?" His words hold a hint of humor.

My face heats up, recalling him sparring without his shirt, the way his muscles stretched and danced beneath his skin, even as I feign indifference. Lightly I say, "I'm not sure what you mean."

"So, you are a voyeur."

"Ha! I'm the one performing for you day after day, without a hint of encouragement. Yet you must not mind so much, or you'd have me stop."

"Ah, well, perhaps I've been needlessly cruel about that."

"Oh." I stare at his face. It's hours, the way he sinks his black eyes into me. Days, weeks. I wait for him to say something. Anything. To do something.

I'm reluctant to accept the feeling...desire, stretched between us. Yet how, after everything, can that be true? Have I forgiven him so quickly after all he's done? I'm not so easily bought. Books and easier conversation shouldn't sway me so soon.

If only my body knew that!

He moves closer, then murmurs, "I meant what I said when I saw you dance on that stage."

It takes me a minute to let that sink in. Then the words come to me, a faint echo of his deep voice in the shadows of the theatre: *You dance beautifully.*

But then a frown etches into his face, like he's angry at himself for saying it. He *is* angry. It's one thing to apologize, to even help me. What he just said is another. He doesn't *want* to be nice to me. He doesn't *want* to want me.

He turns and strides out of the ballroom, nearly slamming the doors. But then I run after him, wondering if, perhaps, I'm no longer afraid of the beast. In fact, I don't wonder. I search my soul and find no fear inside.

"Wait!" I call, chasing him down as he rounds the corner to take the stairs.

Orrin turns, frowning again. "Yes?"

I finally ask, dying to know, "You brought me books?"

"No."

"But you had them brought." When he nods curtly, I ask, "*Why* did you?"

Motioning me toward the staircase, walking at my side, he says, "I need to leave. If you wish to speak, we can talk on the way to your room."

Surprised, I pause on the step. He's never walked me out before, always making Mr. Brown do it. But I don't question it, or the fact we left Mr. Brown behind. We continue upward.

"If I recall, you asked several times. I heard it from maids, as well as directly from you," he finally answers as we move through the second-floor hallway. "So, now you have nothing to complain about."

I say, temper flaring, "I wasn't complaining. I was simply curious. I love the books. I did nothing but read all morning."

We walk up the steps to the third floor, side by side. Orrin pauses, meeting my eyes, his own glinting. "Well then."

"Well then," I repeat, suddenly nervous. I try not to wring my hands. He's just *staring* at me. I almost trip up a step as I move forward. "Can we talk about everything? About *her*."

He leads me down the hall toward my room. "I must go—"

"Please," I beg, as we pause outside my door, remembering the feline look of Elisavet—the way she seemed to see inside of me. "Anything. Just one thing. I still don't understand why or how my sister got tangled up with her. You told me so much and yet nothing at all."

Reluctantly, he explains, "Elisavet is a queen, a magical one. She rules the Court of Death, one of them anyway."

"*One* of them?" I repeat, incredulous.

"There are queens over the whole world, from the sea to the sky and everywhere in between. They rule where they please and try to stay out of each other's way, more or less." He seems agitated, speaking of her. Is it because he isn't supposed to tell me? Or because he truly hates her so much?

She terrifies me already. And my dear, beloved Aven is with her.

"Can we speak again later—dinner again?" I request. "Please."

"Tomorrow evening we can. There is much to discuss, though tonight I will be out. Tomorrow we'll talk about it. Until then—"

He opens my door and waves me in. I enter alone then turn back to look at him, questioning him silently. He's never walked me to my room before. And he still hasn't made any motion to leave.

Clearing his throat, he says, "You may come and go from your room as you please. From now on, I mean. The mansion is yours to explore—and the grounds, though I'd caution you from wandering off the property. I don't want you meeting her outside of my protection."

I stare after him, rendered speechless. But even as he disappears, down the hall, down the stairs, I feel him, his essence, inhale his scent, wrapping around me.

Barely an hour later, Mr. Brown knocks on my door—unlocked, I might add—though I had already heard him creeping down the hall. I rise from my chair and open the door.

He stands on the other side of the doorframe, his white hair windswept, and beyond his own smell, the hint of salt hangs on him.

I also catch the whiff of Sélie's charcoal, and the teasing soft citrus of her perfume. I ask, almost instinctively, "You went to the cottage?"

"I did. I was told I should check on your sister and bring some things back for you, personal effects. She packed it for you." And with that, he holds a bag out to me.

I snatch it up. "Oh! Did she seem okay? Did she ask questions?"

"Not that I answered," he says, cracking his own smile. "Which didn't please her, but yes, she seemed fine, if a bit ornery. I just said I've seen you, been helping you in a way."

I somehow manage not to roll my eyes. "Right."

A laugh barks out of him. The bruise on his temple has shrunk and faded to a nasty yellow-green. I look away guiltily and rummage inside the bag, recognizing several things: my old, worn, pink ballet shoes and a bundle of lambswool; some of my favorite cosmetics, earrings of Aven's, then there are drawings from Sélie—a whole pad worth. I flip through, catching the fairytale drawing she did for me the night of Aven's funeral. I tuck the pad away, for later, when I can savor the artwork. I hug the bag to my chest; it smells like home. Tears spring to my eyes and I don't bother wishing them away. Even though I'm free now, I can't go home, not with the possible threat of drawing Elisavet to the cottage. I won't endanger Sélie like that. So, this will have to do for this moment.

"She found my slippers."

He clears his throat, avoiding my eyes. "I found them, actually, just lying in a heap in the woods. Figured they were yours."

With a grateful heart, I say, "Thank you, Mr. Brown, for bringing all of this. Can I see him now, to thank him as well, if he's still here?"

He gives me a nod and takes me down to the second floor. We walk into a sitting room, clearly Orrin's private sitting room, which feels oddly intimate.

"Why here?" I turn to the butler.

"You won't be bothered in here. He'll be along shortly," Mr. Brown says, then takes his leave.

We're never bothered in the ballroom, but I just shrug. Alone, I walk around the room, taking it in. It feels like Orrin, dark and moody and rich. The wood walls, the shades of deep blue and forest green, and hints of black. It's entirely masculine, from the stately fireplace to the furnishings. I peek through one door at what I already know is on the other side—his bedroom.

"Looking for me?"

I don't jump when he speaks; I already sensed he was here.

"Not at all," I say in a cool voice, turning. "I was just, uh—"

"Spying?"

A smile starts, I can't help it. "Fine."

"Do you want to sit while we talk? Or would you like to go through my drawers next?"

I purse my lips and take a seat in one of the fine, heavy chairs.

He sits across from me and glances down at the sack I'm still clutching. "What's this?"

My mouth softens. "Mr. Brown said you told him to bring some of my things from home. I wanted to thank you for that. I've been so worried for my younger sister—I'm glad he was able to make sure she's okay."

"Oh, yes. I just thought you'd be more comfortable if you had word of her and some things of your own. I have a bit of time now before I must leave, so we can talk. Do you want me to call for coffee?"

"Why not tea?"

"You don't drink tea."

"Now who's spying?" I find myself teasing.

He looks away but not before I catch his wry smile. He looks brighter, more alive. Maybe having a goal means more to him than he's said. Maybe taking Aven from Elisavet is a way of him hurting Elisavet without doing so outright. I know he hates her, after all.

"Can you explain more now? I don't think I can wait a minute longer."

Only silence threads itself between us. I freeze, holding my breath. Is he going to back out of our deal? A part of me still doesn't understand why, after everything, he is finally going to help me. I won't rest easy until I have Aven alive in my arms.

"Yes. You've been patient," he says, breaking the silence. Relief fills my heart. Hesitating, he goes on, "You like books. So I will tell you a story, part of one. Then perhaps you will understand a few things."

"Once upon a time…" my words are laced with a sudden, light mockery. I was never one for fantastical tales, but obviously, now, some of them aren't quite so unbelievable.

His stare has me shifting in my seat, abashed. "This is no fairy-tale, but there *is* a villain."

"You mean two?" I challenge. He and Elisavet, of course.

His lips pull up just the tiniest bit, cracking his hard facade. "Yes. Many, in fact."

"Tell it then." I try not to look as intrigued as I really am.

"Very well," he obliges me and begins his tale. "A long time ago, many decades back, I was a desperate man, just like any other desperate man."

"Why?"

"For many reasons, which I don't care to explain to you now. Then I met Elisavet. She has a knack for finding desperate souls, you see. She hears them calling to her…." He seems to recall some distant memory, then goes on, "We made a deal. She gave me power in exchange for taking my soul, which is how I became what I am. Though," he adds, thoughtfully, "still a sliver remains."

"A sliver of soul? I thought you were entirely soulless. All of your kind are, no?"

"No. Even with my kind, a small bit remains. If it was all gone, we would cease to live. In any case, in return, I became a subject of hers, tasked with her messy errands. A puppet, if you will. And a symbol of our trade was a certain pair of ballet slippers."

I lean forward. "Really?"

He grimaces. "They're a reminder that hurts…for many

reasons. I don't care to get into all of it now. But they have their own sort of magic, and it seems to be connected to whatever is left of my soul."

My mind races. I ask, "Why do the slippers affect *me*? Or am I not the first one to have wanted them?"

After a long moment, he admits, "No, you are. I don't know why they've attached themselves to you."

"That's exactly how it feels." I scrutinize his face, and add in wonder, "It's as though they want me as much as I want them. But why the slippers in the first place?"

"That doesn't matter," he replies in a way that indicates it very much *does* matter. When I open my mouth, he shakes his head curtly. No more questions about that. "I've gotten an invitation for Elisavet's next party, the evening of the full moon. You're to dance for her court."

I have to dance *for her*? Remembering her dangerous smile, the bone earrings she wore, the way she supposedly had a man ripped to pieces for merely annoying her, I'm not sure I'll survive such a performance. What if I don't please her? "At the Court of Death? What is that, like hell?"

"In a sense, yes." He nods. I count the number of eyelashes as he blinks. "It's her domain. She moves as she likes, and the court moves with her."

"But how can hell move?" I fidget with the straps of my bag, trying to comprehend this, trying in my frail, human way to understand the ways of demons.

"Hell is anywhere that people suffer, and death is anywhere that death resides. The court isn't a location, and neither is the hell you are thinking of—a tale created by churches and men. Hell is misery, and it happens in our human world. It's wherever she is, holding residence. Wherever she goes, wherever the queens like her go, only suffering and rot thrive."

Dread fills my thoughts. We've picked quite a formidable foe.

"What is the plan, exactly? I'm assuming we're going to get Aven out at the party, yes?"

"No. I will."

"How?"

"I'll do something to lead your sister to the door. While you dance, and Elisavet and everyone else is distracted, I'll take Aven away and Mr. Brown will bring her here."

"That's it?" It's too easy. "What if Elisavet knows? What if she finds her here?"

At my frown, he says, "Why would she look for her here? I'm hoping hiding Aven here long enough will enable any connection between them to fade, and Elisavet shouldn't be able to track her, especially with my magic muffling their connection, so to speak. Then, when it's safe, we will move her."

"Oh." His plan is not exactly failproof. "What do I do? Besides dance? It hardly seems that important."

"It will distract everyone, which is *extremely* important," he corrects. "Another crucial thing is you must conduct yourself perfectly at the party. You must not speak to anyone, not about your sister, nor anything personal that may give you away to Elisavet. If she knows anything, she won't hesitate to dangle your sister in front of you in the worst way, or to try to trap you in a bargain. Be polite yet reserved. And if you see Aven before we enact the plan, you'll have to pretend like you don't know her, in case anyone is watching, otherwise someone may become suspicious."

"I can't do that!" I argue. "It took all my strength not to ask Elisavet about her, to beg her to give Aven back! If I see Aven in the court, I'm going to carry her out of there my own damn self!"

"You think you'll steal her right from under Elisavet's nose?" His doubtful frown is infuriating. "Why is it, with all the super senses you have, you lack common sense?"

I shoot a glare at him.

"Don't," he warns.

"Why not?" I lift my chin defiantly, though I find my indignation fading. Despite my frustration, what he says makes sense, and at least we have a plan—one he seems confident in.

"Because, for now at least, we're on the same side." He stands, as if restless.

I watch him walk around the room leisurely, perusing the antiques and beautiful furnishings. I find it spellbinding, the way he walks as though he owns everything—not just the belongings in the room but the whole world.

"Will you join me for supper tomorrow evening, as discussed? We can talk more then. I'll be leaving shortly."

I accept, rising from my seat. "If that's all for now then. I'll leave you."

His voice stops me. "Actually. There is something else. Before I go..."

"What?"

"You're not frightened of me anymore." He runs his perfect fingers along a vase, and I find myself staring at his hand, the way he strokes the glass.

It's a statement, not a question. I confirm, "I'm not."

"Then what would you say if I asked you to dance right now? If I *told* you to?"

A smirk spreads across my face. "I'd say the red slippers are in my room, and I don't feel like fetching them."

He looks at the bag Mr. Brown brought, the bag I still hang on to, then back at me, one dark gaze. "I'm curious, then. What if I asked you to dance in your own shoes? Would you do it? Now? Here?"

The words escape me before I can think. "Yes."

He doesn't smile, doesn't speak. But I can tell he is pleased by my answer.

I warm up, roll my shoulders back with a sigh, sink into deep pliés well aware of his eyes on me. It is just the two of us. The walls of his sitting room seem to inch closer to us by the minute, though he's scooted the furniture to the perimeter of the room. I'll have enough space to move if I forgo grand leaps, however, I can't ignore how his eyes are pinned on me in such a close space. Nerves zip through my body.

"I'm ready," I say, soft, and he nods.

For him, I dance. In my own worn shoes, I move to music that is not there. It is rougher without the red shoes, it is more raw, less elegant. Yet, it is me, laid out and flayed open for him. My steps are not perfect, yet there is a softness and hardness I've missed these past months of dancing in the red slippers. With those, I don't fear imperfection because it doesn't exist. With those, I am brave but a bit of a liar, if I'm being honest now. Because there is a beauty in being truthful, in baring myself and my insecurities. In my own slippers, I can't lean on magic, on enchantment. I can only do my best, and if it's not my best, I know that is only because I am an imperfect human, and that's alright. I can still be proud of myself—in fact, I'd argue, I should be even prouder on my own. *Look what I can do. Look at me trying*, I say with my body.

All my senses tingle as I catch his eyes on me, as he sits there watching my vulnerability. Why I'm allowing it, I can't say. Only that perhaps, no longer being afraid of him, I'm ready to be unafraid in other ways. When, and if, he finally releases me from captivity, when and if I can go back to the Clover, would I have the courage to do this? Dance as myself, without the aid of the magical slippers? Would I dare to think myself good enough?

I thought I was nearly naked in the bath the other evening, when I cried in front of him, when I stood bloodied and broken after being attacked. But I've never been as open as this. I am truly naked as I dance for him. I spin, and though he blurs, I know his eyes are still scorched into me.

When I finish, he rises. Clearing his throat, he walks over to me as if he's about to say something, frown on his face. I brace for his critique. My resolve to be proud fades, doubt overwhelming me. I know the performance was flawed. I shouldn't have said yes.

Then he is right before me. He leans down, voice rough, "Corliss?"

His skin is so beautiful, I bite my lip, staring at his mouth, inches from mine, then his eyes. I couldn't look away if I wanted. When did I decide they were mesmerizing instead of monstrous? Just this very second? "Yes?" I breathe.

A moment's hesitation, then he tugs my body in, holding me in place. I stare back, swallow hard, heart hammering as I try to make sense of the way he digs his fingers into my hips. I'm frightened...I think.

Or frightened by how much I want him.

"Corliss," his voice is a whisper against my neck, my ear, then my mouth. His arms tighten around me, then he pauses. The words are unspoken.

They hang between us. His eyes search my face, and I give a small nod.

I don't want to fight anymore. I want to surrender.

He pushes me back against the papered wall, gently but so sudden, I catch my breath.

Orrin. Demon. I war with myself. But he's not a demon, not the way I thought.

All at once he leans down and brushes his lips against mine. I curl my fingers into his hair and pull him down again. *Yes*, another *yes. Kiss me.*

First, soft, exploring my lips with his own, then he increases the pressure, slanting his warm mouth on mine. I gasp at his skillful kisses, the feel of his desire, and I kiss him harder, arching my body against his. He responds with a low groan, tugging me up higher against the wall so that my feet actually come off the floor.

His hands support me, lifting me under my thighs, his hardness presses into me, and I gasp yet again. He tangles his fingers into my hair, dragging his lips across my throat. I take his face to bring his mouth back to mine with a greedy tug. I want this. I need this.

He kisses me until I can hardly breathe. I can't think, can't hear, can't see. Can only feel in this moment, every nerve in my body pulsing with need, blood firing through my veins, pooling in one aching beat between my quivering legs.

And then, just when I can hardly stand it any longer, when I'm slick with need, when I'm about to pull off my own dress to make him take me against the wall, to beg him to do it, he backs away, breath ragged, sliding me so my feet touch the floor again.

Orrin rubs at his chest, his eyes wild. "Fuck."

Then he hurries away, slamming the door behind him. One of the paintings on the wall falls to the floor with a crash.

I slump down to the carpet, chest pounding, heart beating out of control.

Closing my eyes, the expletive echoes. *Fuck.*

I try to think of every reason this kiss was ridiculous, mad, foolish, twisted. After everything we've been through. After everything he's done. I still hate him. Don't I? We are allies, unwilling even in that, and that's all. Right?

I try not to want him, try not to wish his lips were back on mine.

I fail.

Chapter Nineteen

I don't see Orrin the next day as I already expected, and I almost make an excuse to reject his dinner invitation but stop myself. There's no point being embarrassed, and we need to work out the details for Aven's rescue. I can put aside the kissing…can I not?

After Jinny does my hair—again, I am allotted loads of pins—and helps me into yet another new dress, this one a lovely grayish-lilac that enhances my gray eyes, I shoo her out so I can have a moment of peace before I go down. I use the cosmetics from the bag Mr. Brown brought. I happily take in the scents of the stains, the powders, the way one might take in the familiar smell of their place of worship. God, it smells just like the Apothicaire. With shaky hands, I put on Aven's earrings, the pair Sélie packed for me, and take a deep breath for courage.

I pause at a full vase one of the maids must have brought up and placed on the mantel, the scent of soft pink roses perfuming the air. I pluck out one rose, avoiding the thorns, and tuck it into my hairdo, just like Jinny once did. And then I leave my room.

Mr. Brown is waiting for me in the hall. He stares at my nervous smile. "What's the matter with you now?"

"Nothing," I snap, as if I'm a schoolgirl hiding stolen affections and not a grown woman all flustered over a mere kiss.

He only shrugs, and we head down the hallway. I glance over at the older man as we go down the stairs. The clean-cut butler garb, the smell of him: furniture polish and smoke and somehow, beneath all that, something delicate and sweet.

"Cream puffs?" I tease as we reach the grand staircase. "Is that what I smell on you?"

Mr. Brown scowls at me, and I laugh. It's enough to ease my nerves as we keep moving closer to the dining room.

Once outside the room, he opens the door, and nudges me in. Orrin is already there waiting for me. I hold up my head and walk further inside, casually, as if I'm not bothered at all by our kiss yesterday. I take a seat, the same chair I took the last time.

"Good evening," I say politely, as Mrs. Minthy pours my wine and then disappears again.

"Good evening," his tone is slightly mocking, partly amused. He glances at the flower in my hair, and I lift my chin, daring him to tease me for it. He says nothing. But I can tell he likes it, as well as my new dress.

I take a long draw of my wine, sighing at the rich taste—the hints of berry and tobacco—that pinches my mouth with plea-sure. It's the best wine I've ever tasted.

Then I notice his eyes on me. God. I think I moaned out loud.

I stumble out, "It just tastes so good. I mean, the wine. Every-thing tastes better now, from the magic." I grind to a halt before I say something really stupid, like the thought that's circling through my head.

Even you, Orrin, your lips, your tongue, your skin.

My cheeks heat and I glance away before he can read my con-fused desire. I try not to search his emotions—is he regretful? I don't regret the kiss. I'd like to do it again. My intuition—my body—tells me that the two of us could start a fire if we ever joined together. My face heats even more at the image. Not because I'm embar-rassed, but because every inch of me would like that to happen.

Ignoring my reaction, he gets right to business. "I've learned additional details since we last spoke. The party is the night of the full moon, just two weeks hence, and I want you to prepare in the meantime. Emotionally, I mean."

"Because of Aven." Miserably, lustful thoughts fading, I say, "I won't ruin our plan. Don't worry."

"Not only that. You may see or hear disturbing things. I'm not sure how Elisavet or the others will treat you. Stay calm. Don't lash out at anyone, especially not at her."

"How could I? I can hardly speak when she's near." Just picturing her has me jumpy.

"And when or if you see your sister? You'll have to fight your instinct. That will be difficult, to not go to her or acknowledge her."

"I've already said I won't." My heart actually aches. "But what if Aven comes to me?"

Quietly, he says, "I doubt Aven will even notice you. She's been there nearly two months now, hasn't she? Over time, humans lose who they are there."

That hurts, thinking of it. I ask, still concerned, "What if she already told Elisavet about me? What if *that's* why Elisavet's interested in me?"

"I don't think that's why. She wants you." He stares into my eyes, and heat floods me at what he doesn't say.

I change the subject. "Is it just demons in the court?" Before he can correct me, I add, "I know that's not what you call yourselves. But is it?"

"Mostly, but also humans, servants, and those in the process of trading."

"Wait. Trading what?"

"Their souls, of course."

"Their *souls*?" He doesn't need to elaborate; I've already realized what this might mean. How foolish I am, not to have put it together before! "Oh God. You think Aven might intend to make a trade?"

"Eventually," Orrin answers, solemnly. "Most people do, and that's what Elisavet wants, to build her power. She uses the souls she takes for energy, she feeds off of them."

"How does she decide who to keep and who to kill?" I wring my hands together under the table as this new information comes to light. If we can get to Aven in time, we can save her from this threat. But what if Elisavet's already made up her mind?

"They have to want to trade, for one thing. Her power may be great, but she can't *force* someone to become like me."

"So Aven chose to go to Elisavet." I blink away the tears. She did choose to die, in a way. "Why? Why would she?"

"People often want to trade their pain away. Others trade for riches, for power. I don't know what her motivation might be."

I do. I squeeze my eyes closed a minute, a hand at my heart, the feel of it breaking a little more. Opening my eyes, finding him again, I manage, "Well, we have to get her out before anything worse happens."

"Yes." He nods. "We will. Last I saw she was a human servant only. But healthy enough. I believe you still can save her. I believe we will."

He quiets as Mrs. Minthy enters to serve dinner. Now that food is being served, we can't speak of such matters, though I doubt she'd hear us anyway with the glamor he's placed upon the household. I want to ask him about the Court of Death, what it's like. But I've met him and Elisavet. I fear I already know. She would kill you with a smile on her face. She might even make you think you liked it.

Orrin and I manage some small talk, and although the food is as fantastic as always, I can hardly eat, my nerves shot for more than one reason.

We say nothing of the kiss.

What in the Devil's name do you wear to hell? Or, as Orrin calls it, the Court of Death. The contrast of imagery is not lost on me. I've had fourteen days to ponder this and still am no closer to knowing the right thing to do here. I stand in my corset and drawers, aimless. My dressing gown, untied, floats around me in a silky caress.

Carefully, I consider each of the four dresses I've tossed on the bed. I twirl one freshly washed curl between my fingers and force my brain to only think about shallow details. Only the clothes I'll wear there. Not the chance we'll rescue Aven—or worse, that we won't. Not the certainty that I'll see Elisavet, speak with her, get close enough for her to run her cold fingers along my cheekbone.

I quake and decide to do up my face for distraction. As I rifle through the small supply of products I have now, thanks to Sélie and Mr. Brown, the scents of the cosmetics come through again so clearly, a memory flashes through my mind. Seven years ago, but I remember it as yesterday.

"Beetroot powder is expensive!" Aven yelped as I over-measured and spilled the vividly hued powder. I was trying a new recipe. She'd always been best at the recipes—not just in recreating the ones Mavis had come up with but with making her own. In the time we'd been apprenticing there, she'd flourished, a natural at the art of beauty. Matchmakers hired her to paint up their clients. Mistresses and wives and would-be-sweethearts asked her advice on which color or style to purchase. Mavis had been proud, if a bit flustered, when someone came in, asking not for her, but for her oldest ward to help them. Aven had a gift of alchemy.

"Sorry." I cringed at her reprimand. I looked down, the reddish-purple powder all over the black-and-white penny tiles, dusting my new boots—a present for my fifteenth birthday: burgundy and cream leather, soft as butter, buttons all the way past my ankles.

Aven smiled at me, exasperated. "You have to be more careful."

Her sapphire-blue eyes reflecting the light, the sun, my life, our hopes.

I shut my own eyes tight to hold onto the memory for as long as I can before it fades, until I'm clinging to the last fragments of it, until the last bit of smell and taste and sight of her smile slips from my mind. I open my eyes reluctantly. Gone.

After a deep breath, I carefully make up my face with the rouge, a cherry lip stain, and a plum eye color. I line my lids with a black kohl stick then dab my rose-perfume oil on my wrists, in the deep swell of my cleavage, and behind my knees.

Just as I'm finishing, a sharp knock on the door makes me jump. Even though I know it's not Elisavet, of course not. I am still so on edge. Jinny peeks in the room and says, "Mister Orrin said I should come do up your hair."

"Oh." I flutter my hands, a little helplessly. "That would be nice."

Jinny motions for me to sit at the dressing table. I take my place on the velvet stool, and she yanks her fingers through my hair. "Mrs. Minthy told us you're off for an outing this evening?" The smell of chamomile tea lingers on her breath.

I only nod, afraid I'll give my fear away if I speak. An outing to see someone who could strip the marrow from my bones, gleefully.

"A supper picnic by the sea?" she nudges. "That sounds nice."

I murmur something noncommittal back. I don't actually know where we're going. Orrin hasn't offered up the information and I was too wary to ask, yet I highly doubt there will be a picnic involved. Just as Jinny jabs the last pin into my twisted-up hair, another someone steps up outside the door. *Him.* At the knock, she rises and opens the door, but quickly steps back in surprise, dropping into a tidy bob visible in the mirror's reflection. "Oh, sir. I was just finishing up her hair."

Orrin. Jinny glances back at me with a worried smile, as I'm in nothing save my underwear. Worried about propriety. Ha.

With a disappointed twinge, I turn back to the mirror and think, *he's probably never going to kiss me again.* I remember those black eyes burning into me, the curse right after. I wish he'd kiss me, right now. But I shouldn't wish for that, and anyway, it's not going to happen, is it? If it was, it would have again by now. It's been over two weeks since that first one. The only one. And he's seemed to carefully avoid being alone with me since.

My lips tingle, and I avoid his searching gaze in the mirror. He is puzzled by me.

Finding my focus, I give Jinny a reassuring smile and dismiss her with a thank-you. As she walks out, he comes inside the room, a wave of heat and darkness. He leaves the door open. I try not to notice that too much.

"I didn't ask you in, you know." I rise from my seat and walk over, cool and collected. I don't stare at his lips at all. Not his mess of hair. Not his straight nose or strong jawline. Not at his hands, large, long-fingered, both strong and gracefully made. Not at his form, which I still remember shining in the moonlight, shirtless, lean. *He is beautiful, even with those eyes.*

"Should I leave?"

I snap my gaze up. "Hmmm?"

"You seem distracted."

"I'm fine, besides being scared out of my wits." I shake my head, a few strategically placed curls tumbling around my shoulders. "Why are you here?"

"We're late. I see you're not dressed yet, unless you're going to go in that?" His eyes rake over my body so fast I might not have noticed, had I not been staring at him so intently. He swallows so quietly only I would be able to catch it.

My breath catches. I answer hastily, tugging my pale blue dressing gown closed. "Of course not. I was just trying to decide what to wear. I'm not sure what's appropriate." I gesture to the dresses on the bed. "I've never been to a court before, obviously. One of Death or otherwise. I'm picturing kings and queens, and nothing I have is grand enough."

He looks over the choices. "The black is the least-flattering."

I try not to feel insulted. "Well then. That settles it."

"I don't mean it like that. Black is an excellent color." He points to himself—in black trousers and a matching coat, an ebony tie, a silver pocket watch that glints like a blade. His dark boots polished to a shine, the spatters of those men's blood cleaned up, as if they were never there. Or he could just have several pairs of the same style, which I wouldn't be surprised by, with his money. He always is dressed in pristine clothing, impeccable fabrics, tailored to perfection. Clearing his throat, he adds, "And you look beautiful in it."

He means that, I can tell. His voice is serious when he goes on to explain, "In the others, though, you look too innocent."

"I hardly am." I half-laugh. Almost a challenge. *I'm a well-loved woman. You don't scare me. I can meet you halfway.*

His mouth twitches. "Looking too innocent is dangerous today. Elisavet loves breaking the innocent. She considers it an amusing challenge. You will appear less tempting in the black."

With lightning speed, he glances up and down my body again. I'm frightened by what he said of Elisavet and, of course, our errand at hand, yet also flattered by his subtle attention. I inch closer before realizing what I'm doing. Trying to get nearer to smell him—the richness, the clean herbal scent of him mixed with moody undertones. To touch him—feel his hard chest against my hands like before. To taste him, or, to entice him to taste me. To drown in his dark eyes.

But that is not what is important right now. I'm so afraid of what we're about to do—there's so much hinging on it. We'll either save Aven, or we won't. I step back firmly to remind myself of all that is at stake, and say, rather primly, "Thank you. I'll get dressed at once, and we can be on our way."

He, sensing my change in mood, gives a small nod, walks out, and shuts the door behind him.

I sit down on the bed, stealing one indulgent moment to pray for strength. Then I follow his advice and put on the black dress. He's right. I don't want Elisavet to want to take me anymore than she already might.

Knowing we're late and not wanting to draw any more attention to our entrance as we might already, I hurriedly slide the pearl ring from Aven onto my finger and lean down and kiss it for luck. I pull on my boots, buttoning them in haste, and then pick up the red slippers, gripping them to me to keep my trembling hands busy. Finally, I take one more quick breath before opening the door and stepping into the empty hall.

Orrin is not waiting there for me, though the smell of him in the air teases me. Nobody else is waiting for me either—no Mr. Brown making sure I don't try to run. I almost forgot, I have a freedom now I didn't before. I dash down the stairs, both sets, to find Orrin standing in the foyer, which is all shiny fixtures and glossy flooring these days—a far cry from the first time I entered this house.

He looks up at me as I take the final steps down the staircase, and I catch his lips bowing just a bit. He *does* think I look beautiful in the black—and in the matching outfits, I note with a sort of discomfort, we almost look a pair.

I take the arm he holds out chivalrously, reminding myself we are only playacting for the staff.

"We're going out," he says to Mrs. Minthy. "We'll be late."

"Of course, sir. I've packed a basket for you, as I've said. Have a lovely time," she answers merrily, catching my eyes as we pass. "You look very pretty, Miss Corliss."

"Thank you." I give her a smile and then walk out the door on his arm. As I clear the threshold, I glance backward at the mansion, which I've tried to escape from twice. Now how I wish I could run back into it instead of facing off with a demon queen. Although, hopefully, we won't be facing off. I rerun the plan through my mind. While I dance, when Elisavet is distracted, Orrin will lead Aven to the entrance where Mr. Brown will sneak her out. Later on, after the party, Orrin and I will meet them at the mansion, all the while hoping—praying fervently—Elisavet doesn't track Aven here. Is this the best plan? It's the only one we've got. He seems to feel it's a good one, so I try to pull some of his confidence out and drag it into me.

Orrin helps me step up into a sleek carriage. The same carriage, I assume, I was kidnapped in. It's nicer with my eyes open and my hands free. He follows me inside the expensive vehicle, and Mr. Brown shuts the door. It takes me a moment to notice what's missing—horses.

I mention it and Orrin says shortly, "Mr. Brown will hitch them up now that we're inside. Animals sense magic. They don't like it, specifically *my* magic—I doubt they'd be bothered by yours. They don't like my sort. They don't usually linger on the property, wild ones at least."

That explains why the grounds are so quiet. I study his face, noting, "You sound resentful."

"I liked animals when I was human. Horses, in particular. I had a dapple gray I especially loved."

"Oh." As much as I want to ask more about that—*him*, when he was human—in the privacy of the carriage, garnet-silk curtains outlining his form, I inquire, "Will she try to keep me there?"

His look is long, penetrating. "I don't think so. She's not a fool. She knows that taking you from me would be an aggressive move, and I haven't done anything to warrant that. She likes to keep control by controlling her strikes. She hurts when warranted—usually—and then rewards—in the way of money, jewels, power, sex, vices—to gain favor back."

"She is abusive." My ears catch the horses' shoes clip-clopping as they approach, my nose the sweet, warm smell of hay and carrots.

"She commits horrible abuses," he agrees darkly.

I withhold another probing question. He'll tell me when he's ready. "How can she keep a loyal following if she does such things?"

"I don't bother to guess. Elisavet is powerful, and people revere her. I've seen someone turn on her before. It didn't end well. There's nothing she won't do to hold her power, and everyone either respects that, or they fear it. For most, that's enough."

I frown, stroking the red shoes in my skirts for comfort. He glances down, and his own hand in his lap twitches. *He wants to hold my hand.* But he won't.

I swallow down a question.

"What is it?" He sighs at my unspoken words.

"Are we going to talk about what happened?"

"You'll have to be more specific."

"You know what I mean. I can tell by the way you're not look-ing at me." I throw up my hands in frustration. "You've been avoiding me for days."

"What would you like me to say? That I'm sorry for kissing you?"

"Are you?" I ask, holding my breath.

Finally, he gazes at my face. "No."

"I'm not either." My voice is faint. "I almost wish you'd do it again."

"I can't." He looks at me earnestly, regret palpable on his words. "I'm concerned Elisavet would see something tonight between the two of us. It's dangerous."

I nod. Then flare my nostrils. "I smell the ocean. Are we going closer to it?"

He draws up the shade of the carriage. With the first warmth of sunset streaming through the trees, I can see that the woods have thinned.

I stiffen in alarm. "We *are*. And we're close to my cottage."

"That's only a coincidence, being that it is near the sea. Elis-avet draws power from the elements. She likes to reside in court near water, or mountains, or other natural spaces. She draws power from settings in their raw state, untouched by man. It's... complicated."

The carriage stops with a shock. I whisper a secret, "I'm fright-ened."

"You must relax. You look beautiful." But his mouth is drawn.

"Why must you seem so angry giving me a compliment?"

Orrin meets my eyes again, his brows furrowed. "Because. I could kiss you right now...among other things."

"And you don't want to?"

"I cannot," he answers simply, but there's something ragged about it. "As I said."

I stare at his mouth, remember how he pressed his hard body into mine as we kissed in his sitting room, how gentle yet urgent his hands were as they ran up and down me. My lust is a flame that won't extinguish now.

"You're blushing." He gives me a knowing look.

"I'm not!" I protest. As if I'd blush from such a thing.

"Afterward, if we get out of here as planned with your sister, then I will kiss you," he promises, and his teeth flash white. "Use that knowledge to fuel your performance."

"You're so infuriating." Ignoring his teasing, I push down a fearful understanding. If we get out of here *safely*, he means. Alive. If we get Aven. God, what if we don't? I sober immediately. I can't believe this night is finally here.

"Let's go." He gives me one last smile, encouraging me.

We exit the carriage as Mr. Brown holds something over the horse's faces. A blindfold. I glance at Orrin, catch him toss the beautiful beasts a slightly mournful look, so quickly I wonder if I imagined it. He walks ahead, separating himself from me by distance and emotion. I catch up only for him to pause.

We have stopped on the rocky shore near the edge of the sea, not so close for me to see the cottage, but close enough to know it's near, one sister tucked away safely inside. I draw strength from Sélie's love, from the fervent hope I hold to return Aven to her as well. The marrow-deep desire to have the three of us together again.

Then I step forward with Orrin, gripping the red slippers like a lifeline. They have magic. They make me dance like a goddess. Can't they protect us both somehow, regardless of Elisavet being at the root of their power?

We leave Mr. Brown and the carriage behind.

I try to leave my fear behind as well.

CHAPTER TWENTY

We inch down with careful steps.

"I should not hold your hand," he says in apology as I struggle down the rocky sides, trying not to slip. It's far wilder here than the beach at our cottage. He adds, "In case someone is watching."

"I understand." I ask him in a barely audible whisper, "You promise that you'll try not to leave me alone with her?"

We step onto a sliver of beach, rocks all around.

His black eyes meet mine. "I promise."

I roll my shoulders back and take a steadying breath, inhaling the fresh, wet air as ocean spray splashes at my ankles and new boots. The sun lowers over the horizon, casting its glow over the water. It's so beautiful I could stare at it for hours. But there's no time. I push the gift of beauty aside. "I'm ready."

"Good." He jerks his head past me to what I now recognize as the mouth of a cave. "Because we're here."

I follow him into the shadows, my sixth sense screaming not to. After a few steps, my skin prickles with the chill of the air as the temperature drops several degrees. I steady myself by placing one hand against the damp, cool wall, and my heart whispers another prayer. I could be holding Aven in mere hours. I feel the echo of the ocean waves through the stone. Mixed with the sea salt is something sweet and slightly rotten, like grave dirt, like the dead mice my sisters and I used to find in the walls of one of the houses we stayed at as children. Death.

As I stumble over a crack in the stone, Orrin reaches out to help. I give him a quick frown and he drops his hand. We keep going further into the cave, and the sounds of music and voices grow louder. I remind myself to breathe. This place feels unending, but the flicker of light ahead promises that we are almost where we need to be.

I rearrange my face into a mask of polite interest as we wander in, weaving around the candles laid out in clusters on the floor, dripping out in puddles of wax. I step cautiously, so as not to catch my dress on fire. The cave itself is too dark for me to make out more than a pulsating mass of shapes, yet the flames reflect in pools of saltwater on the stone floor. Then, we enter an open area. A room, I suppose I should call it. There's even furniture in it. But it's not the increase of light by even more candles and lanterns that catches my attention. It's the dozens of people who draw my eye. No, not people. Demons. Beings.

Whatever you call them. A lack of souls. That feeling of nails down my spine when their black as ink eyes meet mine.

I find myself scanning the room anxiously for any humans at all. Here. There. A shirtless man with goosebumps dotting his skin, his lips gone blue, balances a tray full of golden goblets. When he comes to us, Orrin takes a goblet, but I don't. I'm not even the least bit tempted. I already know it's full of wine—deepred, and old. Very old. I am too afraid to eat or drink a thing in this court, let alone something that might make me drop my guard. I need all my senses working this evening.

"No, thank you," I tell him before I recall I'm not supposed to speak unless it's unavoidable. *Not even to the servants*, Orrin had said. Still, the young man doesn't open his mouth to reply. I am not sure he heard me.

I turn my uneasy eyes to Orrin. He takes a long draw from his goblet, licks his lips. He mutters, "You're not my equal here. Stay behind me." I flush and nod at his regretful correction. I should know this already.

He turns from me, and I trail him as we make our way through the room. I walk with cautious steps to avoid slipping on the smooth stone floor, shining wet in the spots not covered with thick, ancient rugs reeking of mildew. There are even more candles in here, hundreds of them scattered around. The chandelier affixed to the stone ceiling above holds dozens of tapers, whose flames wink and sputter with the cool bursts of air. And all through the cave, the stench of rot, desolation, and desperation mingles like the worst perfume on earth. Still, I catch the scents of flowers too, actual perfume, good food, wine. It's not all terrible. This place is thick with power, with magic. With lust. I could imagine losing myself here, finding a deliciously dark new self. If you ignored all the bad, the temptations could draw you in. Enfold you. They would stroke you from the inside out.

I follow Orrin meekly as we pass throngs of demons. I'm grateful for the black dress I wear, as it allows me to blend into the shadows. Though it's nothing grand. I certainly don't fit in among most members of the court. To my side, twin women clad in gold and silver wear rich skirts so voluminous they take up the space of four people. Their eyes are fully black—though they each only have one, the right and left, paired up, a matched set. They open their mouths, but no words come out, only a harsh, guttural croaking. *Perhaps you can take his tongue*, Elisavet once said to Orrin about her valet. Their empty sockets seem to search me through. I turn hastily from their sharp gazes, feeling sick with pity for what's happened to them—though they don't seem to mind.

I scurry to catch up to Orrin as he moves in a fluid motion through the crowd. In this horrible, unknown space, I cling to him as my only safety. Whenever he stops to speak to someone, I pause a few paces behind. I turn halfway to assess the room while keeping him nearby. The room is awash in carnal pleasure and other, more twisted things. Some of it benign, all of it is fascinating, in a disturbing, haunting sort of way.

In front of me is a human, her midriff and legs bare, gold chains roping up her ankles and wrists. Her movements are slow and seductive as she dances to the music playing—a harp is plucked by a bare-chested man with cool-black skin and a dull smile, and a frail-looking young woman with no hair at all plays the lyre, skin so white it's nearly see-through. A wave of remorse pours over me at the three of them. *If we could take you too*, I think in their direction. But we can't. The mission is clear: get Aven. Don't get caught.

Scattered around the cave, on cushions and low, dark benches, are the rest of the crowd. Mostly the soulless, wearing suits, robes, and gowns in all lengths and volume, from eras long past or those I suspect have yet to be, in the colors of shadows and rotted fruits. There are several other humans besides the dancer and musicians; the servants are easy to pick out—hungry, wan, gazes cast downward, shabby clothing. Then the others, those in the process of trading, those who are close to becoming demons. They even move in a desperate way, thirsty looks in their eyes, so emotional in a sea of all-black stares. They mostly wear simple dresses or trousers, although some wear no clothing whatsoever.

A demon in an impeccable black suit with a blue-silk square and a gold monocle blows smoke rings as he lounges on top of a bearskin rug, flicking the ashes of his skinny, dark cigarette onto the lap of a human man sitting at his side, who is tenderly stroking his ginger hair. Another someone empties their bladder in the next room—I can smell the urine and hear it spattering against the stone. More moans further away, a rhythmic slapping. Raucous laughter.

Far below, deeper into the cave, someone screams—not in a good way. I can't help but shudder at the desperate sound.

It feels at once tawdrier and more beautiful than I expected. The Court of Death is a perfect description. It's gorgeous and horrifying simultaneously—as are the beings. I feel disgusted, and a little intrigued. Because there's a power here. I can feel it tugging at me, just like the red shoes. What would I give to take away all my pain? To forget all the worst parts of being human? The thought frightens me, and I tighten my smile as I look over at Orrin, who is glancing back at me. He's speaking to a demon with a sharp jawline, black eyes with lashes so long I can even see them from here, bracelets stacked up on their long, wiry arms. The two chat like good friends, shoulders at ease, smiles on both their faces. When they say good-bye, Orrin claps them on the back in a friendly gesture, and moves on, jerking his head toward me.

A demon woman intercepts him, a fine fringe cut short on her pale unlined forehead. She leans her lush figure into his side, whispering something into his ear so low even I miss it. I watch, already disliking her.

Orrin raises a brow, tells her, "Perhaps we can arrange something for another time." His lips tilt up in a rakish smile. "Tell your friend to come too. I haven't seen him in ages."

"Keep moving," he mouths, returning to my side and leaving her behind. I try to lose that momentary flash of jealousy. It's not like he's *mine*. My skin tingles as we get further into the room. Elisavet finally comes into view. She was his lover once, wasn't she? More than once, I'm sure.

You can't help but notice her. She sits on a throne carved right into the stone wall. Tall iron candleholders flank either side, standing nearly as tall as the high seat, the flames dancing, tinting the air with smoke and vetiver. There's something crudely beautiful about it, this spot meant for her. Their queen. She wears a diadem, glinting gold in the low light.

Elisavet stands, looking every inch a royal. Her dress of tight, deep-purple bands falls in panels which slip this way and that, exposing her skin in tantalizing flashes. Her hair is slicked back from her face and hangs in a colorless sheet down her back. Around her neck, a stack of golden necklaces, fat rubies dripping from the strands of gold. Compared to her, even Orrin in his expensive, immaculate black looks cheap. Compared to her, everyone seems small, benign, powerless. My breath catches as she spots us.

"Orrin, you've come!" Elisavet cries, sweeping across the floor. She's standing in front of us before I can blink.

She takes Orrin's face, forcing him to bend low, cupping it in her ringed hands almost lovingly. The glint of a wasp ring on her finger catches my eye, the inch-long stinger needle-sharp. "I'm pleased you could make it, darling."

"I'm happy to be here," he lies smoothly. "I've been waiting for a party."

"I thought you might be! It's been too long since you've attended one." She drops her hands with one last caress across his beautiful face. Excitement hangs on her voice. "I'm especially glad you made it for this party."

He smiles at her, eyes shining with mirth. Yet I can read the bitterness that burns behind them, clear as day. I'm glad she can't read minds because she'd certainly see his hatred. It's not difficult for me to sense, now that I'm in possession of these gifts. Or perhaps it's simply that *he's* easy for me to read now. He doesn't look at me or even acknowledge my presence. I stand silent and demure, a well-behaved pet.

"And you, my pretty little dancer!" Elisavet coos as she moves him to see me better. "I'm thrilled you decided to join us."

"Thank you for the invitation." I smile politely, dip my head as I curtsey.

"Orrin!" She smacks his hand playfully. "Why haven't you given her some wine? She may be your captive, but she's *my* guest."

Then she reaches toward a passing tray, grabs a goblet, and

puts it in my free hand—the other still holding my slippers. The weight of the goblet is almost soothing, something hard and tangible I can squeeze. I press my thumb into one encrusted jewel and pretend to take a sip, the scent of the wine flooding my nose with its richness. "Thank you."

Elisavet doesn't reply. She moves closer, taking my arm tightly in her own, pulling me away from Orrin, as though we're confidants. The side of one of her half-exposed breasts brushes against my arm, and there's a horrible part of me that would love to trace my fingers along the soft globe of it. Her breath is a dark poem against my ear, "I'm very much looking forward to your performance."

"Oh?" I ask in a feeble voice, hoping I sound humble rather than terrified. Behind me I can sense Orrin's concern, his stare at my back. I pray she doesn't move me much further from him. What if she tries to drag me away to a private area? Would he follow, to keep me from being alone with her, as promised? It would draw her suspicion. It could ruin everything.

Just when she's about to reply, a drunken, passing demon trips over her own feet and falls into me, knocking my wine glass, spilling the liquid onto my dress. I step back instinctively as the demon slumps to the ground with a slurred titter, while the crowd roars with laughter—at her, or me, I'm not sure. Orrin doesn't alter his mild expression.

"Oh, what a shame," Elisavet observes. "Your dress is ruined."

"It's fine." I shake my head, trying to sop up the wet dripping across my front.

She turns to the demon lying on the stone floor. "Clumsy fool." Then, picking up her skirts, her very tall, heeled boots visible, she stomps the female in the face. The crack of bone, the blood spurting...I face away, nauseated. *Is she dead? Are those brains...?*

Elisavet snickers, turning back to me, pulling me from the carnage. "Yes, well. Orrin seems captivated by you. Drink your wine, now, and then start, if you please. I can't bear to wait much longer to see you perform." She smiles generously, but there's no mistaking the order in her words. Her plump little mouth parts to reveal a flash of teeth.

Desperately, I find Orrin, who has drifted casually along our path and stands just feet away, speaking with a bone-thin demon man with a one-winged hawk perched on his narrow shoulder. But Orrin stiffens when I look over, and I know he's barely listening to the man. He's watching me instead, making sure I'm handling this, hating that I witnessed such casual violence. I straighten my spine at his questioning look. *I'm fine. Or at least, I can pretend.*

A voice jerks my attention back to Elisavet, and I panic momentarily, hoping I wasn't distracted more than the half-second I thought I was. She is busy, though, looking at the demon woman who has come to join us.

"Introduce me, Your Majesty?" the woman asks Elisavet with a submissive bow of her head, claret waves falling in a sheet down to her knees. Her glittering eyes pin me with a dangerous curiosity. "I haven't seen such a healthy-looking human here in ages."

Elisavet laughs cruelly. "This is Orrin's little pet, at least for now. You know how he has a thing for dancers."

Her statement has curiosity zipping through me. He refused to answer why ballet slippers were chosen as the symbol for his trade. Why exactly would they be? There must be something more to this. Like the woman in the locket...

"Do you have a name, pet?" The demon grins at me, revealing pointed teeth, filed-sharp.

I nod, meeting her eyes. Chin high. I'm not terrified at all. "Corliss."

"Well, are you going to dance for us, then?" she demands, fully ignoring the mess behind her, one of her peers murdered only feet away.

"As soon as I warm up, yes. Is there a place where I can do so?" I direct the question to Elisavet, adding politely, "If it's not too much trouble."

"Not at all." She snaps her fingers. At once, two human servants are at her side, eyes flat. She commands them, "Take my guest to a private chamber to ready herself. When she is finished, bring her back at once."

I have just a moment to find Orrin's face, the subtle look of reassurance he gives me, and then the servants are leading me away.

I paste a placid expression on my face as we move, feigning indifference. There's a human who vomits in the corner—the smell of strong alcohol and a hint of poison are undeniable. A demon giggles as she holds the human's hair back. I don't react to them, to anything. I can't shake the feeling that, if the lights were brighter, I would see streaks of blood, dried on the walls. The coppery stench is heavy in the air.

On the way down a narrow hall, the scent of blood increases—metallic, hot, rich—and I stifle down the urge to retch. As we pass one quieter room, the origin becomes apparent. I walk by with hurried steps, but it's not fast enough to miss the shallow pool of blood on the stone floor, two beautiful nude bodies rolling around in it. I snap my eyes away and follow the human servants with my stomach somersaulting.

I can do this. I move deeper into the cave, taking everything in. I don't see any sign of Aven. But this place is large. She could be anywhere. If she's even here.

We come to a private area, although the servants remain on guard. I have to bend over, catch my breath, and wipe away the tears in my eyes, welling from the brutality I witnessed minutes ago. It was so violent…so unnecessary.

I straighten, realizing how long I've been just standing here, not doing what Elisavet expects. I try to steady my mind, my belly. I'm relieved I was too nervous to eat today. I take off the black boots and tie up my red slippers, the questions swirling in my mind as I warm up, utterly inadequately. What if Orrin was wrong? What if Aven doesn't even want to trade her soul? What if Elisavet has already killed her?

Desperately, I turn to the two servants. Their dirty dresses might have been white once but are nearly black in spots. I scan their expressionless faces, take them in. They reek of despair and sweat, saltwater tears. Misery adheres to them like a second skin. But they weren't always like this. The one on the left, the smaller of the two, has a small birthmark on one brown shoulder, such a human reminder. It hits me, these shells were people with families, with loves and dreams. That they are trapped now, in the sad, lonely place between demon and free. I search her blank eyes, looking for a spark of humanity. Surely, still being human, she has some left?

"How long have you been here?" I ask.

Silence. They both stare vacantly, like they can't even hear me, just as Orrin's maids do when I speak of certain things. Or perhaps *they* can't speak.

I try again. "I'm looking for someone, a human woman. Do you know Aven? She's got dark hair and fair skin, blue eyes. Do you know where she is?"

Silence.

"Do you need help?" I whisper.

They don't respond. I try to let them drop from my thoughts, but it's difficult. I can't save everybody. They chose to be here, it's just they lose themselves over time, like Orrin said. I just didn't fully understand what he meant until I saw it firsthand.

Aven, where are you? If I close my eyes, if I try hard enough, I can feel her, can smell her in the catch of the air: strawberries and pine and saltwater and the memory of flowers. It's not just wistful thinking. She's here, I *know* it now. My magic tells me so, and I trust it.

Too soon, I am warmed up, limber. Anyway, who cares if I pull a muscle, so long as I make it out of here alive, without Elisavet snatching me up to be one of her playthings, so long as Orrin gets Aven out of here safely. In mere hours I could be reuniting with her at his mansion. I close my eyes tight and hold onto that hope.

The servants escort me back to the main room, which has transformed into a stage in my brief time away. Every person—being, creature—has shifted to the outside of the room. They disappear almost, into the shadows. The middle is empty, waiting for me to put on my most important performance yet. If I dance poorly, will I anger Elisavet? Embarrass her for inviting me? But what if I dance too beautifully and it makes her want to keep me for further entertainment? Would Orrin intervene? I scan the crowd for him, but the faceless mass of demons doesn't reveal him. My skin beads with nervous sweat, even in the chill of the cave.

"Now, my loves," Elisavet calls to the room so that it stills, even quieting the rampant questions in my head. "I've invited a very special guest here today. She comes to us with Orrin, who you all know I *adore*. We're quite lucky, indeed, because she's agreed to grace us with a performance, which will be a special treat. It's especially appreciated on a night like tonight."

Before I can wonder too long about her meaning, a round of applause—either on my behalf or hers, I cannot tell—and I step out onto the damp stone floor, praying I don't slip during my dance.

Red shoes, take care of me, I beg silently. "Music?" I look to Elisavet. I could do without, but I'd rather not. I feel as though everyone in the room—demon or human—can hear my beating heart over the silence.

"Play!" She claps her hands once, and the lyre and harp start up again, in a rhythmic strumming beat I can't say I recognize, yet I can certainly dance to. I count down and then step into a sous-sous, then a series of chaînés, and a triple pirouette. I hold an arabesque with my arms in a graceful attitude. Each movement seems to captivate the audience. They look intently at me, pairs of black, hungry eyes, watching each move I make, following me across the floor. It brings me a surprising amount of comfort to know among them, somewhere, is Orrin, steadying me with his dark gaze. But he will be slipping out at any second, grabbing my sister—I hope. Taking her to Mr. Brown, who waits with the carriage, with the horses, who will take her to safety, to Colehart Mansion. I relish the thought and push on.

Never once do I falter, yet I'm aware my movements are slightly tighter, less free, my limbs taut. The fear reins me in, even with the magic of the slippers. I end in a final flurry of leaps across the wet floor. When I drop into a curtsey, the applause breaks through the instruments still playing, and Elisavet is at my side once again. My ragged breath catches when I meet Orrin's eyes across the crowd, see the look on his face. He didn't find my sister. Our plan failed. I can read him like my favorite book.

She pulls me up, twisting me to face her. "Beautiful." She smiles with glee, kissing me on each cheek, then pauses to graze my ear with her teeth. "I meant what I said. I'd love to have you..."

I can hardly breathe.

Elisavet pulls away and says, "Come back soon, understand?"

Luckily I'm spared a response as she's tugged away by a demon couple, making a fuss to speak to her. They practically fall over themselves, bowing, slurring from the effects of too much wine. Somehow, this is one of the things that shocks me most. I knew demons ate, that they slept, even that they could bleed. But I thought other human vulnerabilities would have disappeared. Will they feel the effects tomorrow in the way of headaches and upset stomachs, I stupidly wonder. The vague thought is pushed aside by the intense pain of knowing we didn't get Aven out tonight. By the aching unknown. Why not? Where is she?

Something is wrong.

More demons move between me and Elisavet, and I let them do so, gladly. I creep back into the edges of the cave, toward Orrin. I slink his way casually, pretending to sip a new goblet of wine, not meeting anyone's hungry eyes.

Laughter breaks through my pinpoint focus, Elisavet's, loud and bright. It shatters in my ears. I search the cave miserably. Where is my sister?

Orrin makes his way to me as well, slowing to speak with other demons, to sometimes laugh or clap them on the back, almost affectionately. He's captivating, the way he lights up the dark cave. But I can see it in his eyes: he's troubled.

Then he is at my side. "We need to go," he murmurs, hiding his lips behind his goblet.

I stare at him. Something in me hurts. Warning. Premonition.

He's about to speak when Elisavet claps her hands and breaks the chatter in the cave once again.

"My loves," she begins. "I hope you enjoyed that beautiful performance. Tonight is particularly special because we announce our newest members. I know you will show them the same affection that was bestowed upon you when you were changed. Now, please welcome them into our family."

From the back room of the cave comes first a man, with a naked chest and loose light pants, and then four women wearing long, silk robes in pale shades, the first old enough her graying hair hangs silver in the light, her skin papery and faded. My breath catches amidst the mild applause and encouraging cheers from the demons in the room.

Because the last woman in line is my sister.

Even with her head slightly bowed, I recognize her. I know her walk, her profile, her dark hair. I know her. It's Aven. Or, it is what is left of Aven. When she looks up, I step back. The ink-black eyes. The nothingness behind them.

The pain engulfs me, threatening to crack me in half and spill me out on the ground.

"No…" I hold back a cry, a scream.

Beside me, Orrin tenses. We're too late.

My sister has traded her soul.

CHAPTER TWENTY-ONE

Orrin takes a step in front of me, shielding me, I suppose, but over his shoulder, I keep my gaze locked on my sister. Her eyes rest on me yet there isn't even a moment's recognition, warmth, love, and she moves her attention away brutally fast. She does not know me. My heart breaks a little more. A lot more. This can't be real. This must be a nightmare.

Orrin mouths as he turns back to me. "Come."

Woodenly, I follow him to the center of the room, then watch him greet the human recruits, including my sister. As hard as it is, I keep my distance.

"We must be leaving, my queen," he says to Elisavet, cutting smoothly in front of a group eagerly welcoming the five new demons.

"No, it's still early!" She sounds offended, though after a moment she smiles begrudgingly. "I hate to see you leave so soon."

"I'll stop by tomorrow or the next day, if you're agreeable to that. As much as I hate to go so soon, I have matters to attend to at home." The lie of regret is smooth on his lips.

"Home, really?" Elisavet pouts in an exaggerated way. "What is home away from family, darling? I shall never understand why any of our kind prefers to live apart. There is so much fun to be had here." When she says the word "fun," she shifts her eyes to me.

"I'll consider it. For now, though, I bid you farewell." He lifts her hand, and kisses it gently, lovingly. There's blood on her wrist.

"Congratulations on the newest members. I'll be sure to acquaint myself with them next time."

Elisavet drops her pouty face. "Thank you. Take good care of your pet." She stares at me, telling him, "I wouldn't let beauty like that slip past me, if I were you."

He nods graciously, takes my arm, and pulls me toward the entrance. A departing demon trio trails us, reeking of wine. On our way out, a burly male demon heads in, his eyes frightfully sunken and pinned upon me, his mouth turned in a menacing sneer. He rushes as he gets closer, nearly slamming into me. I dart swiftly to the side to avoid him, pressing myself into the wall of the cave, hair sticking to the dampness, just missing his aim. The demon throws a grin back at me. Orrin's fists tighten at his sides in fury.

The demons behind us burst into mocking giggles, and I nearly black out from the grief as reality washes over me, but not for my sake. For Aven's. I swallow her name with a sob.

I can't leave her, I can't leave her here, with that monster. With those monsters. I slow, turn to go back. I have to get her. I have to make her change her mind. Somehow…I have to…

"Why can't you do anything right, you insolent thief?" Orrin's voice turns cold, and I stare at him in dull surprise before realizing the demons behind us are listening, still laughing at me almost being plowed into. He's only doing this for their benefit. He snaps, "Keep moving!"

I don't have to play along. I don't think I could move without him forcing me. He physically steers me out of the cave, though I feel nothing. I step forward, red slippers soaking in the cool seawater, not that I care.

"Almost…" he whispers in apology.

I turn back in time to watch the three demons disappear into thin air the second they step outside. I'm in too much shock to even ask Orrin about it. I'd forgotten that they could do that.

The full moon sags over the sea, water so still now it's like glass, reflecting the white orb. Aven traded in her soul. For what? What did Elisavet promise her? But beyond the disbelief, the judgment even, there is a dull acceptance, an understanding. What would I have done to save Aven, if the choice had been offered to me? I would have given my life for her; of course I would give up my soul.

Silently, Orrin and I climb up the rocky slope in the dark, and I'm so distracted that I slip, catching my palms on a jagged edge, letting out a cry. My hand bleeds crimson as dark as my slippers.

"Are you alright, Corliss?"

"No." I pull myself up, don't look at the blood in my stinging palm. "I'm not."

We make it up over the edge. Mr. Brown stands there in a stream of moonlight, arms folded. His face is unreadable, but I sense the worry. As soon as he sees us, he turns to cover the horses' eyes, who already shift around, jittery. Orrin helps me into the carriage, already turned away from the sea, set to carry us home.

When we are inside and the door is shut, he yanks down the one slightly opened shade. In the dark of the carriage, he drags me onto his lap. I'm too broken to even be surprised. Somehow, he went from someone I feared and abhorred to the one I feel safest with. And if he wasn't here, I don't know what I'd do, having seen what I just saw.

I can't even cry. I only shake, violently, unstoppable. Shake like a ship going down. His arms wrapped around me like an anchor.

"My goodness," Mrs. Minthy cries as Orrin carries me into the mansion. I bury my face into his shoulder—to cover my emotions, to take in the warm, herbal smell of him and push aside everything else.

"She's not feeling well," he tells her.

With a worried coo, she fusses at me as he passes. I grip him tightly as he carries me up the grand staircase. I want to say I can walk myself, that I can manage. But the words don't come. If they did, I don't know that they'd be honest.

"Draw her a bath," he calls gruffly to the housekeeper.

I close my eyes tighter against his chest as he keeps moving, blocking out the memory of the sights and sounds of Elisavet's cave. I'd like to forget I was there. I'd like to imagine Aven is just on holiday. I tell myself that this isn't real. Except I listen to the sound of Orrin's heart beating against my ear. I wouldn't undo him. Not this moment. *I hate him, I hate him*, I said so many times, out loud, to myself. And I didn't just say it—I truly felt it. That, however, has changed. He has. I have. Something has shifted.

The only thing between me and complete and utter despair right now is him.

Up another staircase, down a hall, and finally, Orrin carries me into my room and deposits me on my feet in one fluid motion. But his arms stay on me, so that I don't fall over. I worry I might faint. He must know it.

"I want to get this dress off me." I finally open my eyes. "There's blood on it, isn't there? I can smell it."

Nodding, he doesn't elaborate, only helps me tug off the dress, averting his eyes, though he's obviously seen me in just a chemise several times. He wraps a blanket around my shoulders. "Are you cold? You're still trembling."

Jerking my head in what is not quite a shake, I let out a quivering breath and wrap the blanket tighter around myself. Even if my skin has warmed, the chill of fear has settled in my bones. I blink away the tears. Orrin keeps quiet. He's waiting for me to speak, when I'm ready.

"I know it sounds crazy," I start, my voice breaking. "But I thought the plan would work." I squeeze my hands into the blanket and wince at the wound on my palm. "At least, I hoped it would. But we were too late. And the way Aven looked at me... like she didn't even *know* me."

"Shhh. Bath is here." His voice is low.

"I know," I whisper back. I already sensed the pitchers of steaming water changing the air beyond the wall.

He shifts, turning away.

"What are you doing?" I say, following him, panic pitching my voice higher than I mean it to.

"I'm leaving so you can bathe." He pauses at the door as I meet him there. "Mrs. Minthy will help you, like always."

"No, please." I cling to his shirt, as though he's the only thing standing between me and Elisavet, as if he's the only thing keeping me from getting hysterical with the reality of this whole thing, and he is. "I don't want you to leave me."

"You're perfectly safe here." His eyes are like black velvet, voice soothing.

"I feel safe when you are by my side. Please." I have to look down when I say it.

A gust of night wind from outside blows against us as we stand there, as I stare back up at him with unspoken words. *Don't make me ask again.*

He nods. "Of course. I'll stay."

We step out of the way as staff fill the bath with pitcher after pitcher of water. They add rose-oil soap that foams up in fluffy white bubbles so full I can no longer see the water. Last to leave, the red-haired maids finish up. Hana sets two large towels onto a low stool near the tub.

"Please tell Mrs. Minthy that we do not need her help with the bath," Orrin tells her brusquely, then adds, in a softer note, "and thank you, all." Both cousins curtsey and walk out the door. The maids cannot approve, of course, of me in here alone with him, nothing except a tub between us, but they don't get a say about it. Not only am I at least four years their senior, I'm their guest. And they'd never reprimand him. Besides, it's not the first time he's been alone in here while I was in the bath!

As the fragrant steam rises from the tub, waiting for me, I glance at Orrin, slightly awestruck. As if I'm seeing him for the first time, separating the hatred I felt for him, the fear. Taking away the lust, even. Just noticing. How he stands, how he moves, his messy hair falling against the side of his high cheekbone. The way the candlelight glows on his dark-honey skin. The safeness of him. His height, his power, his tattoos, the way he looks at me. He turns, perusing my bookcases, allowing me modesty while I drop the blanket around my shoulders and maneuver out of my corset and drawers, slip off my chemise. Then, only when I've sunk into the bath—wincing when the water stings the cut on my hand—and covered my nakedness with a mound of bubbles, does he turn. He stands still, appearing almost unsure.

"Sit by the bath. So we can talk." I lean back with gratitude, soaking in the hot water, washing the sickening smell of blood from me.

He sets aside the towels, pulls up the small wooden stool, and sits. "Do you want to talk about what you saw tonight?"

My wet waves trail around my shoulders when I shake my head resolutely. "Not now. Tomorrow I will face what I saw, what is ahead of us."

"Yes." His eyes reflect me. "We will make a new plan. Maybe one utilizing your skills."

"The 'gifts' thing? Having *slightly* increased senses isn't very helpful." I suds up my hair, blanching at the crusted blood at the back. "Even if it is interesting."

He shakes his head, reaches out and begins to wash my hair for me. I let him, shutting my eyes, forcing myself not to moan from the pleasurable feel of his fingers against my scalp. He didn't even push up his sleeves—his cuffs will be soaked, but he doesn't seem to mind.

"You have more than that. You have power in you, Corliss. Whether that's from my sharing magic with you, or whether it comes from you alone."

I open my mouth to dispute that.

"Don't argue." He rinses my hair for me. "Look at the shoes."

"What do you mean?" I gaze up at him, shiver as he drags a sponge along my collarbone, slowly. Deliciously slow.

"The slippers attached themselves to you. They found magic within you. They recognized something. And they've become connected to you as well."

"But how?" I ask, frustrated.

"I don't know, exactly," he admits. "Though I've been trying to understand. Besides, look at how you followed me in dreams, not once but twice. You and I are connected, in some way. The shoes drew us together—I feel they have a sort of will of their own. Their magic is beyond what I can fathom, I suppose. They're a powerful gift in their own right. And I believe yours is as well."

I frown, and say, with the last bit of stubbornness I can cling to, "I still don't know if I believe in magic. Not like this. You have magic because you traded for it. You're a demon, or whatever! Humans don't have powers like that."

"You've never seen it? Felt it?"

I shrug. "I mean, there are people in The Pins who *pretend* to have magic. But it's not real." Or is it? Even now, I'm not sure how I feel.

Orrin doesn't reply, but he takes my injured hand in his, concentrates his power on it, and seals the skin back together in one hot second. Fixed.

I meet his stare, trembling again, though not from cold. "I'm ready to get out now."

He hands me a towel and stands, shifting his gaze to the bathwater. His pulse quickens so abruptly I *swear* I can hear it speed up.

As he strides toward the door, he says, voice pained, "I'll just be in the hall if you need me."

The door shuts, as if he's hurried to get away from me.

It's only when I look down at the water that I realize all the bubbles have dissipated.

CHAPTER TWENTY-TWO

I dry off with anxious hands and settle my hummingbird heart. Then I get in my nightgown and, still cold, wrap a fresh blanket around myself. I think about all the things that have changed between the two of us, all the ways I have changed. I know it's partly the trauma of the night's events that has me anxiously pulling Orrin back into my room. I also know it's partly something else.

He comes in willingly, allowing me to grab his arm. After being bathed, with my skin now clean and floral, his wild scent is even stronger to me, more enticing. How could I ever have feared him? I'd like to crawl inside his veins, make a bed inside his heart.

He says, "I'll leave you for now—we can speak tomorrow, if you're ready."

"No."

An almost-smile quirks his mouth. "No? To which part?"

"First, can I say how nice it is to hear you suggest things lately instead of ordering me?"

"I'm trying. It's not easy," he concedes.

Sitting on the bed, I point out, "You like to have your way."

"As do you. Now, would you like anything to eat? I can have them send up a tray for you with some food. Or a whiskey to sleep? You look exhausted."

"I am exhausted. I don't need a whiskey though. And I'm not hungry."

"Goodnight, then. You have only to call for me or Mr. Brown if you need something in the night. We'll be listening for you."

"No. I meant 'no' to you leaving me. Please stay. Just for tonight. I'm still so cold. And I don't think I will be able to sleep if I'm alone." I add, softly, almost embarrassed, "Can you just hold me?"

Orrin doesn't hesitate at my request, nor balk at how scandalized his innocent maids might be at us sharing a bed. He pauses only to kick off his boots. He does exactly what I need him to in this moment as he takes me in his arms yet again and scoots us back on to the bed.

He holds me. I listen to him breathing, the expansion of his lungs, sounding much like the swell and give of the sea.

Sometime in the dark of night, I wake with a scream. My own.

"Corliss." Orrin's ragged voice, thick with sleep, is a steadying whisper. "You were dreaming."

Blood, sheets of it, walls of it, pooling around my ankles, hot and fresh. Those men in the woods. Elisavet's cruel laugh in my hair. Aven's white face. Beasts chasing me off a cliff. Pain and pain and pain forever.

I nod, even though it's pitch black—though he can likely still see me. Just a nightmare.

Orrin calms me, running his hand up my thigh reassuringly. I let the nightmare melt away and this moment seep in. This is real. He is real. And I know exactly the magic he's doing now, to distract me, to root me into my own body.

I breathe, focusing on the way his fingers trail up and down, up and down my skin—my nightgown has twisted up in the night. The heat of his sleepy hands warms me. I can almost taste his longing, the itch he has to move his fingers further up. I swallow a sigh, part my knees a little in invitation, but he doesn't reach for me, no matter how long I wait.

I try to fall back asleep, only it feels impossible. I can't tell if it's because of the nightmare, which is already fading from my mind, or if it's because of those damned fingers running along my leg. What they're doing to me. What they're not.

I wake with a beam of sunlight in my face. I roll over, trying to find some darkness to ease the intensity against my lids. Then a sense of someone near me. Recalling last night, I peek open my eyes to find Orrin, sitting upright on the bed, dressed in fresh clothes, watching me.

"Morning," I croak, my throat scratchy.

"Morning." He smiles, lighting up the room even more.

"What is it?" I ask, sitting up, studying him. "You want to say something."

He hesitates for a fraction of a moment. "Do you remember how I said you had something special, and that's why the slippers attached themselves to you?"

"And you believe it's because I have magic?" I try not to sound sarcastic. By the way he tightens his eyes I know I've failed.

"*Yes*," he enunciates. "You are special. Just look at what you've done to me."

"What have I done?"

"You've changed me. I feel as though…" Frustration creases his face. "Words can be so inadequate sometimes."

He takes my hand in his own, sets it against his chest, directly over his heart.

The beat of it twangs against my hand, and I stare into his eyes, fully aware of how his heart speeds up the longer we look at each other. "What are you saying?"

"I think you've made some of my soul regrow."

"Regrow?" I don't drop my hand, though he releases it.

"Reattach, regrow, return. Whatever terminology suits you. Does it matter what you call it? My kind isn't supposed to feel, not good things anyway. Now I do."

Some kind of emotion I can't name floods me—pleasure? Disbelief? Happiness?

"You've not felt like this before?"

"No." He shakes his head. "Not like this. When I first changed, I cared about nothing at all. You'll find your sister is probably the same. Though over time, some of my humanity came back. It's how I could remember...things. I felt twinges of compassion—it's why I took Mr. Brown in, talked him out of trading with Elisavet."

Oh.

"This is different. I don't just remember my old life, I feel like I am actually living again. I know I'm not human. Whatever is happening to me isn't strong enough to release me from my trade. But it's the closest I've felt to human in decades."

"Oh." The word comes out this time. I don't know what else to say, and he allows me the space to mull this over. I finally voice something that is nagging at me. "I don't want to be your savior, not like that. I don't want to think you're only good because of me because it's not true. Besides, it's not like you were unredeemable before."

"Perhaps not. Even before you..." he hesitates. "I was hating what she had me do, toward the end. The killings. That's why I was trying to leave the court. It didn't sit right. I was starting to feel..."

"What?" I prod.

"Guilty," he eventually says. "I left her court, moved city to city for a while, before coming to The Pins. I thought I'd found some peace, that I could settle into a quiet life. But she wouldn't let me get away with that. She followed me here, not long after."

It fills me with sadness, thinking of it. But then I just keep thinking in the span of our silence. He takes my hand, squeezing for my attention.

"What is it?" Orrin asks.

"Probably nothing," I muse aloud. "But you said your soul is growing, whether that's because of me or I simply nudged it along, what matters is that if there's a way your soul has regrown, what if there may be a way to make you human once again? To actually reverse the trade you made. Do you think it's possible?"

After a thoughtful pause, he shrugs. "I've heard things. But I've never seen anything."

I catch his uncertainty. "What?"

"I *believe* if Elisavet is destroyed, that she'd release the souls she's taken. Killing her would be a way to reverse the trade. I think."

"We could steal the souls she has," I offer. Who could kill Elisavet? The idea is frightening in scope. I may not have witnessed her full brutality, but you don't have to see something to believe it. I know she's dangerous. I feel it.

He half-smiles, like he might call me a thief, and I glare it away from him. An amused smirk pulls at his lips. "She holds them in a spiritual sense, as in, they've become a part of her. They're not locked away somewhere. It's tricky, even if we could do it. I'll have to plan carefully. It might be harder—worse—than I anticipate."

"How could it possibly get worse?" I say, exasperated. "My sister literally has no soul."

"Oh, she has a sliver yet, remember."

"It seems too dangerous. What if I talk to Aven to try to make her remember? I could help her soul regrow too. Maybe in time, it would be enough."

His eyes are heavy, weighed down with knowledge I don't yet have. "It has taken me many, many decades to get here, Corliss. I'm afraid you'd be long gone by the time your sister remembers— or cares—about you again."

I nod my agreement, heart aching.

"It'll be okay." He runs his thumb along the top of my hand. "And we can talk more tonight, make a new plan together. After you dance—if you would like to? But in the meantime, do whatever you like while I take care of some business—for the mansion, I mean. Nothing nefarious. A walk perhaps?"

I try to smile. A walk does sound nice. I'd like to explore the house more. Even though I've had free rein to move about, I haven't taken full advantage of it yet.

And then he is gone, and I am alone. To get my mind off of him, off of everything, I first grab the ballet shoes and tie them up my ankles. I want their magic. I want the courage they give me. I dance myself into a state of bravery.

Later, I wander around the mansion, a little aimlessly, peering into rooms, sparkling and vast. There is still work to do but so much has changed just in the time that I've been here. I step into a study on the main floor, which I glimpsed once before, when it was worn at the edges. The last time I saw it, on that day I snuck in, the heavy curtains reeked of mildew, the chandelier was strung with cobwebs, and the thick-gold frames on the wall hung askew. Today, it is bright and clean, vases of pink roses everywhere, perfuming the air.

Roses make me think of flowers in general, which remind me of gardens, which remind me of Aven. Though Sélie and I have grown comfortable identifying flora over the years for business purposes, it is Aven who has a natural gift with growing and cultivating green things. The gardens at home—the source of most of our raw products—are entirely her doing. There must be a garden on the grounds here, or at least something in the greenhouse, which I would like to see, but just when I'm about to head outside, the afternoon rolls in gray and rainy. I sigh. I don't mind the weather, but I'd rather not get soaked. Grumpy, restless, I head back up to my room to write a letter to Sélie. If I can't see her yet—by my choice, to keep her safe—this is the next best thing.

Sélie, I'm close to finishing up what I'm doing away from you, I write her, ending with: *I hope to see you in person soon. I am safe, and doing fine, except I miss you tremendously. I think of you every day and night. I adored each and every one of your drawings. Take care of yourself, love.*

It's brief, but more encouraging than last time. I don't mention anything substantial in the letter—because it sounds strange, unbelievable, even to me, living through it, and I think the less I say, the safer she is from Elisavet's clutches and the Court of Death, only minutes away from her, from our cottage. Yet maybe, in some way, she'll read between the lines and understand I'm more hopeful than last time at least. That I may be able to actually pull this off.

Then Mrs. Minthy is here to ready me for my dance. I rush her through the bath, and when Jinny offers to do my hair, I wave her away thankfully.

"I'll wear it down tonight," I say, eager to get downstairs. Not only to have my letter delivered and have Mr. Brown check on my sister once more, but, of course, to see Orrin. But when I go into the ballroom, he isn't there yet. I put on the slippers and slide down onto the floor to stretch as the sky outside opens up for another round of rain. It drips down the windows like tears. I shiver, uneasily.

When Mr. Brown comes in, I slump, disappointed it's not Orrin.

"He's not here. He went to see Elisavet." How grateful he must feel to Orrin, for keeping him from making a trade with her. But why would Orrin go back so soon? He did mention stopping by there when we were at the party—but why keep it from me?

My senses are tingling. Something is different about this time.

"Do you know why?" My voice wobbles, startled. What if Orrin took our conversation as an opportunity to go do something spontaneous—to try and kill Elisavet? Something that might get him, or my sister, killed? Maybe both of them. "I thought he was occupied with business—personal business, I mean."

"Earlier, yes."

I stand up, nausea rippling through me. He promised to watch me dance tonight, and he indicated we'd make a new plan. Together. What if he changed his mind?

I believe if Elisavet is destroyed, that she'd release the souls she's taken. Killing her would be a way to reverse the trade.

"I'm worried too, you know. He saved me from trading my soul a long time ago." Mr. Brown goes on, rushing out the words as if the faster he says them, the less vulnerable he'll feel. "He saved my life. I don't want anything to happen to him. I've seen the good behind him just as you have."

I open and shut my mouth.

As if embarrassed, he looks away. "You can wait here or go back up. I'll let him know you were waiting when he returns."

He doesn't say *if* he returns, which is reassuring. But I make out the undertone of fear anyway.

"Mr. Brown, wait," I start, slow, something he's not saying making me uneasy. "What did you mean by 'you don't want anything bad to happen to him'? Do you mean he might have gone there tonight, in the hopes of trying to kill her *now*?"

The man gives me a short nod, reluctant. "Yes. And…"

"What?" I cry.

"It's not only the risk of trying to kill her. It could be dangerous if he actually succeeds. According to him, destroying her *could* destroy other souls right along with her. But don't worry about your sister. He was certain that she'd be the safest, with other newly changed ones. The ones who've been with Elisavet the longest would most likely be the ones destroyed." He's looking at me like he doesn't want to look at me. "They've been tied to her longer. Are almost a part of her at this point."

"You mean Orrin?" The meaning sweeps over me and I'm afraid I might fall over.

With nothing more helpful than an awkward pat on the shoulder and a verbal reassurance that things will *probably* be alright, Mr. Brown leaves me, my stomach all in knots.

Back in my room, the time passes too slowly, the thoughts crawling in and out of my brain, festering, the anxiety sickening me. I cannot distract myself with books nor dancing. I watch out the window, leaning over the cool, wet sill, hoping to catch the sound of horses coming, then I realize Orrin mustn't have taken the horses, since Mr. Brown is still here. He must have just shown up there, materializing at the cave, with magic.

I still wait, I still listen, for hours. It feels like centuries.

When a knock comes on my door, I rise, hurrying toward the sound. Relief coursing through my blood like a current. I throw the door open, senses all aflutter, because I already know. It's Orrin.

"I didn't know if you'd be back," I whisper as I stare up at him, suddenly self-conscious of my concern. Was I wrong to be so afraid?

"I'm fine."

"We were worried." Something in my voice breaks. I didn't know until this moment how much. I almost want to cry…which makes me wish I could hide.

"Corliss." He draws in a breath, as though it hurts to speak my name, like he's wounded. There's something in his voice as he gazes at me. Something hot and sharp and immediate. It breaks through the barrier and I fall into him.

Orrin meets me halfway, sweeping me into his arms. He kisses me like a starving man, like he isn't just kissing me but tasting me, like my touch gives him life. Gathering me closer, he tips back my head, to nibble his way along the column of my neck the way he did in the sitting room, gripping my hair in one hand so that I sigh with delight. When I do, he tugs, getting slightly rougher. The chills run down my skin, the heat floods low in my belly. He pulls away to close the door before drawing me into his embrace once again.

I tear him back to my mouth and kiss him until my lips bruise. I can taste the wine on his tongue, the need teasing me so that I let out a gasp of want. Orrin slows down then, frustratingly slow. He reaches around, gently unbuttoning my green dress. Kissing each inch of skin he exposes in the process. I almost stop breathing as he spins me so his deft fingers work the laces of my corset. Something about the intimacy of him releasing me from the corset has me dizzy with anticipation. He tosses the garment on the floor and nestles his face into my neck from behind.

"Hurry," I demand.

A low laugh as he tugs off my chemise and drawers, peels off my stockings, tosses my garters aside. Then he turns me slowly, naked. Drinks up every inch of me with those bottomless eyes. First my face, then on down, taking it leisurely all the way to my toes. His breath catches in his throat and his eyes darken even further, if that's possible. "Beautiful," he says in a husky whisper.

"Please, Orrin..." I strain out, remembering once again his words. *I'm going to make you cry for it.*

A wicked smile, like he's remembering too. I thread my fingers into his long hair, pulling him forward, kissing him again. Again. Again. Tongues tangling, and his bite grazing my bottom lip.

Then we're in my bed, red curtains pooled around us, and his hands trace the skin of my neck, down to my chest. He rubs the pad of one finger against my breast, circling my nipple, making it pebble under his touch.

I gasp again as he drags his tongue against me. "Corliss..." He buries his face into my breasts, sucking at me, grazing my skin with his teeth. I writhe beneath him.

His hands are everywhere. They run along my skin, in me, his hands become me. Bucking my hips, I cry out low as he reaches for the heat of me, rubs against the center of me so softly I push against him. I need more.

He pauses, letting me catch my breath, touching the autumn leaf on my shoulder. "What's this one mean?"

I look up at him, lust making my voice thick. "For my aunt."

He traces the flowers, the vines on my arm. "These?"

"For myself."

Then he moves downward, pausing at the roses trailing over my left hip, lush and ruby-red with leaves green, open and curled. "And these?" He licks the outline of each flower until my toes are as curled as the leaves.

With a shudder, I say, "A lover. Tanna." Her black hair tumbling down, her mouth, her hands, the way she showed me how to hold this leg, or that hand, or that pose. The way she'd smile if I got it right. The way she said good-bye when I couldn't be what she wanted. But all I hold now is a memory, like it was another life. In a way, it feels like it was.

Trailing his fingers down my legs, he glances at my feet, at the sweet pea on one, the paintbrush on the other. "And these?"

"My parents."

As he touches my ankle, for some reason, a throaty laugh escapes him. "An anchor. Who is this for?"

"Another lover, Wil. We can talk about the rest later. Now come back here, let me undress you. I need to touch you. To feel you."

But he searches my face, without words making sure, asking me to be certain.

I meet his eyes, nod. *Yes. Keep going.*

And somehow, the magic takes over. I let each one of my senses work with the other, to take him all in: the rich, moody scent; the wine lingering on his breath; his heartbeat, quick; his mood— want and desire for me; then sort of hidden below all that, a pulse, like energy, like the snap of a flame, warm and fierce, and *alive.*

I pause, sit upright and let out a low breath of awe.

"What? What's that face you're making?"

"I'm not sure. I noticed something. I thought I saw something, like in my mind's eye. Let me try again."

He closes his eyes. Waits.

I start over, this time trying from his head down: the dark, long hair of his, smelling of herbal soap and wilderness and, I realize, hints of me. Note his long black lashes, his handsome face. The white of his shirt, just the top few buttons undone. His warm skin peeking out, inked with several tattoos, his heart thumping below his chest. And there, there it is again, that feeling of energy, and fullness, like gold light, radiating against me. It's small. But strong. I blink, sit back more.

"I…" I start, catching my breath. "Felt something. What is it?"

His eyes are deep, he's almost panting from the intense connection we shared. "I think you felt my soul."

"Oh." I let out a breath, of wonder. Of something else I can't name.

I lean up and kiss his throat, nip at it gently. I barely have time to explore his body or even glance at his own art-covered skin before he lets out a rasp of a breath, lifting me up, scooting me back farther onto the bed, naked, laid out in front of him.

"Not yet." Orrin nestles himself between my legs, leans in and kisses my thighs. I fist my hands into the sheets, and pray he'll keep going. In the candlelight, in my red-curtained bed, his dark head between my white thighs makes me wish I was a painter, that I could immortalize this moment.

He centers himself with a satisfied sigh, tasting me in slow licks, unhurried and patient, as though he has all the time in the world to pleasure me in this way. I go from aroused to almost boneless with desire, feeling him tentatively swirling his tongue. He continues on and on—looking up every now and then to grin wickedly at me—until I think I'll go mad from the need to let go.

"Orrin," I pant, on the verge of exploding. "Please. I need you…I can't."

"You can't?" He sucks now, and I cry out, legs shaking from the pleasure. He pauses long enough to torment me, drawing out each second. "I think you can."

My release is hard, and I freeze, tighten up, call out his name as it undulates down each limb, shaking me in pulsing waves that seem to go on forever. Vision black, I lie there, limp, knees falling together as the pleasure echoes for minutes. Vaguely, I realize he's taken off his clothes, golden body sliding against me. He parts my weak legs, and I stop him with a shake of my head.

"Not yet." I reach between us to stroke the thick heat of him. "I want to touch you first. You're beautiful too, you know."

He throws back his head in pleasure as I slide my hand up and down his velvet skin, jutting toward me. I stare at the beauty of him, his jaw, his cheekbones, his lips, still wet with me. I touch his chest with one hand and keep my other on the rhythmic motion until he shoves it away, tugs me by the hips. My protest that I wanted to taste him too goes unheard. He's ready—we both are.

Caressing me, rubbing me with the hard length of him, he spreads me open as he glides back and forth a bit, not even going inside yet. I whimper, clench my hands into the blankets, and demand that he enter me, words harsh. "Now."

"Don't tell me what to do," he responds with a dark smirk.

Then Orrin pushes in, slow, his face contorted with pleasure. I look up at him, and he down at me, and the rest of the world falls away. He steadies himself, his forehead against mine, and it takes everything in me not to unravel immediately, not only at the shock of rapture from him inside me, but at the vulnerable display of his own. He is patient, letting me adjust, stroking me from the center outward until I explode for the second time. But still, he is not satiated, and in a way, neither am I.

We stare into each other's eyes, lost. Found.

Minutes blur, and once again, I am gone.

TWENTY-THREE

I n the dark of night, moon shining in the windows, Orrin wraps
one black-banded arm around me, caressing the gentle curve
of my soft, warm stomach. For a minute I still, worried that he
will pull away from me, leave to go sleep in his own room. Because
I never expected this, because I know he didn't either. However,
he doesn't leave. Instead, he brushes his warm lips against the
back of my neck, whispers my name once more, gently lifting
me up and turning me onto my knees. I let out a sigh of sleepy
eagerness as he touches me from behind, running his rough hand
between my legs, across my bottom, nudging the slick heat of me
apart in a tantalizingly slow way, bringing me to the brink but
never allowing me to find my release. Not yet.

I lean further forward, onto my elbows, offering myself to him.
I don't tell him this time. But with my prone position, I let him
know he can have me, that he can *take* me. That this time, maybe,
I don't need as much tenderness; he can do what he wishes.

Then Orrin is joined to me, holding my wrists hostage, pushing
my hair aside to kiss the nape of my neck, then grabbing my hips
hard as he pushes forth again and again. The movement teases my
already taut nipples which scrape up against the bedding, my heavy
breasts swinging with each of his deep thrusts. I ache with the need
for him. Even as he is inside me, I ache. He leans forward, bites
the side of my neck, and I find my voice, screaming out his name.
Minutes later, he whispers mine.

The sun shines in my eyes. Throwing one arm over my face, I try to block out the light. Wil—the same handsome boy who'd started off with winks when I passed by the docks at sixteen—used to laugh at me when I grumbled in the morning about bright light or loud noises. I'd sneak onto his ship late at night and spend hours there, as the night faded and brightened into morning, learning how to be a lover. Learning how to be loved.

"You're a nighttime creature, huh?" he'd tease, pulling me in, warm, sticky breath on my neck, wide mouth pulled into a grin. "Not much for mornings, are you?"

I'd crack a smile, for him, say something like, "I can't help it. My eyes hurt."

"Your senses are just stronger." Then he'd pin me under his lanky frame, help me to wake up with the ease of his warm body, which was covered in tattoos, The Pins sailor's symbol on his torso—an anchor with a heart, crossed with three large pins, the words *courage, heart, home*, scrolled across in a banner.

My own skin was free of ink until Wil took me to get the first tattoo—an anchor on my left ankle, not the sailor's one, but a miniature anchor, for him. Then, I wanted more. Each time, Aven would glance at my inked skin, lips pursed. But she never said anything. Mavis had died already, and at that point we were old enough to be on our own, to make our own choices.

Then Wil sailed away for grand adventures I wasn't ready to have, and that was that.

After him, there were a few less sentimental memories. Then came Tanna, who started as my teacher, and then became my lover. My dark beauty, my bright flame. Where Wil had been jovial, laughing, she'd been difficult and abstract, always speaking in poetry, always a riddle for me to figure out. The roses I got after she left. Beautiful, but painful.

I knew loneliness after each of them left my life, after any person I loved went away. Mavis, Wil, Tanna, Darius. Aven. The empty feeling of not having parents. I've known the find and lose, find and lose of each home the three of us girls went to, were kicked out of, were removed from, were thrust into. I've known pain all my life.

But I've also known great love, joy, passion, and hope. When Orrin settles back onto the bed, mattress sinking slightly under his weight, I remember that hope, the same that has carried me through the ordeal of Aven's death and not-death. Somehow, we will get her back. I nestle into his hard body, and I trust.

"Morning," he says low.

I slowly peel open my eyes and turn to him. He's dressed and clean. So beautiful I almost can't stand it. "Morning."

"Breakfast is here, if you're hungry." He gestures to the food laid out on the table.

I wrap a sheet around my nudity, climb out of bed, and walk over with him, where we both sit.

"Last night was…" I begin, shocked to feel a flush creeping along my skin, as if I were some blushing virgin and not a woman of experience. I pour us each a cup of coffee then look back at him.

"It was." Orrin grins roguishly, eyes teasing along my décolleté.

I shake my head at his naughtiness and get to the point. "Tell me what happened while you were gone. The truth. Did you go to kill her?"

"Yes." He takes a drink from his cup, serious now. "But it was foolish. I thought she'd be taken unaware, asleep. I thought I could get past her guards. She never used to be so paranoid, to keep them with her at all times—as we already saw. I didn't realize how difficult it would be to get her alone. In any event, I stumbled upon one of her private parties. I stayed, to make her happy."

"Did you see Aven while you were there?" I hold my breath.

Shaking his head, he says, "No. Not this time."

"And why didn't you tell me the danger to you? Mr. Brown made it seem a whole lot worse than you'd implied."

He hesitates. "Because it's not certain. I'm going off of story, centuries-old rumor. It is a reasonable theory that the connection to my maker might put me at risk, given we've had that connection for so long. I have no proof, but I have to be realistic." When I open my mouth, he adds, "I believe with every fiber of my being, that the newest changed wouldn't be affected. It makes sense, given Elisavet's connection is stronger with those she's been with longer, our souls are entwined, in a way, after so many years. The newest should be safe. I just…cannot promise the same for myself. Elisavet and I sometimes seem to share thoughts at this point. It is not out of the scope of possibility that I might suffer should she."

"Then we won't do it!" I shake my head, stubborn.

"Corliss." A rough whisper. He grabs my hand. Leans down and kisses my knuckles. "Please trust me. I have to do this. I don't *want* to die now that I feel like I'm living again. I'm not being foolhardy, I swear to you. If at any point, I hear something or feel something that changes my mind, I will follow that to a new plan. Do you trust me?"

I sigh. "I do."

Our breakfast sits between us, untouched. He gently releases his hold on me, and I rise from the seat with my coffee in hand. I have to move. Then I turn back to him. "What was it like, when Elisavet took your soul?"

"It…wasn't pleasant." Which isn't exactly an explanation.

I place my hand over my chest, where I'd imagine a soul to live, nestled in there somewhere in the middle—that is where I felt the flicker of his own in his body. "I suppose it hurt."

"It hurt tremendously, although the details are a bit hazy. There was a period of nothing. Emptiness, if you will. When I woke—became aware, that is—I was changed."

"Were you lovers? You alluded to it."

His fingers tighten on his cup. "We were, and we shared many lovers between us, human and non-human alike. But there was no tenderness between us at all."

Hearing that discomfits me, but I push it aside because he looks willing to volunteer more information to me. I recognize the heavy look in his eyes, and step closer.

He speaks, softly, "I made the trade because of a woman. Glisa. I'd hoped to make her my wife." Orrin cracks a bittersweet smile, looking like he's seeing something far off.

"She was a dancer," I guess, taking his hand. This is what he was holding back. "That's who the portrait was of, in the locket. And *that's* why the ballet shoes."

Nodding, he says, "She was. Although not nearly as talented as you. She was quiet, shy. But she had a wicked sense of humor. And such grace. But she was ill, terribly so—fatally, in fact. I hated to see her in pain, and I *did* bargain my soul away for power, but not in the way you probably understood it. In actuality, it was that I wanted the power to save her. I made the trade to save Glisa's life. Me for her."

I hesitate, seeking words to keep my query sensitive. I take my seat again. "I take it things didn't go as planned?"

"No. I traded my soul in order for Glisa to be free from pain, to heal from her illness. But in my despair, I perhaps worded it inadequately. Elisavet took my soul, but she neglected to inform me that she wouldn't be fulfilling the deal in the way I expected. She made it with a loophole, knowing full well she could not complete her side of the bargain. Though she claimed it *was* honorable."

"How?"

"Oh, she said Glisa *was* free from pain, because she was dead. Died while we'd made the trade. And she'd died alone because I was with Elisavet, bargaining for her. Elisavet knew the whole time."

Rage fills me on his behalf. "That monster. What did you do?"

"Nothing. First because I literally couldn't even think straight—didn't *care*." Bitterness taints his words, his body stiffens as he recounts, "Once I realized what had happened, woke from the fog, so to speak, I wanted to die, in that moment. I was bereft, but at the same time, I was filled with enough rage to keep me alive, and to keep me from doing anything stupid. I knew I couldn't do anything. I knew even then how turning on her would go. On my first night I saw someone try. Elisavet obliterated him. I won't describe it to you, that's how gruesome it was. And, perhaps selfishly, I wanted to survive. I shouldn't have cared, after what she had done to Glisa. But I did, in a way, and the rage never left me. Still, I learned to hide it."

"And the slippers?" I gaze over at them, placed on the velvet stool of my dressing table. Blood-red. Powerful. Beautiful and horrid all at once. Like Elisavet. "I take it they were Glisa's?"

"They were, barely worn. She'd been too ill to even dance the last year of her life. Elisavet gave them to me to taunt me, mock me—and Glisa's memory. I could never bear to part with such a petty gift, but I also *couldn't*—though she never stated so, I presume Elisavet enchanted them as a symbol of our trade. When you took them, it pulled at me. It hurt, like the rest of my soul was being ripped out. I think, given enough time, I would have died without them near me. I was dying. Each minute they were away from me. But I was still curious enough about you—and angry enough—to wait it out."

"To fuck with me," I say, before I can help it, thinking of the bird woman and everything else he did to torment me.

He smiles, a little abashedly. "Yes, perhaps. Although I did like watching you, even then. Even in another form." When I narrow my eyes, suspicious, he adds, "I can change forms, briefly. I'm fond of crows, in case you didn't notice."

"Oh." I'm momentarily speechless, recalling the bird perched outside the dress shop.

"I do apologize, though, for scaring you." Leaning across the small table, his lips brush mine. "I am sorry for so much. Sometimes it's too overwhelming, thinking of the things I've done since I traded my soul. How much humanity left me, and how for so long, I became a beast. And I liked it. Not because I *did* like it, but because the alternative—the truth—was far too painful, if that makes sense. Even when I tried to run from Elisavet, to be normal, she chased me down. It made wanting anything different, or anything good, hurt. That included you."

"I rather wish I hadn't hated you so much," I say, a touch bashfully.

"I never hated you."

I scoff. "Liar."

"I didn't. When I discovered the shoes were gone, I was too perplexed—then stunned—to be irate. I was incredulous that they were stolen from beneath my bed!" He laughs lightly. Then grows serious, thoughtful. "When I discovered you—dancing in them, that fevered look on your face, I was consumed, fascinated. That's why I watched you. Why I followed you. A slip of a woman, audacious enough to steal from me, brazen enough to dance her way down the streets, beautiful enough to shock my senses. I hated that I felt that way. But, despite all appearances to the contrary, I never hated *you*. You drove me absolutely fucking crazy—that wet chemise, that face." He swallows, desire darkening his eyes even more intensely. "I hated that I wanted you. I never hated *you*, even if I was an 'unfathomable bastard' most of the time."

"Thank you for telling me that." I kiss him in return this time, then sit back, thinking. After a moment of reflection, I change the topic. "So, what do you think she offered Aven? Do you think it's another trick, like what she did to you?"

"What would Aven want? Power? Wealth?" As I shake my head, he pauses. "Tell me about her?"

He asks with so much gentleness, I explain, briefly, about what happened to her. "Her husband died at sea—though he was never recovered. He was a sailor, his whole ship went down. Everyone dead."

Orrin winces but gives me space and quiet to go on.

I continue, "She was due to give birth within less than two months when we heard the news. She suffered a stillbirth instead, just days after Darius died." I blink the tears away. I can't recount it without emotion. It still hurts *me* too much. What must it have been like for her?

"Sometimes people trade the pain away. To forget," he says, taking the white napkin and dabbing away the tears from my cheek, bringing my small hand into his large one, the rose on the back as black as his eyes. He pulls my palm to his lips, kissing it gently. Tenderly.

I don't ask if Aven has a token of her trade like he has the slippers. I'm not sure I want to know any more. I'm not sure I have the strength. Understanding this, Orrin rises from his seat and tugs me into his arms.

Beholding my face, he smooths my hair at my temples. Kisses me there, on my nose, on each cheek, trailing his lips up and down my neck. He does not disturb the sheet around my body. This is not a seduction but a comforting. "Corliss, I did not expect this. I did not plan it nor ever think it would happen—much as I may have secretly craved the feel of you. But I don't want to lose myself again. I have to do this—beat Elisavet or stay in her grasp for the rest of my days—and I have no doubt she would be responsible for the end of me, eventually. I know it now—the realization I've been putting off for years. I *have* to kill her. It is the only thing that will free me, one way or another. And you must understand—it is the only way to free your sister. I am confident she'll be unscathed. As for me? I'm willing to accept the consequence—my very life—if it goes wrong."

No amount of arguing will change his mind. Much as I don't want to move forward, he's right. Elisavet must die.

Sighing into his arms, I accept this truth and push aside the apprehension. One way or another. His soul is freed…or he dies? Yet I accept this is how it has to be. We have no other ideas. I pray this is the right thing to do. "You'll kill her, and we'll win." I tip my chin up and search his face. "Won't we?"

Orrin nods. "At the next party, I'll sink my knife into her heart. I don't know how, but I'll make it happen. You have my word."

His eyes are darker than dark. I think they are darker than ever before. But I imagine rage there. Fear. Doubt. Mirroring my own. When he leans down to kiss me once more, I think perhaps there's something else there, but he turns away before I can decipher it.

Each morning I rise, resigned to just how dangerous Orrin's plan is. To kill Elisavet in front of a crowd of people. To get away with it, not just Orrin's life, but the remainder of his soul, and Aven's too. And each night, I fall into bed, sick with worry. Besides, what if a knife to the heart doesn't kill Elisavet? What if she's too powerful? He was shot in the stomach and survived. What if she can survive an attack to her heart? Even one that would end any other creature?

I stop myself from talking him out of it. I don't stop the doubts I have. The urge I have to *do* something to help.

"I hate this." I pick at the bedsheets with a grumpy sigh as I recline on him, in the crook of his arm, his face so shadowed in the dark of night I can hardly make him out, even with my *gift*. "I just wish I could see Aven, to speak with her. Perhaps, somehow, if I spark some sort of recognition within her, it'll help. I wonder if I could change her on my own."

"I don't know." I imagine him frowning. "But we can't do anything about it now."

"I know." I sigh, leaning into him, feeling helpless.

In answer, he kisses me. Somehow, like the red slippers, his magic on me renders my worries null and void. Everything melts away. There is only him and me. Tonight, in his room instead of my own—we've been alternating. Making love every evening, often each morning.

Only now, just when things are getting interesting, a knock on his door. I push up.

"Mr. Brown," I whisper to Orrin.

He rises and goes to the door. "Yes?"

"A message for you. A messenger, I mean. From *her*. For you both."

I get out of the bed, glad I'm still dressed. "What should I do?"

"Come on," Orrin says, and slips his hand into mine. "Let's see what the message is."

We go down the grand staircase and into the main sitting room, where the messenger waits in the dimly lit room, just one candle flickering. She's standing, back to us. A deep red gown the color of garnets, braiding all along the sleeves and hem. Thick, dark hair falling down to the small of her back. She turns, and my breath catches. Sapphire eyes turned obsidian, whites gone black as the night outside.

Aven.

A breath escapes me; I step forward, but Orrin places a swift warning hand on my shoulder. I meet his eyes, understanding. Steadying my heart, I inhale and stay where I stand, just in front of Mr. Brown, who is waiting in the hall, stationed still as a statue. I, on the other hand, tremble. Seeing Aven, like this, so close, and without Elisavet hovering in the shadows. If only I could reach her, her memory, her heart. Remind her of our love for each other. All the years of laughter, of joy. The way she took care of Sélie and me for so long. Tell her all the things, all the memories, all the details. That she hates peas. That her favorite color is blue. Her favorite flower a daisy. That she hums while she's hemming. That she can't dance at all—but doesn't care a fig—and even if she's clumsy in her attempts, her face lights up when she moves so that nobody even notices she's off-beat. Her smile could save lives. She loved her husband fiercely. She loved their baby. I would tell her that she was the glue that kept our family together. Even when our parents died. Even when our guardians left us. Hated us. Thought we were burdens. That she protected us. Always wanted us to be safe. Happy. Loved. That she was—is—the most wonderful sister, the greatest friend. That I wish—

"What can I do for you?" Orrin jolts me from my thoughts, asking her, smoothly, "You have a message from her highness?"

Aven nods stiffly. "She's decided to have another grand party, on the full moon next. She is far too busy so sent me to offer her invitation."

I just stare at her. There is nothing of Aven here, not in manner, not in speech, not in appearance. Where is the one who dug splinters from my skin? Who scolded me for spilling beetroot powder? Who wore a daisy crown for her wedding, cried to God that she was the happiest woman in the world? Her soul—her life force—is *gone*. Extinguished. And the strength and purity of it is what gives Elisavet her power. As if she needed any more.

"Sounds wonderful. I'll be there," Orrin tells my sister.

"You're to bring your pet too." Aven doesn't even look at me when she says it.

With a benign smile, he says, "Of course."

When Aven sweeps from the room, I follow her, consequences and Orrin's advice be damned. I run after her to the foyer.

"Wait," I call, breathless, just as Aven reaches for the doorknob. She turns, tightens her mouth. "What?"

I swallow, sense Orrin approaching, know what I'm doing is unwise, perhaps, but I can't help it. "Aven, it's *me*. Corliss. Don't you remember? Don't you—"

"I remember you," she interrupts, coolly.

I stare at her in shock. There is nothing there. *Nothing.*

Then she gives a half-shrug to me, to Orrin, who has come up behind me. She steps outside the door, and with it still hanging open, in a whoosh of magic, is swallowed by the night.

My sister is gone. There is nothing of her left.

"Come on," Orrin says in a gentle voice. "Let's go upstairs."

Nodding, I bite back the tears. All the way back to his bedroom, I keep thinking of Aven's cold eyes, the way she looked at me. Like *I* was nothing. I know Orrin warned me of this—told me her humanity would probably be gone. That she wouldn't care at all. But it still hurts.

Once we're back in his room, Orrin holds me again, nestling us into the bed.

"I'm sorry. I never should have said anything to her. Do you think Elisavet knows she's my sister?" I finally manage to ask. "And that's why she sent her here?"

"I don't think Aven cares enough to tell her," he answers carefully, like he's trying not to hurt me. It does sting to hear him say it, but I nod. The fact she doesn't care for me at all makes me think she wouldn't even think to bother mentioning it to her queen. He goes on, reassuring me, "Elisavet always has others run her little errands. I'm not that concerned, so try not to worry. It won't be long now, and it will be over."

"What if we do it before the party?" I ask. "I hate the idea of waiting, and won't it be safer for you if she's alone?"

"She's never alone," he says grimly. "Which I was reminded of the other night. And I think the more people there, the less guarded she is, actually. Only a fool would dare to attempt to harm her in that sort of situation. It will catch her off guard because she'd never expect me to be a fool."

"And she won't expect you to harm her," I add.

"Right. Only I won't *attempt* to. I will. Please, don't fret. I swear to you, I'll be careful. And I'll do everything in my power to make certain Aven is safe and returned to you, whole."

I bury my face into him, closing my eyes. Soon, one way or another, this torment will be over. Though there've been things beyond torment, of course. There's been us, whatever it is we've shared. I don't want to lose that. I don't want to lose him.

I want you to return to me too.

I tug him down, pull his lips to mine.

He responds by gripping me to him, as though he can't stand to let me go. I don't say it aloud, but I feel the same.

Chapter Twenty-Four

In anticipation of the party, Orrin and I settle into a routine. In the mornings, we wake together, whether in his bed or mine. We eat breakfast, then spend the day together or apart. If apart, he trains with Mr. Brown, practicing his fighting, though I wonder if it's simply a way for him to channel his energy because how much better can he get? Still, I worry he won't be good enough, even though he's had over a century to hone his skill, give or take a few decades—I'm not entirely sure how old he is, come to think of it. I only hope that if it comes down to a physical struggle that he can best Elisavet's brawny guards. My anxiety tells me that she is unbeatable, that we're fools to even try. To distract myself, I read or flip through Sélie's drawing pad, even though I think I've memorized each sketch. There are several portraits of Pearl, which lead me to think, rather gratefully, that she's joined Sélie at the shop, that they've become friends—which means my sister isn't alone after all.

And I practice my dancing, pushing so hard I astound even myself. I count down the hours until I can be with Orrin again each day.

As we spend time together, the stories of our lives unfold naturally. A beautiful comfort develops.

Splayed across Orrin's lower body, my chin on his thigh, I stroke his skin absentmindedly as the morning dawns; it's been about a week since Aven came here.

I say, glimpsing the book on his side table, the spine stamped in gold with one word: Lowell, "I forgot you had books in here, that you like to read too. What is that one about?"

"It's poetry."

"Poetry? You continue to surprise me, Orrin."

"Do I?" he muses, fingers tenderly playing in my hair. He waits a beat, then his sleepy voice starts:

"Hold your soul open for my welcoming.
Let the quiet of your spirit bathe me...
Let the flickering flame of your soul play all about me,
That into my limbs may come the keenness of fire,
The life and joy of tongues of flame,
And, going out from you, tightly strung and in tune,
I may rouse the blear-eyed world,
And pour into it the beauty which you have begotten."

He finishes reciting, his hand pausing in my waves.

We don't say anything for a few moments.

"I love that," I tell him. "I didn't know you liked poetry."

"I like that one," he answers, meeting my eyes. A hint of nervousness comes over me, and I look down, uncertain what to reply. I move my fingertips along his nude body, finding my own form of poetry in the tenderness of touch.

When I graze his navel, he sucks in a sharp breath.

I look up, smiling innocently. "Ticklish?"

"You could say that."

"I wouldn't think you would be." I run my fingers along the tattoos on his torso, getting a proper glance at them in the light. I don't know why I haven't studied them before. Maybe because we've been so hurried. So full of heat, and mostly making love at night, in the dim light of candles, or in the sleepy haze of morning, barely coherent.

"You have a soft touch, despite your sharp tongue," he says sternly, a playful glint in his black gaze. He unabashedly admires my nakedness.

One tattoo catches my eye, and I pause my seduction, looking up at him in surprise. "A Pins anchor?" It's the same one Wil had, and Darius too—an anchor with a heart, struck through with three pins, the banner cut across it: *courage, heart, home.*

Orrin says, musing, "I was a sailor. In The Pins. I grew up here."

I don't even attempt to hide my shock. "When?"

"About a thousand years ago."

I sit up, gaping at him. "Really? That old?"

He laughs, reaching over to pinch my plump backside. "No."

"How old are you?" I study his handsome face with curiosity, his dark hair, his lean, beautiful body. "You don't look old."

"I was twenty-eight when I changed—not much more than you are now. And now I'm one hundred and…fifty-two, but only just."

"Oh," I say faintly. "Well, I'm sorry I didn't get you a gift."

He dances his fingers over my collarbone, down to my breasts. "You did." Then he pulls me up to sit astride him, my full thighs on either side of his hard, naked body. "Now give it to me again."

"Did you live in this house when you were here before, as a human, I mean?" I ask as we wander the grounds a few days later, passing the fountain. My new cloak flutters in the breeze, as deep green, as rich as a summer forest. It is fall in the here and now, though. The leaves have been changing, turning brilliant red in spots, tarnished gold in others. The air is cool as it whistles through the trees. If I'm not mistaken, I think I notice a squirrel perched on one branch. It's gone before I look back at it. "You are a Colehart."

Orrin shakes his head. "I am, but no, I never lived here as a human. It belonged to other Coleharts, distant family. I was poor. I lived near the docks when I was a boy, with my mother, whose family was still in the East. I grew up with boats. The ocean was practically my father."

"Where was your real father?"

"He died when I was a baby. Lost at sea."

"The sea takes a lot of people." I think about Darius.

I squeeze Orrin's hand and will him to speak so I don't have to. He takes my hint, nodding in sympathy. If anyone would under-stand it would be a former sailor. "It does. But I missed it. I've moved a lot and not always near the ocean."

"Moved to be with Elisavet?"

"Sometimes following her, yes." A wry smile. "Sometimes run-ning from her, as I told you. Such was the case in the last few decades."

"Did you have friends there in the court? Not just lovers?"

"Many. But not like Glisa. Not like you." He looks off in the distance, at the sky. His tight inhalation of breath tells me he is not sure he should have said that. There's still a way he holds back from me.

He pulls me into the abandoned greenhouse, one of the few parts of the grounds I have yet to explore. It is thick with heat and the wilted green smells of herbs, dried flowers, mildewed soil, heavy, however still pleasant.

I lean into his side as we stroll through the greenhouse. "You should fix this up," I say. I pause to lift a scraggly vine between my fingers. I release it to pick up a small pot with a dead flower, dried and brown in the middle.

"You think?"

"It makes me melancholy, seeing this place. It could be really beautiful." I look up, and in an instant, the greenhouse trans-forms. Instead of the broken, dirty panes in the windows, light streams through sparkling glass. Instead of wilted greens, forgotten flowers, and the hint of decay, everything is green, healthy, lush. The pot in my hand contains a fully bloomed dahlia, petals pink as a sunset.

"Oh!" I blink. Then it is all gone. I stare at Orrin. "What was that?"

He shrugs, but a smile tilts one side of his mouth. "Nothing, only a parlor trick."

"What else can you do besides parlor tricks? Can you really bring people back from the dead? You never actually said."

"Theoretically, I believe so, except it's a messy art, playing with death, and I'm not sure even Elisavet knows how to fully do it. She may have mastered the art of cheating it, leaning into immortality…but reversing it? I don't know that it's something she would do a trade for, to be frank."

"Then she probably wouldn't have told Aven she could have her husband and baby back?"

"I doubt it." He shakes his head. "Death is best left alone, even for our kind."

"What is it like, do you think? Is there a heaven and hell?" I ask him.

"I'm still not sure. Probably darkness, nothing. Until we return again. I believe our souls live many lives. Some of us more than others."

"I've always been curious about that. Living again," I say. "I believe so too. But I do like the idea of heaven as well."

"I know. Though I think heaven can exist on earth sometimes." His eyes hold mine.

Suddenly shy, I set the pot with the pitiful flower down where I found it, and we keep walking. "You should find a gardener."

"A level of anonymity has kept me secure, not to mention the fewer staff, the less work for me to manipulate their…understanding of me. But, for you, I will find someone, whether local or not. Do you know anyone good with plants and flowers?"

Voice soft, I say, "Aven."

Bittersweetly, I remember her tending her lavender and her roses and her lilies. Her strawberries and herbs for our apothecary. Remembering her barefoot in the garden Mavis started so many years ago. Remembering her bringing bundles of flowers into the cottage, setting them on the table with a broad smile, so pleased with herself, with the world itself.

Orrin stops walking to wrap his arms around me. "Then I will ask. After we rescue her, when she's feeling better. She can bring this broken place back to life, as you have done for me."

I lean up and kiss him. Words are, as he said before, so inadequate.

Weeks pass by in a breath, and finally it is the afternoon of the full moon. I come to the ballroom to dance, as I have so many times before. Though our relationship has taken on a completely different form than how it started, enemies turned to allies turned to lovers, I've kept dancing. It brings us both comfort, a routine he appreciates for the entertainment and the beauty, and for me, the act of dancing itself. I use the red and pink slippers interchangeably now.

Orrin has been wild all day, pacing and desperate, but when he takes his seat in front of me, he visibly relaxes, waiting for me to move for him. I'm grateful for the chance to ease his anxiety.

I go slow, taking tiny steps across the floor in the red shoes. I twirl then lift my arms gracefully in attitude, holding each pose just so. Taking the ache of my heart along with the steps. Because this can't be *it*. Because I don't want it to be. But also, because I'm not a fool.

It's a long routine, unplanned, but somehow perfect. I see it on Orrin's beautiful face as he watches me, and I think, maybe, in this moment, he is truly happy. That his soul is happy.

Something within me breaks open and I could weep, even as I spin.

He is not so much a demon as a broken spirit. I do not seek to fix what is broken, and I never set out to do so. I don't pretend to be his savior. I will, however, allow myself to celebrate what has been salvaged. And I refuse to let it go now.

With a sharp realization, I know the truth behind this dance. The way the slippers tug me toward the movements, as if there's a secret behind it all.

I love him. So I pull all the power from the shoes that I can, to show him, to let him see what I am feeling better than I can say myself. I dance it for him.

I dance for his greatness, his passion, his wicked grin and gentle touch, his words, his truth, his darkness. I dance for his kisses, and his black gaze, and his power, and his weakness. For the piece of his soul I have discovered, that I refuse to surrender. My whole body goes warm, his own seeming to brim with a golden aura, a magical light that makes me ache with its beauty.

Orrin grimaces suddenly, and I drop out of relevé, something snagging at me, sharp and painful.

"What? What'd I do?" I ask in alarm.

Still cringing, he murmurs, "I think you were, um, touching my soul a bit again. Sort of pulling on it or something."

"Oh." I take a step back, the intensity that was blooming in me softening. "I'm sorry. I didn't realize. I didn't mean to hurt you."

"Don't apologize. That was incredible, your dance." Orrin smiles, eyes shining. "Just get over here already."

I don't bother with a curtsey, something that went from a reluctant formality to an impertinent finish over time. I walk over to him, as he sits in the chair at the head of the room, lean down to kiss him before straightening up. He draws his hands up my skirts, yanks my drawers down, reaches for me with greedy fingers. I cast my eyes to the door, where Mr. Brown has already slipped out.

Orrin nods toward the doors and the click of the locks are audible. I raise a brow. "Really?"

"Easy. Another parlor trick."

"Now what?" My breath is a whisper.

Then he makes love with me, in the ballroom, dying sun outside the windows, autumn leaves falling through the sky, leaving the last of the trees bare. I want it to be happy and light, to be centered around passion instead of fear, but there is a heaviness, a desperation to our coupling. Though neither one of us says it aloud, it feels like the last time.

Chapter Twenty-Five

"There's a gift for Ms. Corliss, Sir." Hana comes to interrupt our supper.

I set my fork down while Orrin pushes out of his chair and then walks out of the dining room.

"A gift?" I say.

The maid sort of half-shrugs apologetically before asking if I need anything.

"No, thank you." I give her a smile, hoping she won't see how troubled it is.

Orrin comes back just as she walks out. He carries a large, white box, wrapped in a crimson ribbon, the same shade as the red shoes. I stare at the gift, then back to his hard face. I can smell her.

"Elisavet." He shuts the dining room door behind him. Sets the box on the table.

I cannot say I'm not curious, or frightened. I look up at him once, and he nods. Then I unwrap the package, open the box to reveal a black bodice, dark against the white tissue paper. When I pull it out, I observe how the black bleeds into a deep and brooding red at the scalloped bottom, with ribbons to tie it up and shorten it so it's fit to dance in.

The ballet slippers will match the hem perfectly. I run my fingers along the dress, admiring the craftsmanship. It's made of yards of delicate tulle layered over a satin underskirt; the boned bodice is a deep, narrow plunge, which I imagine would end up diving almost to my navel—so scandalous I gasp, thinking of it cutting down my body, how the demons will stare. Straps the color of my skin would hold the dress up in place, with tiny beads dotting all along it, winking in the light of the dining room. Every eye will be drawn to me in this color, in this dress. Black to red, dark to rich. Almost violently beautiful. It's something Elisavet would wear.

She's also sent a pair of black opera gloves, silk stockings, a velvet choker necklace with a single ruby drop and matching ruby earrings.

Orrin clears his throat, and I turn back to him.

"You don't have to wear this." His soft voice doesn't quite match the anger in his eyes.

"No," I answer, tucking the dress back in the box with one last glance. "She'll expect it. It would be rude not to. I don't want to make her suspicious tonight."

"Yes." His nod is resigned, resentful. He hates her so.

"I guess there's no hiding tonight, not in that dress," I try to joke, putting away the accessories alongside it.

He doesn't laugh. There is nothing humorous about this situation. Nothing.

However, it's just as well I draw attention in this dress. When I dance, I need all eyes on me—so that nobody sees Orrin sneak up on Elisavet. We've already established there's no way to get her alone. At least during the bustle of a party, we can hopefully slip out in the chaotic aftermath of his attack. Hopefully.

We give up the pretense of supper and step away from the dining table with our plates untouched, carry the box upstairs to my room, and leave it on the table. I walk to the open windows to take in the brilliant sunset, to stand there as the cool sky develops its color—the most beautiful sunset I think I've ever seen. Orrin follows me, winds one arm around my waist and I lean into his chest, tuck my head under his chin. Without words, we watch the deepening sky, the saturated colors: gold and lavender and brilliant orange sinking into the horizon. We stand there for long minutes. It doesn't feel long enough.

Then it is time for me to dress. Atop the gown, which only hits a little below my knees, now that I've fastened the ties, I wear my cloak for warmth.

We leave as soon as the sky fills with stars. It is darker than the first time we went, partly because the seasons have shifted from summer to autumn, partly because clouds obstruct most of the full moon. Still, it feels hauntingly familiar. The horses are again hooked in after we enter the carriage. I spread out the skirt of my dress uneasily. There's no sound but our breath, a stillness in us both.

Orrin takes my hand and presses the back of it, gloved, to his lips.

I nod.

The ride is faster than I'd anticipated, with my nerves shot like this. I'd think it would drag, now that we're so close. But it's as quick as a flash, and soon Mr. Brown is muttering a low "whoa" to the horses. Again, he covers the animals' eyes as we leave the carriage together. I have a sudden wistful thought—I would love to saddle up Orrin's beautiful horses one day and ride them across the land together. His soul repaired, his humanity restored. I want it so much that it almost makes me cry.

"Ready?" Orrin nods to Mr. Brown. The horses move nervously at the sound of his voice. They smell of apprehension.

"Yes. I'll be waiting," Mr. Brown says.

I reach out with a gloved hand and stroke one of the horse's velvety noses, trying to steady myself. It breathes against me.

"Alright," Orrin says.

There's an unspoken moment between the two men. Mr. Brown offers me a brief, encouraging smile. I return it, and exhale through pursed lips. My fingers are cold in the flimsy satin gloves, and I tighten them into the folds of my dress to hide how they shake.

Then Orrin turns to me, voice soft, reassuring. "Are you ready?"

"I am." The slippers are already on my feet, grounding me a little, though I still choke down the fear. We have to go in with masks on, acting like all is fine, like we're not afraid. We will lie in wait, for everyone to let their guards down. And then, late into the night, he will take Elisavet down.

His knife hides in his boot. It's honed, silver sharp. He wants to use it. I can sense the impatience in the hand clenched at his side. We walk together, wordlessly.

The only time he speaks is to murmur a low, "Careful," as I step down the steepest rocks.

The ocean air is cold here in the night, even with the cloak. The cave will at least be warmer, with all the demons and people inside…and Aven. Even if hardly anything of my sister remains now, even if she's so lost and desperate that she traded her soul to mend her broken heart. Even if she hates me, or worse, doesn't care at all. Inside, it's still her. The thought gives me courage, and I speed up, ready to get this over with.

Orrin and I make our way across the shallow steps of cool water—he helps me over any that might dampen my slippers, watching eyes be damned—and into the cave. The walls, again, cold, dark. The smells, all the same—or even worse. There's an energy in the air, a sort of crackling nervousness that I sense. I want to tell *him* to be careful. I want to tell him so much. I want to hold him to me, to shut my eyes, to pretend like none of this is real, like he's not in danger at all, like I might not lose him. Only I don't. I step forward into the cave and pray we will step back out later.

This time, when we enter the large, open room, Elisavet is already standing. The music is louder, the guests more intoxicated, uglier in behavior. There's even a fight in one corner between two demons who are actually drawing blood. I look away in disgust.

Elisavet walks past them disdainfully, lips tight as she stalks over to us. "They're restless, Orrin. Please tell me your pet will dance for us later?"

"As you desire," he says in a smooth, rich tone, kissing her hand as he did last time.

She laughs, throwing back her head, drunk with power and wine. "Oh, good!"

I stare at the ropes of pearls wrapped around her throat, at the swell of her high breasts peeking out the top of her bruise-colored gown, which appears to be at least a hundred years old by the style. Her hair is down again. Long, shining. Smelling of jasmine and sweetness, of the salty air and the bloody stone.

I lean into her without meaning to. I *hate* how tempting she is.

Elisavet turns to me with a coy smile. "Good evening."

"Thank you for the dress. It is really lovely," I murmur politely.

She rakes her nails teasingly down the neckline, around the indecently low edge of it, staring at me thoughtfully. "The wearer makes it more so." I am spared forcing a response because she continues, "Have some wine. Food. Enjoy yourselves, both of you. I'll be back later."

I turn to Orrin as Elisavet walks away. My stomach rolls with nerves.

"It's fine," he whispers. "Keep the mask on—stay calm." His expression is pleasant, relaxed. Yet I see the rage which simmers behind that smile. He hates that she touched me. I wonder if he smelled the desire on her as she gazed at me. I swallow the thought uncomfortably.

Nodding quickly, I trail him as he moves. He smiles, greeting half a dozen beings, all in various stages of intoxication, undress, and play.

There's dancing again. A pair of demons take the stage, falling over in giggles as they wind in and out of each other's arms. The music plays harder tonight, more insistent. The hollow-eyed harpist doesn't even look up. Upon closer inspection, I glimpse broken skin on her fingers, as though she's been playing the last month straight. I choke down a gasp and speed up to keep pace with Orrin. I am careful to sidestep the demon sprawled across the stone floor, willing my feet and eyes to stay steady. I try not to stare at the desperate human woman who strokes a demon between his legs as he plays a game of cards with three others. He reaches out, smacking her face hard, but her hand never stops, not even when blood runs from her nose. She runs her tongue across her upper lip, tasting it away.

Choking down a mix of pity and revulsion, I keep moving, pausing when Orrin does, always staying back a couple feet, trying to look submissive, head bowed. I take a goblet when he offers it to me, but I do not drink, as planned. He grows bolder as the night wears on, clapping his cohorts on the shoulder, jesting with them as if he's at ease, flirting like a rake, as if he's getting drunk and comfortable. Only I know he's not.

When he throws back his head and laughs, the way his face catches the light has me breathless. He looks so young, it's easy to see what he once was, what he could have been, if Elisavet hadn't stolen it from him. I envision him with white threaded through his black hair, and something in me yearns to see it manifest.

I despise her with every fiber of my being. If he weren't going to kill her, I'd like to tear her apart myself. If only I could!

Elisavet is at the head of the room, seated on her throne, drinking from one of her goblets as a human servant rubs her calves and thighs, massaging them with oil. She meets my gaze, lifts one eyebrow and doesn't look away until someone obstructs her view, crossing in front of her.

But where is my sister? I sense Aven, I do. But I need her visible, in my sight line, and preferably, near the door, so that when Orrin strikes, she will be easy for me to get to. Because when he kills Elisavet, there may be chaos, violence. I need to keep her safe. I squeeze my shaking, human hands into the folds of my tulle skirt. I wait.

As hours pass, the rowdiness picks up. The demons are cruder than they were at the last party, in manner, in spirit. At last, Aven appears, wearing a gown the color of fresh snow, silver bracelets snaking up her arms, a delicate circlet of diamonds upon her head, ruby-red lips and lids shaded and smoky, looking like an angel of death. I can hardly keep my eyes off her, though it's obvious she doesn't care that I'm here. I stand, miserably, waiting to dance. To get this charade over with. The other demons keep me fairly distracted. But their antics irritate Elisavet, it seems.

Her eyes flash with annoyance, all signs of her easy manner gone when she motions me over. "Get ready. It's time. We need some entertainment. Everyone is getting bored."

Again, two of her servants take me to a room to warm up my muscles. They do not speak to me, and this time I don't speak to them either. There's no point. They're too weak to even ask for help, let alone help me.

They wait outside the room, a bedroom of sorts. I can smell Elisavet in here, on the white blankets laid over the cold floor, in the sheer curtains that give it a degree of privacy. I twist my mouth, imagining her lying in here, tangled up in lovers, in death.

I let out a low breath of despair and vaguely warm my muscles without caring. I can't cry now. It is time to perform. I have to be amazing. I need to awe them all. Orrin's safety depends on it.

The silent servants gesture at me from beyond the curtain, and I follow them back into the main room. The demons slumped around the room don't even wake with Elisavet's piercing voice as she orders everyone to quiet down, to clear the floor for me. The rest of them stare at me, waiting. It's so silent, I can hear the drip of water, the ocean outside lapping at the shore, the breathing of each demon. I don't look at Aven.

"Before she begins," Elisavet states, voice thundering in the cave, "I hope you will all once again welcome our favorite dancer!"

Many of the demons clap or whistle, a few look hungrily at me as though starving for some kind of brutal pleasure...or brutal pain. The rest sit, nursing their wine, smoking from golden pipes, disappearing and reappearing in a thick haze of sweet smoke that stings my eyes.

Elisavet claps the longest of all, the sound grating my ears. Her eyes dig into mine. "And now, a gift for you, little pet, for regaling us with your talent. From one of our newest members."

She snaps her fingers, and out of the back of the cave comes Aven, blue gaze gone dull and black. She carries a tray, and on it, a single rose lays. Not red, like my shoes, like the ones thrown on stage at the Clover, not pink, my favorite, nor yellow, but white. Bone white.

Aven crosses the floor toward me, same expression as last time she looked at me. She says methodically, "A gift for you, from Her Majesty."

My heart goes cold. I jerk my eyes to Orrin, who slinks closer to Elisavet, casually. Goblet in hand. Knife hidden. Just beyond him, Elisavet sits. Watching me, darkly, waiting. She *knows*. She has to know what Aven is to me. Still, I pretend, just in case. There is too much riding on this act.

Looking back at my sister, I take the rose with trembling fingers. "Thank you, it's beautiful," I manage in a whisper. I want to scream. I want to grab her by the wrist and run, whether she's willing or not. Aven steps away, turns her back to me.

"A beautiful flower, though it's hardly enough, given your performance." Elisavet smiles when I look back at her, trying to gauge her tone, her meaning.

I attempt an innocent expression. "Thank you. I'm glad you liked my dancing last time. I hope you will again this evening."

"The dancing?" Elisavet strokes the arms of her stone seat. "Dancing. Hmmm."

I don't reply. Just beyond, Orrin lies in wait, taking silent steps in the shadows, toward her throne. Nobody else seems to notice. All focus on me, on Elisavet, even the demons who were lazing around, intoxicated, seem to perk up. They sense the tension. It's sharp, obvious. I taste it in my mouth, coppery, a burning on my tongue, stifling my cries. I want to tell Orrin no, not now, the moment is not right. I want to shriek and run and run and run away, hand in hand with him, with Aven. I move closer to her, and she turns to face me, sensing me. Her eyes empty.

Elisavet plays with her pearl necklace thoughtfully. "Do you know, there was something about you that drew me in, little dancer? When I first saw you, I was quite taken with you, you know. But there was a familiarity about you. Now, I quite feel silly for not realizing."

I don't reply, only hold the rose so tight the thorns gouge into my skin. Hana and Jinny appear more like sisters than Aven and I do, at least if you don't look closely…as far as coloring and build and personality, but she must know. There's enough about us that is the same.

She goes on, "A couple of months ago, I came across a desperate soul. The want in her was powerful enough to draw me from a dead sleep." Elisavet casts her eyes to find Orrin, who freezes just in time, sipping his goblet casually, leaning against the stone wall. The knife behind his back, visible, I hope, to no one. "As fate would have it, I'd only just arrived, to follow my most faithful friend. In any event, she was so desperate, she would have given anything for me to take away her pain.

"You see, this woman had lost both her husband and her child, a baby boy." Elisavet sneers, and I resist the urge to reach across the room and strangle her as Aven's hollow eyes flare with something that resembles pain.

Could she be remembering?

The way my tiny nephew slid warm and motionless into my bloody hands as I lifted him from Aven's body, then buried him for her in the garden behind the house. While I sobbed, digging out a rectangle of dirt, she lay there in her marriage bed, numb, and poor Sélie wept in the back room as she washed the sheets then ended up tossing them in the fire when she couldn't get the stains out.

Aven must remember some of it. Must remember losing Darius. That day was her real death.

Elisavet continues, "Being a merciful queen, I took her in, allowed her the space to make her deal. Put her to work in the meantime, because nothing is free, of course."

Across the room, in the shadows, Orrin gets closer to Elisavet's throne. *Do it*, I think frantically. *Do it now.*

"Imagine my foolish surprise," Elisavet says in a sickly sweet voice, "when I discovered she was the sister of the same dancer I'd come to admire so very much, whom I had invited to my home, whom I had welcomed amongst my family."

I open my mouth to protest but her sharp eyes snap to me. "I know you asked about her at the last party. My servants are my eyes and ears, and extremely loyal to me. It didn't take long to figure out why or to confirm it with your sister."

What have I done? I look desperately at Aven, but she stares resolutely ahead. Away from me.

"Humans are such stupid, spineless beings," Elisavet says. "I know there is one of my own behind this deception. Someone who knew that we had a *very* coincidental connection among one of my new members and their captive. Someone who knew that it wasn't coincidental at all. And I would very much like to know why you didn't tell me you were up to something...Orrin."

Before I can deny his involvement, two demons step out of the shadows and grab him, ripping the knife from his hand. He struggles but the bigger demon squeezes him tighter—the same demon who tried to run into me last time. I step forward, panicked, before Orrin freezes me with a short shake of his head.

The second, older-looking demon brings the knife up to Orrin's face, and I swallow a scream as he drags the blade from temple to jaw. Both brutes grin, mean, as the blood runs down Orrin's face. It's not deep, just enough to bleed. To scar.

I hold my mask. I stare into my love's eyes, forcing myself not to run to him, to shove them away from him, to fight for his life.

Although he is seething with rage, his eyes also hold a note of reassurance, even now. *I'm alright*, they say to me. *Stay still.*

Elisavet laughs a vile laugh. "Did you really think you'd stick a knife in me, Orrin?"

His teeth glint in a sharp smile. "I damn well hoped so."

She gives him a wounded look as she rises from her seat and wanders closer to him, tsking. "After so long together? More than a century. Do you know what it is to be betrayed thusly?"

He doesn't reply, but I doubt she expects him to. He only stares, bleeding jaw tight, a muscle in it ticking.

She points to another demon, one waiting by the entrance. "Bring him in."

A few moments of confusion later, and the demon returns with a human man, grappling against his hold, bloodied at both temples, one eye already swelling purple. The shock of red matting his snow-white hair. Mr. Brown.

"No," I whisper. *Don't hurt him.*

The demon man jerks him to the center of the room, just feet from me, so that he stands in between Elisavet and me. Mr. Brown gives me one stricken glance then stares at his boots. Orrin's eyes are raging as Elisavet spins and walks over to pause right in front of him. Only a few inches, only one motion away, and Orrin could end her, if only he had his knife. Parlor tricks, magic, what good is it all? Can't he do something? Can't Orrin make them let him go? I watch, breath spastic. I can't watch. If she does something to him…

Elisavet holds out her elegant hand and one of the demons manhandling Orrin passes over the knife. She turns the weapon over in her palm considering the blade. "It is so very difficult to lose those you love and trust. It *really* hurts, Orrin, my darling. Don't you know that?"

No. No. No, I pray. *No.* If she kills Orrin, I will lose my mind.

But she turns away from him, and I let out a sharp breath of relief, before realizing she's headed back in our direction—Aven's, mine, Mr. Brown's…

"Hello, Rupert." She smiles at him. Without another word, Elisavet plunges the knife into his throat and jerks it across.

I vaguely register Orrin's roar as the spray of hot blood floods Mr. Brown's clothes, then mine, then Aven's. I grab my sister and yank her down, despite her resistance, dropping to my knees. I shut my eyes, squeeze out the image, the surprise in Mr. Brown's eyes, the sound of his body thumping on the hard, stone floor, the last gurgle erupting from him. The demon laughter rings in my ears. They think this is funny, most of them. They think it's *funny*.

Aven struggles to stand back up. Glaring at me, she mouths, "Let me go."

"No," I whisper, gripping her with all my might. "I love you, Aven."

"Poor man," Elisavet says sadly, theatrically loud. "It's hard losing anyone, isn't it, Orrin? Especially such a loyal servant."

I tip up my face from our crouched position to watch the way she circles the room, and ultimately, me and Aven, at its center. The way Orrin's knife is still gripped in her hand. I can't breathe. I can't think.

"Don't you touch her!" he spits at Elisavet. She only throws back her head, a mean laugh erupting from her.

He is fighting now, to get out of the demons' grip, to save me. *No.* I shake my head at him, the same way he did to me. *They'll hurt you more.*

My movement draws Elisavet's attention. She stares over at me. "I do not like people trying to take what is mine."

"I don't either." I lift my chin. "I will *kill* you before I give up my sister, you soulless, evil bitch."

"Such hatred." Her light brows rise. "That surprises me."

"Of course it does. You don't know how you've hurt me or anyone else. You don't care."

"Oh, my. Do you even know what it is to really hurt?" she asks, still stalking me like I am prey. "Do you know what it is to be so desperate you rip out your own soul?"

"So you made yourself into a monster?" I taunt, turning to keep her in my sights.

She scoffs. "A monster? Everything I had was taken from me. I became a pioneer. Nobody else has done what I have. Every other queen was made by another. Only I made myself. Birthed myself. I am my own mother, a goddess, a god, a king."

Her heels click on the floor as she walks, the tightness in the air increasing. All eyes are on her as she moves, telling her story. "Centuries ago, my village was at war. My people lost, and my family was trapped in a church, burnt alive by soldiers, a group of men so inhumane they listened to the screams of people turning to ash and did nothing but laugh. Only I was spared, so they could each take a turn with me."

I squeeze Aven harder. She eases, settling beneath me. I count her breaths, count my own. I find Orrin. Then look back to Elisavet.

"In the empty days later, while they left me to bleed out from the injuries I'd sustained," she continues, "I took my own humanity, ripping away my soul. I turned myself, the first to turn on their own. I am made by rage alone. I have given the gift over and over to those who couldn't do it themselves. You see, people seek power. They want to forget the agony of being human, and I give that to them. I can give them revenge too, if they desire. Like how I had revenge on those men, on their sons, on their daughters. I watched them burn, all of them, and I danced in their ashes and spit on their bones."

What she's been through turns me inside out, because she didn't deserve such cruelty, and I can't help crying. "You were hurt so much, but why would you do the terrible things you do? Why would you take my sister from me?"

"I didn't *take* her. I took her in. I took away her pain too."

"Like you took away Glisa's?" I counter. Because no matter what Elisavet's been through, she's no innocent. The slippers seem to pulse on my feet.

Elisavet waves a hand, smirking in Orrin's direction. "That was a shame, wasn't it?"

He yanks forward, snarling. The brutish demon struggles but manages to hold him.

"Aven's mine," Elisavet says. "And whatever plan you and Orrin were enacting is not going to work. Besides, dear pet, I'm not afraid of you. Either of you."

Truth. I hear it in her voice. And now that she knows I mean something to him, she's going to make me pay. Make us both pay.

"I have big plans for you, and Orrin over there. The things I'm going to do to you both!" Elisavet warns me, eyes flashing. She steps over Mr. Brown's body. "That man's death was so quick, so very unlike what yours will be. So stand, now."

I listen, and somehow, I forget to be afraid. I rise with stable legs, and my breath steadies. Elisavet is no match for my love.

"Come." She motions to the demons holding Orrin to bring him to her. Then she beckons to me. "It's time to teach you a lesson."

"Yes." I nod. "But after I dance. That's why you invited me, isn't it? One final dance to entertain your guests?" I only have one plan, one stupid, impossible idea. I don't look at Orrin as I ask.

She waves me on, handing the bloody knife back to one of her burly guards before taking a seat once more on her throne. "I'm generous. Go on then. One dance because it would please *me*, and then you're done. And I do mean done."

At the cold finality of her words, I take a breath. Then I rise up on my toes, and I begin dancing. I tip forward, allowing my bust to push against the barely-there bodice, and I slowly tangle my arms up in the air, letting my hands reach. Elisavet's sardonic laugh, the demons murmuring around me, the jeers and the emptiness alike. Orrin's silence. It's all too much.

But I keep moving, feeling my body, letting the enchanted slippers lead me.

Elisavet's soul, they seem to cry.

I dance through the confusion, Elisavet's features blurring as I move: delicate yet sharpened face, lips pulled into a mocking smile, her black eyes, her gown and jewels. Her scent envelops me even from afar: jasmine, red wine, blood sprayed down her front, speckling her skin, the scent of hate and emptiness. Though it's not only her body, her face I sense. It's her soul—pulsing energy, a sliver, much smaller than Orrin's, but ten times as strong, as stubborn, tied to the cave, to the sea, to the dark of the night and the power of the moon, as old as five centuries, as lost as any lost soul. She ripped most of it out, from rage and pain, but there's enough left for me to sense it. But only barely.

It is hidden, protected.

Try as I might to narrow in on hers, focusing on what is left, I cannot touch it. I cannot reach it. Whether on purpose—most likely—or accidentally, she has surrounded it with the souls she's taken.

So what can I do?

The answer comes to me, unbidden. It's a risk—but it might be the only thing that works. The flurry of pulsing energy enveloping her lifeforce tells me what I need to do. I prance around the circle, searching with my eyes, connecting *this* soul with *that* demon.

The claret-haired woman who stands off to the side, jeering. As if there were a thread connecting the sliver of her soul within her to the remainder Elisavet holds, I connect them. Hers is weak, dried and brittle.

The slippers on my feet grow warm. Seem to guide me, not just into which movements to dance, but in what to do.

Grab it. Pull it toward her.

And where I unexpectedly touched Orrin's last night, I purposefully do it now.

If I can touch it, maybe I can do more.

I'm no demon queen, and this isn't a trade…it's an undoing of one. I can almost sense how desperately the soul wants to be back to its demon. Like a magnetic force, aching to be back where it belongs.

Without removing my eyes from Elisavet, I use the magic of the slippers, all of my own, and the simple desperation of my own goddamned will to tug on the demon's traded soul. My mouth fills with ash and copper, but the soul gives easily, breaking away from Elisavet.

A shriek in the area the woman stood, a thump like she's fallen. Elisavet's sliver beats bright—as if uncovered a fraction. But there is still so much more, more to go. And where is Aven's soul? And where is Orrin's? And if I grab at them, will they survive?

The claret-haired woman is moving again in the corner of my vision, weeping in a puddle on the ground, which bolsters me on. If I was successful—and I don't sense her soul with Elisavet any longer—and if she survived the returning of her soul's remainder, that means I can save my sister and Orrin too.

Elisavet casts an uninterested look at the woman before turning back to me.

Her presumption that her demons are simply misbehaving again is what will benefit me.

The next, Orrin's demon friend from the first party, off leaning against the wall, watching me with interest. I connect their soul right away, a tang of citrus in my mouth, a sharp ringing in my ears. I pull it hard, imagine it as a child's ball, tossing it back in their corner as I leap. They crumple with a silent cry, and I go on, quicker now.

This one, that. My throat going dry and black, like I swallowed burnt toast, my nose filling with the stench of rot, my fingers numb, my feet burning. The shoes pulse, pulse, pulsing as I pirouette. Again, again, again, bodies falling, bodies groaning.

Out of my peripheral vision, I catch Elisavet motioning one of her brutish guards over, frowning. More demons whimpering, exclaimed cries of fear and surprise. Elisavet stands from her seat, scanning the crowd in suspicion.

I stare at my sister, who's moved off to the side. I dance for her.

I spin out our memories, as I did for Orrin last night. But this time I know what I'm doing. I hope.

Aven. Aven. Aven. Strawberries, warm from the sun, grown right in the patch of grass near our cottage. Pine needles in her pale hand. Pulling weeds, tending her garden with such care. Her blue eyes flashing, quick, smart. Her laugh, wide open smile, white teeth. Dark lines of brows. Hair down past her waist. Big belly, thumping baby below. Thin band of gold on her ring finger. Wreath of the flowers she'd grown herself, placed just so on her head, her face made up in rosy cosmetics we made together. Teaching me to read when I got kicked out of school. Clapping for my graceless first attempts at dancing, encouraging Sélie's drawing. Our makeshift motherly sister who held the three of us together, so easily. Willingly. Who never once made me or Sélie feel like burdens.

I can feel it—see it—that part of her, being held by Elisavet.

What is left of Aven is weaker, soft and fluid, but it is there. I focus on that. I will it to grow. I will it to come back in full. I use the power of the red slippers—and the power within me—to take from me and give to her.

Focusing on her silvery, beating soul, I spin, and I spin some more. Leaping, I move, feverish, dancing so hard my chest burns, and I choke in some air. But still, I cannot stop. I think of flowers. Warmth. Love. The magic burns within me. Not just the gifts now. Something more. Something that can heal. Something that can break. *Go back*, I urge her soul. *Go back!* I silently scream, begging it to comply.

This is all the magic that I have to give. It is my love, and I give it willingly, joyfully. Take it, take everything from me. Save my sister, save my sister.

I can feel when it gives, almost leaping its way back to her in its own dance.

Aven's face tips up and she falls backward, swooning.

I pierce Elisavet with my gaze now. Holding hers. Just as the red slippers won't let me go, I won't release her.

I dance for her too. For her pain, her beauty, her sadness. I dance with empathy, even as I hate her. Because she wasn't always this. Because maybe, somehow, she is still redeemable.

Even as I dance, I know—the red shoes are sharing their power, but they are also taking something they've never taken before. My energy drains with each step. Just as I can feel the souls of the others, so I can sense my own, and it is dwindling. Yet, I move on. I jeté, I spiral, I chassé, I piqué arabesque. On and on and on I go, back aching, arms weak, legs like jelly, and still I go on, just as strong, just as powerful somehow. My body may be weak, but my dancing isn't.

The slippers keep going, *making* me jump, making me twist and turn, making me dance harder than I've ever danced before, harder than is humanly possible. I dance until my heart starts to slow and still they force me on. I won't stop, not if I can help it. I'll die before I give up a way to get Aven back home, die before I let Orrin die. And as if in answer, a trade of another sort has been made—between me, between the slippers, between the magic binding all of us together—and my life begins to slip away. I offer my soul up, propose my own magical trade to all the powers that be. *Take my life, let me follow Elisavet into death if I get her there. But spare Orrin.* But where is *his* soul? I frantically try to sift through the rest of the energies surrounding Elisavet, Aven moaning on the ground. I send her a silent apology for any pain she may be feeling, but panic seizes me. I'm running out of time.

I've run out of time.

"Stop dancing," Elisavet's cold command, her eyes slitted at me in hatred.

That's when I notice the seawater pooling at my feet and the chaos created by the humans in the cave who finally seem to have come to their senses—some of them cry with gratitude, some scream hysterically, lost in their own minds again. It's dizzying.

One of them runs right into the stone wall so hard he crushes his own skull, the horrible sickening crack of it echoing through the cave, even above the racket. I shake my head. *No. No. No.*

But I keep dancing.

Bile rises in my throat, my stomach twists, my hands and arms and legs shake, my heart slows so much, I think it'll stop, and I'm cold, desperately cold to my bones, so cold now I suddenly can't feel a thing, my body is not mine. My life is not either.

I meet my Orrin's black eyes. Send him all my apologies. I didn't find his soul—and now Elisavet knows what I've done—stolen back her demons' lives, weakened her. But I didn't kill her.

Now we're probably both dead.

I love you, I love you, I dance the words. I give it the last of what I have. It is the love and the passion within me that meets the magic. That strengthens it. My heart slows some more. It stutters out of rhythm.

Beat.

Beat.

Beat.

And then…something flashes light and darkness both together, something burns, smelling of burnt flesh, rot, sour undertones, and still, the smell of jasmine and poison. The water keeps rushing in.

"No!" With one quick and horrible scream, Elisavet lunges forward, weak, face ashen. She looks weak. She looks like she's dying.

Because of me, she is dying.

I dance on, giving it my last few stilted breaths, my limbs so weak I can hardly move now. I will meet her in death if I must. I am not stopping. For one moment, her eyes meet mine. She looks confused. Broken. It's too much for her. She's too far gone to save, even if she'd wanted that. Somehow, I doubt she would've wanted it.

Beat.

Beat.

Beat.

And as Elisavet stumbles toward me, Orrin manages to wrestle his knife back from the demon, hurtling it with all his might across the cave.

"Elisavet!" he calls. Behind him, in the shadows, slump the two demons that held him, that cut him. Elisavet turns just in time. The knife lands squarely in her chest, in her heart.

With a scream, quick and horrible, Elisavet deflates…her skin caving in around her face, eyes sinking into her skull, body turning small and withered as all that remains of her is a shell…a bag of skin and bones. She, what is left of her, falls on the floor in a flash of light and darkness, cocooned in her bruise-colored dress, pearl necklace shimmering, her body lying next to Mr. Brown's corpse. Just an empty shell, sad and lost. Dead.

I grab Aven to me, finding the last bit of my strength. I tug her away from the smoking, putrid pile of flesh behind her, away from Mr. Brown's bloodied corpse. I clutch my sister to me, not caring if the world around seems to be trembling. "Aven," I cry, rocking her back and forth like a baby.

She holds me so tightly I can hardly breathe—her wiry arms wrapped around me like they will never let go. *This* is her.

And Elisavet is no more.

The shoes pulse on my feet, one weak but triumphant squeeze, and realization strikes me.

There is a *soul* in these slippers. Or something like one. I don't know what to name it. A soul, a heart, a lifeforce, a spirit, a ghostly presence. A dying wish. A sacrifice.

Or maybe, unfinished business. I sense the truth now, so obviously.

All this time, the red slippers weren't enchanted by Elisavet.

They were enchanted by *Glisa*.

With tears streaming down my face, I wrap all of my intentions around the slippers, give them a squeeze, and gently, I let go. I release what is left of her, send it to the beyond.

Someone screams. More now, shocked, horrified, delighted.

There's a terrible sound of something cracking, something breaking—the rush of energy bouncing around the room, some of the candles snuffing in the whoosh of crackling air. The people starting to run, startled like horses. But where is Orrin? I search the crowded place frantically, screaming for him.

"Get out!" someone shrieks. "The cave is coming down!"

I look up as another loud crash sounds, and a giant chunk of stone falls from the ceiling to the floor. More shrieks as people shove each other aside to scramble out of the cave, knocking over the last of the still-lit candles, fire trailing along the fine rugs.

"Fire," Aven finally says, eyes wide, frozen in fear. *I lost you in a fire, I lost you in a fire*, she used to say. That's how our parents died, and that's what her nightmares were made of.

"No," I say, my stomach dropping. We didn't get this far to lose everything now. I scream for Orrin again. Did he survive Elisavet's death? Where is he?

"I'm here!" A familiar presence presses tight behind me. I cry out my relief, as Orrin's arms wrap around me, heaving my weak body up. His panicked hands patting me down.

"I'm okay," I reassure him, hobbling toward the door, his arms propelling me and Aven forward.

"Move!" he screams, as more water rushes into the cave, thankfully extinguishing the flames. Fear gives me speed and the strength to move. We race toward the exit, the light from outside streaming its way in, showing us the way. Our arms flung over our heads in feeble protection, Orrin's arms huddled around us both as we run. Rocks thunder as they hit the cave walls and floor. If we don't get out soon, they'll block the door, trap us.

I move, I move as fast as I can, despite my utter exhaustion, my skirts weighed down with water. I drag my sister with me to the cave opening, while there still is one, reaching an arm out to the dazed harpist with the bloody fingers, the dancer with the golden bangles. "Go!" I scream, pushing them as we struggle against the water pouring in.

There are people behind us, but when I look back, Orrin heaves me forward faster. "There's no time."

"Mr. Brown…" More water rushes in, reaching our waists, my already-heavy gown weighed down even more, making me sluggish, panicked.

Orrin doesn't have to answer, Mr. Brown is dead. I saw it.

We reach the mouth of the cave, and I shove Aven through it with the last of my strength. Orrin grips my wrists, pulling me along as another cascade of rocks comes down behind us—a crash, a scream, the splash of water, the taste of salt as I trip and fall under a wave, his cry of alarm ringing in my ears, his fingers yanked from my wrists. I reach, grabbing nothing but air.

I've lost him.

I choke the water down, I choke again as it sucks me under, dragging me away from Orrin's grasping hands, dragging me from the cave, dragging me out to the sea.

In the haze of drowning, I watch my feet moving eerily through the cold water in the slippers, as if in slow motion. There is no sound except a roaring in my ears. There is no feeling except the burning in my lungs, the muscles in my body screaming. Then crying. Then silence. The waves toss me like a rag doll, and I slam into something hard, my vision blurring. I've done too much. I can't fight anymore.

Beat.

It's enough.

I have nothing left to give.

That's my last thought, before the water spits me out.

CHAPTER TWENTY-SIX

The waves come through first, the lap of them at my legs, at my feet. I blink, face against the sand. The taste of blood in my mouth, saltwater bubbling out of my lungs. I'm freezing and sopping wet, weaker than I've ever felt before, but I'm alive. My *everything* aches, still I don't care. I blink again against the dizziness, search the expanse of shore, the rocky cliffs in the barely there light. I feebly manage to stand, though every bit of me aches. There are people wandering up along the shore, past me, lost and dazed, backs to me as they climb, wet—and some of them—bloodied. I even glimpse the dazed, bloody-fingered harpist and Orrin's demon friend with the citrus-tinged soul.

But not the two I'm seeking.

Then, behind me, someone calls my name. I turn, and Orrin is carrying Aven out of the ocean. My heart stops in my chest. He sets her gently down, and I cry out in gratitude as she races toward me. Aven is alive. And Elisavet is dead, and I killed her. And I'm alive. Am I alive? The red shoes killed me.

The red shoes saved me.

I look at my sister, cry as I take in the beloved sight of her before me, herself once more.

I fall to my knees, weak, and I retch seawater onto the sand.

With my eyes shut, and the tears streaming down my face, I sob out as my sister reaches me, takes hold of me. "You're alive!" I cry. "Thank God. I love you, Aven."

She wraps her thin arms tighter around me and whispers, "I love you too. Are you okay? Your head is bleeding. For a moment there, I thought you were gone."

"I don't care. I'm fine."

Then I open my eyes, to find Orrin standing over us, the earliest light of dawn just breaking the ocean's horizon behind him. I catch my breath as I stare at his face up close. Not at the blood caked from the cut on his skin. Nor the beauty of the rest of it—the fact that we survived—but at something else.

As though I'm seeing a stranger, or someone I've always known, it's unclear. I yank off my gloves and touch the side of his face in wonder, reveling in the feel of him, awed by an unfamiliar sight. It's different than seeing my sister back to herself. This is him for the first time.

"Your eyes…" I say, soft.

Green, like the sea.

Wet, washed ashore, far from the carriage and the horses who must still be waiting, we head to the cottage, only minutes away.

"Are you hurt?" I ask Aven as she walks, exhausted but eager. Orrin carries me, and I hang one arm over his to touch my sister, so that I'm connected to both of them. I hold Aven's hand, the cool skin against my own. "He can carry you instead."

"I can manage perfectly fine. You're the one who nearly died."

Nearly danced myself to death in order to save those I love, I wonder silently. That's what I was willing to do—and the slippers heard my plea.

She tightens her hold on my hand then glances at Orrin, who stares ahead, looking for the cottage. Her eyes hold a question when she turns back to me, asking. But there will be time for talking later, time to explain everything. I lean into Orrin's chest and breathe slowly, still dizzy, spent.

The cottage finally comes into view as the sun rises, and life is fine again. Energized at the sight of our beloved home, I motion for Orrin to set me down. I jog the few remaining steps, faltering, staggering, grasping at the frame of the door for strength. I bang at the door, voice hoarse. "Sélie! Let us in! It's us!"

Within a minute, Sélie has swung open the door. She stares at me and Aven, mouth gaping in shock, and bursts into tears.

Aven pulls her into her arms, and then grabs me right before I fall, my legs still weak. We lie in a wordless jumble of grateful tears across the threshold of the cottage.

Sélie leans out of our embrace to look at Aven, crying, "I thought all this time, you were dead."

"I was among the dead," Aven whispers. "But Corliss saved me."

"What? What do you mean? Where have you both been?"

I hug her to me, hard. "It's a long story. We will explain everything. Later."

"Alright." Sélie frowns, glancing at my soggy ball gown, then over my shoulder.

Orrin, leaning against the front gate, somewhat awkwardly, looking utterly human. Clad all in black, his face bloody, hard features but soft eyes.

"Who is this?" Sélie sounds a little wary.

I look back at Orrin. He appears completely benign to me. My safety.

"That's an even longer story," I say.

"I'm sorry about Mr. Brown." I take Orrin's hand in mine when we are outside the cottage, to say good-bye, not long after he returned with the carriage and horses. It was impossible not to grin at the sight of him leading the gentle creatures who followed him willingly, if a bit hesitantly. But now, soberness has descended on us both.

"He shouldn't have gone like that." His voice is heavy. "I suppose it was quick, at least."

"Are you sure you won't stay with us tonight?" I nod toward the cottage.

"No. I should go—let you have time with your sisters. I don't want to intrude."

"You wouldn't be."

His green eyes are soft but no less deep than the black eyes had been. "It's fine. I should go back and see if anyone needs help."

"How do you think you survived?" I ask, wondering if he has a theory of his own. I add, "And do you think most of them did?"

"I'm not certain." Orrin ponders this. "Maybe I was wrong about it all. Maybe we were never at risk. Or maybe, somehow, you saved us all."

I shake my head. "I think it was the slippers."

"Maybe that too." He smiles softly.

"I think—" I study his face, wondering how to say it. "When I was dancing, I got a feeling that I wasn't alone. Like, that the slippers *did* have a life of their own. Or a soul. At first, I thought yours—you'd implied that they were attached to your soul. But it wasn't yours."

His eyes widen at my implication. "Glisa's."

"Yes. The slippers, all this time, they *wanted* to dance—because they held, somehow, the spirit of a dancer!"

"I believe you." He looks off to some faraway place in time, shakes his head slow. Comes back to me. "It would explain so much. The slippers' connection to me and my soul—I literally gave up my soul to save her, and perhaps a part of her could never part with me because of that."

"Or maybe she didn't want to," I gently say. "And being a ballerina, the slippers called to me. Through me, she got to live again."

"It's a nice thought." Orrin's expression goes a touch bitter-sweet. He squeezes my hand. "I must go. Come to me, though, when you're ready. If you want. I'll be waiting for you, Corliss."

Then he lifts me off my feet and hugs me to his chest. I bite back an argument. I want him to stay, but I want him to *want* to stay, not to do it for my sake.

Can we go back to what we were before this? Or have things inevitably changed? I rest my head against the crook of his shoulder and breathe him in. *Stay, stay,* I silently plead. *Or take me with you. Or at least, beg me to go.*

But he doesn't. He sets me down, tips my chin up, and gives me one chaste kiss, only one.

I reluctantly move away, stepping backward. I watch him from the doorway as he walks, turning to look back at me, even as he climbs onto the driver's seat of the carriage, the horses nickering pleasantly. He clicks his tongue, and they begin trotting away. His eyes stay locked with mine until he's too far. Until I can no longer see him. Back to the mansion he'll go. Without me.

I have my sisters, I have my life. I breathe, trying to push back the feeling of loss. Will I have him again? Will he have me? Or has that which drew us together been irrevocably broken? The ache in me is so great that it is a wonder I don't shatter to pieces. I picture the ballroom. The way he watched me dance. His hands, tracing the lines of my body. His laugh, a secret, sudden thing. As if it were for me only. I think of the shape of his soul.

It is only when I enter the cottage and glance across the room, to where I kicked off the wet ballet slippers, that I realize they have faded, the rich red turned to a sickly brownish-orange.

Glisa is free.

The magic is gone.

For many days and nights, my sisters and I do not leave the cottage. We don't do a thing but eat good food—Aven lets Sélie do all the cooking now that she's proficient at it—and laugh, and cry, and hug each other, and stroll around the garden. Aven doesn't want to walk by the water.

"I'm not ready yet," she says. I know she's upset, even if my magical senses have dulled. I still seem to know things, to see things, to sense them, in a way that doesn't feel entirely normal. Then again, perhaps I never was normal—and Orrin had to show me that.

I wonder, if given practice and time, my gifts could be as strong as they were before. Maybe it's only a talent I must hone, no different than ballet.

"She's never going to come back for you, love," I tell Aven in a soft voice, as we sit, bundled in the garden in wicker chairs, without saying who I mean. We both know. "She's never going to hurt you again."

"It's not just that…" Aven hesitates, a gust of cold salt-air lifting the hair around her face. "I don't think I've forgiven the ocean yet. For what it took from me. Besides, I'm not exactly afraid of her."

"How did it happen?" I finally ask, after so many conversations of holding back.

She stares away from me now, into the beds, long past their prime, flowers wilted or browned, dry bits and stalks, most of the colors faded save for a few hearty varieties I struggle to name. "I was going to go into the water, walk until I was under, and I just remember feeling numb. I couldn't cry at all. I felt empty. I wasn't thinking of you or Sélie, which I know sounds horrid. I was only thinking that I'd miss you both, and not the other way around. I was nothing, nothing but a burden, so why would you miss *me*?"

It breaks my heart, hearing the quiver in her voice, hearing those words.

She goes on, wiping at her eyes. "But then she found me. It was the strangest thing, like the ocean was calling my name, asking if I was sure."

"I thought you called her," I say.

"Maybe I did. Even if I didn't know exactly what—or who—I was calling for. But in that moment, I knew I had a choice—three of them. I could turn around to safety, to the cottage. I could keep walking and drown myself. Or I could stop and answer the voice. So I answered. And she took me. I let her take me."

"I understand, love." I scoot my chair closer and embrace her. "I understand completely."

"I miss Darius so much. And the baby—I miss not getting a chance to know him."

Gently, not sure if it's the right thing to say, I tell her, "They can never be replaced, but I know you'll find happiness again, another family someday, if you wish. You're so easy to love, Aven. And maybe in another life, you'll meet their souls again."

"I'm glad you didn't give up on me."

"I did." I look down, kick at a small stone near my foot. "I gave up hope. I really thought you were dead. We all did."

"It doesn't matter now," Aven says, blue eyes shining. "I'm back, thanks to you."

Just when we step back into the house, a horse neighs. I snap my gaze out the window eagerly, but it's not Orrin.

"Constable Elden," I say to my sisters as I peek out the curtain. "Shit. I suppose I should have informed him you were back, Aven."

"He'll find out now," she says, the blanket still wrapped around her.

When we let the man in, he does a double take at the sight of Aven. "Mrs. Winter!"

Aven tips her head. "Constable."

Sputtering, he takes off his hat, stares at Sélie and me, and then back at Aven. "You're alive?"

"It appears so." She cracks a wry smile.

"Yes." He still stares at her in wonder, I suppose, thinking about the misidentified body, and about his mistake in closing the investigation, even if it wasn't totally up to him. I pray for that woman's soul to be at peace, whomever she was. For her family to discover her outcome at some point.

As if reading his mind, Aven says, "I'm sorry for the confusion. And of course, my condolences to the family of the woman found." She bows her head earnestly. "I hope that can be settled now, the confusion cleared up. But what can we do for you?"

"I come with news, Mrs. Winter, which I was going to tell your sisters, but since you're here…um, you may want to sit."

Aven does, and Sélie and I flank her, protectively.

He looks at her. "Your husband's ship has been recovered, just a few miles outside of Salille."

You could hear a pin drop in the cottage. On the beach. In town. We are so quiet I wonder for a moment if I imagined his words.

"Aven." Sélie squeezes her hand. "The ship…"

"It has?" Her voice is breathless, a hint of a whisper. "Darius."

"Yes, ma'am, and on board, the poor departed souls—all twenty-eight of them. It might take a minute, but we'll get them sent back for burial. Mr. Winter can rest in peace now, along with his comrades."

Darius, lost and found. My heart clenches, but mostly in relief for Aven. I flutter my eyes shut a moment, fondly picturing his kind face, beard of gold, the black earrings he wore in both ears, how merrily he loved my sister, loved us all, tugging on Sélie's braids when she was young enough to wear two, teasing me, kissing Aven's neck as she laughed out loud. I open my eyes again.

Aven's face is so white, I speak for her, trembling, tell Constable Elden, "Thank you."

He jerks his head in a ghost of a nod, black mustache twitching. I can tell he is *dying* to ask us questions, but instead he just tips his hat respectfully and leaves. Glancing back once more as he rides away.

I turn to Aven, grab her tightly. "Are you alright?"

She looks wide-eyed at me and Sélie. And she manages a relieved sigh, peace crossing her fine-boned face. "The ocean returned him."

"I think I should handle the shop without you tomorrow," Sélie suggests to us a day later, after dinner, when the topic of work comes up. "You've both been through so much. Besides, you know how people will be. You'll be answering their prying questions all day. You should stay home and rest. Pearl would be happy to come in for the afternoon." Her eyes light up when she mentions her friend—her best friend now. I was right about Pearl helping out at the apothecary. She became an anchor for Sélie in a way I could have only hoped. She got her through this time of missing us.

Aven shakes her head, and I'm pleased to see some color on her cheeks again. Even her frame seems to have filled out a little more in the last few days.

"No," she says to Sélie. "I'll be fine. I want to get back to normal life, to living. Of course Pearl can stay on and take shifts—I'd never take that from her—but tomorrow I'd love to go myself. I want to work."

Sélie frowns, not hiding her doubt. "You and Corliss both showed up here looking terrible, and you were weak, and I don't want you to push yourselves. We have plenty of time to catch up and get back to normal. Stay home."

"I'll be lonely," Aven argues.

"I'll be here, goose," I jab at her a little.

She grins at me. "Fine. Then I'll be bored."

"Ha. Funny." I turn back to Sélie. "Anyway, we're not sick! We're coming, and that's that."

Sélie throws up her hands in exasperation, fire lighting up her eyes. "Fine! It's not that I don't want to have you back, you mules. It's just that I'm worried for you!"

Then the three of us fall into merry laughter.

"Mules?" Aven giggles, staring at Sélie with delight. "You cheeky thing."

Tomorrow we will get back to the Apothicaire, into our work again. Somehow, I will find a way to repay Marieta for planting the idea of Aven's return in my head. Then, finding the courage, I will go to the Colehart Mansion, in search of a former demon, who has, quite inexplicably, ripped out, not my soul, but my heart—in the best possible way.

I will ask if he wants me.

Lord knows I want him. With all of my being.

Chapter Twenty-Seven

*A*fter we close the shop, on a day that couldn't have been any more perfect—just being there with my sisters, even with the curious customers gazing at both Aven and me—we pause at the door as I lock it, pocket the keys. I'm going in a different direction.

"Should we expect you for dinner?" Sélie asks with a teasing grin, the pretty blue of her dress just visible under her heavy cloak.

I try not to sound so uncertain, nervous. I only answer a mild, "Either way, you'll know what happens." I turn to Aven, her eyes bright, her cheeks rosy. She looks so *alive* I could cry. Grief doesn't simply just disappear, but healing comes to soften it over time, and hers has begun. For that, I could cry even more. "I suppose you're exhausted, with all that."

"A little." She laughs at my meaning.

It was intense, but not as bad as it could have been. Constable Elden must have alerted someone of the mistaken presumed death, that Aven is, in fact, alive, and town gossips spread it wide. There was no shortage of people coming into our apothecary all day, just to get a glimpse of Aven, to tell her how happy they were that she was actually alive. Most of them—not all—kept their questions to themselves. But that doesn't mean it wasn't a lot for her.

I shift from foot to foot. "Maybe I'll go tomorrow instead."

"No." A shake of her head. "You said today. Well, I didn't forget. Go, now. Go to him. It's been long enough."

I hug her so hard she coughs. I apologize, smiling, then take Sélie into my arms next. "Wish me luck," I say.

She says, "The way that man looked at you, dear sister, I hardly think you need it!"

They leave me in a peal of smug laughter. I watch them go, my soul fed. And I walk on, alone, in the other direction.

At my back, by the docks, seagulls squawk. A ship calls out. Children play in the street, and it is all perfect. I'm glad to be back here in the mess of The Pins, I'm so glad. The wind calls, the cold breeze of autumn. The air whispers to me. And it doesn't feel odd anymore. Or it does, but no odder than I am.

Because I've had magic. I've lived it. And I belong here. Life feels right again. Full of possibilities. Before I go to the mansion, I have three places to go.

First, I stop to visit Marieta, bringing her all the treats my arms can hold, and a healthy dose of thanks for encouraging me to find Orrin—which she eats up faster than the caramels I hand over. Afterwards, I go to the Red Clover. My own pink shoes are tucked in a bag at my side. Julian will either have me, or he won't. But I've lost a lot worse. Besides, several times, someone made me dance when I didn't want to. Yet no matter what, no one could ever make me stop.

Julian is calm as I explain as much as I can.

"Your sister mentioned a family emergency." His eyes hold concern.

"Yes," I say. "I had to get my other sister from a dangerous situation—it was life-threatening. I never would have left so abruptly otherwise. I just wanted to come in person, first to apologize for leaving without a word of explanation. Secondly, for taking so long to return. And third, to beg you to let me audition again. If you will consider having me back."

He frowns, stroking his smooth chin. "Why would you have to re-audition?"

"Because." I look down at myself. Back to him. I take a breath. "I've changed, and I don't think my dancing is as strong. So perhaps you won't want me after all."

"Dance, then, please." He waves a hand and ushers me out of his office, toward the empty, unlit stage. "Afterwards, we will talk."

I wait while he finds Dina and brings her to play. My stomach still twists nervously as I dance in my own, worn shoes. I try not to compare the music of Dina's perfectly fine playing to Mr. Brown's delicate fingers on the keys in the ballroom. I try not to compare anything.

Instead, I let the music wash over me, the sound, the joy. I am here, I am alive. I dance gratefully, like I've just been reborn. My dancing is alive, too, lit with passion, wild with it. So what if it's not perfect? I'm scared, too, but I dance through the fear. Orrin loved my dancing, no matter what I had on my feet. Maybe Julian will as well. I don't have to be Bell with the red shoes. I can simply be Bell.

When I'm through Julian simply nods. "Welcome back."

A smile spreads across my face, and we discuss my return, the sets I'll need to make up for the next show. Before I leave, I run to the backroom to see who is there, even though it's a bit early for practice. I stop first in the men's dressing room, and Lysander practically tosses me up in the air.

"We were worried about you." He tugs me to the women's dressing room and flings open the door dramatically. "Look who's back!"

Pearl tightly hugs me, wrapping me in her strong arms and sweet perfume.

"*Thank you*," I gush, then pull away and look into her warm, sparkling eyes. "I appreciate you looking out for Sélie while I was away. She's told us so much, and I am so thankful that she's got a friend like you."

"I'm lucky to have her too! Though, I suppose you won't need my help anymore at the shop." Her face falls.

"I wouldn't say that." I grin. "Sélie would be crushed if you didn't come back. We'll work it out—today was just important for the three of us to be together. Tomorrow come by, if you can, and we'll figure out proper shifts."

"Alright." She nods brightly.

"What'd you do, Corliss?" Tanna blurts out, edging forward, curiosity coming off her in waves. "Go off and have a baby or something? Commit a crime and have to run from the law?"

"No." I laugh when I realize she's teasing. "Definitely not. Neither. It was just some family business. It's taken care of. So now I'm back. Aven is as well. She didn't die after all, which I'm sure most of you already heard. Everything is good." I can't help the tears that spring to my eyes. I don't mind weeping in front of them though.

"Stay for a while, Corliss? I know you're not dancing tonight, but you can talk to us while we get ready?" Lysander cajoles. "Tell us what you've been up to? Maybe go down to the tavern with us after the show? Star is taking us out tonight—her treat!"

Regretfully, I shake my head. I'd love to stay. I'd love to deepen all these connections of my own, one day. Except there's something else I want more right now. "Not today. I can't wait to get back here to work, to hear how you've been. But I have to be somewhere right now."

I hug them each one more time—even Tanna. When she embraces me back, I smile fondly.

I only have one final stop before I get to the Colehart Mansion. I walk fast.

It feels so strange to knock on the door. The only other time I knocked, Mr. Brown answered.

This time, a tall, handsome young man in a crisp butler suit answers, his skin dark-golden brown and his eyes a striking pale blue.

"I'm here to see Orrin. Is he home?" I ask, somehow nervous. I fist my white dress in my hands to keep them busy.

"Yes, Madame," he says, formally, nothing like Mr. Brown. He's a proper butler, I'd wager. The young man allows me in and leads me through the foyer. God, it looks the same, only shinier, somehow. Only different.

On the way to the sitting room, Mrs. Minthy meets us in the hall, duster in hand. She stops with a little gasp at the sight of me.

"Why, Miss Corliss!" She reaches over and smiles as she pats my arm fondly. "I'm so happy to see you! We weren't sure if you'd be back."

"We?" I ask, even happier to see her than I thought I'd be.

"Well, Mister Orrin said you might not be."

At the mention of his name, my heart flutters.

"Can you bring me to him?" I glance to the butler. "If that's alright?"

Mrs. Minthy tells him, in a friendly way, "This here is a good friend. I'll take care of her. Thank you, Joe."

He bobs his head and his Adam's apple moves in unison. He grins at us both. Something in his smile is familiar, though I can't quite place it. He adds, agreeably, "Of course, Mrs. Minthy."

She gestures at me to follow her, tucking the duster under one arm. "He's out back, having a walk through the grounds. I'll take you to him straightaway."

"How have you been? How has he been since I left?" I whisper as we walk.

Her eyes widen. "Well, we were a bit surprised not to see you back with us, when he returned, all chilled to the bone and wetter than a drowned cat! And bleeding, no less! I had to sew his face shut myself."

"Ah." I wince, remembering the dagger down his face. He wouldn't have been able to hide his injuries from her, being human again. And he wouldn't have the magic to heal it, either.

"Since then, we've not seen hide nor hair of Mr. Brown, though Mister Orrin didn't say exactly where that man ran off to, only that he wouldn't be back. I take it he was probably dismissed, or maybe he just left for a life elsewhere," she muses, and then says, almost to herself, "I never cared for him much, but it's odd without him here. I hope he found something better."

My throat clenches and I nod, thinking of Mr. Brown's white hair, his piercing eyes, his crooked smile. That lingering scent of cream puffs under the furniture polish and smoke. We'd liked disliking each other. "I hope so too."

"You know Joe?" She knocks her head backwards, leaning in to whisper, "They say he's Mr. Brown's grandson."

"No!" I answer, delighted to hear it. I knew something about him was familiar! Those icy eyes should have been obvious.

"He is, least that's the story I heard, though Mister Orrin has yet to confirm. Anyway, he's just right there." She points as she stops in front of the double-French doors leading to the back. Framed by clusters of pines and spruce, I spy his tall figure walking along the grass, beyond the fountain, and my heart, God, my *heart*…

"Thank you," I say, passing Mrs. Minthy in a rush.

I don't waste time walking.

I run to him, across the grass, past the forgotten greenhouse, to where he wanders at the edge of the paved walkway.

"Orrin!" I call and he looks up in surprise. I stop abruptly, just shy of leaping into his arms.

He wasn't sure I'd be back. Does he truly want me back?

"Come here," he demands.

I do, throwing myself into his open arms, hesitation gone.

"You've gotten less stubborn," he teases as he tugs me in tighter. I inhale his scent, bury myself closer to his warmth, the chill of autumn against my back. I can still sense so much about him, even now. He is as glad to see me as I am to see him.

Smiling, I draw back. Then I frown, pausing to run my finger along the jagged scar, stitched shut along his face. Still healing.

He flinches, and I stop. "Sorry."

I stare into his green eyes, discovering him anew. Do I miss the black after all this? He's beautiful, in a different way now. What does he see me as?

"Do you want me, still? After everything?" I ask, holding my breath.

Orrin stares at me and his mouth falls open, incredulous. "I want you more than anything, Corliss. But the choice is yours. Last time, I made you come here, and you stayed for a long time, out of fear, and obligation to return your sister to safety—then, perhaps, for lust."

"It was more than lust."

"For me too. But this time, the choice is yours alone." He pulls me in for a kiss. The touch of his mouth on mine makes something in my belly flutter with delight. Reluctantly, like he doesn't want to let me go yet, he lowers me to my feet. "Stay for as long as you like. My heart is yours, and my home as well."

At his fiercely stated, open admission, I ask, half-teasing, "Have I tamed you then?"

"Only a little. I can still be wild, brutally so. You may find that out tonight."

Laughing, I slip my hand in his, tug him toward the house. "Your room or mine?"

"We haven't tried the dining room yet." His lips twist with mirth. I can still taste those lips on me.

"The ballroom wasn't scandalous enough for you? You'll have to kick everyone out of the house if you want to have your way with me in each room."

"That could be arranged." Orrin's eyes twinkle like the sun cast on the sparkling sea.

We are still smiling at each other as we walk up the stairs—to his room. Still smiling as he tosses my cloak down, where it puddles on the carpet. As he kisses me, the smiles fade, to seriousness, to sighs full of longing. As he touches me, to moans and gasps.

He kisses me all the way to my feet then pauses. With tender fingers, he removes my shoes and stockings, lifts my feet to his lips, kissing each one reverently. Then my white dress and undergarments follow the rest of my clothes to heap on the floor.

On the way back up, he stills, eyes glued to the bandage on my rib cage. "Are you hurt?"

"No." Shaking my head with the secret, I reach down and peel the bandage off. Underneath, my fresh ink bleeds a bit, but I don't mind.

"A crow," he muses. "For me?"

"I made a stop before I came. I had to do something for you. And I'm quite fond of the little beasts now."

He laughs as he gently reapplies the bandage to cover the crow inked on my skin, in black, black as night. Black as ink, as black as his beautiful eyes when I first hated him, when I first loved him.

"What?" I say to his smirk. "What's so funny?"

Then he lifts off his own shirt, and I see it, on his lower rib cage. A lush pink rose, with plenty of thorns, more healed than my tattoo. Without him saying a word, I know it's for me. This is how he sees me, beautiful and wild and soft and full, all at once.

I only shake my head, press my lips to his. I love him, I love him. He kisses me back and teases me, talented fingers pausing to stroke and divide me so that I shudder.

To tease him back, I run my fingers along his hard body. "I missed this."

"Just this?" He shuts his eyes with pleasure.

I kiss him chastely, though my words come out breathy and weak. "No, not just this, you fool. This, you, everything. I missed it all. I feel as though I've been gone a year instead of days. I so desperately wanted to be back here, with you."

"And are you happy now that you are?"

"I am." I pause, voicing my concern out loud, "But are we safe now that Elisavet is gone? She's not the only queen we have to fear."

Orrin nods, running his hand along my naked back. "There will always be evil. I don't know that there will ever be anyone like her though. But there will also always be hope and love and beauty. Sometimes, only a sliver. Still, even that is powerful. Even that can win."

"I'm not gifted anymore, not like how I was, with all the magical senses. Or at least, they're muted now," I tell him. "And the red shoes don't work."

"I was wondering."

"They turned brown. The magic is gone."

His eyes are intense when he tugs me back into his inked arms. "Not all the magic."

I smile. Perhaps he's right. Sometimes I still feel as though there's more to me. More within me. I glance down at his forearms and wrists. "I'd have thought these tattoos would fade as well. Like the other magic."

Shaking his head, Orrin frowns. "No. These were never magic, never a symbol. They're real, as real as any of the others, a part of my past. I can't erase who I was in every sense."

"Nor would I want you to."

He hesitates, voice gruff. "I'm not perfect. You may yet find me hard and cruel in ways."

"You're no more a beast than I am," I argue. "And I like you that way. Now shut up and kiss me again."

"You kiss me," he challenges back.

Laughing, I lean up to him. Sigh. "If you say so. I suppose you've tamed me as well."

As he moves to join me, he says, "No, neither of us really are.

We are just two wild hearts who find calm within the other. Two old souls, made the same. That's why the red shoes loved you; you and I shared each other even then. Fated to find each other one day."

"I agree," I whisper, closing my eyes. "And I believe you're right. The magic isn't gone."

Chapter Twenty-Eight

I revel in the deliciously cool air, a perfect excuse to burrow closer to the heat of Orrin's skin, the windows flung open to let in the chill. It's been three weeks since I returned to him. Though I've gone back to work and the Clover to dance, beyond that we've hardly left the bedroom.

"Again?" he cocks one dark eyebrow.

A smirk lifts my mouth. "Are you having trouble keeping up with me?"

He laughs, his throat working, the joyful sound filling my heart. Every moment is like this, fuller and fuller and fuller. It's a wonder I don't explode with happiness. With awe.

"No," I sigh. "I'm so comfortable, I have no desire to leave this bed, but it's time. My sisters will be here within the hour."

This morning we are giving Aven a tour of the grounds, to see if she wants to take over the gardens. To see if she has the interest and the energy.

"I'll call for baths." I bound out of the bed, feeling renewed energy. I give Orrin a naughty smile and twirl away so he has a full view of my backside.

He lets out a low rasp of approval. "Come back."

"You'll muss my hair too much."

"Get away from the window—do you want to shock the neighbors?" he calls, huskily.

"There are no neighbors."

"I know." After a pause, he says, "There could be though…if you like? If you wanted to go somewhere, travel, we could. Make our home anywhere."

I ask, "Is that what you want?"

"After decades of doing just that, for my part, I must answer you a decided no. But I would go if you wanted."

"No." I shake my head. Return to the bed and into his arms. I stretch my tired limbs out, pointed toes and all, the warm sheets decadent against my naked skin. "I love it here. I love The Pins, in my own way. And—"

"Your sisters." A loving understanding fills his eyes. Though he's yet to get to know them, and they him, it will happen, and I cannot wait. He nods. "I'm glad you have each other. I didn't think you'd want to leave them, but I had to be sure. I want you to be content here, with me."

"I'm more than content. I love this place. I even loved it when it was covered with dust and grime. I love it all the more because it's where our story began. I love this bed. I love the ballroom. And you know I love *you* like mad." I push up to kiss him, leaning over his body.

He threads his fingers into my hair and tugs my head gently back, his lips going to my throat. I sigh contentedly and wriggle my hips.

"I actually didn't call you back to bed for that," he muses. "Though you're making it rather hard to stay the course."

Another naughty grin. "Am I?"

He groans and sits further upright, carefully adjusting me, so I am cradled in his lap—his very hard lap.

"I have something for you." He grows serious, and I hold back the wicked thought. Something in his gaze, the deep, loving green of it, has me straighten up, curious.

"A gift?"

"A question, really. I realize it's very traditional—something neither of us particularly are—but my heart wants it anyway. So…close your eyes a second." I do, and after a moment he tells me to open them. He places a ring in my open palm. Closes it. Kisses the knuckles. "It's yours if you want it."

I unfold my hand and stare at the ring, stunned into silence.

"I know it might seem fast," he adds softly. "We've only known each other for a few months, but I feel as though you've been in my life so much longer, after what we've been through. And, I don't expect anything quickly. We can wait as long as you need. I just hope you'll want to eventually. I hope you'll be my wife."

I admire the pink stone, surrounded by a sunburst of diamonds, the band a shining silver, filigreed. The second the shock fades, I slide it on. Look at him. "That wasn't actually a question, you know."

He breaks into a grin. Swallowing the sudden lump in my throat, I whisper, "But my answer is yes. It's always yes."

Later, my sisters will come to the mansion, marvel at how lovely it all is, the fresh paint, the things that have been fixed, though they never saw it as broken as I did. Joe will let them in, and Mrs. Minthy will serve us refreshments in the sitting room. They'll watch Orrin and me with grateful tears in their eyes, watch the miracle that we've become. We will give Aven a tour of the sad gardens, and she will tell us all the ways she will make them bloom again. How she'll bring them back to life, save them, just as she was saved. We will eat, and we will all laugh and hug and dance, tipsy on champagne and whiskey. The sun will set, and my sisters will retire in the rooms we aired out for them for their overnight stay, and in the morning, we will break our fast all together before they leave me—but only until I meet them at the apothecary later. It is the three Bells, no matter the name. No matter the circumstances. It always will be.

But there are still three-quarters of an hour before that begins, and so I curl my fingers into my fiancé's hair, and I tell him I love him.

He takes me. I take him as well.

We take each other. We break and mend each other.

The birds chatter as the sun rises in the sky, its glow kept company by an orchestra of hidden stars, which, even to my ordinary human ears, seems to sing with joy.

Epilogue

The fluffy snow patters against the windows of the Apothicaire while my sisters and I set up for the day. It's just us three here for now, until I go to the Clover to dance later. Tomorrow, as she does a few days a week, Pearl will take a shift so Aven can go work at the mansion. Even in early March there are steps forward to revive a garden, apparently. Not just in the repairs of the greenhouse, which is nearly complete—mostly at the hands of handymen—but in propagating seeds and planning beds, both inside the greenhouse and outside.

It has been months since Orrin's proposal. Christmastime has come and gone. Sélie has had her twenty-first birthday. Aven has gotten stronger every day. The nightmares of my encounters with Elisavet and her court come less and less. And my fiancé, my wonderful fiancé, continues to astound and delight me, continues to grow into his most alive and grateful self.

Behind the counter, Sélie and Aven giggle over something while I happily sweep the floor. I get a sudden sense they're laughing at me.

"What?" I turn in suspicion, one hand on my hip.

"Nothing," Aven clucks, eyes happy. "I love seeing you this way. You're thinking of Orrin, aren't you?"

"No." I pause, finally admitting, "I was thinking of that lemon cake."

The three of us laugh, and I shrug, taking up the broom again. "You would too, if you'd had the sample! I had some this morning and I can still taste it!"

Aven holds back a naughty retort, I can tell.

"Soon, we will," Sélie replies, agreeably. "Summer can't come soon enough for you, I'm sure. Or even next month! I cannot wait for the party."

"Me either." I sigh in contentment, anticipating April. "The renovations seemed to take forever, but it's all finally finished. Just wait until you see everything."

The mansion has been transformed, every room, every closet, every nook and cranny, and on top of that reason to celebrate, there will be the party—our engagement party. A few months delayed, but for purely practical reasons. Orrin and I wanted to wait until the place was in its former glory. We wanted to sink into our engagement together, in each other's arms, and enjoy it before opening up our home and lives. But in only three weeks, we will.

Everyone in The Pins—even the gossips—are invited. We wouldn't have it any other way.

Sélie echoes my sigh and says, for the millionth time, "I'm just so happy for you, Corliss."

The wind picks up outside, the snow flurries swirling wildly, but in our shop we are cozy and dry, everything smelling like zest and rosemary. I'm so happy too, so incredibly happy that I could burst. However, I look to Aven, as I always do. Making sure it's not too much for her. That my happiness won't drag more grief out of her—not because she doesn't want such a thing for me, but because of all she went through, mere months ago. Things are better than they were, though she has her low days, still. But today is not one of them. The lightness in her gaze as she agrees with Sélie has me sweeping happily again, the taste of lemon curd—and Orrin—on my tongue, my sisters' merry conversation the most comforting background noise as I tidy and they brew face cream and hair oil.

I'm cleaning near the door when the bell rings, and someone enters.

"Hello, Bells!" a jolly voice booms. The courier, a Mr. Hoblan. His black hair is dusted with snow, and his eyelashes are wet.

"Hello," I greet him, smiling. My sisters echo my sentiment. "You have something for us?"

"I have mail." He shakes his head, rifling through his bag. "Such a fine looking letter. Gold seal and everything!"

When he pulls it out to flash it my way, a twinge of curiosity runs through me. This isn't our usual invoice or order-by-mail. It *is* fine. The envelope feels important, somehow.

I reach out my hand, impressed—my pink diamond sparkling—and he gives me a coy smile.

"Oh, it's not for *you*, or the shop, Miss Corliss." I get a glimpse of delicate, elegant script before he whisks it out of reach.

"Who is it for?" I ask him.

He gives me a smile, turns from me. "It's for her." And he hands it to Sélie before tipping his hat and heading out with a cheerful hum, leaving snow tracks on our floor, which I'll have to dry up so nobody slips. But that can wait.

I step closer to the counter, curious. "Well?"

Sélie looks at the almond-colored envelope and then at both of us, exasperated. "Stop staring at me. It's only an envelope, not a singing bear!"

"Aren't you going to open it?" Aven asks.

"I think I'll keep you both in suspense and save it for when I'm alone," Sélie teases. She tucks the letter into her apron pocket, only one edge sticking out.

"You…are a brat," I tell her, returning to my broom.

"I learned from my sisters," she retorts, spirits high, cheeks flushed as peach as her dress.

"You *are* cheeky!" Aven bursts into a laugh. I twirl to watch her.

The sound of it, the sight of her, head tipped back with wicked glee, fills me with such joy. We're here, the three of us. We're here, and we're not going anywhere. I might not live at home anymore, and Sélie's already talking about moving in with Pearl to her rooms above the fishmonger's shop. But not living in the same house won't change us. There's nothing I wouldn't do for them. Nothing they wouldn't do for me. Nothing—not even hell—could part us.

Dropping my broom with a thud, I stride over and reach across the counter to hug them both to me, so eternally thankful to have them back. Aven laughs again, open and gay.

You were embracing. She was laughing, Marieta's premonition echoes, one I've so far kept to myself.

I pull away, startled, and they stare at me.

"What is it?" Sélie asks.

"Nothing." I only shake my head, smiling. I tug them in again, gratitude filling me once more. I'll tell them the whole story, one day.

THE END

Dear Reader,

A Dance With Death is a love letter to ballet, though it's been many, many years since I last tied up my own pointe shoes. The only dancing I do these days is twirling about in my kitchen while I'm waiting on dinner to cook, but it is with a bone-deep admiration for the art of ballet—and all dance—that I share this book with you today. One of my early memories is being a four-year-old telling people I wanted to be a ballerina when I grew up. Though I got to experience the joy of sporadic dance classes through-out my childhood and the elation (and hard work) of being on a very successful high school dance team and even a college team (however briefly), I never quite got to where my four-year-old self wanted. But in a past life, I know I did—and I don't mean past life *figuratively*. The love of ballet is in my soul, and to this day, my throat gets a lump when I watch ballerinas on stage. It is one of my deep regrets that I never got to be a part of a show like *Sleeping Beauty* or *The Nutcracker* or *Swan Lake*, and, well, now I'm aged out and lost my skill. But while I have a bittersweet feeling toward it all, I ended up exactly where I was meant to be—writing books, something else I feel soul-deep. All that said, dancers past and present, I ask that you please forgive any inconsistencies in technique or portrayal during dancing scenes and know that I deeply admire you and your dedication and grace.

As for the lovers of history, this book had some leeway given it's a fantasy world, but I did do my best to research some aspects of the early 1870s while also enjoying partaking in artistic license. You'll find that one long-dead character in the story is mentioned having a certain pair of pointe shoes, which would have been well before they came into fashion in the nineteenth century. Lovers of *Beauty* by Robin McKinley, a book whose existence has had a hand in making *my* existence as a writer possible—and greatly inspired this particular story—may recall when our main character, Beauty, is given access to the beast's library, including some books which "haven't been written yet." There is a small nod to this in the scene that features an excerpt of Amy Lowell's poem, "The Giver of Stars," which was not published until 1914. It is with great passion for McKinley's story that I shared this little Easter egg.

Finally, content guidelines can be accessed on my website for those who desire them.

Thank you for reading and sharing a piece of my soul.

Amanda

Acknowledgments

To my editors, Amanda Chiu Krohn and Ashlyn Inman, for giving me the gift of believing again that dreams do come true. For loving this story and the characters and for giving this series a home—a *great* one. Thank you to the entire Turner and Keylight team that have had a hand in this book coming to life: Kendal Cliburn, Jane Flautt, Claire Ong, Aric Dutelle, Christine Balsley, proofreader Marilyn Gillen, Olivia Brothers, Melissa Schneider, and Todd Bottorff. And a big thank you to Faceout Studio and William Ruoto for such a gorgeous cover design. And to Charlotte Slegers for the beautiful map!

To my agent, Juliana—we did it!! I really have no words. You know what this meant and I'm full of gratitude that you didn't give up on this story.

I've been really lucky to find such an incredible writing community and I can't imagine doing this job without the support and encouragement from my peers and friends—thank you so much for it all. First, to Jamie McLachlan for the crucial help you gave me in the early version of this story. Thank you to Kelly Cain and Bianca M Schwarz for your unwavering support, and to Cathie Armstrong for help with querying and submissions over the last several years even though you are absolutely *horrid* at checking into our DM—and yeah, I mean that a touch snarkily haha. To Adrienne Young's *Writing With the Soul* alumni and absolute gems of humans, Jennie Grace James, Alexa Manz, Amanda Murphy, Anna Leighten, Rachel Jenkins—especially for your aid with brainstorming—and to Ande Pliego for your help with my rusty French. There are so many other alumni I could list here that have been such loving and warm cheerleaders—and who are all talented writers. Again, thank you all so much. To the lovely Zeyneb Holdridge, for keeping me mostly sane during the long, arduous process of being on sub. Thank you to my sweet pub sib, Teagan Olivia King for all the commiserating and encouragement as we send out our books into the world. And to Autumn Lindsey, who is one of the kindest souls to exist. I'm so glad to know you all! To the friends who keep me grounded in the real world, and who are the type of people to sneak into your house when you're feeling lower than low and whisk you off to a surprise getaway out of town and make you laugh so hard you fall onto the floor and almost pee your pants, and by that I mean thanks to Theresa, Lindsay, and Melissa. And to Nicole, for sharing a deep love of romance novels with me ever since we were far too young to be reading them, and, if I remember right, going to see Disney's *Beauty and the Beast* with me in theatres when it first came out—oh, how time flies! I'm blessed with true friends, old and new—you know who you are.

To the talented, amazing writers who blurbed this book. When making the list of dream authors to send this story to, I never imagined I would get such lovely responses. I look up to you all very much in different ways, but the heart of it is, you all are *excellent* storytellers, and your work has shaped me in some way, and I'm humbled by your kind words. Thank you to N.L. Shompole, for letting me use one of my favorite poems, from *Lace, Bone, Beast*.

To Beth Check, for your insight into my ballet terminology. I appreciate your corrections that strengthened the dance scenes.

To the readers—what words can I share here to tell you how much it means that you are a part of this story's (and others') journey? Your support of my work in this early-ish stage of my career means the world. I hope you'll be around as long as I'm writing.

The fact you picked up my book and supported it through either renting from your local library (yes! Please utilize your libraries) or buying new or secondhand, or borrowing from a friend, it means so much. To the librarians and booksellers and educators—you are as crucial to the book world as the ones writing them. Thank you for your work, your joy, your dedication.

To my family—we've really been through it lately, huh? I'll keep it simple here and say two things I mean from the bottom of my heart: Thank you. I love you.

To my love, and to my loves: S, B, M, & S. Oh—and Maggie, Luna, Mouse, Pancake, Mercury, Bear, and Mystery! Life is a beautiful chaos, and I wouldn't want to go through it with anyone else. Thank you for choosing me.

About the Author

Amanda Linsmeier has been a book nerd as long as she can remember, and it was that great love of reading—especially R. L. Stine novels and fairytales—that eventually brought her to writing her own stories. In high school, she won the senior class vote for "Most Romantic Girl," a title she's still ridiculously pleased with. She feels most joyful when writing, scream-singing her favorite songs, playing in the water, and laughing with her beloved family. She lives in a magical place with a man who smells like maple syrup and woodsmoke, their wonderfully wild children, a dog, and an assortment of half-feral cats.

www.ingramcontent.com/pod-product-compliance
Lightning Source LLC
Chambersburg PA
CBHW032207010726
47493CB00008BA/2869